NICCA'S LIGHT

THE SOPHIE'S HAVEN SERIES

MEREDITH HOWLIN

For Philip, my Irish Angel

NICCA'S LIGHT

THE SOPHIE'S HAVEN SERIES

By
Meredith Howlin

PROLOGUE

*I*reland 718 AD

Nicholas stood at the edge of the cliff. The irony of his current position wasn't lost on Niamh. They both knew he was standing on the edge of something much bigger than the massive valley before him. Even with his back to her, she could read his emotions.

Anger.

Hurt.

She wanted desperately to comfort him, but if she pushed, he would shut her out completely. He was being asked to bear a burden too heavy for any one person.

The sun was setting in the afternoon sky. She needed to hurry, but without Nicholas, their plan wouldn't work, so she waited impatiently until he finally turned toward her.

She knew what he saw. An old woman. Her body, a used up shell, was close to its expiration date, but inside, she still felt as young and sharp as ever. Her eyes held wisdom that came with years of studying and meditating.

Niamh was a powerful druid, although today she didn't feel very powerful. All the ancient wisdom had failed her. She learned today that when faced with a decision based on wisdom or love... love often won.

Very few people outside of the village knew about the group

of druids she called her family. They lived out here in peace, fulfilling their purposes in life—collecting and protecting knowledge, observing nature, healing the sick, and keeping the balance.

Niamh's life had been going exactly as planned, but with an emptiness inside that wouldn't ease. Then one afternoon, eighteen years ago, Niamh had found Nicholas wrapped in a blanket and tucked at the base of an oak tree. In an instant, the emptiness had disappeared, and her purpose had felt certain. She'd raised him as her own, teaching him their ways and rituals. The strange name "Nicholas" had been sewn on the blanket, and it was the only connection given to his origin.

Until today.

Nicholas's voice jerked her out of her thoughts. He was using the old language preferred by the druid women. "Have you known all along exactly who I am? *What* I am?"

Niamh studied the beautiful man in front of her. He'd been the biggest surprise blessing of her life, and she'd enjoyed every second of raising him. He was brave and strong, but also kind. He already looked like the warrior he was destined to become. Well over six feet with massive shoulders, he blocked the view behind him. The braids in his long dark hair fell over his shoulders, whipped by the wind rising over the cliff. If she hadn't raised him, she'd be terrified of him, because he looked like he could burn the world with a thought.

But she *had* raised him. She knew he had a gentle and protective spirit, and turning his world upside down was the moment she had dreaded for years.

Maybe that's why she had put it off for so long.

Too long, as it turned out.

She took a determined step toward him. "I haven't known since the beginning, Nicholas, but I have suspected since you were a young boy. We were out in the woods collecting for the Beltane rituals, and ended up by the ancient site. You strayed from me, and when I found you, you were about to touch the gate. Nicholas, you understand those sites are designed to repel most people, and the spells are put in place to hide them from human inspection. When I found you not only drawn to it but about to touch the stones, I panicked. I yelled for you, and you turned away from it to look at me, so you didn't see, but I did. The stones reacted to your touch, and that's when I suspected the old stories were true. That's when I knew what you must be."

"Don't you think that knowledge might have been helpful to me?" he said bitterly. "Before I did what I did? Before I became the one responsible for destroying *everything*?" He turned away from her again to face the valley. He looked unreachable, and in a flash of panic, she wondered if she had lost him forever.

She tried to calm her raging emotions. "Nicholas," she whispered. "Nothing that happened was your fault. It was the result of decisions made by the people around you. I wish I could fix it myself. It shouldn't even be your mess to clean up, but unfortunately, you are the only one that can make this right again." She reached out to touch his arm. His body stiffened.

"I thought—" His voice cracked. "I thought she loved me."

Niamh bit the inside of her cheek. "I know," she admitted. "It's proof to me she was the worst kind of monster, Nicholas." She grabbed his hand. "Anyone that would use love as a weapon is the most awful evil I can imagine."

"I was a fool," Nicholas said tightly. He pulled away from her and crossed his arms.

"No. It's never foolish to love. It's a gift. How she handled it was foolish," Niamh insisted. "The location ritual we performed today will lead you to the girl who can fix this. As soon as she's born, the magic will draw you to her. Once you find her, perform the binding ritual and it will finish the connection."

"So now I'm stuck until this girl is born? How long? Ten years? A thousand years? I find her and then what? Protect her while she cleans up my mess? That doesn't sound fair." He squeezed his eyes closed, clenched his fists, and let out a loud frustrated groan.

"You'll fulfill the role of a guardian," Niamh explained. "You were always meant to do this, Nicholas. You're just changing what you're guarding. Instead of the portal, it'll be a girl."

He pivoted and sliced a hand through the air. "How? How is a simple girl meant to stop the darkness if I couldn't even recognize it?"

"That's what I'm trying to tell you. We have to perform another ritual. Tonight. The sisters and I all agree that we need to send her every bit of power we have. You'll be able to help her learn how to use it," she explained anxiously.

Nicholas scoffed, "Yeah, because I've been so helpful."

"You were made to do this." Niamh grasped his chin in her hand. "This was always your destiny. You can be upset with the abrupt change, but then stand up and embrace it."

Nicholas tugged away from her. "I thought I was a simple orphan. One who had been lucky enough to find a home, and the love of a kind woman I had planned to marry. My life was planned out and settled. In a flash, it all disappeared." He looked down at her with pain-filled eyes.

She took a few precious seconds they didn't have to tap into her power, looking into his future. Scenes flashed through her mind with alarming speed, and it was too much to grasp. He had such a long journey ahead of him.

She desperately tried to grab hold of something good she could use to give him hope, when suddenly, the rapidly moving scenes froze on the image of a beautiful woman. A wild mane of curls flowed around her smiling face and shining blue-green eyes. The overwhelming love she felt was breathtaking. Niamh sucked in air. "I see her."

Nicholas froze. "Who? The girl?"

Niamh brought her focus back on him. The love she felt for her child, plus the love from her vision, still coursed through her body, bringing tears to her eyes. "She will need you more than you can comprehend, my son. All the world will depend on her, yet she will feel alone. You have a long journey ahead of you, but it will all be worth it."

"Tell me everything you saw." Nicholas leaned toward her, his despair fading a little.

"I wish we had more time, but we just can't wait any longer. We must perform the ritual tonight if we want a chance at fixing this. I may not have another year to wait and try again next Samhain. We *must* set it all in place tonight."

Nicholas looked resigned, "Will I have to leave now that everyone knows what I am?"

Niamh gasped. "What are you talking about? You're a gift straight from the heavens. You're a guardian, Nicholas. The only chance we have of saving our world from unimaginable evil."

He jerked as if she'd hit him. "You mean from the evil I let loose?" He was a wounded animal striking out. She had taught him to love and respect all of nature—knowing he had played a role in its possible destruction was killing him.

"Nicholas." Her voice resonated with all her love, sadness, exhaustion, hope, fear. When he looked at her again, she saw him pause. She held her breath as she watched emotions run across his beautiful face. Anger and hurt were still there, but there was something new now. Curiosity.

Hope bloomed in her chest.

"You keep calling me a guardian. There's a word for what I am?" he asked.

Niamh sagged with relief, but there was no time for soft words. "Nicholas, come. We have so much to do."

PART I
FINDING SOPHIA

CHAPTER 1

*P*resent day: Nashville, Tennessee

*N*icholas walked down the sidewalk the same way he walked everywhere—like he owned it. He liked the way people seemed to cower when he walked by, because it kept him from having to be social. He could pull the shadows around him and make himself invisible, but this took less effort.

He'd been on this mission longer than he ever dreamed possible and now, after all this time, he was so close to something finally happening.

Niamh explained to him all those years ago that his existence was a good thing, that when the world leans too far toward darkness, a guardian comes to protect the balance. He hadn't known what he was until it was too late, and instead of saving the day, he had accidentally—but very royally—fucked it up.

Niamh should have told him as soon as she suspected so the location and binding rituals could have immediately been performed. Then he would have fulfilled his life's purpose and spent his life as intended, on a mountain overlooking a beautiful valley in his beloved Ireland.

Instead of protecting the portal from darkness, he'd been

tricked into helping evil find and use it, changing what he needed to protect. The druid women performed the location ritual, and that's when he learned he was searching for a girl.

The problem was she hadn't been born yet.

Nicholas was frozen in time. He hadn't aged and wouldn't until he located her and completed the binding ritual. All he knew was that he was looking for a girl. He had a sense of her even though he didn't know who she was or what she looked like.

Waiting for her to be born, he'd spent the time learning. He'd tracked down ancient texts and people who could teach him anything about guardians. He'd planned for every outcome, honed his skills as a fighter, and amassed a small fortune so he could take care of what mattered when the time came. He'd learned new languages and adapted the best he could to the world around him as it changed.

Aside from temporary immortality, the location ritual had given him other powers. His sight and hearing were heightened, and he moved faster and was stronger than other humans. His body had always been built like a warrior, but after the ritual, he'd grown even bigger. He also learned, purely by instinct, that he could be invisible and even influence the emotions of others.

Waiting had been frustrating, and over the centuries, he had given in to depression and anger many times, but overall, Nicholas thought he had done well to get ready.

All of that changed, however, the moment she was born.

The instant she took her first breath, the location ritual powers kicked in and Nicholas began the fight of his life—for his sanity. The primal instinct to protect with no way to reach her felt like ripping his insides out. He went mad for months and was ashamed to admit he couldn't remember much of that time in his life.

Slowly, he'd learned to control himself, but it hadn't gone well, and he'd spent most of those days in isolation out of fear he would kill someone. He could feel every moment when she was hurt or afraid, and being unable to help her caused him to fly into rages that destroyed everything. He would wake up from those episodes with no memory of what he had done.

Eventually, he learned control, because he awoke from a rage to find himself locked in a prison cell. He'd destroyed a lot of property, and the man he'd attacked pressed charges, resulting in a hefty sentence. While locked up, he'd learned he could use the power when it surged to point him in her direction.

It was almost like playing a massive game of "hot and cold." When he was moving away from her, a force pulled at his feet, like moving through water. When he moved toward her, he got warm and everything sped up like life was in fast forward. He noticed the change while pacing his cell, but unfortunately, he had to wait two years to get free and test his theory. He wandered Ireland for a couple of more years, unwilling to leave the country.

Once he admitted to himself that she must be outside of Ireland, he finally gave up pretending he was in control and followed his senses without question. Two more years passed before he reached the southern states of America. Every time she was afraid, and the power swelled, he would make as much progress in her direction as he could. While he waited, he worked on learning to control his emotions and actions so that when he finally found her, he could function. It was like learning how to be normal from the ground up. Or at least to act normal so he wouldn't scare her.

His senses were on fire, so he must be close. He hiked his backpack up a little higher and looked up at the tall buildings around him. How was he supposed to find her in all of this? He knew he was close, but he didn't know what to do next.

He recognized the familiar burning that began deep in his chest when a surge was about to hit him, so he turned down the alley to his right and stopped just beside a stack of boxes. They made a haphazard pyramid against the wall and around an overly full dumpster.

He leaned against the warm bricks and listened to the sounds of country music drifting along the night air. It was the beginning of fall and only just starting to feel cooler in the evenings.

He breathed in the air deeply and tried to get his emotions in check. His bond with her was weak until he could find her and finish the ritual, but he could feel her, and she was scared. It was better to get away from people for a minute and try to calm down.

He dropped his backpack and bent over to brace his hands against his thighs.

He was just about to stand up straight when he heard a noise. Just a slight little sniffle. He turned his head slowly to the side and looked into the alley, his increased senses on high alert.

He focused his eyes and saw slight movement down low, just beside a box. It was a tiny hand. His entire body hummed, and he sucked in a lung full of air. He crouched down, his guardian instincts focused and intent.

"Hey," he whispered, low and soothing. "Ye don't have to fear me. I won't hurt ye."

Her fingers moved back, and he heard her whimper. This had to be her. It *had* to be. His powers were surging through his body.

"Come on out, and sit on a box." He held his breath while he let her think about it. "My name is Nicholas. What's your name?"

He knew he needed to slow down and gain her trust, but he had been waiting for so long that his emotions were clouding his judgment. He'd spent centuries training to protect her, but it had never crossed his mind to learn how to *talk* to her. His colossal size probably didn't help matters either.

The top of her head popped out from behind a stack of cardboard. Beautiful golden honey and caramel curls. A crowd of loud drunks walked by the end of the alley, and she ducked back out of sight.

Dammit.

He sat all the way down on the ground and scooted closer to the boxes, putting his back against the bricks. He tried his best to make his massive frame look as small as possible.

"I won't let any of them come down here. I promise." He tried to lean forward to get a glimpse of her, but all he saw were tiny dirty feet in torn pink flip-flops. He stifled a growl as he leaned back against the wall and looked up at the dark cloudy sky. He closed his eyes. Maybe if he just talked a little, she would calm down enough to come out.

"You know," he began, "when I was your age, and scared or mad, I used to run to this beautiful cliff outside of my village. It had a green valley with a lake of blue water at the bottom, and I used to imagine myself diving off and swimming into the middle of the lake. Sometimes I would focus on that lake and imagine myself there so hard, I would actually forget I was still sitting on the cliff. Kind of silly, I guess."

He heard a rustling noise as she moved and remained still so he wouldn't scare her. Holding his breath, he heard a wooden crate scrape on the cement and sensed her sitting next to him.

He slowly opened his eyes and looked at the tiny feet right next to his motorcycle boots. They were connected to tiny legs with scraped up knees. Even the sight of the small wounds gave him the urge to kill. He squeezed his eyes shut to force the emotions back down and heard her little voice for the first time.

"That's not silly," she said.

His eyes shot open. Her arms were folded across her body as if she were trying to protect herself. She had a little grin on her face, but she was looking down at her feet dangling off the crate. Her mass of curls fell in matted tangles around her shoulders and down her back. She looked like the breeze would knock her off the crate any second, and he had to fight the urge to grab her up and take her out of this dirty alley.

"It's not?" he asked.

"Nope," she claimed. "I do that all the time." She uncrossed her arms and started fidgeting with her fingers. "I dream about a valley too. It's prolly the same one," she said sincerely.

She avoided looking up, and he wondered who'd taught her to keep her head down. Instead, he asked her, "You know my name. What's yours, little one?"

"Sophia Snow," she said in a sing-song manner that made him smile.

13

"Well, Miss Snow, it's nice to meet ye." She covered her mouth and giggled.

"What's so funny?" he asked.

"You called me Miss like an old lady. I'm just a girl, silly." The smile on her face disappeared, and she jumped as she heard a noise down the alley.

"Well. I'm a little old-fashioned, I guess. Don't worry, Miss Snow. No one is comin' to hurt ye. I've been trying to find you, and I'm sorry it took me so long, but I had to come from very far away. I promise everything is going to be ok now." He stilled and waited to see how she responded to the truth.

She looked straight at him.

Her turquoise eyes were the most intriguing shade of blue-green, and he swore for a second they even glowed.

He couldn't breathe.

Suddenly, that cliff he felt he had been hanging off of for so long, disappeared and finally—he fell.

CHAPTER 2

"*Y*ou talk funny," Sophia said.

Nicholas tore his gaze away from her and focused on breathing. Almost seven years of not protecting her rushed up at once, causing him to lose his grip. He forced a smile. "I'm from a different time and place, Miss Snow. It makes me sound different, I guess." He glanced back at her. She was muting her eyes somehow, and it made it easier to focus.

"I like it," she declared finally with a smile.

"Good," he said, "because yer kind of stuck with me."

"I am?" she said, her eyes growing bigger.

"Yep. If that's ok." He shot her a hopeful grin.

"I think I knew you were coming," she said.

"What do you mean?" He looked at her curiously.

"Someone told me you would come to help me, and that I would know it was you because you would be blue. And you are... blue. It's pretty." She explained to him as if he would know exactly what she meant.

"I'm *blue*? Who told you?" His power prickled along the back of his neck.

"I don't know. She visits me sometimes and tells me things," she said seriously. Then she leaned over with wide eyes and a hushed voice, like she was sharing a special secret with him. "She's a fairy godmother."

He had to smile a little at her innocence, but he didn't believe in fairy tales. "Miss Snow, what do you mean I'm blue?"

"It's not all the time. It just sparkles around you like a princess. Well... not a princess 'cause you're a boy." She giggled. "But maybe you're a prince. A prince that sparkles." She looked down at her hands and then began carefully. "I never had a friend. I always wanted a friend, but I never got one before." She looked back up. "No matter how good I am or how hard I tried." He couldn't help the shot to the gut he felt when she looked straight at him. "Nicca? Maybe you could be my friend... if you felt like it, I mean."

That brought him up short. "Nicca? Why did you call me that?"

She stood and rested her hand on his shoulder. The moment she touched him, the guardian within him reared up and he almost did the binding ritual right then. The knowledge that it would scare her to death was the only way he stopped himself.

He looked up just in time to see her eyes fading. Had they glowed again? They were the color of his lake back in Ireland. She tilted her head to the side and answered him finally. "Nicholas doesn't fit. Nicca does."

"Ok, Miss Snow. Nicca then." She was right, he thought. With her, it seemed to fit. "I would be happy to be friends." He watched her face as a genuine smile transformed her. He knew in that instant that even without the binding ritual, he would do anything he could for this girl to be happy and safe. Knowing how he felt now, he couldn't imagine how strongly he would feel after they were bound.

"Miss Snow, can you tell me why you're out here in this alley?" He braced himself, because there was no way the reason would be a good one.

She took her hand away and turned to look at the alley and then kicked the edge of the crate she had been sitting on. "My mom needs money," she sighed. "It's my fault. I keep getting hungry. Which means I need food. Which cost money." She looked so mad at herself as she kicked at the ground. "I try so hard to not be hungry, but I just can't do it." She flopped back down on the crate and looked frustrated. "My mom has to make money, so I have to wait here until she gets back. It's for my own good."

He surged to his feet, a growl deep in his chest as he started for the end of the alley, intent on ripping the woman's limbs off and shoving them down her throat. He only made it about ten feet when he heard her small voice behind him. "Nicca?"

He froze. It took him an entire minute to bring himself back to reality. What was he thinking? He squeezed his eyes shut, clenched his fists, and tried to even his breathing. Here he was heading off into the unknown to kill some woman he didn't even know. He didn't even have a clue what she looked like, much less where to find her. This entire street was full of bars. She could be anywhere. His anger was so intense he was walking off and leaving Sophia in the very alley he had found her. He turned around and saw her standing a few feet away. She was looking up at him with a curious stare.

"Are you going? Will you be back?" She had such a hopeful look on her face. His heart cracked a little at the sight of her. She was so small. This girl had to save the world. How could she bear that burden? It was too much to expect from her.

"I was hoping you would come with me?"

"I can't. My mom wouldn't be able to find me. That would hurt her so bad. Maybe you could wait until she gets back and then we could both come with you?" she asked with such hope.

He felt an intense hatred for the woman she was trying so hard to protect, but he could tell by looking at her she loved her mother. He would have to be very careful here because he needed her trust. It would be hard to protect her if she hated him. He pulled from his power and began searching for wisdom.

Just then his senses prickled. He turned to see a woman standing at the end of the alley looking in her purse, and he instinctively moved to block Sophia from her view. She couldn't be much over five feet tall. She had the same caramel-colored hair as Sophia, but it was straight and only fell to her shoulders. Her face was worn and tired beyond her years after too much sun and smoke. She had a cigarette hanging from between her lips and heavy eyeliner smudged on her face. He could see how she might have been pretty once, but her lifestyle had stolen her beauty.

She pulled an apple out of her purse. "Hey Soph, I found you some—" She froze when she saw Nicholas. He watched a slideshow of emotions play out over her face. First it was shock, then fear, and then she eyed him up and down as a smile tugged at her lips.

"Hey mister, you are one tall drink." She gave him a wink while taking a drag on her cigarette.

Nicholas had assumed he would want to kill her as soon as he saw her. Instead, he felt his power sizzle, and instantly he saw exactly what he had to do. He looked over his shoulder at Sophia and whispered, "Wait here while I talk things through with your mam, ok?" He saw her nod and head back to the crate to sit delicately. He couldn't help but smile watching her, but when he turned his smile back to her mom, his eyes had hardened to green glass.

"What's your name?" His words dripped with power and authority. He was asking... but he wasn't, really.

The smile slid off her face, and she pulled up straight. "I don't think that's any of your damned business, mister. What are you? A cop or something?" She looked like she was about to take a step toward Sophia, but with one look at Nicholas, she stopped.

"Name. Please." He said it politely but with authority.

She got the point. "It's Lorraine, geez, ok? What do you want?" She tossed her cigarette down and smashed it with her foot.

He gave a brief nod of his head over his shoulder. "I wish to adopt her, and I will compensate you well. She will never have to sit in another dirty alley."

Her eyes grew wide as she comprehended what he was saying. She hesitated only briefly before lunging at him with her purse. "You perve! Who do you think I am? Get the hell away from us!"

He caught her purse, wrapped the straps around her hands, and pulled her close. Her toes were barely touching the ground.

"I give you my word that no harm will ever come to her. She will have a life you'll never be able to give her, and you'll no longer have the burden of feeding her." He saw her face fall a little in shame, but not before he saw the spark of interest. Somewhere in there, she loved Sophia, but this was a lost woman, and he'd be damned if he would let her drag Sophia with her. He pushed his power out over her, letting his influence sink into her as he set her down gently.

"Lorraine, look at her. Six years old in a dirty alley. Hungry. Scared. She deserves better, and you know it. I understand you do the best you can, but your best isn't good enough." He let his point sink in before declaring, "I am trying to help." He kept pushing his magic over her to help her understand he meant Sophia no harm.

She looked at him then. Really looked at him. "Who are you?"

"I'm someone who will guard your daughter with my life," he said, as if that settled everything. In his mind, it did.

"You can't really expect me to just walk away without her. That's my daughter, mister." She tried her best to look indignant, but he could see she was already spending the money. It made him sick, but his power told him this was the right way for Sophia.

"I don't expect you to just walk away, Lorraine. That would devastate Sophia. I'm sure you wouldn't want that," he said, failing to hide the sarcasm in his words. He went back to the spot he'd been sitting earlier to pick up his backpack. He gave Sophia a quick wink which got him another adorable grin before heading back toward Lorraine.

She pulled up to her full height. "Of course I wouldn't. She's my life."

He tried not to roll his eyes. "Yeah, I'm sure she is, which is why yer going to do right by her now." He handed her a large bag he pulled from the backpack and let her look inside.

She couldn't hide the look of excitement that flashed across her face.

"Shit! How much is in here!"

"More than you deserve." She at least had the decency to

temper her excitement at his remark. "This is how it's going to work, Lorraine. You're going to explain to your daughter how much you love her, but that you need her to come with me. You will make her understand that you'll be ok and that this is the right thing for you both. Then you'll leave with the money. My contact information is in the bag, as well. If you ever want to check on her and make sure she's ok, I expect you to call." He leaned down close to make his point stick. "But it better be the mother of the year act or ye won't get a penny. Are we clear?" Just then he felt a tug on his pants. He looked down to see Sophia peeking around his leg.

"Hi, Mama," Sophia said. "Can we go with him? He's really nice."

Lorraine looked at Sophia hard for a minute. Then at the money. Then at Nicholas. "My grandmother used to tell me stories about the women in our family. I never believed her. Then when Soph started showin' how different she was, I wondered. Is my Soph the one?"

Nicholas wasn't sure what she meant by 'the one' exactly, but he could guess. "Yes, she is," he said quietly.

Lorraine looked around the alley for a minute before she took a deep breath and gave him the slightest of nods. She clutched the bag close as she crouched down to Sophia's level. "Come here, sweetie. Let's talk for a sec."

It took every ounce of control he had to let her get close to Lorraine, but he stepped aside and watched as she moved into her mother's arms.

Lorraine held her for a minute. Then she pulled back and looked at her with bright eyes. "I have some exciting news. We're going on an adventure. You always wanted to go on one, didn't you?"

Sophia clapped her hands together. "Yes! Oh yesssss! Let's do it, Mama! Pleeeease?"

"Well, we are. Isn't that exciting? But here's the thing, since I'm the mommy, I'm going to go first to make sure everything is ok. You're going to stay with him, and he will keep you safe for me."

Sophia stopped jumping with excitement and stared carefully at her. "We aren't going together?"

"No, baby, but it's ok. Mama will be fine. I have money now. Look!" She held the bag up a little. "And you will have everything you ever needed or wanted. It'll be so great!"

Sophia looked at her mother for a long time. She put her hands up to Lorraine's face, and it was so tender and loving, Nicholas had to look away. This woman didn't deserve tenderness. "Will you be happy, Mama?"

Lorraine's eyes filled with tears as she looked into her daughter's for the last time. "Yes, baby," she whispered. "God forgive me, but yes." She hugged Sophia tightly.

"Ok, Mama," Sophia whispered into her mother's neck.

Lorraine wrenched herself away with a sob. And walked away.

Sophia watched until she disappeared around the corner. Then she looked up at him sideways. "Are you my dad?"

Nicholas choked. "No, Miss Snow. I'm not." He thought for a second. "But I would've been proud to be your father. You're very brave."

"I am?" she asked, her eyes getting wide.

He leaned down and touched her nose with the tip of his finger. "Yes. You're *very* brave. What do you say we get out of here and find some proper food? Whatever your favorite thing to eat is, that's what we'll order." He took a chance and held out his hand.

She took his hand timidly. "Pancakes?"

Her tiny hand felt so fragile. He started walking forward slowly so she could keep up. "Pancakes it is!" They had made it almost to the corner when he felt her slowing to a stop. "Miss Snow?"

"You gave my mama money for me." She looked up at him with a blank stare.

She wasn't asking him. She seemed to need him to tell the truth. "Yes."

She looked away for a second and when she looked back her eyes were full of tears about to burst like a dam. "I think Mama loves money more than me, Nicca." Tears rolled down her cheeks silently.

Impulsively, he picked her up. Her little arms went around his neck and she buried her face and cried. He held her as he continued down the sidewalk. He wanted to say something to comfort her, but he couldn't bring himself to lie.

CHAPTER 3

She cried herself to sleep as he walked through the city. His assistant, Martin, had booked them into a hotel in the city so he didn't have too far to bring her. He didn't even take time to look around the lavish rooms as he gently laid her on the couch and pulled his cell phone out to ring Martin.

"Yes, sir?" He answered on the first ring.

That's what he loved about Martin. Straight to the point. Martin had been tagging along with him for several years. He was brilliant with finances and research, and he didn't ask questions. He was the only person Nicholas considered a friend.

"I have her, Martin. I need you to get her some clean clothes." After thinking it through a bit, he added, "Toys. Buy toys for a six-year-old girl. I think she likes princess stuff. She definitely mentioned princesses."

There was a long pause before Martin calmly asked, "Do you know what size she wears?"

"Size?" He knew nothing about little girl clothing.

"Is she wearing clothing now?" Martin asked, as if this was a normal conversation.

"Yes, of course." Nicholas's head hurt.

"Perhaps you could check the tag in the clothes she currently wears?" Martin explained politely.

"Oh yeah! Just a moment." He quietly walked to where Sophia lay sleeping. His gaze softened as he took in her peaceful state. Curled up on her side, he easily peeked at the tag in the back of her dress. "There's a number 6 on the tag. Whatever that means."

"I'll take care of it and be there shortly." He immediately hung up.

Nicholas once again gave thanks for Martin. He was only twenty-three, but age didn't seem to be a hurdle for him. He never had to worry; if Martin said he would take care of something, it just got done.

He had been wandering Scotland still struggling with his control when he came upon Martin being beaten to death by a group of men. It had been impossible not to respond. Even though Martin wasn't his assignment, the fact remained he was a guardian. It was his nature to protect. Without even realizing what he was doing, his instinct had taken over, and he had attacked. Martin had returned the favor with companionship.

Even though Martin had seen him use his powers, he had never confronted him about it. He knew the time was coming soon to tell Martin everything, because it was only fair to give him the chance to decide if he wanted to be a part of it or not. He just hoped it didn't cost him his friendship.

He shook off the negative thought and faced Sophia. She had a calming effect on him. After six years of torture, he welcomed the reprieve. He made one more call to room service before collapsing onto the sofa.

He took a deep breath.

Well over a thousand years of waiting, planning, hoping, searching—and she was finally right here in front of him.

Safe.

He'd done it.

Emotions welled up inside him, and he struggled to push them back down. He watched her sleep and felt at peace for the first time in centuries. Life was finally going to move forward.

He dozed until a rustling sound brought him awake sharply.

Sophia was sitting up and looking around the suite with wide eyes. He watched her patiently until she swung her gaze to him. He didn't think he would ever get over those eyes. "Miss Snow, are ye feelin' better?"

She gave him a small nod and a gentle smile. "Is this a castle, Nicca?" She slid down from the couch slowly and wandered around the living area.

The suite was tastefully decorated in varying shades of brown. The couch and chairs were covered in expensive pillows and cosy throws in front of a faux fireplace. Battery operated candles lined the inside of the fireplace, flickering gently. He could look through the "fire" to see a dining area similarly decorated on the other side. It was nice, but he had seen much more lavish places. To her, it must seem extravagant. She held her hand over one of the flickering candles, and the light reflected in her eyes.

"Not a castle, Miss Snow," he explained. "We're in the Sheraton. It's a hotel."

She looked up at him then. "I've never been in a hotel." She looked past him to the windows that formed the wall behind him. "*Oh!*" she gasped and ran for the window. "Nicca, did you see this? It's so pretty! I've never been so high before!"

Nicholas turned in his chair to watch her press her face to the window and look down on the city. She deserved joy. He wasn't sure how to handle what came next, so he was more than happy to just let her enjoy this moment.

There was a knock at the door, and he cringed when he saw her jump. "No worries, Miss Snow. It's only our food."

She smiled with relief. "I'm really hungry."

Nicholas went to the door. He felt his instincts prickling and naturally noted her location by the couch before he opened the door. It seemed his guardian instincts didn't rest, not even for room service.

When the server rolled the cart into the room, he felt her move behind him. She peeked at the food curiously. The server set the food on the dining table and then passed him the bill to sign and add the tip. He sensed the moment the server took notice of Sophia.

He leaned over a little toward her. "Hey there, little cutie! Are you having fun here in Nashville?"

Sophia dove behind Nicholas and buried her head in his legs. His heart swelled.

"My girl is shy like that too," the server said, shrinking at Nicholas's intense look.

Nicholas handed the bill back to him with a dismissive nod. He took the hint and scurried out as quickly as he could. Turning to Sophia, he gave her a smile. "Ready to eat?"

She nodded and ran for the table. "What are we having?"

He pulled the lid off her plate and watched her eyes light up. "*Pancakes!*" she yelled and threw her hands up in the air. "You 'membered." She looked up with such adoration that Nicholas couldn't wipe the grin off his face.

"Of course I did. Now dig in and enjoy!" He sat down across from her.

She paused while looking down at her plate. "Is this 'spensive, Nicca?"

She was worried about him the way she worried about her mother. A flash of fury washed over him, but he reeled it in. He leaned over to look in her eyes. "Miss Snow, I have more money than I could ever spend in three lifetimes. Ye will *never* have to think about money again. I don't want ye to worry. I want ye to enjoy your pancakes, ok?"

She looked down again but didn't start eating right away. "Miss Snow?"

She looked over at her fork and picked it up, "I was just wondering. I mean... do you think my mom is eating supper tonight?"

Nicholas wanted to yell at the top of his lungs that he hoped she was choking on it, but he couldn't do that to Sophia. Instead, he said softly, "Your mother isn't hungry. I promise you, I gave her enough money to eat for a very long time. You never have to worry, Miss Snow. Not about food. Not about money. And not about your mother." He sent out soothing vibes to comfort her. She seemed to calm, and then her entire body relaxed.

"Thank you, Nicca. Not just for pancakes either." She stuck her fork in the pancake.

He looked at the precious girl in front of him and felt his heart thump in his chest. "You are most welcome, Miss Snow."

CHAPTER 4

*N*icholas listened to Sophia ramble on about her favorite Disney princesses. She had very detailed pros and cons for each one, and he could tell she took it very seriously. He wondered how she would handle this next part.

He was nervous because he needed to have the final binding ritual, but he'd never seen it done before and didn't know if it would be scary or painful for her. The sooner it happened, the easier it would be to protect her.

He was just working up the nerve to tell her when there was a noise at the door.

All of his senses sharpened, and he leapt from the table. It took him over before he could stop it. Martin stepped inside the room with bags hanging everywhere on him. Nicholas looked back to Sophia to see she had jumped up to get behind him. He had scared her with his reaction.

He turned and held his hand out to her and calmly told her, "No worries, Miss Snow. This is my friend Martin MacLane. Can ye say hello to him for me?" He gently pulled her toward the door where Martin was untangling the bags on the floor.

She looked up at Martin, and he smiled at her when she mumbled, "Hi. I'm Sophia Snow."

Nicholas could see Martin stiffen as he took the brunt of Sophia's stare.

"Hi, Sophia. It's verra nice to meet you, lass." Martin smiled at her.

She looked at the bags and rubbed her palms against her legs. "It's nice to meet you too. You have really nice toys. Could I play with them sometime?" she asked with so much hope on her face.

Nicholas smiled to himself. It seemed Sophia worked her spell on everyone. Not just him. He could see Martin melting.

She looked at them both and then said, "You talk funny too. Kind of like Nicca but not the same."

Martin looked at Nicholas and mouthed "Nicca?" to him before saying, "Well lass, I'm from a different place. So, my accent is a wee bit different." Sophia seemed to accept that as a reasonable explanation.

Martin gestured toward the bags. "These are yours, Sophia. I bought some clean clothes and toys. I thought you might like something to play with while you're here."

Sophia's eyes got big with shock. "These are all mine?" She looked up at Martin.

He smiled at her and nodded.

Nicholas crouched down. "Why don't you search through everything and see if you like any of it. I'm going to talk to Martin for a bit, ok?"

She surprised Nicholas by jumping into his arms and knocking him off balance. He caught her up and hugged her close. She just kept whispering, "Thank you! Thank you! Thank you!"

Nicholas hugged her tighter. "No worries, Miss Snow. I told you."

She looked up at Martin and exclaimed, "Best. Adventure. Ever!" She jumped into the center of the bags and started pulling things out.

The two men watched her with goofy grins on their faces.

Nicholas caught Martin's attention and motioned for him to follow. They went to the desk in the corner. "Thanks for that, Martin. I'm sure it wasn't easy to do. She really seems happy with your choices, though."

Martin looked back at Sophia, who had her hands buried in a

bag of dress-up clothes. "She is—different—Nicca," Martin drawled.

"Yes, and if you call me Nicca again, you will regret it," Nicholas said good-naturedly. "I need you to get the files. Didn't you tell me we had it narrowed to three families?"

"Yes," Martin explained. "The Smith family had a child and were no longer looking to adopt, so we took them off the list."

"Ok. Get the others for me to look over. I need to make a final decision," Nicholas said.

"Are you certain this is the best thing? You spent so long looking for her. You donna think she would want to stay with you? What about her parents?" he asked tentatively.

Nicholas stopped short and looked at Martin. He was a couple of inches over six feet. His hair was a rusty red-brown color. He had cut it short recently, and it made him look older. "Are you sick of just having me for company?"

Martin grinned. "I get plenty of company. The ladies love me. I just thought maybe it would be nice to have her around. I find it hard to believe her parents just let her come with you with no resistance. What happens if they change their mind?"

"I'm not abandoning her, but she needs a stable place to grow up. We travel too much. Finding her was only the first part. I don't think her father is in the picture. Her mother cares for her, but she never really wanted to be a mom. I offered her a way out, and she took it. She has our contact information. If she needs to check in, she will, but I wouldn't hold my breath. I don't want to do this, but it's the right thing for her. That's the only thing that matters." Nicholas said it to convince himself as much as Martin. "Look, just get me those files ok? The sooner I decide and get her settled, the better it will be." He hated how angry he sounded. It wasn't Martin's fault, but already the thought of letting her leave his sight set him on edge.

Martin straightened. "Yes, of course. Be right back." He disappeared into his room and came out with a stack of files. Nicholas took them and picked a chair in the corner where he could still see Sophia, and began going over the information.

Martin walked over to Sophia, who had a hot pink feather

boa wrapped around her neck and bracelets covering both arms. "Martin! Do you want to have a tea party? I have the most beautiful tea set ever!" she exclaimed.

Martin looked a little lost. "I donna know how to have a tea party. I've not yet had one."

Sophia giggled. "Me neither, but I dreamed and dreamed about it. Come on, pleeeease!"

Martin sat cross-legged across from her. "I'm at your mercy, lass."

CHAPTER 5

*N*icholas didn't need to read the files again. He had spent decades upon decades dreaming up all the different scenarios in which he might find Sophia. Best case had been a loving family and a happy life, of course, but he had planned for everything. He had prepared himself for the possibility that she would need to be in a safer home.

Martin had researched families from adoption agencies for the last year. Every time Nicholas got a step closer, he would revisit the pile and eliminate the ones that lived farther away or were no longer looking to adopt.

In the last three months, Nicholas had known he was seriously close to Sophia and had taken more time to research the families left. He looked into every aspect of their lives to make sure they were perfect in every way. Finances, health, religion, and even daily habits were monitored to make sure they were happy, healthy people.

Now he was down to three families, and they were all good people, but he knew only one would be perfect for Sophia. He just didn't know how to pick the right one. Would it be better to put her with siblings? Would she like that? Or would her special powers make her the outcast in a group of brothers and sisters? Or maybe the family with the farm? Would she love being outside with animals? He just didn't know how to choose. What if he made the wrong choice? It would affect her entire life. His head was pounding again.

He looked up at Martin and Sophia playing on the floor. It calmed him to see her happy and safe. She already had Martin wrapped around her finger. He was wearing the feather boa now and drinking imaginary tea, pinky out and all. Sophia was in a fit of giggles over Martin's impersonation of a fairy princess.

Maybe Martin was right. Maybe she could just stay with them.

As soon as he thought it, his power surged painfully, almost as if to punish him for even thinking it. He knew what he had to do. It didn't make it easy though. He spread the files out on the table and took a minute to center himself. Searching for wisdom, he slowly held his hands over the files and waited for some sense of guidance.

Just when he was about to give up, he felt a tingle in his thumb on his right hand. He paused and concentrated a little more. The tingle spread until it covered the entire finger. He looked down and saw that his thumb was over the file in the center. He moved his hand closer and laid it down on the file. The power hummed through his hand, up his arm, and settled with certainty in his heart. As simple as that, it was over. This would be her family. This was the one.

He turned to check on her. His power pushed out to sense her mood. She was happy, but he could feel her tiredness too. He checked the time and realized she needed to sleep. The ritual had waited six years. It could wait until morning.

He went into the bathroom and started some bathwater. He didn't know how to care for the daily needs of a six-year-old, but he knew the basics at least. When he went back to the living area, Martin and Sophia were folding all of her new clothes and putting them into piles according to her favorite colors. "Miss Snow, I think a bath and sleep are in order."

Sophia looked up and smiled. "Ok, Nicca. Have you seen these beautiful clothes? I've never seen so many beautiful things. And they really belong to me?"

Nicholas smiled. "Yes. That and anything else you need." He

leaned down to her level and put his fingers under her chin to bring her eyes up. "Miss Snow, I need you to remember this. It's very important. If you ever need anything, you only need to ask me. Ok?"

She looked at him in that direct way that sent shock-waves through him. "I will."

Nicholas looked over at Martin. "I thought maybe since you have been bonding with Miss Snow, she might be more comfortable with you helping her."

Martin looked like a deer caught in headlights. "Um..."

"You know, with her bath and stuff?" Nicholas explained. Both men stared at each other in silence. Nicholas didn't know where to begin with helping a six-year-old girl get ready for bed. He had been hoping Martin would just take care of it, but Martin looked just as mortified.

He felt Sophia's hand on his leg. "I don't need help, silly. I'm a big girl." She headed for the bathroom. Nicholas looked at Martin, and he was certain the relief he saw was mirrored on his own face.

"Maybe you could just stay close in case she needs something," Nicholas stated.

"Yes. That I can do," Martin agreed.

He held up the file. "I have to make a call. I will be in my room for a moment." When he got into the bedroom, he sat on the edge of the bed and opened the file to see which family he had chosen.

Jon and Penny West from a town close to the city. Jon was a surgeon here in Nashville, and Penny was an English teacher at a local high school. They were, by all accounts, decent upstanding citizens. They weren't able to have kids, so Sophia wouldn't have siblings. He didn't know why this family was better than any of the others they had found, but he never doubted the magic, and it told him this was the one. He lifted the phone and called the number in the file.

"Hello?" A polite female voice answered.

"Yes, hello," Nicholas began. "My name is Nicholas Stone. Is there a Penny West I may speak with please?"

"I'm Penny. May I help you?" she asked.

"This is going to sound a little bizarre, but I got you and your husband Jon's names from a local adoption agency. I have a beautiful little girl who desperately needs a home. We took great care to study everyone and after very careful thought, we selected you. I will be completely honest with you, Mrs. West, this is a delicate situation. I require an interview, and there are some stipulations before completely agreeing; however, after that, if you and your husband are still interested, you would have the opportunity of raising a wonderful child." He held his breath.

There was a long pause.

Finally, Penny answered, "I'm not sure how to answer you, Mr. Stone. I would love more than anything to raise a child, but I'm not sure you will still be interested once you find out that my circumstances have changed."

She sounded nervous. "What do you mean changed?"

"Well, I know that it's very hard to adopt sometimes, for single people. My Jon passed three months ago in a car accident." Her voice broke off. She took a moment to gather her emotions before continuing. "It's just me now. I would really love the opportunity, but I understand if you are no longer interested," Penny explained.

He was confused. Why had the magic told him to pick this family? Was he really going to put Sophia in a home with a single mother? He centered himself to look for wisdom. Yes, he thought. He was. "Ms. West, I'm so sorry to hear about your loss. I will have to take that into account; however, I see no reason to cancel a meeting at least. I would still like to interview if you would."

"Oh my! Why yes, of course," she stammered. "You name the time and place, and I will be there."

Nicholas rattled off the directions and then said goodbye. He really had to wonder what was going on here. He had to believe there was a bigger picture he just couldn't see yet.

Suddenly, he felt Sophia's worry. He jumped from the bed

and went to the living area. Martin was on the couch reading a magazine.

"Nicholas?" Martin asked.

He just walked by him and knocked lightly on the door. "Miss Snow?"

"Just a minute." Her voice sounded strained.

"Miss Snow, I feel like there might be a problem. Would you please let me help?" he tried.

After a moment, the door cracked open. She was in her new pajamas. It was a pink shirt with purple flowers and the words "Too Cute" on the front. Her hair was wet and in knots. She had a brush hanging from one side of her head, and big crocodile tears filled her eyes. "I tried to fix it, and the brush got stuck. I think I ruined my hair. I can't get it out."

Nicholas went to his knees, and she walked into his arms. "It's ok, Miss Snow. We'll fix it together ok?" He took the brush and began trying to untangle it. For a moment he was afraid she was right, but he finally managed to get most of it free. He brought her in where Martin sat and worked at it some more.

Martin interrupted his concentration. "Actually, if I may, I happen to be verra good at detangling curls."

Nicholas looked up in shock. "Excuse me?"

Martin took the brush from Nicholas and began gently easing sections of Sophia's hair apart. Nicholas let him move Sophia in front of him and watched as he indeed seemed to know what to do. Martin leaned over and smiled at Sophia while explaining, "I used to do this for my sister. It's easy once you know how. I'll teach you."

Nicholas sat in shock as he watched them. He never knew Martin had a sister because he'd never asked. He'd been so driven and focused, it made him wonder what else he didn't know. Martin had always respected his privacy, so he had returned the favor. Or maybe, he thought with guilt, he'd just been a selfish friend.

Martin worked the brush through small sections of curls and then twisted them around his fingers before moving to the next section. Sophia stood very still and listened to him explain what he was doing. Finally, Martin asked her, "Would you like to try it now, lass?"

"Yes, please," she said as she turned to face him. Her hand touched Martin's as she grabbed for the brush.

Nicholas felt the power surge out of her. He could see her eyes as she looked at Martin. They had an iridescent shimmer to them that caused Martin to freeze like a statue. Nicholas watched in complete fascination as Sophia moved her hands to both sides of Martin's face. After a moment, she said very calmly, "It wasn't your fault, Mac."

That seemed to unglue Martin. "Wh... what?" he stammered.

But Sophia was back to normal. Her eyes muted and her attention focused back on her hair. Martin looked rattled. He looked from Sophia to Nicholas and then got up quickly and mumbled, "Excuse me." He went straight to his bedroom and shut the door.

Nicholas looked at Sophia, brushing her hair. "What did you mean by what you said to Martin?"

She turned to him. "I don't know. Sometimes, I just have to say stuff. Mama says I'm weird."

He stifled a growl of frustration. "Not weird, Miss Snow. Special. Very, very special." She smiled at him.

"I think it's time for bed, little one. Let me show you to your room," he said softly.

Her eyes got big and round. "By myself? My own bed? My own room?"

"Yes. For tonight, it'll be your room. Tomorrow we will talk about your future." He could see she had no energy for that talk tonight. He led her into the bedroom and pulled back the covers. "Hop on in, Miss Snow."

She walked to the bed slowly, and he could feel the fear creeping into her heart. "I never had my own bed before, Nicca."

He lifted her gently onto the bed, pulled the covers over her, and smoothed a curl out of her eyes. "No worries, Miss Snow. I will be here in seconds if you need me. I promise." He stood to walk out and got nearly to the door when he heard her.

"Will you sleep with me, Nicca?" she asked in a quivering voice.

Nicholas coughed. "Um, no, little one. I cannot sleep with you. You need to learn to sleep in your own bed. But if it will help you, just for tonight, I will stay until you sleep."

She smiled over at him. "Thank you."

Nicholas pulled the chair close to the bed and turned the side lights off. "Good night, Miss Snow."

He could feel the fear leaving her body and the calm of sleep already sinking in. Her small hand reached out and grabbed his fingers. "Good night, Nicca." He stayed long after she fell asleep, just enjoying the peace of being near her.

CHAPTER 6

*N*icholas wasn't sure what time he finally crashed on the couch. He hadn't been able to sleep in his bedroom because he was afraid it would take too long to get to Sophia if she needed him, and he didn't like being too far from her now that he had found her.

A small shuffling sound brought him out of his fitful sleep, and he knew it was Sophia without even looking. Pressing his palms to his eyes, he tried to get rid of the sandpaper grit on the back of his eyelids. When he turned his head, he came face to face with her.

Apparently, she had been standing right next to him, patiently waiting for him to wake up. He had to smile because her hair was a crazy mess of curls going a million different directions. "Miss Snow?"

She smiled. "Morning, Nicca. Do you want to play with my new toys?"

She looked so excited that he hated to tell her no. "I cannot just this moment. I need to shower, and then I would love to talk with you about our day today, ok?"

She nodded and put her hand on his cheek. "You're pretty, Nicca."

Nicholas smiled and reached out to brush her hair back from her face. "It's only your reflection you're seeing, little one."

She giggled. "No, it's not, silly." She bounced over to the toys Martin had bought for her and picked up a doll.

Martin opened the door to his room. He looked at Nicholas, "Morning. I apologize for my fast exit last night. I was feeling a little off."

Nicholas suspected it was more than that, but he didn't push. "It's fine, Martin. I hope you're feeling better."

"I'm grand. Is there anything I should start with this morning?" Martin asked.

"Maybe you could order some breakfast for us? Whatever she wishes," Nicholas suggested.

He looked over at Sophia and smiled. "Of course."

Nicholas hit the shower to wake himself up and focus on what he needed to do today. He needed to have the binding ritual. That meant explaining to both Martin and Sophia more than he had ever explained to anyone before. He didn't want Martin to think he was crazy. His friendship had become important. And Sophia. She was the sole purpose he existed, and it would be hard to accept her being afraid of him.

He dressed in a pair of jeans and a blue t-shirt. He figured he might as well be comfortable because he didn't think being marked would be pleasant. The moment Sophia had been born, he'd felt the driving need to take the guardian mark. He'd known exactly what to do instantly, but he hadn't been able to do it.

Those first few weeks after her birth were a blur of pain and desperation he didn't like to think about. Usually, the binding would have happened immediately, but he'd been waiting thirteen hundred years, the last six being the most brutal. It was time to fix that. He looked at himself in the bathroom mirror as he took a deep breath. "Now or never, I guess," he said to himself.

When he got to the dining area, Sophia was giggling at Martin. He sat down across from Martin and looked at her. "What's so funny, little one?"

Sophia looked up with sparkles still in her eyes. "Martin's favorite color is pink. What's your favorite color?"

Nicholas didn't even have to think about it. "Turquoise."

She frowned in serious thought. "What is turk-toys?"

Nicholas leaned over and winked. "The color of your eyes."

She grinned and started eating her eggs again. "How old are you? I'm six-years-old."

Nicholas couldn't very well tell her or Martin he was thirteen hundred years old. Besides that, once bound, he would age normally, so he went with the easiest answer. "Well, I'm eighteen, but I'm very responsible for eighteen. I promise." He caught Martin staring at him strangely, knew he was doing the math, and it wasn't adding up. Martin had been hanging with him for almost four years.

She regarded him. "Where are your mommies and daddies?"

It was a fair question because both he and Martin appeared young. Most people thought he was just a rich man's son spending family money. People didn't question you for long when you threw money at them. "Well, Miss Snow, my parents are long gone. Martin's too. We take care of each other like a family."

Sophia seemed to ponder that information before adding, "Kind of like me. I can be y'all's family too." Nicholas couldn't help but grin at her sincere offer. So innocent and eager to love and be loved. He hoped she would understand why she had to stay with Penny. "Well, I need to talk to you both about that, actually, but how about we finish breakfast first?" he suggested.

"Sure, I'm finished anyway," Sophia said as she put down her fork.

"Well, I'm just starting. So how about you play while I go over some things with Martin? Then you and I will make a plan," he said.

"Okie Dokie. I have to organize the dollhouse, anyway. It's a mess," she said with a serious expression.

"Well, we can't have that, can we?" he answered.

"No. We. Can't," she said affirmatively. She hopped down and went to work on her dollhouse in the next room.

"Martin. This is going to be a hard conversation for me. I know we rarely delve into each other's pasts, and I have always appreciated that—depended on it," Nicholas said carefully.

Martin stopped eating. "Look, Nicholas, if this is about last night..."

"No, not at all," Nicholas interrupted him. "I don't know how much you've seen, but I'm hoping that you've noticed there are some things that are different about me." He paused and looked at Martin to gauge his reaction.

Martin grew quiet and looked down at his hands. Nicholas kept going, "I'm starting this conversation now because we've reached the point where you may start seeing a lot more. I need to know if you can handle that. If ye can't, this would be your opportunity to walk away."

At that, Martin's gaze jerked up to meet his. "You're firing me?"

Nicholas jumped. "No! Not at all. I'd be fucked without your help. But Martin, I value your friendship more than having you as an assistant."

Martin looked at him seriously before he answered, "You saved my life. I owe it to you." At Nicholas's shaking head he added, "No. Seriously. Even after you saved my life physically. I had nowhere to go. No family. No money. No purpose. You gave me that. I value our friendship as much as you do."

Nicholas hadn't known Martin thought of him as a friend too. "What's coming isn't nice. It's evil and very dangerous. It would be safer if you left, and I want you to have that option, but once you choose, it's done. You can't unsee what's coming. So it's important to choose what's best for you. Not me. You."

Martin hesitated before he admitted, "I've known since the beginning that there is something 'other' about you. I have noticed... things. I haven't understood completely why we searched for the girl, and I noticed your age, the lack of family, but the abundance of resources. I have had questions, but I never doubted your character. I was just hoping you would tell me when you were ready. I'm an excellent judge of character, Nicholas, and I've met no one with more honor, integrity, or goodness. I may not know exactly what you are, but I know who you are, and I donna know exactly what we are doing, but I know whatever it is, it's for a good reason. I like knowing I'm helping do something good. And lastly, even if you doubted I would help you, you canna think for a moment I would walk away from that little girl in there, knowing she needed someone to help. So answering your question, I am in this one hundred and ten percent." Martin finished with a definitive nod of his head.

"Well," Nicholas said, "that settles that, I guess." He gave Martin a lopsided grin of thanks. Then he remembered something. "Hey, you said last night you had a sister. Just now you said you had no family?"

Martin looked away and explained in a flat voice, "I had a sister. I donna anymore."

"I'm sorry. I didn't mean to drag up painful things." Nicholas apologized.

"It's fine. A story for another time, perhaps," Martin said dismissively.

Nicholas took Martin's cue and changed the subject. "Now for the weird stuff. I will explain more to you later, but for now, I need to focus on Sophia. How much do ye know about druids?"

Martin's face frowned in thought. "Nothing, really. I mean. I know they were a group of people, but I couldn't tell you anything about their religion. They were early pagans, right?"

Nicholas cringed. "Sort of, yes. It wasn't a religion so much as a way of viewing the world and all the life in it. Although my mother would hate being described as a pagan, they believed in the existence of other gods. Some early druids had great powers and gifts of magical abilities. A group of powerful druid women raised me. One in particular took me under her wing and taught me the ways. She found me in the woods as a baby. Her name was Niamh, and she was the only mother I knew. Sophia is her descendant." Both men looked over at Sophia playing in the living room.

"So," Martin began, "Sophia is a druid?"

Nicholas tried to think of how much to say at this point. "Yes, she is a druid. Besides teaching her everything she needs to know about being a druid, I am charged with the very important

43

task of protecting her. I can't go into everything right now, but there is a darkness coming, and Sophia is the only one left who can stop it from completely swallowing the entire world. She's so important that certain things have been put into place to ensure she has the best chance possible of returning the balance. I am one of those things."

Martin seemed to take in everything, so Nicholas continued, "I'm a guardian. The druids performed a ritual to help guide me to Sophia, but that's only half of it. I have to complete the ritual to bind me to her. Then, I will gain all of my abilities. I'll always know where she is and if she's in trouble. And Martin, if I have to, I will kill anyone who threatens to harm her. My life will be forever tethered to hers. I've put it off for six years. I cannot put it off any longer."

Martin studied him for a moment. "You're not eighteen, are you?"

Nicholas just gave a slight shake of his head.

Martin paused a moment longer and then with a sigh he said, "Just tell me what to do."

Nicholas felt like a ton of rocks just lifted from his shoulders. "I need you to find a couple of houses. Find a home you think Sophia could be happy growing up in. Look at school systems and neighborhoods with high marks in the area Penny lives. I want the second house for us to stay in while we are here. It needs to be close to hers. See if you can work your financial magic and close as soon as possible. The quicker we can get Sophia settled, the better for her. Also, I want you to research Sophia's family tree. I know her mother's name is Lorraine Snow, but that's it. I want to see how Niamh's line got from Ireland to America. It won't be easy and you probably won't be able to get much, but one day Sophia might want to know where she comes from, and it could be useful."

Martin nodded. "I can do that." He stood to get to work but paused. "So if she is a druid, does she have powers?"

"Martin, she has *all* the power."

CHAPTER 7

*N*icholas took a deep breath and walked toward
Sophia. He was excited that he was finally fulfilling
his destiny and worried that he would scare her. She had set all
her dolls in a line along the couch and was teaching them how to
curtsey. With a tiara on her head and a wand in one hand, she
looked exactly like a six-year-old should look. She had on a pair
of cropped jeans and a pink t-shirt with a unicorn on the front.
Her little tennis shoes were white with pink flowers. Why did
she have to be the one? Why couldn't he just do it for her?

He got down to her level by sitting on the floor with his back
against the sofa.

She smiled and put a hand on his shoulder. "You look
worried, Nicca."

Nicholas hadn't realized his emotions were showing. He
would have to work harder at keeping control of that. "I have to
do something that might be a little scary for you, but I need to
do it so I can take better care of you."

She leaned back against the couch so they were shoulder to
shoulder and looked over at the fireplace. "I know," she said
matter-of-factly.

Nicholas looked at her. "What do you mean?"

"Ney told me you would have to do it. She already explained

everything." She looked over at Nicholas and must have seen his shock because she smiled. "No worries, Nicca."

Nicholas couldn't believe it. "Is Ney the fairy godmother that visits you sometimes and tells you things?"

Sophia started twirling against the edge of the couch. "Yep."

He reached out and pulled Sophia back to him. "Miss Snow, is her full name Niamh?"

She looked at him. "You know her too?"

Knowing that his mother was helping brought him such comfort and relief. "Yes, I know her very well."

She leaned over and said, "I am very glad because I thought maybe she might be pretend."

"No," Nicholas agreed. "She is not pretend. I need to make sure she told you everything you need to know though, ok? So just listen to me for a moment." He waited for her to nod before continuing. "My job is to protect you, Miss Snow. I will always be here to make sure you are safe. You will always have everything you need to be happy, ok?" He waited for her nod again, "In order for me to do that we need to use some magic. Do you believe in magic?"

She thought for a second and then explained, "My mama told me there was no such thing, but I think there is. Are we really going to do magic?"

"Yes, little one," Nicholas said. "After we do this, I will always be able to get to you if you are in trouble and need me for anything."

"Ok." As simple as that, she accepted it.

"Ok. Just a moment, Miss Snow, and we will get started. It helps to be high up. So how about a trip to the roof?" Nicholas asked her.

"Cool," she said. "Sounds like an adventure!" She started twirling around the couch.

Nicholas grabbed a cup and went into his bathroom to put some water in it. Then he picked up a little bag in his suitcase and met back up with Sophia. "I'm ready, Miss Snow. Let's go."

She set her wand down, waved goodbye to all her dolls, and grabbed Nicholas's hand. "Ok. I'm ready too," she said bravely.

He led her out the door and down the hall to the stairwell. Once at the top of a smaller set of stairs, he came to a door that said emergency exit. He put his hand to the door and centered himself. The power surged out of his hands and surrounded the door to hold the alarm in place.

With a wink he said, "Here we go, little one."

She smiled up at him as he pushed open the door and led them over to a place at the center. They were nowhere near the edge, but it still made him nervous.

Sophia looked around at the taller buildings in awe. "It feels like we are in the clouds, Nicca."

He smiled. "I need you to hold still for a moment. I'm going to set up everything." He walked a few steps away, and after checking the sky to find North, he opened his bag and pulled out a small piece of oak, a candle, and a lighter. He placed the oak to the north, the water to the east, and the candle to the west. He lit the candle before walking to his bag and pulling out a longer piece of oak wood and two smooth river stones.

He explained to Sophia, "This is a druid circle I'm drawing. It will help keep us centered and calm." She watched him as he walked to the south point and set the stones to make a door into the circle. Then he began drawing in the gravel connecting the points going clockwise to make a circle. At each point he murmured a phrase in his native tongue.

Sophia watched with curiosity until he reached the south point again. "What are you saying, Nicca?"

"I'm wishing peace for all the corners in my original language. Does it sound weird to you?" Nicholas asked.

"At first it did, but then I think I understood you," Sophia explained.

"It's in your blood, Miss Snow. That's a good thing," Nicholas said as he walked toward the two stones that acted as a gateway. He motioned for Sophia to walk into the center of the circle, and she timidly walked toward him with her tiara still on her head. She looked so small.

When she reached the center, he got on his knees so he could face her. He took both of her tiny hands as he explained, "Now we wish peace for the center." He uttered the same phase while she listened. "This circle is like a bubble, Miss Snow. All the world is moving on around us, but here in this circle, it's timeless. No past and no future. Just now. I need you to forget everything but here and now, ok?"

She took a moment to concentrate with her eyes closed. When they opened, they had a slight shimmer to them. "Ok. Only now. I got it."

He brought his hands up to frame both sides of her face. His hands were so large they seemed to swallow her entire head. His fingers slid into her curls and his right thumb landed just behind her left ear. "Miss Snow, this might hurt a bit, but I promise I will protect you. I may be in some pain also, but don't let that frighten ye. It will only be for a bit."

She smiled even as her eyes shimmered, "No worries. Right, Nicca?"

He smiled and felt his power rise from his chest. "No worries, Miss Snow."

After six years of torment, of holding his power down, he finally gave over to it. His head fell back, and he felt power sizzle down his arms into Sophia. His body was vibrating, and at first, it didn't hurt. It felt good. He looked at Sophia. Her eyes were like blue diamonds. She was staring back at him as the power kept building.

Suddenly, he felt Sophia's power pushing back up his arms and humming through his body. It felt like tiny pinpricks all over his skin, and it was getting hard to breathe. He saw her raise her right hand and hold it over his heart as her eyes took on an intense turquoise glow. He felt like she was pulling him into her soul. His lungs were burning from holding his breath. And then she spoke. Her voice raised goosebumps along his skin. It moved over and around him like smoke. He even felt her voice inside of him.

With her hand still on his heart, she began, "You are..." A shot of electricity hit his chest where she touched him. She moved her hand to her heart. "I am..."

The electricity burned his chest and moved down his arms.

His right thumb burned behind Sophia's ear. And then the pain hit him. He had just enough focus to see Sophia falling, and he eased her to the ground while a ferocious growl erupted from his chest. He rolled over next to her and gave into the pain. Clawing pain ripped at his chest and up the left side of his neck. He lay there in agony trying to focus and center his mind, but the pain was too intense, and he was certain he was going to pass out because he couldn't breathe. He burned inside and out.

Then suddenly, without warning—it stopped. Just a mild burning left behind. He took a deep breath and looked down at his chest. Shockingly, his shirt looked fine. It'd felt like something had ripped his body open. He lifted the shirt to see an intricate tattoo on his chest.

It looked Celtic, with bold dark lines and sharp twists and turns. It started at his heart where she had touched him and spread over the left side of his chest, disappearing over his shoulder. His fingers traced it, going up the side of his neck. He looked at Sophia, still lying peacefully on the gravel. Leaning over to check her more closely, she looked like she was sleeping. He was just about to wake her when he heard a voice behind him.

"Well, it's about time. I thought you would never mark the girl."

Nicholas whirled around with a growl, ready to fight. He straightened in shock. "Martin?"

CHAPTER 8

*N*icholas saw a gold spark flair in Martin's eyes. Instead of being alarmed, it seemed familiar.

Martin took a step closer to him. "It's Martin's body," he said. "I'm just borrowing it for a few moments. I'm Jophiel. Think of me as a guide. I've been waiting quite some time to guide you too."

Nicholas was trying hard to process everything he was hearing while still monitoring Sophia and not focusing on the burning in his chest. "I don't understand what's going on. Where's Martin?"

"He's here. He's fine, don't worry. It's easier to borrow a body. It's hard for human eyes to see an angel." Martin leaned over and winked, "We *are* kind of bright."

"What? An *angel?*" Nicholas felt lost.

"Yes. An angel. Sophia is fine, by the way. The mark on her will burn for a bit. Letting her sleep spares her the pain. Also, the ceremony you performed has shielded her powers. It will protect her from accidentally revealing herself to others, at least until she is older and learns control," Jophiel explained. "How about you close the circle, and we get off this roof and back to the room? Sophia would be more comfortable in a bed, I'm sure," Jophiel suggested.

That Sophia might not be comfortable snapped Nicholas into

action. He quickly went counter-clockwise, wishing light and life in his native tongue, collected his things, and gently lifted Sophia.

It took only a couple of minutes to get back to the room with him carrying her. He laid her on her bed, took the tiara off, and set it aside. Checking behind her right ear, he saw a small triskelion. Three bold lines moved out from the center. Each line curved back on itself, making three spirals in a triangle shape. He knew without looking her tattoo would fit perfectly in the hollowed-out triskelion over his heart. It was all overwhelming, but he needed to hear what Jophiel had to say.

When he got to the living area, Jophiel was leaning against the fireplace. He looked casual with his suit jacket off and his tie loosened. It was strange because it was Martin's body, but it didn't look like Martin anymore. The way Jophiel carried himself and the gold shimmer in his eyes made him look completely different.

"You know," Jophiel began, "you're an angel too. An archangel at that."

"*Me?*" Nicholas choked, "I'm starting to think I know nothing."

"We found ourselves in a unique situation, my friend. I'm not allowed to guide you until you've been marked. That's the rules. Normally, I would have appeared much sooner, but you had to wait for the marking, therefore, you had to wait for the guiding." Jophiel walked over to the couch.

Nicholas flopped down in the chair, "So I'm an *angel*?"

Martin laughed. "Well yes, you *were* an angel, and when this assignment came along, you volunteered. Demanded it." He looked at Nicholas for a moment before asking, "Where did you think the term guardian angel came from, my friend?"

"Guardians are angels that become human?" Nicholas asked.

"Most humans have an angel from time to time. Invisible help to answer a prayer, show an open door of opportunity, or just lend support or comfort. You know, just keeping the balance. A few times, we have been sent straight from God in our angelic forms to strike fear or give life-altering messages.

Those times make the headlines." Jophiel leaned back on the couch and put his hands behind his head. "But sometimes, when the balance swings too far and fast toward darkness, a person becomes too important to the light's cause. That person needs a full-time guardian to devote every second to his assignment. It's much easier to protect if you are living on the same plane. So, it falls to the highest of angels, archangels, to become guardians. When you looked through time and saw Sophia, nothing could stop you from being her guardian, Nicholas. You insisted. I can see why too. Her light is beautiful, and the times have never been closer to darkness prevailing. It was a job for our best."

Nicholas sat still for a moment and let the story sink in. Somehow what he was hearing felt right. He knew it should sound crazy, but his senses could feel the truth in what he was explaining. One thing didn't make sense, though. "I caused this problem, Jophiel. I brought this evil here. Why would I volunteer to come protect her, only to be the very reason she's in danger?"

Jophiel took his hands down slowly. "That was an interesting turn of events, for sure. The danger was coming to her, Nicholas. How it got here was up for debate, but the endgame was always going to be the same. It's a complex puzzle that even angels aren't meant to understand, much less humans. Man always has a choice, Nicholas. Darkness, and light for that matter, have a million avenues to get to where they want to go. Man's free will determines the path. If you had chosen differently, then it would have come here a different way, but it still would have come."

Nicholas leaned his head back and shut his eyes. The knowledge that he couldn't have changed the outcome should have made him feel better, but it didn't. He wasn't sure what to do with all of this new information. "What did she mean earlier, Jophiel? When she said 'you are, I am'?"

"How well do you know your Bible?" Jophiel asked.

"Well enough, I guess. Are you thinking of the part where God tells Moses his name is I AM? Was Sophia calling me God?" Nicholas said in shock.

Jophiel laughed. "No, my friend. They are words from God, though. If you haven't noticed already, names mean a lot to her. Do you know what Nicca means?"

Nicholas shook his head. "I just assumed it was a nickname for Nicholas."

Jophiel nodded. "It is, and in an ancient Celtic language, it translates 'guardian.' She recognized you the moment she saw you. The moment you were assigned to her, your lives became forever entwined. God in all of His brilliance does not waste words. Ever. 'I AM that I AM' What a lovely way to explain His position of greatness. His absoluteness. He is because He is... period."

Nicholas frowned. "So she was saying she recognized I was from God?"

Jophiel shook his head and sighed. "You misunderstood her, Nicholas. She didn't say 'You are, I am.' She said 'You are,' but when she said 'I am', she was referring to herself. It's beautiful, really. A profession of how closely you are tied together. You see Nicholas, God is because He is... but not you. You are, because she is. As long as she exists, you exist. It's the tightest bond known. Closer than parent/child, husband/wife, or even brotherhood. It's a gift of complete devotion."

Nicholas was finally understanding. "So, what now?"

Jophiel leaned forward and placed his forearms on his thighs. "Exactly what you're doing. You get her settled into a nice stable life and then disappear and let her have that life."

Nicholas jerked his head toward him, "What do you mean *disappear*? I can't go altogether. The last thing she needs is someone else to abandon her."

Jophiel grinned. "You disappear, yes, but you don't really go. Look, you already had that very instinct. That's why you are putting her with Penny. A guardian isn't meant to be seen all that often, really. Some assignments live their entire lives just thinking they're really lucky people. Now that you're marked, you will feel when she is in trouble. You just imagine her mark fitting into yours, and it will pull you to her instantly. You'll probably be able to dispatch the danger and leave again without her even knowing you were there. Having a relationship gets messy, Nicholas. It gets complicated when your assignment becomes less like a mission and more like family. It clouds judgement. Just make sure she gets the training and education she needs. Her battle, her purpose, will not happen until she is grown. Protect her from all the ways darkness will try to defeat her, because it *will* try. She is as close to pure as a human can be, Nicholas. She's almost completely light, and that will turn her into a magnet for the dark. It will be drawn to her, and she will constantly find herself in trouble."

Nicholas couldn't argue with his logic. He just thought it would have been nice to have had the information before he'd met Sophia. Staying out of her life would be hard to do. "You said this was a unique situation, though."

Jophiel grinned again. "Look, I get it. I truly do. I've been a guardian before, but trust me. You'll be able to protect her better from a distance. Getting close makes it near impossible to let her fight when her time comes."

Nicholas looked at his new friend. "You're using Martin's body... I didn't know angels could possess people. I thought that was just a demon thing."

Jophiel stood slowly. "Well, we don't get the bad publicity demons get. First, we ask permission before we share a body. Second, we don't destroy them. In fact, we leave a body better than we found it, which is only the polite thing to do. And last, we don't stay. We give them their space back. Most find it a priv-ilege as your friend Martin has, I think. I've taken the liberty of letting him hear our conversation. It will save you having to explain everything to him. I'll visit from time to time as needed. For now, just keep her safe. Her fight isn't until later." Jophiel looked at Nicholas with flashing gold eyes. "It has been good to speak with you, finally."

Nicholas felt panic. "How can I get in touch with you if I have more questions?"

Jophiel turned back toward the couch and answered simply, "You don't."

Nicholas leaned forward. "Were we friends when I was an angel?"

Jophiel's eyes flashed quickly as he pounded his fist against his chest. "We were brothers."

Then, just like that, he was gone. He saw it the moment Martin was back. There was a shift that most would never notice. Even Nicholas couldn't put his finger on it, but he knew he was looking at Martin now. He looked a little frazzled but otherwise ok.

"So…" Nicholas began. "That was weird."

Martin smiled. "Actually, it was very enlightening."

"How do you feel?"

"Honestly, I feel great! It was kind of like receiving a gift." Martin seemed genuinely happy about the situation.

"Good to hear. I'm glad you know most of the story now."

"I'm not sure I know most of it, but I think I know enough for today. I think we both have a lot to process for now." Martin gave him a friendly smile. "Look, I had an excellent find on a couple of houses. I was in the middle of inquiring about them when Jophiel found me. How about I get back on that and you can rest a bit? I'm sure you have a lot to think about."

Nicholas nodded and watched Martin head out of the room. He reached up to feel his tattoo over his heart and instantly felt Sophia sleeping peacefully. It allowed him to relax enough to fall into sleep. Maybe the deepest sleep he'd had in over a thousand years.

CHAPTER 9

*N*icholas felt her when she walked into the room. He remained still in the chair where he'd fallen asleep, but it surprised him when she crawled into his lap and rested her head against his shoulder. He sensed her sadness as she snuggled into his t-shirt.

Sophia looked up at him and gave a half smile. "I was just thinking about mama. I hope she is ok."

Nicholas frowned. "I'm sure she is, Miss Snow. How about you? Do you feel ok after everything earlier?"

"I feel fine. I can feel you. It's like a warm feeling. Not just on the outside. I feel the warm feeling inside too." She looked up at Nicholas with big eyes.

"It's just from earlier. So, you will always feel safe. I know it's been a hard couple of days for you. I'm sorry." Nicholas pushed her curls back from her face.

She looked at him with that stare he was starting to think meant she was seeing inside him. "Nicca, Ney came to me while I slept. I don't like what she told me came next." She hugged him tighter and buried her head.

Nicholas shut his eyes and held her for a moment. He imagined Niamh was trying to help her adjust to the fact that he would be leaving. He was glad for her support, because he didn't like what came next either.

"What comes next, Miss Snow?"

His shirt muffled her answer. "You are giving me away to some stranger." The last of her sentence caught in her throat on a sob.

Nicholas was torn. He knew it was best, but having her so upset was hard to handle. He let her cry for a moment while he stroked her hair softly. Then he explained as best he could. "Miss Snow, I need you to remember something very important. I will never abandon you. If you ever need me, I will always be there. I am not 'giving' you to anyone. Ever. I will *always* be your guardian." He placed his finger under her chin and tilted her face up so he could look at her. "I promise you." She seemed to relax a little at his words, so he kept explaining. "Martin and I have to travel a lot. It's no way to raise a child. You need to be in one home and one school. Somewhere stable. I'm doing this so you can have the life you deserve."

Her eyes were brimming with tears. "Nicca. I will be the best girl ever. You wouldn't ever have to tell me to do anything twice. I would keep my room clean. I would get a job and earn money to pay for everything..." She trailed off as she saw Nicholas shaking his head. "But Nicca, what if I don't like her? What if she's mean? Mama always told me what it would be like if they took me away from her." She took a deep breath before saying with a shaky voice, "I'm really scared." The tears started flowing again down her cheeks, and she put her face in her hands.

Nicholas's heart ached. He physically hurt to be making her feel this way. He gently pulled her hands down. "Miss Snow, if anyone hurts one little hair on your body, they will have to answer to me. I will not let anyone take care of you that won't love you as you deserve to be loved. Think of this as exciting, not scary. It's an adventure. You'll have a new, beautiful home. New clothes and toys to call your own. We'll get you into a great school and you can make so many friends. You will finally get to have a normal six-year-old's life. You'll get to do all the things you dreamed of doing."

She seemed to think over the things he was saying. He waited patiently while she thought it through. Finally she asked, "Will I ever see you again, Nicca?"

Nicholas thought about what Jophiel had said about being invisible in her life. For the life of him, he couldn't bear to break her heart any further. He wondered if maybe he could compromise. "Yes, Miss Snow. I will come see you on your birthday. Would you like that?"

She smiled a little at his comment. "With presents?" she asked.

He smiled back. "With presents."

She reached up and started tracing the tattoo that appeared out of his shirt and ran up his neck. "What is this, Nicca?" she asked, looking amazed.

The tattoo tingled like it recognized her. "I got it earlier today. Do you like it?"

She looked up at him and smiled. "It's pretty. Like you."

He smiled down at her and said, "Miss Snow, I know it's hard today, but you'll realize very soon that this was the right choice."

She took a deep breath again and wiped her eyes. She put her hands in her lap and stared down for a moment. Then she looked up and smiled. "I trust you, Nicca."

He brushed her hair over a shoulder. "It's going to be ok, little one."

She jumped down. "Do you think I could bring my toys?"

He assured her, "Of course ye can. They're yours." He checked the time, because he was meeting Penny for dinner. He planned to let her go with Penny, but he needed to be sure she would agree to the conditions he had.

He went to Martin's door and knocked lightly. At Martin's command, he entered to find a bedroom covered in stacks of papers. "Did a tornado come through while I slept?"

Martin grinned. "Being possessed by an angel has a strange effect. I've done more work in the last hour than I've done in the last week. I keep waiting for the crash, but it hasna happened yet."

Nicholas didn't know if it was good or bad, but Martin seemed pleased enough with the whole situation. "Well, hopefully it will last until tonight. I have to meet Penny, and I don't want her to meet Sophia until I'm ready. I was hoping you could watch her this evening?"

Martin nodded immediately. "No problem. I think I've found the perfect house. I have two options, though. Maybe she would like to come along and pick the one she wants?"

"I think she might like that very much. I'm going to shower and change. Can you call down and have something light brought up? She's hungry," Nicholas agreed.

Nicholas left to shower but paused when he entered his bathroom and saw the tattoo coming out of the top of his shirt. He removed his shirt and looked more closely. He remembered what Jophiel said about finding Sophia whenever he needed to so he gathered the shadows until he couldn't see himself anymore in the mirror, closed his eyes, and imagined Sophia's mark fitting inside the one over his heart. A slight tug deep in his chest, and he was right behind Sophia, playing on the living area floor with her dolls. She stopped immediately and turned in his direction. She couldn't see him, but he knew she could feel him. After a moment she went back to playing.

With one last look, he went back to the bathroom and showered. He chose a suit for his meeting so he would appear older and more authoritative. Thankfully, he was large, which helped, but if one looked closely at his face, it still held the look of youth. He'd cut his hair over the years, but he still kept it on the long side. It was a little wild and untamed, like his home in Ireland. For tonight, however, he pulled it back and secured it with a leather strap. He checked himself one last time and went to say goodnight.

Sophia was at the table eating a ham and cheese sandwich and telling Martin what all her favorite fruits were. She turned to Nicholas with a smile.

"Nicca, you look so fancy!" Her face lit up. "Guess what?" She didn't actually give him a chance to guess. "Martin is taking me shopping for a whole house." She fell into giggles. "A whole house, Nicca. Like shopping for food or something."

Nicholas smiled. "Well, how else are you supposed to pick out your home?"

Sophia sobered. "I don't know. What if I don't pick the right one?"

"If it feels like home, it will be, Miss Snow. You'll do fine."

"Are you coming with us?" She asked him.

"I cannot, little one. I'm off to an important meeting, but I look forward to hearing all about the one ye like the most, ok?" He watched her for any fear about him leaving her, but she was only a little anxious, thankfully.

"Ok. Maybe we could take some pictures on your phone, Martin?" she asked him hopefully.

Martin grinned at her. "If you can help me then of course we can, lass."

Nicholas gave the top of her head a couple of taps. He got almost to the door but had to stop. This was the first time he was leaving her like this, and it was physically hard to do. He turned and looked at her still sitting at the table eating and talking with Martin. She looked up and grinned with a mouthful of food, then gave a goofy wave. Nicholas gathered his strength, then grinned and forced himself to turn and walk out the door.

CHAPTER 10

*N*icholas moved with a confidence he definitely did not feel. He planned to meet Penny at the restaurant in the hotel, but he was struggling with thoughts of being far from Sophia. He took a calming breath and walked into the bar of the restaurant.

Scanning the seats, he saw a woman who resembled the photo in Martin's file. She was slender with dark hair and blue eyes, and she looked nervous, which worked in his favor. He walked directly up to her and held out his hand. "Hello, Penny West? My name is Nicholas Stone. I believe I'm here to meet you?"

She looked shocked at the sight of him, but quickly recovered and grabbed his hand. "Yes! Mr. Stone. I'm Penny. Sorry, I was expecting someone... well... older."

"Yes, Ms. West, I get that a lot. I'm much older than I look," he assured her.

They were seated quickly, thankfully, in a private corner as he had requested.

"Ms. West," Nicholas began, "I would like to thank you for meeting me so quickly."

"Please, call me Penny. I want this opportunity so of course meeting you was no problem," she said sincerely. "Although, I will admit this all feels a little strange."

61

"Penny, can you tell me a little about your current situation? Everything in the files is current up to the passing of your husband. Can you help me get up to speed?" He hated bringing up painful things, but he needed to know.

The spark in her eyes dimmed a little at the mention of her husband. "Yes. Of course. Well, everything is pretty much the same as far as my job and living situation. Things are a little tighter with only a teacher's income, but thankfully, Jon had excellent insurance. Most expenses were taken care of, so living on my income hasn't been too difficult. It's just me living at home. No pets or extended family. It's... pretty quiet." She paused for a moment and then stated bluntly, "I'm not sure what you want to hear, Mr. Stone. Maybe you could just ask?"

"I know this seems uncomfortable and maybe a little awkward, but I'm actually not looking for a specific thing. I'm looking for an overall sense of your state of mind. The type of person you are to come through the words you are choosing to share with me, if that makes any sense."

"It makes a weird kind of sense. It sounds like you really care about what happens to this little girl. This whole situation seems a little unorthodox. I am a little concerned about the legality of this. Are you a lawyer?" she tentatively asked.

Nicholas saw that despite the sadness that still lingered behind her eyes, and the obvious loneliness she was feeling, this woman still had fight. Maybe that was why the magic picked her. "I'm not a lawyer, and I appreciate your concern. I care very much about what happens to her. In fact, she is the most important person in the world to me. I will stop at nothing to see she has a happy and safe life. You're right. This will not be a conventional adoption, but if you agree to my terms, you will have the pleasure of raising a beautiful little girl. As you stated in our phone conversation, adopting when single can be tricky. This might be a win-win for us both. I can find a safe home for Sophia, and you get the chance to be a mom."

Her eyes teared up. "Her name is Sophia?"

"Yes. She's six-years-old going on forty."

Penny let out a small laugh. "She sounds perfect."

Nicholas gave a small but affirmative nod. "She is." He was about to launch into his long list of conditions when they were interrupted by the server. "Shall we have drinks and place our order, Penny?" he asked instead.

"Yes. That would be lovely. Thank you."

After telling the server their orders, Nicholas spent the rest of the meal asking her questions about her life. It was all information he knew from her file, but he was looking for any inconsistencies or red flags. "If you don't mind my asking, how did your husband pass?"

Penny looked down at her food and explained, "He was in a car accident coming home from work one evening. He had been in surgery all day. I always complained about him driving while exhausted. The accident wasn't his fault, but I've always wondered if it could have been avoided if he had been more alert. He was driving along the interstate and a large chunk of concrete either fell or was thrown from an overpass. It crashed into the windshield, hitting him and causing him to crash. Thankfully, no one else was hit, but he died almost instantly."

"That's awful. Again, I am so sorry to keep prying into such sad topics," Nicholas apologized.

"No. I get it. Truly. After going through developing a file for the adoption agency, I know that it's part of the gig if you want to adopt. Maybe it's time to hear about exactly what I'm signing up for here?" Penny looked at him with a mixture of hope and hesitancy.

Nicholas took a deep breath and centered himself. He wanted to draw from his magic to help keep the conversation calm and hopefully not scare her away. "Ms. West... Penny, I agree you have been most patient with me, so I will explain myself as best as I can, and hopefully we can come to a mutual agreement that will benefit us all. I am Sophia's guardian, and I want to remain her guardian; however, I'm honest enough with myself to admit that I cannot give her the stable life she needs. I travel constantly. She needs one home, one school, friends, birthday parties, and maybe even a pet. She needs a female role model to help her with things I simply know nothing about."

Penny gave a small laugh. "You mean the thought of periods and training bras is enough to send you running for the hills?"

Nicholas blanched white and was speechless for a full minute. "You laugh, but I was a wreck just thinking of helping her get ready for bed. I hadn't even thought that far. Periods? Training bras? Jesus..." Nicholas swore quietly.

Penny laughed. "It's always so comical how such topics can send the biggest, baddest, bravest of men running." She looked out over the restaurant for a moment and then looked back at Nicholas. "Listen, I want more than anything to be a mom, and Sophia sounds lovely, but I wouldn't be able to live with myself if I didn't say this. Every new parent feels overwhelmed, like you do right now, but many single men raise beautiful daughters. All the things you're afraid of can be figured out. If you care about her as much as you say, are you sure you shouldn't be raising her?"

Nicholas saw at that moment why she was the one. She was putting others' needs before her own desires. Sincerely and unselfishly sacrificing her dreams for what may be best for a child she hadn't even met. "I am not—nor do I want to be—her father, Penny. My role in Sophia's life is difficult to explain. Tell me, what are your views on people with... special abilities?" Nicholas held his breath.

"You mean like a kid with a super high I.Q.? Is Sophia a genius? I think that's amazing and as you know, education is very important to me." Penny was winding up with excitement.

"No, Penny. I mean, yes, Sophia is extremely smart, but I'm talking about abilities that most deny exist. Like moving objects, or reading thoughts, or predicting outcomes." He stared at her intently.

Penny sat back, and her eyes widened. She took a moment before leaning forward and placing her arms on the table. "Mr. Stone, I would describe myself as open-minded. I haven't personally seen anything like that, but I do like the idea that they could exist. In fact, there is a long-standing rumor that my mother's ancestors used to have some abilities. My great grandmother told me a story once when I was a young girl. I know this might sound crazy, but she swore they were druids that could control the earth—" Penny laughed nervously. "—or something like that. But it was probably just a story."

Nicholas sat in shocked silence. Of course, the magic would have led him to her. He bet every dime he owned Penny was a descendant of the druid women from his village.

"Penny, Sophia is, in fact, a druid. She doesn't know it yet, but she is extremely important. She is destined to save the world. I know it's difficult to comprehend, but I am telling you the truth." He pushed his influence into his words, hoping she would see his sincerity.

Penny turned white and pinched her lips together and looked down at her hands. Nicholas got the feeling this was the turning point for her. Either she would accept or simply walk away. He kept sending whatever power of influence he had and hoped for the best.

She looked around as if she felt the magic. When she looked back at Nicholas, she took a deep breath. "That sounds like a tremendous burden for a small girl. Definitely not something she should face alone. A girl like that is going to need all the support she can get if we expect her to save the world." She gave him a half-smile.

Nicholas felt his body relax. "Yes, she will. She has certain abilities most people would not understand. I want her to have as much of a normal life as possible, but occasionally you might see or hear things that don't seem possible, and I need to know you can handle that with sensitivity. I don't want her ashamed or embarrassed about how special she is."

"I would never intentionally make a child feel 'less than' for anything," Penny stated with passion.

"Good to hear. I'm going to give you my conditions, but I don't want you to answer me tonight, Penny. Go home and honestly think through all the possible good and bad. Talk to a lawyer and come up with any concerns or conditions you might have. Then sleep on it and tell me tomorrow, ok?" Nicholas asked.

Penny nodded so Nicholas continued, "I have more money

than I could ever want, and I want to make sure Sophia has everything possible. I will provide a home in the best school system, a monthly allowance, and all medical expenses. I will expect a few extras concerning her education. She will be tutored in ancient druid history, and I want her to learn to defend herself. You will be responsible for daily needs and parenting. I have promised I will visit her on her birthday. Other than that, I will only appear if her safety is in question or if there's something concerning her destiny."

"Her safety is in question? How would you know?" Penny asked.

"That is my special ability, Penny, and difficult to explain further than that. I'll know if she is in danger or hurt or scared. It's my job to keep her safe and make sure she has what she needs to accomplish her purpose."

"Ahh...so you're her guardian angel, huh?" Penny joked.

Nicholas froze and stared directly at Penny.

Penny coughed nervously. "Ok, I think this is where I stop."

Nicholas softened his look in understanding. "I'll always do what is good for Sophia, and if you can take on this monumental task, you'll be rewarded with the love and devotion of a wonderful little girl. I would count myself indebted to you. My 'special ability' led me to you, and I never doubt it. I found you for a reason. Please think about it and call me tomorrow with your questions?"

Penny nodded her head as she stood up from the table. "I know this whole situation should probably have me running. I will do some research of my own and call you tomorrow."

Nicholas stood and shook her hand. "Thank you."

He watched her walk toward the lobby. Every moment since he had found Sophia had been one step toward righting a wrong. He felt lighter. It was the first time he felt certain they could do this.

CHAPTER 11

$\mathcal{N}$icholas was heading back up to the room when he got an idea. He ducked into the lobby bathroom and checked on Sophia. Her excitement rushed through him, and it made him smile.

He pulled the shadows around him and pictured her mark fitting inside his. In a blink, he stood behind her in the middle of a kitchen.

Her hands were above her head as she laughed and twirled. The moment her face turned in his direction, she stopped. It warmed his heart that she searched for him.

She turned to Martin, "We have to take pictures of this kitchen. It is so huge." She walked over to the phone Martin was holding out to her and started trying to figure it out.

Nicholas ducked out of the kitchen and walked to the front door. He shook off the shadows and opened the door wide, yelling, "Hello! Anyone home?"

"NICCAAA!!" Sophia came running as fast as she could right toward him. He leaned down to catch her.

"I finished my meeting and thought pictures just wouldn't be as good as the real thing. So tell me. Is this the one?" He put her down and followed her to the kitchen to find Martin leaning against the counter with a grin.

"Yes, Nicca. This is totally it. It has everything a girl needs." She looked so serious it was hard not to laugh.

"You get around fast," Martin said.

"Well, there is no time to waste when looking for a princess castle, is there, Miss Snow?" He looked out to the backyard. There was a play set and a nice fenced-in yard. He could already picture her running around with a puppy on her heels.

"No. There. Is. Not," she said while waving her finger back and forth between the two guys.

Both men chuckled. "What makes this house the one, Miss Snow?" Nicholas asked.

"Well. The other house was beautiful. But this one has a swing on the front porch, and it has a bathroom right off the room that would be mine. I can't believe it! But mostly, it's because it sparkles blue, which reminds me of you." She glanced up and away.

Nicholas crouched down and tapped the tip of her nose. "Then this is the one. How about we celebrate by going to watch a movie? Surely, there is something appropriate showing in the local theater."

Her eyes got as big as saucers, "Oh my goodness!! Yes! Yes! Yes! I've always wanted to go see a movie in a theater." She started dancing around the kitchen and singing an off tune song about going to the movies.

Martin spoke up, "As much as I would love to go, I should start the process on this house if this is the one."

Nicholas nodded in agreement. "Sure, Martin, but Miss Snow and I will need a ride back into the city. I don't have a car."

Martin just shook his head and sighed. "Of course you don't." He headed out the door.

Nicholas looked at Sophia, "Come on. I haven't been to a movie in a very long time, actually. It could be fun for both of us."

Sophia skipped and grabbed his hand. "Best. Adventure. Ever."

CHAPTER 12

*N*icholas reached in his pocket for the hotel key card while he balanced Sophia on his hip. She had passed out as soon as they left the theater. The movie had been a fairy princess unicorn movie that had made Sophia squeal with excitement. He had smiled through the entire thing because of the happiness rolling off of Sophia in waves. Martin was sitting at the dining table with papers surrounding him and his computer on.

"I'm just going to put her to bed, and I will be back out in a moment." Nicholas said as he walked to her bedroom. "How is the house business coming along?" he asked Martin when he returned to the kitchen.

"Well, it took a while to get someone on the phone, but when I finally did, the offer of cash hastened things. It will still take about three weeks to close, but I added a bonus and they will let her move in as soon as we bring the money," he explained.

"Ok. Get a cashier's check over to them tomorrow. Penny will call with her answer as well. If the other house is close enough, why don't you just buy it for us to use when we are here." Nicholas sighed and went to the bar to get a drink.

"Is Penny West the right person?" Martin asked. "Is she going to do right by her?"

"My magic tells me she is the one. She is also a descendent of druids. A different line than Sophia, I think, but it made the discussion easier for her to believe. She was more open-minded than people today." He took a drink and stared at the city down below.

"It seems weird to me. All these years of searching, I had begun to believe we would never find her. But you did. And now we just leave? What happens next?" Martin walked over to the couch and fell down into it. "Why Sophia? Why does the weight of the world have to fall on her?"

Nicholas walked over to the couch and sat down hard. "Because I fucked up. A very long time ago, I sent evil through a type of portal into the future. Sophia was born at the wrong time, Martin. She is 'the one' because we are getting close to the time the evil will pop out of the portal. It's all my fault she has this fight on her shoulders." He leaned his head on the back of the couch and closed his eyes.

"I…" Martin began. "I don't get it. Firstly, I don't believe it was your fault. I remember what the angel said. The evil would have always made its way here to this point in time. I don't know why you had to play a role, but it wasna your fault, Nicholas. What I still don't get is Sophia's role. Why can't you and I just go after it? Why do we need her to be in danger?"

Just the thought of her in danger caused his magic to boil under the surface. Nicholas growled, "I don't have the ability to defeat it. My strength is protecting and guarding. Thanks to the druid women in my village, Sophia has the power to face what's coming. All I can do is make sure she is ready."

CHAPTER 13

*N*icholas woke to the sound of his phone ringing. A quick glance told him it was early, and he didn't recognize the number. "Hello?"

"Mr. Stone? It's Penny. I couldn't wait any longer. I don't quite know how to explain it, but I had a dream——I think it was a dream. Anyway, I woke up even more certain that this is the right path for me. It's.... it's my purpose, I think," she finished softly.

Nicholas perked up immediately at her wording. "We all need to fulfill our purpose, Penny. If you're certain, then I think you should come and meet her today. We have secured a home. The rest of the information you can get through my assistant, Martin. Do you have something to write his contact information?"

"Yes! Of course." Penny said with excitement. "I do have a list of some questions and concerns, if that's ok."

"I would be disappointed if you didn't, Penny," Nicholas confessed. "Send them to Martin, and we will go from there. Whatever you need to put you at ease, we will do."

"Thank you, I will send them now," Penny said.

Nicholas finished up with the details, showered, and got ready. He was certain this was the right thing, but it was going to be more difficult than he had originally imagined. He didn't know the right words to use that would make Sophia not feel abandoned by him. Hopefully, his magic would guide him.

As he left the bedroom, he felt his power twist sharply in his gut. She was frightened. Quicker than he could think, he was next to her. She looked stressed in her sleep, like she was having a nightmare. He put his hand on her face and pushed her hair behind her ear. The tips of his fingers touched the raised mark and immediately she calmed down.

He calmed his heartbeat and slowed his breathing while looking around the room to be sure that everything looked normal. He was going to have to get a handle on this new, stronger bond. He couldn't jump just because she was mad at Penny, or nervous about a test at school, or anxious because of some new experience about to happen. He was going to have to learn what was normal, and what was actual danger. Maybe it was something Jophiel could help him with the next time he popped in.

He slipped away from her to find Martin drinking coffee. "I just talked to Penny. She will contact you to start the setup process. Financials, the move, everything. She'll also be here at lunchtime to meet Sophia. If she feels comfortable, she will take her to the zoo."

"Yeah, she already emailed me." Martin smiled. "I guess it's a good sign she's so excited."

"I know I have been steadfast in this, and I am still, but I've got to be honest. This will not be easy for me. I am going to need..." Nicholas trailed off.

"It won't be easy for any of us. We'll get through it." Martin gave a sad smile.

"Will you get some breakfast ordered? I imagine she will wake soon," Nicholas asked, and then walked over to the laptop on the table. "I am going to do a little work on our next move. Once Sophia is gone, it will be hard to stay here in this room."

"Do you know our next move?" Martin asked.

"Not really, but I know it will probably start with research. Specifically, research of ancient texts about druid lore. Unfortunately, there aren't really any druid recordings because everything was passed down orally. Maybe I can find some books or resources about their ancient traditions. I only know what my family taught me, and they were a little out of the norm, even for their time. Niamh didn't know who or what the evil I described was, and my searches have only hit dead ends. I have to get serious now so I can better prepare her training. The last six years I was too focused on finding her."

"Sounds riveting," Martin joked.

"Honestly, Martin, the best way to help me is going to be keeping the business side of things running smoothly. The less I have to deal with that, the more I can devote to this," Nicholas explained.

"Nothing really to do," Martin pointed out. "All of your holdings basically run themselves. We have good people in place, and your money kind of obnoxiously grows itself. I will keep on top of it, but really you are in a good place to walk away."

"Good. As long as I have what I need, I don't really care about the rest," Nicholas admitted.

He sat down to start his research and left Martin to figure out breakfast. The laptop lit up, and he stared ahead, wondering how he should approach this new leg of the journey.

Unfortunately, druids had held fast to the traditions of passing things down through stories. They could read and write, however, they felt a spiritual connection to keeping the knowledge in a living, breathing form. Also, they felt strongly about controlling who had the information. Knowledge was power.

He held his hands over the keys and tried to think of something to type into the search. After a few searches that got him nowhere, he already felt the frustration rising. He was missing a gigantic piece of the puzzle. He held his forehead in his hands, already at a standstill, when a slow stirring began in his core. Like a glowing ember, it flared to life. Sophia was waking. He smiled and automatically calmed down.

Suddenly, it hit him just how little time he had with her, and he couldn't think of a reason he shouldn't enjoy the few precious moments left. He closed the laptop with a definite force and stood to go to her. He knocked twice and opened her door.

She looked like she had just sat up in the bed. Her hair stuck to the side of her face on one side and went straight up on the other. She was still in a sleepy dozy state and rubbing one eye when she looked over at him leaning against the doorjamb.

"Hi, Nicca," she slurred and sort of waved a hand by slapping the bed beside her.

Nicholas thought it was absolutely the most adorable thing he had ever witnessed in his entire life.

"Miss Snow, good morning. Are ye well?" he asked as he sat on the edge of the bed. She climbed into his lap and put her head on his shoulder. Not sure what to do, he didn't move a muscle.

"Will you snuggle me, Nicca?" she burrowed into his neck and wrapped her arms around his shoulders.

He cradled her as best as he could. "Miss Snow? Are ye ok?" he remembered her bad dream. Maybe she did too.

"I'm ok. I loved the movie so much. Can we go again?" she asked as if she already knew the answer.

"Miss Snow." He closed his eyes for a moment and felt her tense. He took her chin and tilted her eyes to him. "I enjoyed every second because I was with you. You have so many great big adventures coming. When I think about the fun you have ahead of ye, I'm almost jealous. I'm sorry, little one, but there just isn't time for another movie." Nicholas hated saying the words because he could feel how they affected her, but he also did not want to lie.

She reached up and touched his face in that tender way he had seen her use on her mother and Martin. The moment she did, he felt a sizzle along his skin and a quick flash of turquoise in her eyes. Not nearly as bright or as long as before the ritual, it had been subtle enough that he felt sure most people would miss it. She took her hand down and looked away.

He waited for her to speak, but she slid off of his lap and walked away. He felt her sadness, so he grabbed her hand gently to stop her. "Miss Snow?"

She turned to look up at him with a sad, broken smile. "It's ok. I know. I was just pretending for a minute."

He pulled her back to him and wiped her tears with his thumbs. "Miss Snow, trust me ok? Let's get you ready for the day and eat some breakfast. No worries, yeah?"

She gave him a watery smile and agreed, "No worries."

CHAPTER 14

$\mathcal{N}$icholas spent the rest of the morning trying to get as many smiles and giggles out of Sophia as possible. He and Martin were doing their best impressions of princes, coming to slay the dragon and save the princess. It worked for about two minutes before the little warrior princess decided she would do the slaying and save them.

They were currently tied to the dining room chairs cheering her on. Once she had defeated the monster, she turned to them and gave the most delicate curtsy, causing them all to laugh. "Now, Miss Snow, you must free us. We thank you most heartedly and will forever be your devoted followers," Martin declared with gusto.

Sophia looked at them both. "Meh, I obviously don't need protecting. I'm the dragon slayer." She put her hands over her head and started running around the room cheering. Then she skipped into her bedroom and started talking to her dolls.

"Uh. Miss Snow? Little help in here?" Nicholas said with a half-smile.

A knock on the door had Nicholas snapping the flimsy ties and standing between Sophia's door and the intruding knock in less than a second.

"Whoa, man. Calm down. It's only a knock." Martin looked at

76

him with wide eyes. "That was awesome. Totally awesome, but it's ok."

Nicholas was standing in the middle of the room, breathing hard, and hands clenched. He looked behind him at Sophia peeking at him from around the door frame. Again, he had frightened her with his reaction. He forced his features to relax. "Sorry, little one. I guess I'm jumpy. Everything is fine."

She gave a little half smile and came to stand behind him while Martin answered the door. He looked through the peephole and Nicholas saw him pause for a moment. Then he turned to look at him with a sympathetic smile. "I think it's her."

Sophia pressed against him, her arms wrapped around his legs. This time he wasn't sure if the twisting pain in his gut was from her or him.

"Do we have to, Nicca?" she asked with more maturity in her eyes then she should have.

"We have to, little one." Her sadness made his skin feel tight and stretched thin.

She looked at the door and nodded to Martin. "I trust you, Nicca. No worries. No worries. No worries," she kept whispering the mantra under her breath.

Martin took a moment to gather himself and slowly opened the door. Penny was standing there with so much hope on her face it almost dulled the pain. She was dressed casually but still couldn't get away from looking like a teacher in her school spirit t-shirt and jeans. She smiled at Martin but immediately looked around the room.

"Hello, you must be Martin? I'm Penny West. I know I am a few minutes early, but I just couldn't help myself," she explained nervously. When her eyes reached Nicholas, she froze and her smile faded.

He realized he was probably staring daggers at her, so he forced himself to get it together and smile politely. She returned the smile but then noticed the arms around his legs, and she froze again.

"Come in, Ms. West. We have been expecting you. I hope you

don't take offense, but I'm afraid we're all a bit nervous," Martin said and smiled warmly at her.

Penny finally turned away from Sophia and laughed at Martin in thanks. "Yes, no offense at all. I've been nervous too." She turned back to Sophia with a hopeful look.

Nicholas put his hands on Sophia's about to pull her forward when she peeked around his legs. "Why are you nervous?" she asked softly.

"Oh!" Penny gasped when she saw Sophia. All he saw on Penny's face was immediate and instant love. "Well, Sophia, I was nervous you might not like me very much. Hi. My name is Penny. Penny West. I would like it very much if we could hang out today?"

Martin crouched down to speak on her level. "Hey, Sophia. What do you say, lass? Come and meet her properly, yeah?"

Sophia thought it over, then loosened her grip on his legs. Dammit if he didn't fight to hold on to her so she couldn't go. He forced his hands to let go so she could do it on her own terms.

She stepped around Nicholas and slowly walked to Penny, who dropped to her knees. "I like your shirt." Sophia pointed at her t-shirt. "Is that the school you go to?"

Penny looked down like she had forgotten what shirt she even had on. "Yes! Actually, I teach at this school. I'm a high school teacher. Do you like school, Sophia?" she asked.

"I think so. I went a while ago and my mama had to move. She said I could go again, but I didn't get a chance before... well... before now." She looked around the room like she might have said something wrong.

Penny glanced at Nicholas, who remained frozen. "Well, we'll get everything sorted, ok? I will help you."

Nicholas tried to say something, but the emotions were locking him up tight. He was fighting a raging battle inside, and at the moment he was losing. He clenched and unclenched his fists and tried to slow his breathing.

Martin watched him carefully for a moment, and then

nodded as if he'd decided something. "Sophie dear, have you ever been to the zoo?"

Sophia's eyes grew wide, and she vibrated with excitement. She clapped her hands. "Martin! How did you know I always wanted to go to a zoo? Can we? Can we?" She spun around to Nicholas and gave him the biggest smile. "Nicca please? Can we? I've always wanted to see a lellyphant up close."

Her happiness finally gave him the edge he needed to relax. His entire body calmed down, and he looked at Martin in thanks. "Do you mean an elephant?" he joked.

"That's what I said. A lellyphant," she said. "Men," she rolled her eyes, "they just don't get it."

Penny just stared at Sophia with a goofy look on her face. Nicholas smiled because it seemed everyone who met Sophia was star struck. She finally gave a giggle and leaned toward Sophia, "No. They. Do. Not," she said with a wink.

Sophia smiled and put her hand on Penny's shoulder. Nicholas could tell she was getting 'the stare' when Penny froze. Sophia calmly stated, "You won't be alone." Then she bounced over to her dolls on the couch.

"Oh...wow..." Penny whispered. A tear escaped her eyes, and she brushed it away quickly.

Martin touched her shoulder gently before explaining to Sophia. "Sophie lass, Nicholas and I have some things we need to take care of today. We thought, if you felt ok with it, you and Penny could take in the animals at the zoo. What do you say?"

"Where will we take them?" Sophia looked confused.

"I meant visit them at the zoo, silly girl." He ruffled her curls.

Sophia looked at Nicholas. "We'll come back?"

"Absolutely, little one. We'd never sneak away like that. I will always tell you when I am going. And remember," he put his hands on his knees and looked her square in the eyes, "even then, I will never be far from you." He gave her a smile and turned to Penny. "How do you feel, Penny? Are you ok with that?"

Penny looked over to Sophia and gave a thumbs up. "Absolutely."

Sophia gave a nod and whispered to Nicholas, "No worries."

With one last glance, Sophia bounded out the door with a skip. Martin pulled the door almost closed but leaned in to look at Nicholas. "All good?"

Nicholas stared through the door as if he could see Sophia. "Thanks, Martin. I will be."

"Just... I don't know. Think calm thoughts." Martin shook his head and closed the door, taking Sophia and Penny off to begin their adventure--without him.

CHAPTER 15

$\mathcal{I}$t was definitely good they had tried a dry run today, Nicholas thought as he listened to them walking down the hall outside. He had spent the entire encounter stuck to the floor. He centered his thoughts and slowly lifted one foot, putting it in front of the other, shaking the tension from his muscles, and pacing the room. This emptiness he felt when she was away was going to have to be something he accepted; it seemed.

Now that he had begun moving, he couldn't stop. He paced the floor in circles. He needed help from Jophiel. "If anyone out there is listening, I could use a visit from a friendly neighborhood angel," Nicholas requested.

He stared around the empty room. "Well, it was worth a shot."

Sophia would be gone all afternoon, so maybe he could help Martin tie up loose ends. He wouldn't be able to stay here once Sophia was gone. The sooner he could find something to focus on, the better it would be. His phone vibrated in his pocket, making him jump.

"Jesus," he swore and answered roughly. "What?"

"Whoa, man," Martin said. "Reel it in a little."

"Sorry. Did they get off to the zoo ok?" he asked.

"Yeah. All is grand with them. Two peas in a pod they were,"

Martin said. "I'm calling because I thought I would put down the deposits and finish with the house, deliveries, and installations."

"Deliveries?" Nicholas was confused.

"Well, I've been online shopping for two days. Did you think imaginary fairies would deliver princess bedroom furniture?" Martin joked.

"I hadn't even thought about that side of it," Nicholas confessed. "Could we split the job and get done faster?"

"If you want to handle a couple of these, then sure," Martin said.

"I'm on my way down," Nicholas said as he walked toward the door. He was glad to have something to do. As he closed the door and walked to the elevator, he checked Sophia. She was happy. He breathed in deep as the elevator doors opened.

They split the jobs, and Martin took the cashier's checks while Nicholas went to manage things at the house.

One afternoon of receiving packages, overseeing installations, and assembling princess bedroom furniture, and Nicholas was exhausted. He really underestimated Martin and needed to give him a bonus.

Finally heading back, he rang Martin.

"Yes?" His voice came over the hands-free system.

"Martin, you're a godsend. I don't know how you did all of this in two days, but I couldn't have done it without your help. I barely put together one little bed... much less all the things that showed up today. Thank you," Nicholas said sincerely.

"It's all good, mate," Martin said. "Chalk it up to 'angel essence.' Better than energy drinks. I handled the cashier's check. They gave me the keys to the front and back doors, but I would prefer we have the locks changed. Just to be safe."

"Yes. That sounds perfect. I am heading back now. I'll meet you there." Nicholas ended the call.

As he got closer to Sophia, it was hard not to be affected. It was hard to explain how her emotions mingled with his. It was going to take some effort to separate them. Right now he was feeling all over the place.

He had to have another hard conversation with her before

she left with Penny. He needed to lay some groundwork for her future. She deserved a chance at normalcy, but she needed to know some things now. He wasn't sure what Niamh had shared with her already, and he needed to ask those questions before saying goodbye.

Just as he entered the hotel lobby, he noticed a shopping wing to the left. He approached a jewellery store because something in the window caught his eye. Making a decision, he darted inside to make a purchase.

As he approached the door to the hotel, he heard Sophia singing loudly and off-tune. Nicholas paused with his hand against the door. This was what he hoped for her. A lifetime of this. He put his card to the door and opened it to a vision.

Martin was on the floor on all fours with an elephant nose on his face. He was doing a horrible impersonation of an elephant while Sophia danced around him with her princess wand and a stuffed monkey. Penny was sitting on the couch laughing.

When Sophia saw him, she squealed his name and ran at him full speed. He didn't have a chance to speak before she launched into her entire zoo trip.

He picked her up and walked into the room while she talked about monkeys, giraffes, ice cream, and of course, the lellyphants. He just held her while she talked and waited for her to take a breath. Penny gave him a knowing smile.

Finally, she paused, and he took his chance.

"I think we need a membership to the zoo. It's obviously a place you should go often." He sat her down and touched her cheek with his finger.

"Yes. I think I could go every single day and not tire of it," she vowed.

"Well, I'm glad you enjoyed yourself. Have you had dinner?" he asked both her and Penny.

"No," Penny explained. "I wasn't sure what you had planned, and I didn't want to ruin anything."

"Well," Nicholas looked at Martin, "maybe we could order some pizza?"

"Sounds good to me," Martin agreed.

"I am going to head out, actually," Penny said sadly. "There's a lot to finish up to get ready for movers this week. I still have all of my bedroom furniture to pack. But Sophia, I had probably the best day of my life. Thank you so much for spending it with me. I will see you tomorrow, ok?" She opened her arms to Sophia who ran headfirst into them.

"Ok. Thank you for the zoo trip, Penny," she said sincerely.

Penny got up, looking at Martin. "Let me know if I need to get you any other information. Thank you for taking care of so much at the new house. You're making this change much less overwhelming." She gave Martin a quick hug and waved at Nicholas as she ducked out the door.

"Well," Nicholas said as he looked around at everyone, "pizza for three, I guess. Sophia, while we wait for the food, why don't you get your bath. I'll get it started while you pick out some nightclothes, ok?"

"Ok, Nicca." She skipped away to her bedroom.

Nicholas started the water and leaned against the counter, watching the tub fill up. He was just deciding he should probably grab a shower after working at the house all day when Sophia came bouncing in the bathroom with her pajamas held above her head.

She was singing another off tune song. "I got my princess panties, princess panties tonight." She wiggled her body and jumped around. Then she plopped her pajamas on the counter. She looked up at Nicholas and shrugged one shoulder while giving a little smile.

Nicholas laughed and shook his head.

"You're quite the little performer, Miss Snow." He leaned over to turn off the water. When he turned around, he saw her trying to undo the straps on her overalls. "Wait!" Nicholas felt a moment of panic. He wasn't entirely sure of the social rules here, but he was definitely not comfortable.

She looked up sharply and threw her hands down like she was in trouble. "I'm sorry. I was going to take a bath."

Nicholas looked up at the ceiling. He had to stop doing this.

She was overly sensitive to his reactions. He got down on his knees, pulled her closer, and lifted her chin. "Don't say sorry. You did nothing wrong. Here. Let me help you get started." He pulled the metal bits apart on each strap and let them fall to the back.

He grabbed her shoulders. "There you go. Now, you can do the rest on your own. I'll go get ready too. The pizza won't eat itself now, will it?" He smiled at her.

She grinned. "No, it won't."

He ruffled her curls and hopped up.

Jumping in his shower, the water was still cold and shocked his system. He washed quickly and then just stood under the water, feeling momentarily lost. What was he going to do now? He still didn't know what his next step was, and if he didn't figure it out quickly, he was going to be twiddling his thumbs.

He got out and put on some tracksuit bottoms and a t-shirt. In the living area, Martin was getting a drink, and he could hear Sophia singing and splashing in the bathroom.

Martin looked toward the bathroom and smiled. "It's going to be boring without that one around," he admitted.

Nicholas joined him to get his own drink. "Yeah. Maybe you could start singing your own made up songs and wearing princess outfits to entertain me." He laughed.

"Hey. I would make princess outfits cool," he joked.

Nicholas went to the windows while Martin turned on the tv and began channel surfing. "Once we get past this next part, Martin. I think we need to have a sit-down. I need to bounce everything off your brain. Maybe fresh eyes will help with this mental block I seem to have."

"Good to hear we agree," Martin said. "I wouldn't enjoy forcing it out of you." He turned back to the tv with a laugh.

"Hmph." Nicholas smiled. He felt a little twinge in his gut. Instead of jumping to Sophia, he took a minute to decipher the feeling. He knew she was ok, but something was bothering her. He closed his eyes and pushed in deep. Then with a smile, he opened his eyes. "Miss Snow! Could you use help with your hair again?"

The bathroom door opened, and Sophia walked out. She had on a pair of pajamas bottoms and a matching shirt. Her mass of wet curls hung down her shirt, leaving wet streaks and drips. She looked so defeated standing there with the hairbrush in her hands. "I was trying to do it myself." She looked at Martin with an apology.

Martin waved her over. "I'm certain you would have done it too, lass. How about I help since the pizza will be here soon?"

She smiled and ran over to him, holding out the brush. "Thanks, Martin." She turned toward the tv and stood in between his legs. Martin worked on her curls while asking her what she wanted to watch. He gave her the remote so she could flip through the menu. Nicholas just watched and tried to commit the moment to memory.

CHAPTER 16

*T*hey watched movies and ate pizza and tried to keep everything lighthearted, but eventually, Nicholas had to admit that he was out of time. Tomorrow he would hand Sophia off to Penny and charge her with the important daily decisions that would make Sophia the person she was destined to become. If her life went according to plan, she would only ever see him briefly on her birthday. At least until she was older, anyway. He needed to say the words that would sink into her soul and leave a mark. It needed to be words she would never forget.

He leaned on the one thing that never failed when it came to her. His magic. He centered himself and breathed deeply a few times and concentrated on what he needed to do. "Miss Snow, could we have a serious conversation for a moment?" he began.

She stopped bouncing on the couch next to Martin and looked at Nicholas. She looked at the ground and nodded her head. "I don't really want to have this conversation, Nicca. We could just not do it." She looked up with hope for a split second before looking away again.

Already, her fear and sadness were gluing him to the chair. "Come here, little one." He reached out a hand. "Please."

She ran to the chair and jumped. He caught her and pulled her close. Her tears fell down her cheeks before her head even hit his shoulder. "Shh, Miss Snow. It's not as bad as you are thinking." He was struggling with mixed emotions and he paused, hoping she would calm down and his thoughts would clear.

Martin seemed to understand what was going on and tried to be helpful. He got to his knees beside the chair and placed his hand on Sophia's back carefully. "Lass, you mustn't be sad. We're both your loyal followers, remember? You're so special and you have so many great adventures ahead of you."

"I... I just don't understand," Sophia said through her tears. Her hand had tangled in the back of Nicholas's hair and she was pulling at it none too gently while she tried to get out what she wanted to say. "Everyone tells me I'm so special. Everyone says I have so many adventures ahead." She looked over at Martin and back to Nicholas. "My mama, you, Martin, Ney. But I don't understand, why do I have to do it alone? If I am so special, why does everyone send me to have these great adventures by myself? How do I be special enough to get people to want to do things *with* me? I always wanted a friend, but no one thinks I'm good enough to be their friend. I try really hard, but it's just not enough." She squeezed her eyes closed and tears ran down her cheeks, and she buried her face in Nicholas's t-shirt.

Both men were speechless.

Martin leaned over to catch her eyes. "Lass, having friends is a wonderful thing, that's true. But it doesna define your worth. It doesna make you happier or better or more special."

Nicholas turned her toward him. "Miss Snow, if you hear nothing else that I say, hear this. The last couple of days with you have been the best days of my existence. I promise ye that. Listen, try for a moment to not think about that. Let's talk about something different so we can calm ourselves, yes?" Nicholas's heart was cracking.

Martin took his cue and sat back on the arm of the adjacent couch. Nicholas sat Sophia back a little so they could talk better, and he could pull her hand out of his hair. Her face and eyes were red and blotchy. He felt the little pricks of pain along his spine from her sadness. "I would like for you to tell me what

Niamh...er, I mean Ney...told you about why you were special. Can you tell me that?"

Sophia wiped her eyes and sniffled. "Um, she told me that when I get older, I will have to use the gifts she sent me to fight a bad person. She said it's really important for me to listen and learn. She said... she said that the whole world will depend on me."

Jesus, Nicholas thought, did she have to lay so much of it on her so soon? He sighed. "Miss Snow, those things are true, but... and this is important... I don't want you to worry about that for now. Instead, I want you to focus on your new school, make friends, have slumber princess parties, and go to the movies or the zoo with Penny. Have fun, Miss Snow. When you are a little older, we will start working on things to get ready for that day, but that is for later, ok? Do you understand what I mean?"

She nodded her head solemnly. "I do like Penny. I was thinking she could stay with me and we could all stay together? She could teach me stuff, and we could all be a family."

Nicholas shook his head. "You know how you have this big job to do when you are older? Well, Martin and I have to do our job now so that when it's your turn, you'll be able to do your job. Think of us as a team, and Martin and I have parts we have to do now. You'll finish the job later."

"It's just that everyone seems to be leaving at once. Ney says I won't see her much for a while, same as you and Martin, and I don't think Mama was being truthful. I don't think I will see her much anymore either. It feels like everyone is going." Sophia started to tear up and put her face in her hands. "I just want a friend who stays."

"Miss Snow, look at this." Nicholas pulled up his shirt and showed her his mark. She was thrown off for a minute, but as soon as she noticed the empty design over his heart, her hand was immediately drawn to it. "Yes. That's what I thought. Have you felt the raised shape behind your ear here?" He reached her hand to the spot where her mark was. "It fits perfectly. Right here. Does that seem like someone who is leaving you? You might not see me a lot, but every single time you need me, I will be there."

She seemed to settle at his words, and he finally breathed easier. "Nicca? Could you watch over my mom too?"

Nicholas swore to himself. That was the last thing he wanted to do. "For you? I will promise to check in on her from time to time, ok? Martin will make sure I remember to do it." He looked at Martin.

"Aye, Sophie. We will do it, I promise," Martin vowed.

"I... there's something I'm supposed to say but... it's fuzzy," Sophia admitted.

Nicholas went on alert. "What do ye mean, little one?"

"Well, you know how I say stuff sometimes? Usually it's really clear what I'm supposed to say, but now it's fuzzy," Sophia mumbled.

Nicholas was confused but also relieved. She seemed to be working through her emotions and they were leveling out, but then she said something that really shocked him.

"Who is Jop?" She looked at him with a curious stare.

Nicholas froze. How did she know about Jophiel? He hadn't even had time to process him or what he had told him.

"Well... that would be me, my dear!" Jophiel said. Nicholas looked sharply at Martin to see that Jophiel was back. It appeared he came calling when Sophia asked.

He jumped off the arm of the couch and held his hand out as if to touch her. Without thinking, Nicholas grabbed her tighter and a growl began low in his chest.

"Whoa, tiger. In full guardian mode, I see. Ok. Ok. Point taken. Was just saying hello." Jophiel sat back down. "I am Jophiel... at your service, dear Sophia."

"You share a body with Martin?" she asked in a matter-of-fact way.

"Sometimes, I do. It's easier for people to see me this way," Jophiel explained.

"Miss Snow, how did you know who he was?" Nicholas tried to get the conversation back on track.

"I didn't. Like I said. Things are fuzzy now. Not so clear. I asked how to make it not fuzzy, and all I got was J.O.P." Sophia looked frustrated with herself.

"That would be the ritual from the other day. It mutes your powers," Jophiel explained.

"Ah! I almost forgot, little one. I was going to explain that part tonight, as well. When we did the magic on the roof, part of my magic covered you like a security blanket. It will make your magic sleep until you're older and can control it better," Nicholas explained.

"Well, it's making it hard to see what I need to tell you, Nicca," Sophia said while hitting her thigh with a fist.

"That is impressive, my dear, because you shouldn't be able to see anything at all. I could probably lift the blanket momentarily if your guardian promises to behave." Jophiel gave Nicholas a pointed stare.

Nicholas didn't like Jophiel doing anything to her, but her magic must be breaking through for a very important reason. "I will behave, as long as you do," he agreed.

Jophiel rolled his eyes. "Of course. Of course." He touched Sophia's forehead with the tip of his finger.

Instantly, her body went rigid, and her eyes glowed bright turquoise. And then, just as suddenly, it was over. Jophiel stepped back and looked at her in awe. "Stunning, my dear. Simply stunning," he said as he fell back to the sofa arm.

Nicholas glared at him. "Miss Snow, are you alright? Jophiel, you and I need to have a long conversation very soon. Don't forget that," Nicholas said to him as he continued to check her over.

"You feel lost, Nicca?" Sophia said bluntly.

"What?" Nicholas looked directly at her. "What did you see?"

Sophia reached up and touched his cheek. "Stop looking for us. At us. No... *about* us. Don't look in the box. Look for the flower." Sophia seemed confused. "I still didn't see all the words. I only saw some pictures, so I have to guess a little."

"It's ok, little one. We'll figure it out together, ok?" Nicholas had goosebumps. He felt like he was close to something big.

"Sophia, if I may, who was the message from?" Jophiel asked, suddenly very curious.

"It was the last thing Ney was trying to tell me," she explained. "In my dreams."

"Nicholas, were you 'looking into' Ney?" Jophiel asked him.

"I have been researching druids for clues or references to spells or rituals that referred to defeating different evils," Nicholas answered.

"Well, maybe you should stop going down that path, and maybe she meant think *outside* the box?" Jophiel guessed.

"Yes, possibly, but what does the flower mean?" Nicholas looked back at Sophia.

"One moment dear," Jophiel took out Martin's phone. "Can you point to the type of flower you saw? Maybe we need to be more specific."

"Um, it was one like that one." Sophia pointed to the white one halfway down the page.

Nicholas looked over her shoulder. "A Lily? Search for a lily?" He looked at Jophiel. "The evil I encountered long ago appeared to me as a woman named Lily. I just assumed she made it up." Nicholas looked thoughtful. "I guess I should focus more on her and not on finding the druid magic to defeat her?" He was so busy thinking he hadn't noticed how white in the face Jophiel had become.

"Your evil is Lily?" Jophiel's eyes flashed gold, and he jumped up and began pacing. "No, no, no, no…" he was murmuring under his breath.

Nicholas went on full alert. "What is it?"

Jophiel looked back at Nicholas and he looked actually afraid. "I must go, brother. I will return." And just like that, he left.

"Did I say something bad?" Sophia asked, getting upset again.

"No, little one. In fact, you helped us out very much. Now I am not lost anymore. All thanks to you. See what an excellent team we make?" Nicholas gave her a hug while looking at Martin over her head. He just looked at him and shook his head. Whatever this was, it couldn't be good.

CHAPTER 17

*N*icholas kicked himself because he hadn't thought the name Lily meant anything. He assumed evil had been pretending to be a woman named Lily to trick him. He was torn between being elated he now had a lead and terrified that Jophiel's reaction meant bad news for Sophia.

One step at a time was all he could do, he thought. Right now, he needed to tend to Sophia. She was holding steady but on the edge. He stood with her in his arms and began walking to her bedroom. "Miss Snow, it has been a crazy few days. You have had so many changes. Some good and some sad. All of it can be overwhelming, even for me." He gave her a little smile. "I think it's time to relax and try to clear your mind. A good rest will go a long way to heal your body and mind. It will make you feel strong."

"I don't want to sleep, because I don't want tomorrow to come," Sophia confessed, hugging him tightly.

"I understand." He laid her gently on the bed and pulled the covers up. "But tomorrow will come whether you sleep or not. At least if you sleep you will be strong enough to face it bravely." He sat down on the edge of the bed and held her hand. "I'm truly sorry for any role I've played in making you sad. I promise that everything we do is to make your life happy. It's hard right now, and tomorrow will be a little sad too, but every day after will get better."

"I know, Nicca. I will try to focus on the good parts instead of the sad parts." She said, trying to be strong. "Will you stay until I sleep?"

"Of course." he said with a smile. He held her tiny fingers until long after she had slipped into deep sleep. Then he stood and quietly left to see what Martin knew.

He found Martin drinking whisky and staring out into the city. "She's sleeping. Tell me, Martin. I don't understand how it works with you and Jophiel. Did you get anything before he left?"

Martin took another drink before he looked over at Nicholas. "It's hard to explain. He seems to have access to all of my knowledge. I only get small bits and pieces of him, though. Mostly, I only get what you get. I feel a tremendous feeling of love. Goodness. I also get the sense that he is a teacher or guide by nature. He seems very passionate about it––it's not just a job he is doing for you. Other than that, there have been two times I got a feeling that I don't think he meant for me to feel. Like he was genuinely shocked or surprised and accidentally let it slip. When he touched Sophia, he was honestly blown away by her. I got the sense he was not expecting that. The second time was when he saw that damned lily." Martin turned and started pacing. "The name Lily terrified him, and I gotta be honest, Nicholas. I don't know how I feel about something that causes an angelic being to run away. Or how I feel about the fact that whatever that thing is," Martin stopped and pointed toward Sophia's bedroom door, "is something that lass has to face alone."

Nicholas took in all of what Martin said. He didn't like it either. Jophiel had told him that Nicholas was 'one of their best,' and Sophia had every power available at her disposal. He had to believe that counted for something. "I agree, Martin, but if I go into this assuming we've already lost, then I'm going to cause more harm than good. I've got to do everything in my power to make sure Sophia can be successful. All of this is happening whether or not I prepare her. I can ignore it and ensure our destruction, or I can fight with my every breath. I can't bear the thought of her walking to her doom. So I will fight. I will fight like I'm certain we will win. And then I will fucking make it so. It's all I can do," he finished as he collapsed onto the chair. Suddenly, he felt exhausted.

"Well, you won't be doing it alone, that's for damn sure," Martin bit out and walked to his bedroom.

Nicholas stared after Martin with a half-smile trying to decide if that had been a promise or a threat. Once more grateful for his loyal friend, he leaned back and sighed loudly while rubbing his hands over his face. He needed proper sleep. He pushed himself up and went to his bedroom. Falling face-first onto the bed, he immediately fell into a deep sleep.

CHAPTER 18

*N*icholas was having a hard time getting out of bed to start the day. He just wished he could snap his fingers and put the day behind him. He laid on his back, staring up at the ceiling. His hands ran down his chest and over his guardian markings. His left hand came to rest on the space that Sophia's mark filled. He moved back and forth over the space and reached out with his magic to sense her.

She was awake. Like him, she seemed to be stalling. He closed his eyes and tried to imagine what she was doing. Suddenly he had a clear vision of her in her bedroom. He opened his eyes with a shock. He didn't know he could do that. Was what he saw actually happening?

He tried it again and sure enough, a vision of her sitting in her bed popped into his mind. She was looking out the window, murmuring to a doll. She halted and reached up to touch the mark behind her ear. Did she feel him checking on her?

Distracted by his newfound power, he got up and changed into some clothes. He figured he might as well be comfortable, so he grabbed some torn jeans and a t-shirt. Walking out to the main room, he found Martin eating breakfast and answering emails.

"Morning, Martin. What's the schedule for today?" He

thought it would be good to get everything sorted before Sophia came out.

Martin looked up and gave him a half-hearted smile. "Morning. I just finished coordinating with Penny and the movers. They are packing the furniture she is bringing to the new house today. Once she gets them sorted, she will head to the new house. I figured we could bring Sophia over and the two of them could plan together. She would probably enjoy being part of the process."

"What will she do with her home and other belongings?" Nicholas wondered.

"She says that anything she doesn't need to bring over, she would donate to her school's yearly garage sale fundraiser. The clubs at her high school come together every year and put on a big sale to raise money. As for the home, she is fairly sure she will just sell it, but there's no hurry," Martin explained.

"Is the high school she teaches at the one Sophia will eventually attend?" Nicholas hadn't thought about that before now.

"Yes. Sophia will eventually go there," Martin confirmed.

"That could be good. She'll have someone she loves close to her at home and school." Nicholas liked the thought of that.

"Well, yes. It could be good. It could also be a drag. Being a teacher's kid means all the teachers keep an eye on you," Martin laughed.

"Exactly. I'm liking it even more." Nicholas nodded with approval.

"You're going to have to let her be her. It's not fair that she has a built-in tattle tale device. One of the best parts of living is all the crazy, messed up crap you get yourself into as a kid," Martin cautioned him.

Nicholas thought about that. Martin was right. He couldn't always save Sophia from every mistake, because it was part of what would make her strong. "You're right, Martin. I'm going to have to pick my battles. Maybe Jophiel could help me when he shows himself again."

Just then, the sound of a door opening caught their attention. Nicholas leaned around the fireplace to see Sophia's door ajar just enough for her eyes to peek out. When she made eye contact with Nicholas, she quickly shut the door again. Nicholas couldn't help but smile. He knew how she felt. He turned to see Martin was grinning too.

"Gonna miss that kid," he said as he looked back to his email.

Nicholas went to Sophia's door, knocked gently, and entered. Sophia was in bed with the covers over her, pretending to be asleep, complete with a little snore. He had to give her an 'A' for effort at least. He gave a little laugh and walked over to the bed.

"It's a good impersonation of Martin sleeping, little one, but not you. I know you're awake." He sat down gently on the edge of the bed.

Sophia opened her eyes and with a little growl, she turned her back to him and hit the bed. "I am sleeping," she said, pouting.

Nicholas couldn't help it. He laughed, but it was the wrong thing to do. Immediately she sat up and hit his arm with each word, telling him how 'in the wrong' he was. "Do Not Laugh At Me I'm Sleeping And You Are Keeping Me Up With All Your Mean Laughing!" she declared.

Nicholas grabbed her little fists to stop her from hitting. He waited for her to relax her arms and wrapped her up in a hug. She was stiff as a board for about ten seconds, and then he felt his sweet Sophia come back. She relaxed and hugged him back.

Nicholas sat her back on the bed and leaned close to her face. "I know how you feel. It was very hard to start my day too, and I'm sorry if laughing upset you. I was just overcome with how cute you were snoring. I didn't mean to hurt your feelings. But, Miss Snow, don't hit someone in anger. Sometimes hitting or defending might be necessary, but you shouldn't hit a friend just because you're angry about something. You should use your words. Do ye understand what I mean?"

She nodded slowly, but the fighting spirit in her had to get in one more word. "I'm not cute." She informed him.

He smiled again. "Ok. Then what are ye?" he asked her.

"I don't know yet, but it's not that. And you are not my friend, Nicca." She looked up at him with a serious face.

Nicholas wiped the smile off his face. "Then what am I?"

She looked out the window for a moment, then she shrugged one little shoulder. "I don't know yet, but you're not my friend. Martin is my friend. You are... more."

Nicholas felt a little overwhelmed. He understood. "As are you, Miss Snow." He reached over and touched the tip of her nose. "Come along now. Martin is missing ye, and breakfast will be cold. Let's go see what we can find, yeah?"

As he walked away, he heard a big sigh. "Ok, Nicca."

He smiled and kept going, but it was hard to do.

CHAPTER 19

*A*fter breakfast, Nicholas decided everyone should pack, not just Sophia. It only took an hour, and they were ready to go. Sophia watched tv while Martin tried his best to braid her hair.

"I have to run to the lobby for a moment. I'll be right back," Nicholas said. He could take care of checkout and his gift from the jewelry store at the same time.

He felt a jolt of fear coming from Sophia as he reached the door, so he turned to her and winked. "I'll be right back, little one."

She smiled and turned back to the tv.

He checked out, picked up his gift, grabbed a luggage rack and was back in less than fifteen minutes. The three of them sullenly filled the luggage rack and walked to the elevators.

He was sure they looked like three people walking to the gallows. He didn't want their last day together to be this way. Thinking on his feet, he came up with an idea. "Hey," he got Sophia's attention, who was pouting and kicking at the elevator wall. "You know what we forgot to do?"

Her eyes perked up a bit. "What did we forget?"

"Well, Martin ordered you an awesome princess bed, and I put it together for you, but we don't have any bed covers. You can't sleep in a princess bed without covers, can you?" he asked her.

Finally, her smile was back, "No. You. Can. Not," she declared, as if it was law.

When the elevator doors opened, all three walked out much lighter and happier.

An older couple smiled and passed them getting onto the elevator, "Look at that, Gene. I just love seeing gay men adopt. What a beautiful family."

Nicholas choked on a laugh. Martin started flexing his arms. "You would be lucky to get tickets to this show, laddie," he joked.

"What are gay men?" Sophia asked.

Both men looked at each other for a moment before Martin answered, "How about you save that question for Penny, dearie."

Nicholas nodded his agreement.

Sophia just shrugged her shoulders and hopped into the car. Both men sighed with relief and quickly loaded the luggage.

They went to the closest mall and bought bed covers before finding the food court. While they ate, Martin and Nicholas asked Sophia about things she hoped to do at her new school.

Eventually, they couldn't stall any longer, so they hopped back in the car and drove to the house. They pulled into the driveway and Martin cut off the engine.

Nicholas looked it over critically. It looked like a modern version of a farmhouse. It had two stories with shutters and a big front porch with a swing, but it had a new upgraded feel because it was all brick, and instead of being out in the country, it was in a nice quiet neighborhood full of sidewalks and street lights. Soccer moms walked in yoga pants, pushing strollers and waving at neighbors. Husbands pushed mowers and washed cars. He imagined Sophia skipping along the sidewalk and playing in the yard. It felt right.

It *was* right; he kept telling himself.

Everyone sat quietly, not budging.

Just as Nicholas was about to speak, the front door opened and Penny stepped out on the front porch waving.

"Penny!" Sophia called and opened her door. Nicholas and Martin watched her run up the steps and jump into Penny's arms.

"She's gonna love it here," Martin said.

"I know. Let's see if we can help in some way. I don't want to just drop and run." Nicholas got out and walked up to Penny and Sophia. "How's it going, Penny?" He looked up at her and smiled.

"The house. It's so beautiful! I can't believe you did all of this so quickly. There really isn't much left for me to do. Sophia and I will make a big shopping list and hit the store this weekend. I want her ready for school Monday. I've already talked to the counselor at her new school. So really, everything is great. I could use some guidance on the security system stuff though."

"Of course. I'll let Martin help you with that if you don't mind. Miss Snow, could I take you and your new bedding to your room?" Nicholas asked.

"Wait until you see what I got! It's awesome!" She looked over as Martin walked up with the bags.

Nicholas grabbed the bedding bags and held out his hand for Sophia. She grabbed his hand, and they walked up to her bedroom. When they reached the hallway, she ran ahead and skipped through the door. He felt the rush of joy the moment she saw her bedroom furniture. When he rounded the door-jamb, she was staring with her mouth open. "You like it?"

"It's the best bed that was ever created. Like *ever*," Sophia said dramatically.

"Well, you have Martin to thank. He found it for you," Nicholas admitted. "Here. Let's make your new bed up, yeah?"

She snapped back to life and grabbed the bags to help Nicholas open them. Together they made the bed up. Sophia promptly had to sit on it once they made it. She just sat with a smile on her face, looking around the room.

Nicholas sat down beside her. "I think you are going to like it here, Miss Snow."

Her smile faded. "Are you leaving now, Nicca?"

Nicholas nodded sadly. "I think we are making it worse by dragging it out. I want you to get to the good stuff, Miss Snow, and the good news is that your birthday is only a month away, so I will visit you very soon. And remember. I will *always* be here if you need me. Remember to have fun, but work hard to do your best at everything you try, ok?"

"I will, Nicca. I promise." She said bravely.

"I have a surprise for ye. A pre-birthday gift. I wanted to mark our time together with something." He reached into his pocket and pulled out a small, wrapped box.

Her eyes were bright with unshed tears. "An actual present with wrapping paper and everything?" She took the gift into her hands like it was a fragile piece of glass. Her tears finally won out as she looked back up. He wiped them off her cheeks. "You gave me my first ever real present, Nicca. I love it!" she said.

"Well, it's probably too big for now, but you can keep it, and we'll add to it," he explained. "You have to open it, though."

"Oh, yeah!" She laughed and began unwrapping the box very carefully. It took forever, but finally, she was down to the jewelry box. When she opened it, her entire face lit up. "Oh, my goodness!" Inside was a charm bracelet with round delicate links of platinum.

"I hope you keep this tucked away somewhere. It's too much for a six-year-old to wear. Right now, it's empty, but together we'll build it into a bracelet of memories. By the time we fill it, you'll be old enough to wear it." Nicholas suddenly thought it might have been a stupid idea.

She launched herself at Nicholas and hugged his neck tightly. "I love it, Nicca, and I will take special care of it, I promise."

"Well, I wanted to start your bracelet with something to help you remember our time together this week. I want you to have something so that if you ever feel alone or you think I've forgotten you, you can look at it and remind yourself of all the memories we have had, and all the empty spaces for the memories we still have ahead of us." Nicholas reached into his pocket and pulled out the little elephant charm he had purchased. He clipped it onto the bracelet at the first link. "Here is the very first charm to help you remember our first week."

She let out a squeak. "It's a lellyphant." She looked up with complete adoration.

"Turn it over, little one." He held his breath.

She turned over the elephant and engraved on the elephant were two words. She ran her fingers over the words. "Do you know what it says?" he asked.

"I can't read too good yet, but I know what this says. I hear the words in my head when I touch them. It says 'no worries' doesn't it, Nicca?" She looked up at him.

"That's right. If you feel alone or worried, take out this bracelet and remind yourself, ok?"

Sophia just looked at him and nodded her head, fighting tears again.

Nicholas couldn't stall anymore. "Come on. Let's go save Martin." He held out his arms, and she jumped.

He set her down at the bottom of the steps. Penny was standing at the kitchen counter writing the codes and directions for the system. Martin looked up just in time to catch Sophia. He picked her up and hugged her close.

"You be good for Penny, lass, you hear?" Martin said gruffly.

"I will, Martin. Will you visit me too?" she asked, burying her face in his neck.

"Of course! You canna get rid of me that easy," he joked.

He set her down next to Penny, and she took hold of her hand to give it a supportive squeeze. Nicholas nodded his thanks to Penny. He really was past talking.

He needed to get out of there fast. "Remember everything we've talked about, Miss Snow, and listen to Penny, ok?"

She nodded her head silently. Nicholas couldn't stand another moment, so he leaned over and kissed the top of her head. "See ye soon, little one." He turned and walked away.

He got to the front porch and grabbed the post. He just needed to get through this first part. Hopefully, Penny would distract her and things would ease up, because right now it was painful to move away from her.

"What can I do to help?" Martin cut right to the point.

"Get me out of here, Martin. I don't care where we go." Nicholas began trying to walk down the steps. He stumbled a bit and Martin caught his arm.

"Come on. It will get better soon." He helped Nicholas to the car door and then left him to it while he got into the driver's seat.

Nicholas shut his eyes and concentrated on breathing while Martin drove away. He ran his hand over his mark and a picture of her came to his mind. Penny was holding her while she cried her eyes out. It made his skin feel like it was tearing apart at the seams. A deep growl began deep in his chest.

Martin glanced over at him and suggested, "Maybe try to block it out. Just for a few minutes. Just to give you a moment to recover."

Nicholas had never thought of blocking her. It seemed to go against everything. It felt like a betrayal. "She is sad because of me. I feel like I deserve to suffer," he admitted.

"That's crazy," Martin said. "You aren't doing anything wrong to her. She just doesn't understand, that's all. She'll be much better in just a few minutes."

"I just don't feel right trying to shut her out. I will be fine in a few minutes too."

"Alright. Alright," Martin sighed. "Lucky for you, I'm on top of things. We're here."

"What? We're where?" Nicholas opened his eyes to see Martin pulling into a driveway.

"Our home, lover boy!" Martin laughed.

Nicholas let out a shocked laugh. "Wow. Same neighborhood and everything."

Martin gave a satisfied smirk. "Not only is it the same neighborhood but, if you were to look out the back door, you would see a very specific swing set."

"Huh?" Nicholas thought for a second. "This house's back-yard is connected to Sophia's backyard?"

"Yep! The two houses share property lines. We are only a yard away," Martin said with a smile.

"Wow. Martin, you never cease to amaze. Well done, mate." Nicholas looked the house over with interest.

"Well. Don't thank me yet. I didn't have time to get as much for this house, so we'll be slumming it until I can get stuff delivered, but I got the keys and the internet. We can chill here until you feel better. Then we can make a plan." Martin opened the door and jingled the keys in the air.

Nicholas was already feeling better. The initial burst of pain had ebbed. Penny must be distracting her with plans for the new house. She was still sad, but distracted. Thankfully, he could breathe easier. Walking into the house was walking closer to Sophia, so it was simple to do.

The set up was perfect for them because it was a split design so they could both have space on opposite ends of the house. He walked to the back door and looked across the yard. Sure enough, over the fence, he could see the top of the swing set. He closed his eyes and pressed his forehead against the glass door.

He felt overwhelmed and lost. Several times throughout the centuries he had felt this way. A "why me" attitude that only led to more frustration. He also carried tremendous guilt for the role he had played. Everything was getting real now, and it was hard not to give in to the feelings of defeat and depression. He knew he couldn't give up, but sometimes like this, it hit hard.

Behind him, there was a loud noise of something hitting the ground. He opened his eyes and turned to see Martin standing with a determined look on his face. "Ok. Where are we going to get this started?"

Nicholas took in Martin's state. He had changed into workout clothes. He looked down and saw a gym bag at his feet. "Get what started, specifically?" Nicholas asked curiously.

"Well, you were right. We can't go into this acting as if we've already lost. Sophia needs us all at our best. Now, I might not be all of that," he waved his hand in Nicholas's direction, "but I can hold my own. I could be better, stronger, more knowledgeable. Whatever training you're planning for Sophia, I could do too. I know you're her guardian, but surely any help would be good help. So... here I am... let's get started." Martin finished his speech defiantly.

Nicholas smiled. Maybe a good workout would go a long way to get his emotions under control. Martin was right, help was help. He stood tall and gave a quick nod. "Alright then, we need to find a good gym."

CHAPTER 20

*N*icholas couldn't believe almost a month had passed. He was running through the neighborhood to get back to the house after a tough workout with Martin at the gym.

Several times he had wanted to go to Sophia, especially when he'd felt her fear on the first day of school, but he had restrained himself. Once she'd been having a nightmare, so he had visualized her and imagined his magic calming her. It seemed to work.

Things had settled into a type of routine. He and Martin worked out every morning. They spent the rest of the day furnishing the house and researching possible evils that went by the name of Lily or any information he could find on archangels. Nothing solid about Lily had come up, and he was at a dead end.

He was also trying to locate the perfect trainer for Martin and Sophia. None of the existing styles of martial arts alone were enough. Ideally, he wished they could learn all of them, but time was a factor. Over the centuries, Nicholas had mastered most fighting styles, but he could also use some training and conditioning.

He hadn't decided what direction was best for Martin or Sophia. She was so young that maybe he needed to start softer with her and work up to the tougher styles. These were the thoughts he had been wrestling with the last three and a half weeks. He jogged to the corner and turned down his street.

Martin was already home, so he could jog right up to the open garage. He took a couple of minutes to stretch and cool down and then went to see what he could find for lunch.

Martin was leaning against the kitchen counter eating some heated grilled chicken and a mountain of steamed broccoli. "Hungry, Martin?" Nicholas asked with a laugh.

"Yes. You're killing me. I'm filing a complaint with human resources," Martin whined good naturedly.

"Do I have an HR department?" Nicholas wondered aloud.

"You have a few, actually." Martin rolled his eyes and walked over to the newly acquired kitchen table. He had a bite of food halfway to his mouth when he froze into a statue. Nicholas watched curiously as a flash of gold ran across Martin's eyes.

"Jophiel?" Nicholas asked.

"In the flesh," Jophiel said with a half-smile.

"You sure abandoned us in a time of need. Fucking hell, we've really needed your help." Nicholas felt his temper rising.

"Watch it, Nicholas, your Irish is coming out." Jophiel smiled. "I know how it seemed, and I'm truly sorry. It shocked me to hear that Lily was who we were up against. I wanted to be sure, and I didn't want to say the wrong thing. I needed to gather my thoughts and knowledge, friend."

"Does that mean you are here to give us answers now?" Nicholas was trying to calm down.

"I am ready to be more open, yes," Jophiel started.

"Well... open away then," Nicholas waved his hand, telling him to keep going.

"It doesn't quite work that way. How about you start by asking me something?" Jophiel suggested.

"No. Uh uh. I'm not about to sit here and play twenty questions with you." Nicholas was ready for some answers.

Jophiel spotted the food in front of him and took the fork full of broccoli to his nose to smell it. He shrugged his shoulder and took a bite. Nicholas watched in frustrated silence while he chewed. Finally, he said, "Nicholas, let's try this. What have you learned about me in your research?"

Nicholas swallowed his temper and replied, "Not much.

Most sites online are conflicting. The overall gist of them is that you are a protector of knowledge. I also read you have a flaming sword that can cut through illusions."

Jophiel smiled fondly. "Ah yes. That's true. I am, by nature, a teacher and protector of knowledge. It is my purpose. I was charged with evicting Adam and Eve from the Garden and protecting the Tree of Life. Trust me when I say, I know the power of knowledge. But here is the thing to remember, Nicholas. When, and in what order, you receive that knowledge is just as important. Free will is a theme in almost everything we do. It may be our most sacred law. I'm here to guide you. Not to push or pull. I know it's hard for you to understand, but it's very important that you take your own path and make your own discoveries. Any other way would only set you and Sophia up to fail, my friend."

Nicholas clenched his jaw to fight back his reply.

Why does everything have to be so hard? He slammed a fist onto the counter and turned to walk out. Only the thought that Jophiel might disappear and not return for weeks caused him to stop. He had questions, so he might as well try to get some answers to help him move forward.

He turned back around and sighed. "I need help with separating our emotions. I have an overwhelming need to run and fix anything that feels negative. How do I know if what I'm feeling is danger or just normal negative emotions?"

Jophiel nodded in agreement. "Yes. That's always the challenge in the beginning. The connection will settle more permanently inside both of you. As it does, you will 'acclimate' to what you are feeling. It's not separating your emotions that you need to do. You need to combine them into a single seamless unit. Once that happens, you'll know instantly if it's danger, shock, anxiety, or anger... as easily as if it were you feeling it yourself. Stop fighting to keep it separate, Nicholas. It will happen naturally and quickly then."

Nicholas nodded in understanding. He thought of something else. "What if she is in danger but doesn't know it? Or sudden accidents like car wrecks or lightning strikes?" Nicholas was feeling edgy just thinking of these things.

Jophiel smiled. "When you did the binding ritual, that mark appeared on your body because you literally ripped part of yourself out and placed it over her. It is, in essence, as you called it earlier, a security blanket. Your magic is her 'eyes in the back of her head' so to speak. You will feel danger even if it is sneaking up behind her. As for wrecks or sudden death situations, those are a little tricky. Basically, that security blanket will protect her for just a moment until you can get to her. It can slightly deflect a bullet or shift her from flying debris. Just enough to borrow her a second or two until you can get to her."

Nicholas was feeling much better knowing the extra protections in place for her. One more thought occurred to him. "If I have to go to her and handle a 'situation.' Is there a magical way to return, or is it only a one-way thing? I could see myself getting into very awkward situations, and it would be great if I could get out quickly."

Jophiel laughed. "That is a *great* question. Most guardians don't think to ask it. They have to learn the hard way. Yes. You can return to the exact place you were immediately before. It will sound simple to do, but it takes more focus. You simply do the opposite. You envision her mark pulling off yours and returning to her. It sounds easy, but it may take a few tries."

Nicholas sighed with relief. Finally, new and useful information. It boosted his mood enough to ask more questions. "Ok. I will work on that. How about Lily? I am struggling with how to focus my research. Can you at least point me in the right direction?" Nicholas braced himself for the answer.

Jophiel became as solid as stone. It was obvious this topic was unpleasant for him. "Have you ever read in your research about the first human woman?"

Nicholas looked confused. "You mean Eve?"

Jophiel shook his head. "Actually, Eve was second. God made another woman first. He formed her from the earth, same as Adam. Then, that tricky free will kicked up. See, the first woman saw herself as equal to Adam, and she wasn't interested in being his companion at all. She refused and left. God didn't kick her out. She flew out of her own free will."

Nicholas held up a hand. "Wait. Flew? She had wings?"

Jophiel nodded. "Yes. She was a more muted version of an angel. She tried to build her life separately. When God saw, He sent three of our brothers to talk to her. He basically said to return or suffer consequences. She refused. It all went downhill from there. She became twisted and bitter. It wasn't enough to defy God. She had to destroy and manipulate. It was she who whispered to Lucifer how to tempt Eve. If God wanted it to be, then she swore to ruin it. The evil growing inside of her transformed her into a literal monster. The devastation she brought upon the earth was absolute. Can you imagine the type of evil that Lucifer himself would take advice from?"

Nicholas blanched white. "Are you telling me that woman is Lily? This is who Sophia will have to defeat?"

Jophiel looked back with sympathy. "No. I hope not, friend. Because I don't think she can defeat her. That woman was Lilith. There are many, many versions of stories concerning her, and you should definitely research her. Start with the old Jewish texts about her. The woman you call Lily is merely a part of Lilith. She is searching to become whole again. If she succeeds, it will doom this world. You must get to her while she is still just Lily." Jophiel stood as he finished.

"Wait. She isn't whole? How did she get to be... not whole?" Nicholas held a hand out as if to keep him from leaving.

"I'm sorry, brother. You must begin your search. Have faith." Jophiel clapped his fist over his chest and left. Martin leaned over the kitchen counter.

"Are you ok, Martin?" Nicholas asked quickly.

"No. Not really. Adam and Eve? Lilith? The Garden of Eden? I feel like I'm in a terrible movie. I don't know what I thought we were facing, but not that!" Martin looked like he was on the edge of a panic attack.

Nicholas wanted to panic too, but it wouldn't do to have both of them crying about it. He decided to focus on the positive. "It sounds very overwhelming, that's true. But don't you see? We have a place to start, and that means we have a chance. We just have to get to her before Lily becomes Lilith again."

"Sure," Martin said with a hint of sarcasm. "Easy peasy."

"You are one of the best researchers I know. You heard him. Start with the old Jewish writings. Druid writings and experts are almost nil. But Jewish experts? We can do that, Martin. We can move forward and give Sophia the chance she deserves to succeed." Nicholas felt more determined with every word he spoke.

Martin looked calmer. "Yeah. I can definitely dig up resources now. I will get right on it. See where it leads." He looked a little embarrassed. "Sorry for the freak out."

Nicholas laughed. "Don't be sorry. I think we will take turns on that front."

Martin grinned. "Ok. Then I got your back next time."

Nicholas watched him walk to the office, taking his food as he walked by the table. He decided a quick lunch was in order. He had a monster to track.

CHAPTER 21

*I*t was Sophia's seventh birthday. Nicholas remembered the exact moment she had been born. Midnight, exactly seven years ago. He had been leaving a pub in Ireland and her life force had hit him like a ton of bricks. One second he had been walking and the next he had been on the ground yelling like he was on fire. Thankfully, people had just assumed he was drunk. Once the pain had subsided, it had left him with a driving force to find her.

She was born at the height of Samhain, midnight between October 31 and November 1. Her birth certificate says she was born October 31 because she was born in the Central time zone, which is six hours behind. He didn't know what hoops Martin had jumped through to get her official papers, but it was just another example of how he could get things done.

Nicholas sat on the back porch reading yet another rendition of Lilith and keeping his eye on Sophia's house just to keep him calm. He had felt her excitement all day. She was having a party with her new friends tomorrow. Penny sent weekly emails keeping them up to date, but he had Martin read them and just tell him if there was a problem. It had been Martin who told him about the skating party. Nicholas smiled. Her new passion was roller skating.

The research on Lilith was doing his brain in. It seemed

every evil story had a Lilith version attached to it. Some claimed she was just a monster. Some had her as the mother of vampires. Others claimed she strangled babies in front of their mothers. There was no way to know which stories were true. One thing was certain—all the stories were terrible. He was waiting for some resources from Martin and some answers from an expert he'd contacted. Hopefully, they could point them in the right direction. Well... any direction.

Nicholas walked inside to get some water.

Martin came into the kitchen with a gift-wrapped box. "I wanted to be sure you got this before you went to see Sophia."

Nicholas smiled when he saw the glittery unicorn paper. Martin was thorough. "Looks great. I will head over soon."

Martin blinked slowly. "You remember it's Halloween, right?"

Nicholas nodded. "Sure. Why?"

"Well, she will be busy with, I don't know, Halloween stuff," Martin explained.

Nicholas had forgotten about the day's traditions. "Did Penny tell you the plan?"

"There's a Halloween carnival at her school. She'll be there all evening," he explained.

"Well then, I guess I will go tonight," Nicholas decided.

"I have a Skype call with that expert. I'm going to work on my list of questions so I get all the information out of him I can," Martin said.

"Ok. I'll look over the resumes of trainers for the job we posted. Gotta find the person who will get you in line," Nicholas joked.

"Couldn't make her a gorgeous brunette, could you?" Martin asked with a laugh.

"I'll see what I can do." Nicholas rolled his eyes and took his laptop to the table. Might as well get started on it.

CHAPTER 22

*N*icholas stood at the door of Sophia's house. He took a deep breath and knocked.

"Hello, Mr. Stone. I thought I would see you soon. How are you?" Penny said as she ushered him inside.

"I'm doing well, Penny. How are ye?" he asked her.

"Honestly, I'm exhausted, but it's been the best month of my life." She smiled genuinely.

"I'm happy to hear that. I've been checking on her, and she seems happy too. Would it be ok if I give her the present?" Nicholas thought asking would be the polite thing to do.

"Sure! She's organizing her candy haul from tonight." Penny laughed. "I think she has been looking for you."

Nicholas nodded his thanks and ran up the steps to her room.

Sophia crouched in the middle of her bed with stacks of candy all around her. She stood up quickly when she saw Nicholas.

"NICCA!!!" She launched herself into the air off the bed.

Nicholas dropped the present and caught her just in time. "Whoa!" He hugged her to his chest. She wrapped her arms and legs around him and held tight.

"I thought you weren't coming, Nicca," she said into his neck.

"Always, Miss Snow. A promise is a promise." He sat her back

116

on the bed. "Tell me what you have here?" He pointed to her outfit.

"Oh! I'm a G.I. Joe Princess," she explained, as if that made perfect sense.

Nicholas took in her army fatigues covered in glitter. She had combat boots, but they were white with yellow daisies. Her curls were in their usual state of chaos in the back, but the front had been pulled up into buns on top of her head. It made it look like she had little devil horns. On top of them was a beautiful tiara. She had a butterfly painted across her face, but under her eyes were two dark smudges of paint like a football player.

Nicholas grinned. "Your outfit is perfect, little one." He pointed to the piles of candy. "How are you organizing them?"

She squatted back down as she explained. "Well. These here are chocolate kinds. These are suckers. These are crunchy kinds. Then sour kinds. And these are yucky kinds." She wrinkled her nose in the cutest way when she looked at the yucky candy.

"Sounds like serious business. Tell me about school, Miss Snow. Have you enjoyed living here this last month?" He took her hand and helped her to sit. He sat on a desk chair that was beside her bed.

She promptly launched into stories from her escapades at school. It felt like she had been saving them up to tell him, so he just sat and listened. She talked about the different kids at school, her favorite subjects, learning to skate, and shopping with Penny. Finally, she asked him a question. "What have you been doing, Nicca?"

He smiled. "I have been working hard with Martin to learn as much as I can about things that will come later. Nothing for you to worry about. Instead, I think you should open the gift."

Her eyes went straight to the box on the ground. "I did see it before. The wrapping paper is beautiful. Can I open it?"

"Well, I must confess that Martin got the gift, and he wrapped it. He sends his love and says to have an awesome birthday." He leaned over and grabbed the box.

Sophia grabbed the box with considerable strength, making

Nicholas laugh. "I can't WAIT to open this." She began unwrapping delicately.

Once she got the paper off, the box still revealed nothing. She looked up at Nicholas as she opened the top. When her eyes went to the contents, her face froze into shocked silence. He waited patiently for her to process what she was seeing.

Her shout of excitement was ear-splitting. She reached in and carefully lifted one white leather roller skate from the box. Wonder Woman roller skates. At the top of both skates in pink thread was her name 'Sophia' embroidered on them. The dot on the 'i' in Sophia was a little crown instead of a dot. "These are the most beautiful, gorgeous, awesome things I've ever seen!!" she said in awe.

"I'm happy to hear it. We were hoping you would use them at your party tomorrow," Nicholas explained to her.

"I will have the best skates there and I will treasure them forever and ever." She hugged the skate close to her body.

Nicholas reached into his pocket and pulled out another blue jewelry box. "I think it will be hard to follow that present, but I got this for you, little one." He handed her the box.

She glanced over at her nightstand, and Nicholas looked to see her bracelet laying on the top. He picked up the delicate platinum links.

She opened the box and gasped at the charm inside. A little white gold roller skate sat inside. She picked it up very carefully and handed it to Nicholas to add to her bracelet. Nicholas explained while he clipped it on the second link. "Eventually, you will outgrow your real skates, but I wanted you to remember this time in your life. Also, I wanted this to be proof that even though you may not see me, I am paying attention." He finished putting the charm on and handed the bracelet back to her. She took it and held it to her heart.

"I love it so much. I miss you, but sometimes I think I feel you. Thank you so much for my birthday surprises, Nicca. It's been the best birthday ever."

Nicholas looked her over for a moment, enjoying the time he had spent with her. She needed sleep, so he took a breath and stood up. "I have to go, for now, little one. But you have fun tomorrow with all of your new friends. Skate around the rink a time or two for me, will you?" Nicholas ruffled her curls.

He turned to leave but stopped with her question.

"I won't see you again until my next birthday, Nicca, will I?" She looked a little sad, and Nicholas didn't want her to be sad on her birthday.

"That is the plan, Miss Snow. But life is full of surprises, so maybe we will keep our options open to the possibility. If you need me, I will always be around. I promise." He leaned over and kissed the top of her head. "Happy Birthday, Miss Snow."

Nicholas turned and left, feeling the expected hard pull of emotions. He thought back to what Jophiel had said about not fighting it, so he didn't. He just took it in and accepted it. It was still hard to feel, but he could walk and move easier.

He saw Penny in the kitchen and waved, "Everything going ok with her, Penny?"

She hesitated briefly, grabbing the kitchen counter. "I think so, yeah."

He narrowed his eyes. "You can tell me if you have reservations, Penny."

"It's just some general thoughts, Nicholas. Nothing specific. I guess it's more that she's too good to be true. She does nothing wrong. She has had zero breakdowns about her mother or you. She does exactly as she's told and never argues." Penny smiled. "I know it's weird that I would complain about that, and I'm not really. I just don't think it's very normal behavior."

Nicholas looked out the back door into the yard and reflected. "I agree with you." He centered himself while he searched his magic for the answer. He felt the power grow. After a few beats, the answer crystallized in his mind. He turned to Penny and smiled softly. "For a normal child, I think it would be a genuine issue, but Sophia is different. She's almost completely pure light and goodness. It's the way she's built. She'll always strive to do right and not cause problems."

Nicholas stepped to the counter between them and leaned closer. "She'll worry about her mother and me, but it'll be up to you to ask her about it. She won't want to cause a problem. She'll feel sadness and anger and other negative things, I'm certain, but it'll be up to you, Penny, to get her to talk about them."

Penny nodded slowly. "Ok, Nicholas. I'll monitor her and try to draw her out more. I'll let you know if I think she's struggling."

Nicholas smiled and stepped back with a wave goodbye. "Thanks, Penny. I think you're doing great. She seems happy. Be sure to let me know if you need any help here at the house, ok?"

"Sure thing. Thanks again." She smiled and walked him out.

Nicholas could have jumped their back fence, but he felt like the walk around the block would help his emotions.

He made his way to his home and entered through the garage. When he came to the kitchen, he noticed bags packed by the kitchen table.

"Hey Martin! Are you going somewhere?" Nicholas yelled.

Martin came out of the office. "We're going to Jerusalem. Go pack for at least a week. We leave in a couple of hours."

"What? Why? Can't we see everything we need to see on the internet?" Nicholas felt nervous about leaving.

"No, Sherlock. We can't. I got some good info from the expert I talked to, and he gave me a list of texts and people to talk to. We can track most of them down in Jerusalem. The rest, interestingly enough, are in Dublin. So a trip home for you is on the list too. We'll get a better picture of Lilith if we can hang with these people. We need to get our hands on the texts, and we have stayed here long enough. Her birthday has passed. You won't have to visit for another year. We need to look into this."

"I don't want to be far away from her," he confessed.

Martin smiled with sympathy. "Yes. I know. That's one reason I've been putting this off, but it's been a month. She's doing well. Having something more concrete to do will help. It's time."

Nicholas nodded slowly and walked to the back door to look at her house. "You're right, I'm sure. Ok. Time to pack, I guess."

"Great. Don't forget your passport." Martin said as he walked back into the office.

He knew Martin was right, but it felt like he was abandoning her. He breathed in deeply and turned for his room. Guess he was going to Jerusalem.

PART II
SOPHIA'S TEEN YEARS

CHAPTER 23

*S*aving the world sucked! Sophia sighed heavily and flopped onto her bed. Actually, it wasn't the "saving" part that sucked, it was the "knowing". It was a dark, looming cloud that shaded every single thing in her life, making the good times a little sad, and the bad times even worse. When she felt a little down or depressed or anxious, it was easy to wallow in "why me?"

And right now she was anxious.

She looked over at her side table and grabbed her charm bracelet. She always began with the first charm, a little gold elephant that said 'no worries' on it and worked her way down the chain. It took her mind off her worries to remember the reasons behind each charm.

A tinkling noise floated around her as all ten charms moved through her fingers. In just a couple of weeks she would turn sixteen, and she wondered what the next charm would be? The thought of seeing Nicca calmed her down, and she smiled as she looked over her charms.

After the elephant was a roller skate and then a pair of boxing gloves for her eighth birthday. Nicca put her in beginning boxing classes that year. Then a soccer ball for her first year in team sports. She laughed at the next one. It was a garden spade for the summer that she and Penny tried to grow tomatoes and green beans in the backyard. After that she had a Celtic symbol that matched her mark, a triskelion. That was the year she had learned druid history. Her twelfth birthday was a piano, then a cell phone, and a starfish for her first trip to the beach. Last year was a little cat.

She smiled and looked at the foot of her bed where Sam, her pet cat, slept in a spot of sunshine warming her bed. He was a stray that had fast become Sophia's best friend.

She was petting Sam with one hand and rubbing the charms with the other, and it relaxed her enough that she began dozing off.

A knock at her door jolted her out of her reverie. "Yes?" She sat up slowly.

Penny poked her head through the door. "Hey sweetie, can you help me put away groceries in the kitchen? I put them on the counter, but I need to run to school and grab some papers."

Sophia smiled. "Sure, Mom."

Penny had changed her life in an instant to raise Sophia. She tried to be the perfect daughter and never cause trouble, because she never wanted Penny to regret her decision. She often thought of her real mom. Mostly, Sophia just wanted to know if she was finally happy.

Penny walked down the stairs ahead of her, and paused at the bottom. "You doing ok, sweetheart? You seem quiet today."

"Yeah. I'm good. Just feeling anxious about tomorrow," Sophia admitted.

Penny grabbed her hands and squeezed. "You'll be beautiful, Soph."

"You're biased, Mom." Sophia laughed. "I don't know how to dance, and I'm going to look like an idiot."

Penny smiled. "Every girl thinks that. But actually, the boys look way more awkward."

"I just don't want to fall on my face," Sophia joked.

Penny walked to her purse. "Soph, you would make even falling on your face beautiful, and that is not me being biased. It's just the truth, sweetie." She waved and winked as she walked out the garage door.

Sophia went into the kitchen to put away the groceries. She was super nervous about the dance, but for something more than what she had told Penny.

Every single girl in her class had been kissed. She was feeling left out that she didn't have a first kiss story. She got along with people at school, but this 'saving the world' business kind of ruined everything. The kids in her class were great, but they were carefree and immature.

It made her feel different.

Separate.

The things they worried about didn't seem important when she was training to defeat some unknown evil bent on destroying the world.

And the boys? Well. None of them were going to measure up to the role models in her life. Mr. Larry who trained her, Martin, and of course Nicca. She measured every single relationship in her life against Nicca. It wasn't fair. No one could reach a bar set so high, so she just hadn't bothered. But now it felt awkward, so she decided it was time to have her first kiss.

A boy from her class had asked her to the dance. She didn't really like him in that way, but he was nice and decent looking. Before the dance ended, she wanted to be able to say she had been kissed. She was so nervous about it. What if she didn't like it? What if it was gross? What if he wasn't interested?

She cleaned Sam's food and water bowl and then went back to her bedroom. Mr. Larry would be over to train in a half hour, and she needed to change into workout clothes. She had taken boxing classes from eight until ten years old. Nicca had wanted her to learn the basics, develop stamina, and 'toughen up' a little. She met Mr. Larry when she was ten. He was ex-military and had traveled the world. He told her on the first day that they wouldn't be focusing on a single fighting style.

According to him, the person who won a fight nine times out of ten was the person who thought outside the box. He taught her four different moves to get away from any fighting situation. When she got older, they moved from evading techniques to confrontation and attack.

Every situation, he gave multiple ways to get away or overcome. His objective was to make Sophia a creative thinker. It was important to understand that no matter what situation she found herself in, there were always options, and she should never give up.

"We ain't here to earn belts or trophies, Sophie," he would always say. "We're here to survive. You have a much better chance if your attacker can't figure out what you're gonna to do next."

Sophia looked in the full-length mirror that hung beside her closet. Her body hadn't really taken off until the last couple of years. She still wasn't very tall at only 5'4" and her curves weren't really all that curvy thanks to constant training, but she supposed she wasn't half bad. At least she was finally getting some breasts. She reached up and gave them a boost in her sports top. She flipped her massive head of curls over and finger combed them into a scrunchie at the top of her head. One messy bun later and she was bouncing down the stairs to the backyard.

It was finally starting to feel cooler in the evenings. Fall was her favorite time of the year. Something about the air, the crisp blue skies, and the approaching holidays really felt special to her.

She stood on the back porch and began her stretches. She had been doing them three to five times a week before every workout for years. Now she could do them without even thinking.

As she bent over and let her fingertips trace circles on the cement, she thought of how she'd begun feeling differently over the last month. She didn't know what was changing, but it was more than just her physical body.

She slowly stood and then placed her right foot across her left. She bent over and wrapped her arms around her legs, pulling her face close to her thighs. Lately, she had felt different inside. Her dreams were more intense. She had snippets of visions, especially in large crowds, and she thought she had seen something that could only be described as a ghost.

Weird things had been happening, and she was afraid to

mention it to anyone because she didn't want them to think she was crazy. She changed her leading leg and bent to stretch again. Hopefully, it could all be blamed on the stress she had been feeling. Or hormones. Couldn't everything be blamed on hormones?

The mark behind her ear tingled, and she smiled as she sat to stretch her hamstrings. She always thought of it as Nicca saying hello. Something told her it happened when he was thinking of her. It reminded her that she wasn't alone.

She needed that.

Sophia struggled with loneliness more than anything. All she wanted were friends. She had tried so many times. No matter what she tried, she just couldn't connect deeply enough with anyone. No one ever stayed.

It was hard with kids her age, because she had to hide such a big part of herself. She'd always believed if she could just make friends, everything would be better, but making friends was a talent she didn't appear to have. It didn't seem to matter how perfect or good she was.

When she finished her floor stretches, she stood and pushed against the wall to stretch her calves. As she finished, she felt a presence just to her left.

She spun quickly and held up her hands to defend herself. Mr. Larry was only six feet away. His hand was on his hip, and he looked disappointed.

"Girl, if I had a weapon you'd be dead. Where is your head?" Larry scolded.

Sophia bit her lip. "Sorry, Mr. Larry. You're right. I'm distracted today."

He stared down at her. Larry was a mountain of a man. He resembled the actor Dwayne Johnson with his tan skin, bald head, and big arms. He was huge, but fast. Most men would cower under his disappointed look, but Sophia knew his heart. He was a good man.

"Sophie. We could work every day all day for years. Then one second of you being distracted could end it all. All of our hard work for nothing. Learn to focus when you're exposed." He reached up and touched her chin with a finger before turning and dumping his bag of equipment on the ground.

"Got it. What is on the agenda for the day?" Sophia peeked at the equipment. There were sticks, pads, and protective equipment.

"Today is a mix it up kind of day. We are going to learn a little Muay Thai. Then I'm going to attack you, and you're gonna use that noggin of yours to defend yourself." He turned around and tapped her on the shoulder. "But first a run, I think." He smiled.

Sophia groaned good-naturedly. "Ok. ok. How far today?"

"Just a mile. We'll exert a lot of energy when we get back. I just want our muscles warm." He walked behind her.

"You're coming?" she asked. Sometimes he joined her, but not always.

"Yeah, gotta keep this old machine oiled, you know," he joked as he pointed to his body.

They rounded the corner just as Penny drove up in her car. Sophia waved and jogged over to her door just as she was opening it. "Hey, Mom. Mr. Larry and I are going for a warm up run."

As soon as Sophia mentioned Larry, Penny changed right before her eyes. She turned red, smoothed her hair, and dropped her papers as she turned to say hello.

Sophia began running after papers that Penny seemed to have forgotten about completely.

"Oh. Hello Larry. How are you today?" Penny said.

Sophia kept collecting papers.

Larry answered her. "Hiya Penny. You're looking good. I mean, I'm doing good. Are you? Good, I mean?"

Sophia grabbed the last paper and stood to look at what were usually two functioning adults. Mr. Larry had an actual smile on his face, and Penny was twisting and turning like she didn't know which way to look. It was the most bizarre thing, but seriously funny.

"What is happening right now?" she asked. "Are y'all ok?"

Penny spun toward Sophia. "I'm fine. Oh. My papers. Thanks, sweetie. Y'all have a good run. I've got to go."

Sophia watched Penny almost run to the garage door, stumble on the step, and drop her papers again. Sophia turned to look at Larry. He was still watching Penny with that weird goofy grin on his face. Sophia laughed.

"Larry and Penny sitting in a tree," she taunted.

Larry wiped the smile off his face and started walking her way. Sophia began running toward the sidewalk, but she couldn't help but finish. "K-I-S-S-I-N-G." She started laughing as she hit the sidewalk with Larry closing in.

"Shut it, Sophie," Larry said, matching her stride. He sounded so grumpy.

Sophia laughed. Grownups with crushes were hilarious.

After their run, Sophia and Larry were standing in the backyard so Larry could explain the move for the day. "Ok Soph, today we're revisiting the idea of using your opponent's size against them. If someone bigger than you is in your space, knowing how to get in your strikes close range could make all the difference. Remember," Larry explained as he tapped the back of his neck, "the muscle back here is weak, even on a big guy like me. If you can get control of me here, then you get control of the attack."

Sophia nodded in understanding. They had been practicing close range like this for a few weeks. She always felt powerful when she could make a big guy like Larry hit the ground. She sometimes wondered if he let her do it, though.

He kept explaining, "Today I want to put everything together. Most attackers are going to be bigger than you."

Sophia scoffed, "Thanks."

Larry straightened up and corrected her. "No Soph. It will work to your advantage. Men will underestimate you. And you want them to. They see you walkin' around like you don't have a care. Like you ain't payin' attention. It'll make them lead with their egos. You'll use that to your advantage. Look. This is what I mean. A guy who means you harm, especially a guy who doesn't think you are a threat, will gloat. He'll get into your space. Like this." Larry leaned over and got right in Sophia's face. "He will be too busy getting off on trying to intimidate and scare you. He won't even realize he's done half the work for you." Larry grabbed Sophia's hands and put them behind his neck. "You only have to get your hands here. In this position, I'm already at your mercy. His ego served him right up to you on a platter."

Sophia pulled on Larry's neck, but he shook his head. "Remember, Soph. Don't push down on my shoulders. I'm strong there. Jerk down like you are pinning my chin to my chest. Keep your hand on the neck higher up. Here." He slid her hand into place.

Sophia jerked down and his head went down easily. He caught himself and stood up with a smile. "Right. Good. Now, if you have the space, we add a knee. Depending on the situation, you might just need to pull a guy down so you can get away. But if you add a knee to the face and ring his bell good, that will buy you more time. Let's go again, Soph."

Sophia and Larry spent the late afternoon practicing. She wasn't sure if she would ever need any of it. None of them knew exactly what her future would look like. Learning to defend herself was something she was doing "just in case," but it made her feel empowered knowing she had options. Knowing that just because a person might have her beat on size didn't automatically mean she had to be a victim.

It gave her a chance.

And she was glad for it.

CHAPTER 24

*S*ophia stared into the full-length mirror. She was as ready as she was ever going to be for the dance. Her dress was a thin, blush-colored fabric with thin spaghetti straps attached at each shoulder and just under the arm to hold the bodice against her. The back was completely bare. At the waist, the flowy material draped to a little above the knee.

Her heels were a beautiful nude color. They were high but sturdy, thankfully because of the block style heel. Her hair was in a very romantic up-style, and Penny had helped her with soft natural makeup. The only pop of color was her gold eyeliner.

She turned to the side to get a view of the back. Thankfully, her toned arms and back could handle a dress like this. She took a deep breath, and unable to stall any longer, she went downstairs.

Penny was at the kitchen counter reading mail. "Hey Mom. I think I'm ready to go," Sophia said.

Penny immediately teared up. "Oh, my goodness. You're gorgeous! I can't believe how grown up you look. I gotta get a picture. Hold on."

Sophia patiently suffered through the pictures until Penny was finally ready to go. "You sure he's just meeting you there?"

"Yeah. I didn't think he needed to come get me since you were going anyway." Sophia didn't want a big deal made of it.

"Do you like this Jared kid?" Penny asked.

"Um, sure. He's nice." Sophia shrugged one shoulder.

"Ok. Well, you have your phone, so call me if you need. And remember, I'm only a chaperone for the first hour. Are you good to get home?" Penny asked as she gathered up her bag and keys.

"Yeah. If not, I'll call you," Sophia said.

"Ok. Ok. Well let's go get our dance on then," Penny said. "You really are beautiful, Sophia. Inside and out. I'm so proud of you." Penny gave her a quick hug before walking to the car.

The high school was only about six blocks away. Sometimes when Penny needed to work late or had a staff meeting after school, Sophia would walk.

When they drove up to the high school's gym, Sophia felt her face getting warm. Jared was standing at the doors in a suit holding a corsage.

Penny giggled. "I don't know where he thinks he is gonna stick that."

Sophia would have given anything for the ground to open up and swallow her. She was opening the door when a loud rumbling sound came from the ground.

She glanced at Penny, who had frozen halfway out of the car. "What the heck is that?"

Sophia didn't know, but she had the strange sensation the ground was listening to her. Definitely going crazy, Sophia thought.

"Maybe an earthquake? Loud music?" Sophia hoped out loud.

"Geez. That is some loud music, then. It shook the ground." As they walked to the gym doors, Penny waved to Jared. "Hello, Jared. How nice for you to be here early."

Sophia stifled a groan. She put a smile on her face and gave Jared a little half wave. He was nice looking, but Sophia felt nothing around him. The men in her life were large, strong, warriors. Jared was perfect for someone, she was certain, but just not her type. "Hey, Jared," Sophia said when she reached him.

"Hey Sophie. I figured you'd be here early since your mom

had to be here. I got you a flower." He shoved the plastic container at her.

"Thanks. That was nice of you." She took the flower. "It's pretty. I hope you don't mind if I just take it home with me. I don't think it will go on my dress." She held her arms out, showing off her outfit.

"It's cool. My mom made me bring it," Jared explained before turning and heading inside.

Sophia sighed.

The rest of the night was pretty much the same. She sat at a table with a couple of girls she considered her closest friends at school. She hung with them at breaks, and they shared a lot of classes together. Lucy was a beautiful Asian girl who was currently mad at her boyfriend and glaring daggers at him across the room. And Brandy was a plump, pretty brunette girl with blue eyes and a sweet, shy nature. Sophia was pretty sure Brandy and a boy named Shane had feelings for each other, but both were too shy to follow through with anything. Sophia was trying to come up with a way to get them together.

"Hey," Lucy turned to her. "What are you doing over here, anyway? Shouldn't you be over there getting your kiss on with Jared?" She tilted her head to the group of boys stuck in the corner of the gym.

Sophia looked at Jared. He was rough housing with another guy, and they were all laughing. She was pretty sure he had forgotten about her. She should be upset, but she couldn't really bring herself to care. "Eh, I'm just taking a break," Sophia bluffed.

"Mmm hm," Lucy said knowingly. "Look at these outstanding outfits, girls. We look hot! Why did we waste our hotness on these losers?"

Sophia nodded agreement. "I didn't dress hot for them. I did it for you and Brandy." She smiled over at Brandy, who laughed.

"It's wasted on me too, unfortunately. Believe me, If I could switch over to girls right now, I would." Lucy sounded determined.

Sophia caught Brandy looking over at Shane again. "Brandy, one of us should have fun. Go ask Shane to dance."

Lucy looked over and nodded immediately. "Yes. Brandy. Do it. I dare you."

Brandy turned three shades of red. "I can NOT do that, y'all."

Sophia thought for a second and then smiled at her. "Ok. I'll help you. I'll go ask him to dance. You come tell me that my mom needs me after we start, ok?" Sophia got up.

Brandy grabbed her arm. "Wait!" She looked over at Shane and then back to Sophia. "Then what?"

"Just do it, ok?" Sophia smiled supportively and then walked toward Shane.

He was sitting at a table with one other boy. "Hey, Shane."

Shane froze for a moment and then looked around like Sophia might be talking to another Shane. Finally, he got it together and answered her. "H… Hey Sophie. What brings you over?"

Sophie smiled. Straight to the point. She could appreciate that. "I'd like it if you'd dance with me for a moment. Would you?"

He looked over at the corner. "Didn't you come with Jared?"

"I came with my mom, and Jared is doing his own thing. So, would you mind dancing with me?" Sophia smiled and looked directly at him.

Shane got the weirdest look on his face. Sophia was just about to ask him if he was ok when he shook his head a bit and answered. "Sure, Sophie. I'm not very good, but I can try." He stood and held out a hand.

Sophia immediately liked Shane for Brandy. He was going to be a good man, she could tell. Something inside her was driving her to do this. It was scary, but also exhilarating to follow the driving instincts she had been feeling lately.

They reached an empty spot on the dance floor and Sophia moved into Shane's arms. He wrapped them around her back, felt her bare skin, and then jerked them to her hips as if her skin burned him. He looked so uncomfortable that Sophia decided to distract him and plant a seed of knowledge at the same time.

"My friend Brandy adores you. Do you know her?" Sophia asked.

Shane jerked his eyes up from watching his feet. "Brandy likes me?"

"Sure. I think you should ask her to dance next. You two seem like a good match." Sophia smiled kindly.

Shane squinted his eyes a little and asked, "Do you really think so?"

Just then she heard Brandy saying her name, so she leaned over and whispered, "I know so." She turned her head to see Brandy standing shyly.

"Um... Hey Soph... Your mom is looking for you." She kept darting her eyes to Shane. It was adorable.

"Ok. Thanks, Brandy. Looks like I've got to abandon you, Shane. Sorry about that." Sophia kept tilting her head toward Brandy while she was talking to Shane.

It took Shane a couple of beats, but he finally took the hint. "BRANDY!" he shouted so loud everyone jumped.

He looked around embarrassed and tried again. "Brandy. Would you like to dance with me?"

Brandy grinned. "Yes. I would love to."

Her goal accomplished, she skipped off to get some air outside. She was actually thinking of leaving and heading home when Jared stopped her at the door.

"Hey. Where are you going?" Jared asked.

"I was thinking of going home. This dance isn't really doing anything for me," Sophia admitted honestly.

"Um... Sorry about that. I'm not really much of a dancer. I should make sure you get home at least," Jared tried.

"It's ok, Jared. You can stay and hang with your friends." Sophia had given up her first kiss dreams, anyway.

"No. My mom can run us home, just let me text her." He pulled out his phone.

"No need. We can walk. It's just a few blocks away," Sophia insisted.

Jared looked out the door to see it was a pleasant night. Making his decision, he held the door open for her.

They started down the sidewalk toward the main road. "Can I ask you something?" Sophia questioned. "If you don't like dances, why did you ask me?"

Jared looked over sheepishly. "Well, everybody was making such a big deal about it, and I felt like the only guy who didn't have a date. I heard you tell Lucy in class that you didn't have a date, and before I knew what I was doing, I asked you."

Sophia nodded knowingly. "I understand. It's ok. I don't hold it against you. Dances aren't my thing either."

"Well, I couldn't believe you didn't have a date. You're, like, the most gorgeous girl in school. I've been the most popular guy all week. You're good for the cool factor," Jared declared.

Sophia laughed. Poor guy just didn't know when to stop talking. "Well. Thanks, I think. I don't really date. I think I give off a 'friend zone' vibe."

They were only about a block away from the school when he stopped walking.

She turned around to face him. "What's up, Jared?"

He looked super nervous. After a beat, he stepped up to Sophia. "I really like you."

Sophia froze. Was he going to make a move on her after ignoring her all night? Wasn't that a typical immature male thing to do? Sophia sighed. But it would accomplish her goal of getting that first kiss out of the way. Not ideal, but she didn't feel so bad about using him now that he was kind of a jerk about it. "Thanks, Jared. That's sweet to say."

Jared grabbed her hand. It was kind of sweaty, making Sophia pause. She wasn't sure she liked this, but she wanted to get that kiss behind her.

"I think I'm falling in love with you," Jared said so sincerely Sophia had to fight the urge to laugh.

"Wow. Jared. That is a very strong thing to say so quickly." Sophia wondered if he knew anything at all about her.

"Love at first sight is a thing. I believe it." Jared leaned in close. Sophia was locked in a battle of letting it happen or kneeing him in the crotch.

She finally decided to just let it happen when a loud, very

mean, but very familiar animal-like growl started right behind her.

Jared opened his eyes, mid-fishy face, and looked up. Way, way up behind Sophia's head. All the blood drained out of his face, and she watched in stunned silence as Jared let out an ear-ripping scream, turned, and ran as fast as he could.

"Seriously?" Sophia took two steps away from Nicca, still looking after a running, screaming Jared. "That was my first kiss story you just ruined."

"Jesus, what are you wearing?" She heard him mumble under his breath.

A shot of insecurity went through her as she looked down at her outfit. Only Nicca could make her feel nervous. She looked up at him. At least six and a half feet. Long thick dark brown wavy hair, icy green eyes, and a firm jaw with full lips. He clenched his hands at his sides like he wanted to hit something. He was terrifyingly beautiful. The most beautiful creature she had ever laid eyes on.

And he saw her as a child.

And he always would.

He calmed himself and took her hand. Holding it away from her body, he looked over her outfit from her hair down to her shoes. "Forgive me, Miss Snow. It shocked me at how grown-up you look. You're stunning," he said sincerely.

Sophia looked at him doubtfully. She crossed her arms in front of her and asked, "Nicca. Why are you here? It's not my birthday, and I wasn't in any danger."

Nicholas looked back over Sophia's head toward the direction Jared had run. "I confess that I probably overreacted, Miss Snow. I felt different emotions from you that I could not pinpoint. When I checked on you and saw that... boy... well, I probably responded too quickly because of my overprotective instincts." He sighed and looked into her eyes. "Would you like me to go get him?"

Sophia turned and looked. Jared was long gone. She sighed too. "No. I can't unsee that, can I?" She turned back to Nicholas with a smile.

He laughed. "No. You really can't. Please, allow me to walk you home?" He held out his arm for Sophia to hold on to.

She smiled up at him and wrapped her hand around his bicep. They fell into a comfortable stroll down the street. How could any boy in her class come anywhere near this, Sophia thought?

"For all he knew, you were here to kill us, and he just left me here." She laughed.

"Can I ask why you were going to let him kiss you?" Nicholas asked.

Sophia held nothing from Nicholas. "I'm tired of being the only girl in school who hasn't been kissed. I feel so different from them all. I can't make friends. Not real ones anyway. I don't date or go to parties. I just thought this could be one way I could fit in with them all."

Nicholas and Sophia walked along quietly for a few beats before he answered. "I understand. It's nice to feel you belong. But, Miss Snow, I cannot explain how special you are. The person who gets your affections—not just kisses but smiles, laughs, hugs, all of it—will be the luckiest person in the universe. You should be selective with who that person will be. They should at least be someone who tries to deserve that affection. Don't give it away as if it means nothing." He stopped and tucked a curl behind her ear before looking into her eyes. He paused as if he'd seen something and then continued, "Because it means everything."

Sophia nodded in understanding, even though secretly she doubted him. If she were so special, why didn't he stick around? Instead, she said, "I get it, Nicca. I didn't really want to do it once it was happening."

Nicholas smiled and raised one eyebrow at her. "Then I'm glad I interrupted." They turned and walked the rest of the way in silence.

CHAPTER 25

*N*icholas needed the last couple of blocks to get a hold of his emotions. He wasn't sure how he felt about what just happened. Over the years, he'd been protective, sure, but he'd never been possessive. This was a new feeling he was wrestling with, and he didn't like it.

He glanced over at her. She really was stunning. Tonight she looked so grown up. He'd seen her off and on over the years, so of course he knew she had grown, but she had a peculiar dressing style that was very young looking. This dress. It really showed her in a new light. His little Sophia was fast becoming a young woman.

He had to put those feelings away, for now, because there was another problem. He'd noticed her eyes glowing earlier. It seemed her powers were already waking up. He'd been holding off on telling her about her birthday this year; however, since he could see things already starting, he figured now was as good a time as any to give her a heads up. He turned them up the driveway and took her hand to help her up the steps.

"Miss Snow, if you aren't too tired, could we talk for a while about your birthday?" Nicholas asked while indicating the porch swing.

Sophia smiled. "I always have time for you, Nicca." She passed him to sit on the swing.

Nicholas eyed the swing cautiously before sitting next to her and turning her way. He placed an elbow on the back by her shoulder and brought a foot up to rest on one knee. "Tell me honestly, have you noticed any changes in how you feel recently?"

~

Sophia froze. Of course, Nicca would know what was going on with her. He wouldn't think she was crazy. Finally, maybe she would get some answers. "Well," she began, "it's funny you mention that because, yes, I have noticed some things," she admitted.

Nicholas watched her closely. "Could you elaborate, Miss Snow?"

Sophia laughed nervously. "Nicca, sometimes you sound like you are from another time."

Nicholas smiled. "Answer the question please, Miss Snow."

Sophia sighed and leaned back in the swing. "Well, starting about a month ago, I guess, I've had intense dreams. The kind I suspected were true but had no way to verify. I started having visions again too, like when I was young. Visions that tell me things or tell me what needs to happen. Like yesterday, I suddenly saw clearly that Mr. Larry and Penny like each other but need help to get together. And tonight, I just knew my friend Brandy needed to dance with Shane. Not just a guess. I know, without a doubt, that making them dance together tonight set them on a path that will be forever. I know they will be together until their deaths and that it all began with that dance. And then there was some crazier, weirder stuff." She looked over at Nicholas.

Nicholas gave her a stern look. "Not crazy, Miss Snow. Tell me."

"I swear I saw... well... I guess it was a ghost. Maybe?" Sophia felt so stupid admitting that. "I don't know, Nicca. It was only for a second, and then today, I was thinking I wanted the ground to swallow me up and... I think it started to." She looked at her feet.

Her shoes felt tight, so she reached to take them off. She was trying to keep from looking at Nicholas to see how weirded out he was.

His hands appeared and stopped her. He grabbed her hands and made her sit back up. "Miss Snow, I apologize. I should have had this talk with you sooner, and I didn't mean for you to struggle alone for a month. I felt a change in your emotions, but as I said earlier, I was having trouble identifying the change. Do you remember when we first met? We had a type of ceremony on the roof of a hotel downtown?"

Sophia leaned back and smiled. "Yes, I remember."

"I told you that the ceremony covered you in my magic. That it would make your visions sleep until you were older and could control them better. Remember?" Nicholas looked out into the yard.

Sophia understood. "And now that I'm older, your magic is fading, so my powers can wake up?"

Nicholas shook his head. "It's not fading. Just changing. I'm sure you learned in your druid history that a druid comes into their power when they reach adulthood."

Sophia nodded. "Yes, I remember. I just assumed it would be when I turned eighteen."

Nicholas corrected her. "No, not eighteen. That is a very current belief. In many cultures, especially in the past, it is much younger."

Sophia looked away. "Let me guess. Druids become adults on their sixteenth birthday?"

"Yes, little one. This birthday is big for a normal druid. For you, it will be life changing," Nicholas tried to explain. "I don't want to keep you in the dark, but I also don't want to overwhelm you. You tell me. Do you want to hear more?"

Sophia thought for a moment. If he didn't tell her, she would probably imagine the worst potential scenarios and freak out more than she should. She looked over at Nicholas. "Tell me, Nicca."

Nicholas began. "In the beginning, magic was common. Most of today's myths and legends have kernels of truth buried in them. When humans started taking over earth, magical creatures disappeared. Some became extinct by human hands. Some left by choice to live in other dimensions. Humans, for all their goodness, can be brutal with things they don't understand. So it wasn't long before humans with magic began hiding too. My theory is that magic began disappearing in humans at that point because they stopped using it. Eventually, all magic seemed to fade, and the stories became just that—stories for entertainment. Around thirteen hundred years ago, all that remained were a few rare groups of druids that had some magic, but they were fast dying out."

Sophia felt sad that such a unique and beautiful side of humanity was lost just because of fear. "Ney?"

Nicholas perked up. "You remember her?"

Sophia smiled. "Yes. She got me through some rough nights before you found me."

Nicholas growled low in his chest. "I'm sorry, little one."

"It's ok. It wasn't terrible. Just sad and lonely mostly. Tell me. She was in one of these rare groups that still had magic?" Sophia pushed forward.

"Yeah. She and her druid sisters used their magic. Grew and developed it. So they were powerful," Nicholas said.

"How do you know about them, Nicca?" Sophia wondered.

Nicholas looked blank for a moment. "It's complicated, Miss Snow. A story for later. For now, the druids. Each family, there were four, carried a unique power. Ney, she is your blood. You are a descendant of her line. She had the Power of Mind. Visions mostly, as I understand it. The other families had different skills."

Sophia nodded. "Ok. I'm with you, mostly. So I've inherited Ney's magic because we are family, but what about the ghost or the ground shaking?"

Nicholas took a deep breath. "Miss Snow, when it was fore-seen that a horrible evil was coming, the druid women feared there would be no magic left in the world to defeat it. They sacrificed the last of their magic so that we would have a chance."

Sophia was afraid she knew what was coming next. "What do you mean, Nicca?"

"They performed a ritual to bind their magic. One of the four family lines held the Power of Souls. One from that family pulled the bound magic from the strongest of each line and placed them in Ney." Nicholas closed his eyes as if he were remembering a horrible experience. "She immediately passed away. She was very old, and as I said before, druids only carried one magical skill. We've never heard of one with more. Until you." He opened his eyes and seemed to come back from where he was to look at her.

"Me? Keep explaining, Nicca. This will kill me?" Sophia felt a deep sadness for the story. What would cause a group of women to give up their very essence to save a future they wouldn't even be present for?

Nicholas turned her face in his direction. "I'll not let it kill ye, little one." He let the statement sink in before continuing. "The bound magic of all four lines moved through Ney's line, sleeping for centuries. It woke in you because you were born at the right time, Miss Snow. The evil will come during your lifetime. Ney's magic woke immediately. It's yours by birth. The rest of your powers are locked inside and will wake on your birthday. Although it seems they are waking a little early."

Sophia took a minute to accept what he was saying. It felt right. Deep in her bones, she felt the absolute truth of what he was saying. She thought she should be on her way to a panic attack, but strangely, she felt pretty solid about the whole thing. "How do you know I won't die when all the magic wakes up, Nicca?"

"The theory is that your body is used to the magic. It's been there since birth. It won't be like Ney. A shock to an old woman's system." Nicholas leaned closer. "I'll not let ye die."

Sophia stood from the swing. "How do you know all of this? Who told you?"

Nicholas just smiled. "It's complicated, but knowing this and protecting you is part of my magic."

Suddenly Sophia had a very upsetting thought. Which, of course, Nicholas felt instantly.

"Tell me, little one," he demanded.

He seemed very sincere. "Are you doing all of this for me because you have to, Nicca? Because of duty?" She would be very disappointed if that were true.

Nicholas leaned over and picked up her shoes. He walked over and pulled a curl. "Not even a little bit, Miss Snow."

He handed her shoes to her. "This is enough information to lay on you for one night. I will explain more later, but there are a few things to remember for now. Don't forget that your power shows in your eyes. People might respond to that in good or bad ways, so try to avoid direct eye contact until we can work on control. Also, for reasons I will explain later, we must take a trip for your birthday. Pack for cold, wet weather. We'll leave two days before your birthday." He began walking down the porch steps.

"Wait!" She waited for him to stop and turn back to her. "I'm going someplace with you? Like on a trip? Where are we going?" She grabbed the post next to her and hugged it tightly.

He grinned up at her. "We are going home, little one. To Ireland." And with that, he reached up and touched his heart. The moment she blinked, he disappeared.

CHAPTER 26

*O*nce Sophia understood the changes in her were because of magic and not a developing psychiatric disorder, she accepted it and noticed new things. Her observation skills had sharpened. It allowed her to notice patterns and pick up on subtleties. It was shocking the wealth of knowledge that was just lying around waiting for her to notice.

All she had to do was pay attention. Case in point, she was sitting in world geography waiting for the bell and looked up to see Ms. Murphy walk by the door. To most people, that would be nothing, but to Sophia, she realized in a heartbeat, that Coach Tucker's class is nowhere near where Ms. Murphy needed to be. She always seemed to walk by about this time, and Coach Tucker always seemed to look over when she did.

It was knowledge.

It was power.

She didn't know what to do with all of it yet, but for now she just wanted to get through this week and keep her head down until her trip. She'd never been outside of the country, and that she got to do it with Nicca was just icing on a cake.

She brought her foot up to her knee and began doodling on her converse high top shoe with a sharpie. She was rocking an old school look today with her high tops, blue jeans, and a denim jacket she had found at a garage sale and covered with iron-on patches. Even her curls were piled up in a side pony with a big scrunchie. She knew her style was sometimes quirky, but she embraced it, because it was a way she could express how she felt.

Different. Odd. Separate.

But still totally cool.

She looked down and noticed she had drawn her mark over and over. It had been tingling all week, more than usual. She liked to imagine it was because Nicca was just as excited about spending a few days together. She knew it was wishful thinking, but that's what fantasies were for, right?

It's not like it was that crazy of an idea. He was only like eleven or twelve years older than her. That wasn't the craziest age gap, but she didn't imagine for a second that Nicca would ever see her as anything other than a responsibility.

If she voiced how deep her feelings for him were, she could only imagine how he would react. She was sure he would be gentle with her feelings, as always. And to be fair to him, returning her feelings would technically be against the law. So there was that.

Sophia rolled her eyes at her silly train of thoughts. She needed a distraction. There was no need to wallow in self-pity. She reached into her backpack and grabbed the ticket sticking out of the front zipper just as the bell rang. As everyone raced out the door, Sophia walked up to the desk where Coach Tucker sat. "Hey Coach, do you have a minute?"

"Sure, Sophie. I have hall duty, but it can wait just a minute. What's up?" he said as he looked up from his desk.

"Well, as you know, I'm heading out-of-town tonight. I bought two tickets to the Nashville Symphony, and I won't be able to attend. I don't know if you enjoy live symphony, but I've heard you mention Star Wars. It's a night of Star Wars music, so maybe you could enjoy it. If not, I thought you might know someone else who would be interested." Sophie handed him a ticket.

Coach Tucker looked straight at her and paused. Sophia quickly looked away. "Wow. Sophia. That's really generous.

Thank you very much. I'll think about it." He took the ticket and set it on the desk.

Sophia smiled and started for the door when Coach Tucker's voice stopped her. "Sophia, I thought you said you got two tickets. This is just one. Is that right?"

Sophia grinned before she turned with a shocked look, "Oh! I forgot. Yes. I gave the other ticket away. I hope you don't mind. If you go, you'll sit next to Ms. Murphy. She loves the Symphony. See you after Fall Break, coach!" Satisfied with the blush creeping up Coach Tucker's face, Sophia smiled and walked out the door.

It felt good helping people over the weird hurdles they put between them and happiness.

Sophia strolled home. Her body was buzzing with excitement about seeing Ireland. It didn't escape her notice of just how lucky she was. Sometimes she thought back to how her life began.

Time had a healing nature to it. She hadn't been abused, thankfully, but she remembered feeling unwanted, hungry and lonely. Nicca finding her was the best thing to happen.

She wanted to cherish every moment of the trip. That she was a couple of days away from her powers waking up and possibly killing her was just an inconvenient price to pay.

She swung her backpack around to dig out her key as she ran up the steps and noticed Sam laying in the windowsill. "Hey Sam," she said.

He stretched and rolled right off the ledge.

Sophia laughed. "Oh, Sam. You are not a normal cat. I love you." She picked him up as she walked to her room and laid on the bed.

"Sam, I'm going to miss you this week. You'll be good and look out for Penny, won't you?" She leaned over to kiss his head.

She was packed, but she wandered the house looking for things she might have forgotten. Reaching the kitchen, she grabbed some chips and leaned against the counter to think when a commotion at the garage door caused her to jump.

Penny came running through the door. When she saw Sophia

with a chip halfway to her mouth, she sighed with relief. "Oh, my goodness! When you didn't come by my room, I was afraid you'd left already!" Penny collapsed on a chair at the counter.

"Mom, I wouldn't go without saying goodbye." Sophia smiled at her.

Penny laughed. "You're right. I'm just being crazy. It's just that you've never been so far from me."

Sophia hugged Penny. "I have a built-in babysitter with me at all times, and I've trained to defend myself for years. I don't think there's a safer human on the planet."

"I know, sweetheart, but it's just not something I can turn off." Penny grabbed a chip out of the bag.

Sophia smiled. "I think you should use your mini-vacation to do something fun just for you." She opened a drawer next to the frig and pulled out a brochure. "I booked you an appointment for Monday. A full spa day. Get yourself all dolled up, and when Mr. Larry shows up because I forgot to cancel, invite him in for dinner." Sophia smirked at Penny as she blushed.

"What?" Penny seemed stunned as she grabbed the brochure from her.

"Enjoy your time off. Relax. You've earned it, mom." Sophia hugged her again and then grabbed the chips.

"This is so extravagant, Sophie. How did you do this?" Penny still looked shocked.

"I called Martin, and he helped me set it up." Sophia loved Martin. He could always get something done.

Penny looked at the paper in her hand for a moment before looking up at Sophia. "You know what? I think I will be a little crazy. Not with that Larry matchmaking business you tried there, missy. But I will enjoy a day at the spa. Thank you, sweetie."

Both women had their hands in the chip bag and jumped when the doorbell rang.

She followed Penny to the door to see an older gentleman in a black suit.

"Good afternoon, ladies. My name is Aaron. I'm here to drive

Miss Sophia Snow to the airport." He looked over at Sophia and gave a polite smile.

Penny looked a little hesitant. "I really don't like the idea of you going off with a stranger, Sophia."

"Mom, it will be fine. I promise," Sophia assured her.

"There was an issue with the plane that Mr. Stone had to sort out. I assure you, ma'am, he has already threatened me within an inch of my life. I am very aware of what awaits me if Miss Snow's experience is anything short of pleasant." He smiled politely at Penny.

Sophia spoke up. "Let me grab my bag. I'll be right back, Aaron." She ran up the stairs before Penny could stop her.

She grabbed her phone and charger, stuffed them in her carry-on bag, checked she had her passport, and kissed Sam on the head. "See you in a few days, Sam."

One eye peeked open, and he purred loudly.

When she hit the bottom of the steps, Penny was there wringing her hands. "Do you have your phone? Your passport?" she asked.

"Yes, Mom. I just checked. I'll call you when I can. You know Nicca will make sure everything is fine. Try not to worry. I'll see you in a few days with tons of pictures and stories." Sophia hugged her.

"You always loved a good adventure," Penny said as she held her. "Please send me messages when you can, sweetheart. I love you so much."

"I love you too." Sophia opened the door to hand her bags to Aaron. She felt a little sad at leaving Penny behind, but her excitement was so great that she was having a hard time focusing.

Penny grabbed her for a last hug before Sophia jumped into the back of a sleek black Audi. She looked up to see Penny waving and smiling as the car pulled away, but the big tears were hard to miss. When she turned around, she caught Aaron's eyes in the rearview mirror.

"You are a cherished little girl, Miss Snow," Aaron said good-naturedly.

"I know, Aaron. I'm thankful every day," Sophia agreed.

As they approached the airport, she realized something. "Aaron, do you know where I should go once you drop me here? Like a gate or something?"

Aaron smiled into the mirror. "I wouldn't think of just dropping you off, dear. Mr. Stone would have my head. You aren't flying like most people do. You're one of the lucky few who get to fly private. Mr. Stone will be there to meet us," he assured her.

Sophia knew Nicca had money. But not 'rent a plane' money. This was going to be insane. Aaron turned left before they reached the airport. "We aren't going to the main airport? Is it a smaller one close by or something?"

"Basically, all of this is the airport. This is just a side entrance. Only people flying privately come back here," he explained.

Five minutes later, he pulled up to the front of a metal building. Nicca was leaning against the wall with his arms crossed, watching the car as it pulled up. He had on torn faded jeans, an old looking blue t-shirt, and motorcycle boots.

She had to laugh because nothing about him screamed, 'I just rented a plane to fly to Ireland.' Her mark tingled, and she knew he was checking that she was ok. He leaned over to open the door, and she jumped out to hug him. "Nicca. This is awesome. I'm so excited. I can't stand it."

He wrapped an arm around her while he spoke to Aaron. "Valet is waiting for her bags, Aaron." He looked down into her eyes, and his entire face softened.

He touched her cheek. "Your magic is showing, little one. Your excitement is sparking it. I'm so happy you're enjoying this, but try not to look right at people until you feel calmer, ok?"

Sophia's smile fell, and she stepped away, looking down. She had forgotten about that for a moment. She really had to figure this magic business out.

Nicholas grabbed her shoulders and lowered his face to catch her eyes again. "It's gorgeous, Miss Snow. Mesmerizing. I don't like that I've asked ye to hide it, but it's for your protection."

Sophia smiled up at him. "It's ok. I understand. I need to figure out how to control it, but I just don't know how."

Nicholas turned to open the door. "That's part of what this trip is about, little one. You have a big few days ahead and much to learn."

Sophia walked through a long hallway to what looked like a little sitting area. The glass windows against the back wall opened out onto the airfield. She could see airplanes parked in different locations. "Uh, Nicca? Those planes are very small." She felt nervous jitters looking at them.

Nicholas smiled. "Yes. They're much smaller than if we flew commercial, but trust me, they're safe and much more comfortable. I don't fit well in most commercial planes."

"I always trust you." Sophia said sweetly. "I just don't trust those." She tilted her head toward the window.

Nicholas laughed just as a door opened and a woman stepped through. She called them over for check-in, and they promptly boarded. It gave off an office feel with chairs covered in white leather facing different directions.

Nicholas whispered, "Anywhere you like, little one."

On the left was a table with seats around it, but just behind it were two roomy seats. She went straight for them, and happiness bloomed when Nicca sat beside her.

Nicholas explained, "The flight is long. We'll stop briefly in New York to top up fuel. Then we'll fly all night. When we land in Dublin, it will be early morning, Ireland time, but Central time, it will be about two am. These seats lay back to become a bed, and I highly encourage you to sleep. The jet lag will be much less if you do."

Sophia began messing with the seats and playing with the window. "This is so cool."

Nicholas grabbed her carry on and stashed it away. Then he sat down and fastened his seatbelt. Sophia took his cue and belted herself in too. She was looking down at her belt when the most annoying sound hit her ears.

"Oh Nikki! I'm so happy to see you!"

A couple of things happened at once. Sophia had the most intense feeling of jealousy she had ever felt, and she heard Nicholas curse for the first time.

"For fuck's sake," he muttered under his breath.

Sophia had never felt jealous, so it was a new emotion. She tried quickly to reel it in. It sucked to know that he was probably feeling it.

He leaned toward Sophia, away from the woman who looked like a flight attendant. She was beautiful with brunette hair done in big fluffy pageant curls and green eyes. She had on a lot of bold makeup and her nails were long and bright red.

Sophia suddenly felt... lacking.

Nicholas spun quickly and looked at her. She knew he was feeling her reaction, but she couldn't stop it. He looked like he was about to say something, but Miss Perfect popped in.

"It has been too long, sweetie. We have to catch up. I hoped I would cross paths with you again. Is this your little sister?" She gave Sophia a dismissive look.

With every word out of her mouth, Sophia felt worse and worse. Why did she have to dress like a 1990s kid today? What an idiot, she thought.

Again, Nicholas turned and looked at her. Sophia forced herself to give him a sweet smile. He finally turned to the attendant and answered. "No. She's my companion, and unfortunately, we've business to discuss. We have a lot to do once we land. It's not a pleasure trip, I'm afraid," he said politely.

"Oh, that's too bad. If you decide you have a little time, you just let me know and we can pick things up where we left off," she said in her sickeningly sweet voice. She ran a red nail along his arm. "We really should give it another go," she whispered into his ear.

Sophia coughed to cover up a laugh and turned to look out the window. She could feel him looking at her, but she couldn't bring herself to turn around. Part of her wanted to cry, the other part wanted to laugh *until* she cried. All these years, she never thought of the life Nicca led away from her. Of course, he'd be out here living it up. He was a rich, gorgeous, single guy. He probably had women all over the world.

"I think we'll just wait for food until we take off from New

York, Bethany. That will be all we need for now. Thanks." He dismissed her easily.

Bethany, Sophia thought. Of course, she was called Bethany. She felt sullen, and it ticked her off. This was her big adventure, and he had done nothing wrong. It wasn't his fault her fantasy had been tarnished, and she wasn't about to let a beautiful goddess named Bethany ruin her adventure.

She felt him watching her, and knew he was struggling with how to talk to her about what she'd just witnessed.

"Miss Snow," he began with a heavy sigh.

Sophia couldn't bear to hear whatever explanation he felt he owed her. He didn't owe her anything. "Yes... Nikki?" She put a big smile on her face and turned.

His eyes grew large. "Please never call me that," he begged.

"I don't know, I kinda like the sound of it." She laughed.

He stared at her for a moment. "I'm not sure how to talk about this with you. It's... uncomfortable."

She touched his arm. "It's simple. You don't. You don't owe me an explanation, Nicca."

He looked down at her hand and reached over to cover it. "I feel your discomfort. It hurt ye."

Sophia did not want to go where this conversation was going. "I don't want to talk about this, Nicca."

"You never hold back from me." A muscle tensed along his jaw.

"I know, but maybe I'm just growing up. It's not unacceptable for me to want some small part to myself. Have you ever had a silly thought? Something you were thrilled you hadn't said out loud? Now imagine what it might be like to never have your inner thoughts and feelings to yourself?" Sophia squeezed his arm and then let go.

Nicholas leaned forward in his seat. "I'm sorry. It's not something I ever considered. I never want you to feel... invaded by me. I'll try to give you space."

Sophia sighed. This was not at all how she wanted this trip to go. "I never feel invaded by you, Nicca. That came out wrong. I feel... possessive of you." Maybe a little truth would help, she thought. "I never get to see you. This trip is really a dream come true for me. I don't like sharing my time with you. I felt invaded by *her*. It's embarrassing to admit, and I don't want to talk about it, but I understand if you want to 'have another go' with her. She's very beautiful. But I really must caution you about giving your affections away so freely." She smiled. When he grinned back at her, she giggled.

"Thank you for telling me. I feel possessive of my time with you as well, Miss Snow. Trust me when I say that I'm looking forward to this trip with you. Please. Never use the term 'have another go' with me. And believe it or not... I don't really ever do... that," he said.

Sophia scrunched her face. "Do what?"

Nicholas let out a breath. "Jesus... give away my affections, ok?" He looked so uncomfortable.

Sophia laughed. "Well, ok then. Good talk." She turned to the window but couldn't wipe the smile off her face. Sophia would take what she could where Nicca was concerned.

She was a basket case of nerves and excitement while the plane took off. It was a smoother ride than she'd imagined, so she quickly dozed off while looking out the window at puffy clouds. She was so close to sleep she almost missed his comment. She only heard it because she felt him pulling curls off her face.

Nicholas whispered, "She couldn't hold a candle to you, little one."

Sophia drifted off to sleep with a smile on her face.

CHAPTER 27

$\mathcal{N}$ icholas watched Sophia sleeping peacefully next to him. It had been uncomfortable to have two different parts of his life clash together so spectacularly, but feeling the hurt from Sophia had been painful.

Something about Bethany made Sophia feel... less than. Inferior, even. He'd never felt that from her before, and he didn't want her feeling it now.

He'd been looking forward to spending time around her. Over the years, he'd kept contact to a minimum. Sophia's emotions would slide from positive to negative every day, but he only answered the call if it was severe distress or danger. He was looking forward to spending time in her presence and actually learning what things made her feel certain ways.

He closed his eyes and leaned his head against the headrest and thought back to the first time he had stepped in to save Sophia. It had been a few weeks after her seventh birthday. He had been running, and then, in a blink, he'd been at a park under a very tall play set.

He'd looked up just in time to see a bully run straight at her and shove her hard. Nicholas thought his heart would explode watching her small body flying. He'd caught her easily, but the sight had terrified him. He'd wanted to kill the other child, but the sound of her giggle had stopped him cold, and he'd looked down to see her giggling away.

"Good catch, Nicca," she'd said to him.

He smiled, remembering now. He'd kissed her curls and set her down. She had run off as if nothing had happened, and Nicholas had dragged the boy to his mother and given them both a piece of his mind. Then he'd walked behind a tree and tried to figure out how to get back.

Jophiel had been right. It had taken more focus that first time. He had a lovely memory of Sophia looking up and blowing him a kiss just before he had succeeded. He had picked up his jog right where he had left off with a smile on his face.

Over her lifetime, she had needed him more times than he was comfortable thinking about. Jophiel had been right again. He was always saving her from one disaster or another.

He opened his eyes just in time to see Bethany walk by and set a drink next to him with a wink. Mentally, he cringed. That had been why nothing had ever come of his interactions with girls like Bethany.

He had tried to relax and enjoy himself a time or two. But the problem was, it was hard to get... in the mood... when Sophia's emotions were constantly hitting him. He'd been kissing Bethany when Sophia had gotten lost at a festival. Nicholas had apologized to Bethany and run to save a tearful Sophia.

Having sex was impossible. He was constantly aware that Sophia might need him. Just the thought of him "having a go" and snapping to Sophia while naked and aroused had been an immediate buzzkill every time.

He'd always thought of his problem as one sided, though. He'd not thought of this connection with Sophia from her point of view. How would it feel if she found a boyfriend, experimented with sex, or had personal thoughts or fantasies? She was almost sixteen. Surely she wanted to experiment with those areas, but she was probably aware that someone was always listening to her inner emotions.

It just dawned on him now that she probably wanted to

explore those things like every normal teenager, but she was denying herself simply because of him.

He didn't have an answer for this dilemma, and he didn't like to think of her denying herself on his account, but he had to be honest—it felt better knowing that it wasn't one-sided.

This connection was just as hard for her as it was for him.

He wanted her to have and do everything she desired, but their connection robbed her of experiencing life at its fullest. She was, once again, being hurt because of him. His guilt was always present where Sophia Snow was concerned. No matter what decisions he made, she always suffered.

Thinking of what was coming while on a plane heading home was messing with his head. It brought up old memories, and he tried blocking them, but they pulled him under. Suddenly he was eighteen again and in the woods by his village.

"I'm surely the luckiest man in all of Ireland," Nicholas murmured softly in his ancient tongue. His fingers slid down the naked spine of the dark-haired beauty laying beside him.

She turned her head to the side and smiled at him. "And I, the luckiest woman." She turned over and began gathering her clothes.

He pulled some grass from her long hair. "It should be against the law for you to cover this body."

She laughed softly, "It's just a body. A shell. It's not who I am."

Nicholas grabbed her shoulders and kissed her. When he felt his body stirring, he pulled back. "Well, it's the prettiest shell I've ever seen, my Lily."

Their passion had left her lips swollen and face flushed. How did he get so lucky? "You must come to the village and meet Niamh. We'll marry during Samhain," he said, thinking out loud.

She froze. "Marry?" She laughed again. "I don't remember being asked, Nicholas." She finished straightening her dress. "Besides, I can't marry."

Nicholas sat up straight and grabbed her arm. "You give your body to me, but not your heart? You would be so cruel?"

Her gaze softened, and she leaned against his chest. Nicholas's body immediately responded. He couldn't wait to have her again.

"It has nothing to do with you, Nicholas. I don't want to marry

until my brother returns. It doesn't feel right." She pushed back and turned from him.

Nicholas bit his tongue and tried to soften his tone. "You said he disappeared years ago. What if he never returns?"

She looked over her shoulder and gave him that soft smile he loved. "I've heard of a way to find him, but I need help."

Nicholas wrapped his arms around her, clinging to her tightly. "Tell me how, Lily. I will do this for you, and then we'll marry and be happy," he said into her hair.

She turned in his arms. "You promise me? You'll find him for me?"

"If that's how I win your love, then I'll do it." He smiled before claiming her lips again.

Lily ran her hand along his face. "I will give you everything."

Nicholas felt his heart swell. He was so blessed. How could life get any better than this?

Nicholas shook himself. Fucking Lily. What a naïve fool he'd been. It wasn't fair. How many ways would Sophia suffer for his mistake in judgement?

He didn't have an answer for those issues, but he could definitely do something about how she'd felt earlier. He would make sure this trip was as special for her as she hoped it would be, so he pulled his phone from his pocket and began texting Martin.

CHAPTER 28

Sophia slowly opened her eyes and took in her surroundings. It took her a moment to identify the sounds of the plane and remember where she was. She looked over at Nicholas to see him watching her.

She smiled as she sat up. "Hey."

"Hey," he said softly. "The change in altitude woke you. We're landing."

She felt a jump of nerves at the idea of landing. Hopefully, it was as smooth as taking off. She put her seat up and fixed her belt when Miss Perfect approached again.

"Well," she sighed. "Unfortunately, you will finish your trip without me. They need me on a leg from here to Dallas. Stephan is going to jump on when we land. Guess I'll have to do that catching up next time, sweetie." She was leaning so far over Sophia thought she might fall into his lap.

She looked at Nicholas. He was leaning over so far his shoulder was hitting her. She tried not to laugh. She really did.

"I'm sure Stephan will be great. Take care," he said, not coldly exactly, but definitely directly.

Sophia could tell what he was doing, but Bethany seemed to ignore the signals. She took another good look at her. Obviously, he found her attractive. Was this what he liked? She'd heard his comment when falling asleep, but she would never be a Bethany. Did all guys prefer girls like that? Maybe Sophia was destined to be alone forever. Maybe she just wasn't designed to inspire romance or passion in anyone.

"Stop," Nicholas admonished.

Sophia turned and jerked in surprise. He was talking to her--not Bethany. "Sorry?"

His face softened. "Whatever ye are thinking," he whispered. "Stop."

She smiled softly. "Ok."

The announcement to buckle up for landing came on, and Bethany just shrugged her shoulders and wandered off. Sophia had a thought. "Wait, she's getting off when we land? Did you do that for me?" She wouldn't lie. She was glad, but also a little mortified he felt he needed to do it.

"I'm sure I don't know what you mean, Miss Snow. Ye heard her. It was a work thing," he said, staring straight ahead.

"You didn't have to do that," she insisted.

He leaned close, getting into her space. "Miss Snow, there's nothing I wouldn't do to make sure you're happy. If this *had* been me, then it would have literally been nothing. Not a moment's trouble or thought." He paused. "If it *had* been me, I would have been happy to do it."

Sophia sat for a minute soaking in his words. She took her Converse shoe and kicked lightly against his boot. "Thanks, Nicca." She smiled.

She saw the corner of his mouth raise. "Ye are welcome, little one."

The plane landed a little bumpy, but it wasn't too bad. They sat at the table to eat dinner while she told Nicholas about her matchmaking skills.

"Nicca, do you think my newfound desire to help people get together is part of my powers? Or am I just a nosey romantic?" Sophia was hoping to shed light on what was happening to her.

Nicholas thought. "None of the families had specific match-making skills. At least not that I know of. It's possible your visions are just starting, and it's just a coincidence they all seem to concern love." He set his fork down and tilted his head. "Actually, it didn't have to be about love. You took that knowledge and made it about love. You could have equally used that knowledge to destroy, separate, or ruin."

Sophia gasped. "What? Why would I do that to anyone? Why would you want me to?"

Nicholas shook his head. "You misunderstand. I don't want you to. I just meant that knowledge is power. You always have the free will to decide how to use that power, for good or for evil. You're just so pure of heart, it never dawned on you there was a choice."

Sophia thought for a moment while she played with her food. "It didn't dawn on me. You're right. Does that make me pure of heart, or just naïve?"

Nicholas straightened. "Explain what you mean."

"Earlier. I was looking at that woman and thinking that I would never be her. I'm not downing myself, but I don't think age or experience will ever make me into that. But that's what men want, right? I just wonder if being alone is part of my destiny. I can't even make a proper friend, much less a boyfriend." Sophia slumped in her chair.

Nicholas just stared at her with a blank face. Finally, he tried to answer her, but it was obvious he was struggling. "Miss Snow, men like women like that sometimes because it's simple. Uncomplicated. They understand the situation. No big explanations or promises have to be given. They aren't looking for hearts and flowers and romance. It's a physical exchange, not emotional. It's selfish, and no one ever walks away actually fulfilled. Sometimes, if two people are lonely, it can be a way to kind of drown your sorrows, so to speak." He ran his fingers through his hair. "Does any of that make sense?"

"Is that what you did with Bethany? Drown your sorrows?" She didn't enjoy thinking of him as lonely either.

"No, I... I didn't do... what you think I did... with her." Nicholas looked at his plate. "I kissed her, and then I had to excuse myself to help you at that festival," he admitted.

Sophia sat up quickly as realization dawned on her. "Oh, my goodness," she said. "I got upset that you hadn't thought about this from my point of view, but I hadn't thought about it from your point. I'm so completely sorry, Nicca." She reached over and grabbed his hand. "This is hard for both of us, isn't it?"

Nicholas smiled. "It's unique, that's for sure. Don't be sorry. Even for all the awkwardness, I wouldn't want it any other way."

Sophia smiled. "Yeah. Me either."

"You're not destined to be alone, little one. We'll defeat what's coming, and you'll have a happy, complete, love-filled life with someone. When a man is ready to love, to commit, to give his life, they don't look for girls like Bethany. They look for you." Nicholas picked up his fork as if he had just reported on the weather. Not completely blown her mind with the sweetest thing anyone had ever said.

"And you, Nicca? Will you be happy?" Sophia watched him carefully.

He paused. "If you are happy, Miss Snow. I'll be the happiest man on earth."

CHAPTER 29

"Ok, Nicca," Sophia declared. "I'm ready. Give it to me."

Nicholas cocked an eyebrow, "Give you what, exactly?"

They were back up in the air and on their way to Ireland. The next stop was Dublin. Sophia was finally ready to learn more about why they were on this trip. "I want to know why we are taking this trip. I don't think it's just a birthday gift. So, let me have it."

"Ok," he agreed. "I guess we should lay some groundwork for what is coming."

She leaned forward to give him her undivided attention.

"You may not know, but your birth certificate says you were born at 6 pm on October 31." He waited for her to nod and then continued. "If we think of Irish time zones, that's midnight between October 31 and November 1." He looked to see if she caught on.

Sophia's eyes widened. "Samhain," she answered.

"Yes. Exactly. Martin and I have collected every detail we can find about a druid coming into power. Most of what we know had to come from rumors and memories and stories. I've never actually seen a druid come into her powers. It was a secret and private thing."

Sophia wanted to help. Unfortunately, being a druid didn't come with an 'installation of powers' guide.

"What I was told, Miss Snow, is that on your exact birthday, you will enter some kind of trance, or sleep. I don't know what happens in your mind while you're sleeping. I don't know if you'll be in any pain or discomfort. I don't know how long you'll be this way. I don't know a lot." He gave an apologetic smile. "What I have put together is that you'll have more power waking up inside of you than anyone has ever seen. It will happen on your birthday, which is exactly at the height of one of your sacred holidays. If it is possible, Ney will show up to help you through it. I just want to give her the best chance possible to do that for you."

Sophia thought through everything he was saying. "So we are going to your old home to be closer to Ney?"

Nicholas frowned. "I just think we stand the best chance of success if you are in Ney's home village at the moment your birthday hits at the height of Samhain. I think all three together will give you much better odds. Staying in the States is too far from the residual magic. You'll feel it in the land the closer we get to the old village."

Sophia nodded. "We'll be where Ney lived?"

Nicholas stretched his legs. "Yes. There isn't much there anymore, but the magic remains. I think it will bring you closer to her, and she will have to protect the parts of you I cannot. I can keep you breathing, but I won't be able to get inside your head, so I need Ney for that."

Sophia noticed the frown on his face and the ticking muscle as he clenched his teeth. She could see it bothered him to have to rely on someone else to help her. "It makes sense. It's kind of like moving me closer to the cell tower to get the best possible signal."

Nicholas laughed. "Yes. That's a very modern but apt explanation."

"I'm excited. I want to see her again, and I would love to see where she lived. I just hope I don't explode into a million pieces," Sophia joked.

Nicholas jerked in surprise. "Why would you think that? Jesus, don't say that. You'll not explode into a million pieces. I will hold you together myself if I have to. Everything is going to be fine, I swear it. Now, get some sleep. We still have to travel by car once we land. Rest will help. Trust me."

Sophia twisted her legs and laid on her side. She reached up and squeezed his arm. "I always trust you, Nicca." In moments, she was asleep.

CHAPTER 30

"Wake up, Miss Snow. We're landing," Nicholas said as he ran a finger along Sophia's cheek.

Sophia opened her eyes to see him leaning over her. Over the years, his shoulders had broadened, and his face had hardened. He still wore his hair long and had recently added a light amount of facial hair. I wasn't a full beard, but it was just enough to make him look more dangerous. He looked like every girl's dream of a bad boy, and it was definitely a pleasant way to wake up.

She squinted her eyes. "Hey." Her voice was gruff with sleepiness.

Nicholas grinned. "Are ye still grumpy in the morning, then?"

She sat up and looked out the window. It felt like it should still be nighttime, but it was bright out. She guessed flying six hours into the future did that to you. She turned back to Nicholas and processed what he had said.

She scrunched her nose. "I'm not grumpy."

He laughed at her. "Ok, grumpy," he joked. "If you want the bathroom, you have about fifteen minutes before we have to buckle up."

Sophia jumped up and walked to the small bathroom. There wasn't much room, but enough to get the job done. She made the mistake of looking into the mirror before she left. Her side ponytail was hanging limp, and most of her curls had escaped. She heaved an enormous sigh while she pulled the scrunchie from her hair. "Real sexy, Soph." She flipped her head and tried to tame the madness that was her hair. She should probably cut it, but for some reason, she had held onto the length. She wrestled it into a messy bun and splashed her face with water. She was looking forward to a toothbrush and a shower.

She got back to a grinning Nicholas in plenty of time to buckle up. Half an hour later they were on the tarmac waiting for customs. The moment she got to the steps and looked out, she squealed in delight.

"Martin!! I didn't know you would be here!!" Sophia ran down the steps as fast as she could. Martin was leaning against another black Audi with a big smile on his face. She ran into his arms with a laugh. "It's so good to see you. It's been too long this time." She stepped back and looked him over.

He was easily the second most beautiful creature she had ever seen. He had reddish-brown hair currently cut short on the sides and a little longer on top. His eyes were a deep blue color that always had a sparkle, like he was about to crack a joke. He was a couple of inches over six feet and built like a football player. "Martin, you seem bigger every time I see you. What are you doing? Living in a gym?"

"Aye, Lass. I've got to keep fit for the ladies you know." Martin wiggled his eyebrows at her, causing her to laugh.

Martin had a slight Scottish accent, while Nicholas's accent was definitely Irish. Both were mellow after years of traveling outside of their countries, but still extremely sexy.

She turned to Nicholas who was standing behind her frowning. "Hey! You didn't mention Martin would meet us."

Nicholas confessed, "I didn't know, Miss Snow. I'm as surprised as you."

"I was in Dublin anyway, and I thought you might need help. We donna know exactly what's in store, so I wanted to stick close and help if I can," Martin explained.

Sophia jumped at Martin for another hug. "Thank you, Martin. You're the best."

"Well hop in, I'll have you at the hotel in about 45 minutes." Martin turned and opened the door for Sophia.

Sophia got in the backseat. "Great, because I need a tooth-brush and a shower," she confessed.

"Well... I didn't want to say but..." He winked at her when she laughed.

"Hey Nicca, can I use my phone to text Penny and let her know I landed?" Sophia asked as they left the airport.

"Sure. Whatever you need to put her at ease." Nicholas assured her.

Sophia dug her phone out and sent Penny a quick text telling her about the flight. Then she took in the scenery.

Dublin airport and the surrounding city actually looked similar to American cities, but there were distinct differences. It wasn't until they got farther away from the city that she felt it.

The magic.

The genuine beauty.

They were traveling on the M50, which seemed similar to an American interstate. It was truly beautiful. And green. She could totally get behind the whole 'Emerald Isle' thing.

The guys seemed to be talking business, so she tried to let them be. But of course, Nicholas turned to check on her. "You ok?"

"Where are we going?" Sophia asked.

He smiled. "There's a city outside of Dublin called Dundrum that has shopping, eating, and hotels. It will get us much closer to where we need to be by tomorrow. It's still big enough to be comfortable so we can recover from our travels. Today we rest."

She smiled as a response and went back to watching the beauty. "I don't know why I'm so exhausted. I slept on the plane," she said.

Martin explained. "Your body thinks it's two in the morning, lass. Just stretch out and rest. We will be there in about thirty minutes."

That was the last thing she remembered until she felt a hand in against her head. She opened her eyes to see Nicholas reaching over the seat to wake her.

"We're at the hotel, Miss Snow. Let's get you to bed for a few hours. Then you can shower and eat. Ok?" Nicholas asked her.

"Sure. Great." Sophia felt so disoriented. She had never felt so tired. It felt like she had hit a wall and couldn't shake it.

She heard Martin laugh. "Here. I will get her while you check in."

"No," Nicholas bit out sharply.

Martin quickly responded, "Whoa, buddy. Ok. Got it. It's all good."

"Sorry, Martin. I'm... tired. I think. Just... give me a moment." Sophia felt her door opening.

She opened her eyes and let Nicholas help her out of the car. Martin grabbed the bags, and they walked into the front lobby.

If she hadn't been so tired, she would have loved to look around, but all she could think about was a bed. Her eyes were open, but she felt like she was looking through a fog.

It took all of ten minutes to get into the room. Sophia collapsed face-first on a bed she didn't even see and immediately drifted away. She heard Nicholas say something about being right through a door, a blanket fell over her, and then sweet darkness took her under.

CHAPTER 31

Sophia cracked her eyes open and tried to remember where she was. Her eyes felt gritty and her mouth felt like cotton. "Geez Louise," she moaned as she rolled over.

Her room was straight from "Gone With the Wind." The windows were covered in long, thick, floral fabrics. There were huge valances in matching fabrics and elaborate cornice trim going around the room. The furniture was large and dark, and the wallpaper, covers, pillows, and couch were all varying patterns of florals and stripes. Sophia had never seen so many textures and patterns stuffed into one room.

She loved it.

Next to a wooden cabinet that looked like a wardrobe or tv cabinet was a door. She figured that must be the rest of the suite. Not liking the thought of Nicholas and Martin waiting on her, she forced herself to roll out of bed. She definitely felt better, but she was still sluggish.

She went into the bathroom and saw the grey marble shower that was big enough for four people. "Hello friend. I will definitely be back for you," she mumbled before going to see what the plan for the day was.

The moment she went through the door, she realized her mistake. It was not a suite like the last time she'd stayed with the guys. It was two adjoining rooms.

Standing in the room's bathroom she'd just barged into was Nicholas, in only a towel, shaving. When he turned, she couldn't help but notice the water still running down his perfectly formed chest.

"Oh my God," she said before she could stop herself. It was not her best moment.

"Is everything ok, Miss Snow?" he asked while reaching for a shirt.

Sophia finally snapped out of it, closed her eyes, spun, and choked out an apology. "I am so sorry, Nicca. I… I swear I thought the door would open into a living area, *not* your private room." Ground please swallow me, Sophia wished.

A low rumble started beneath her feet.

She felt Nicca's hands on her shoulders and his voice in her ear. "Calm down, little one. Take deep breaths and center yourself. It will stop."

Sophia began breathing in deep gulps of air. After a breath or two, the ground settled, and the sound faded. She hung her head, and couldn't help but think going back to bed might be a good idea. She felt Nicca move in front of her.

"Don't worry, Miss Snow. No harm done. Had you come in a few minutes earlier, it would have been an awkward conversation," he joked.

Sophia was still standing with her eyes closed and her head down. "I'm so embarrassed."

"Look at me, little one," he demanded softly.

Sophia raised her eyes and noticed he had put on a shirt. She relaxed a little now that it was less awkward.

"It was an honest mistake. No worries, ok?" He laughed and added, "You know. For a decade now, I have been taking the fastest possible showers and sleeping in clothes, all to prevent an awkward encounter such as this. Never thought it would happen simply from you walking through the door." He smiled kindly at her.

Sophia laughed. "Sorry, again. I was just wanting to check I had time to shower."

He nodded. "Sure. I'm about to order some lunch. Why don't you get changed and then come eat, yeah?"

"Okie dokie." Sophia turned to head through the door, but she just couldn't let the whole situation go without saying one more thing. "Um, Nicca, not for nothing, you've really got it going on there." Sophia started moving her hand in circles in front of his chest. She immediately felt her face burning.

Could she be a bigger dork, she thought?

"Any who... just letting you know your hard work definitely shows." She chanced a look at his face and saw the grin he was fighting to keep off his face. "Ugh. Don't laugh at me. I was just paying you a compliment. You're... well... gorgeous."

That decided it. Sophia was officially an idiot.

Nicholas walked up to Sophia and slid his hand under her chin. He brought her face up and smiled while moving his thumb along her cheek. "It's just your reflection, little one." He gave her a wink and then turned to order room service.

Sophia stood with her mouth open for several beats before running to her room. The moment she got to the bathroom, she collapsed against the counter. That was either the most embarrassing or most exciting thing ever, she couldn't decide.

One thing was certain. The image of Nicca in a towel was forever burned into her mind. It was the gift she hadn't known she wanted. She caught herself grinning. "Alright Soph, you are acting every bit the teenager you are right now. Get it together, girl."

She threw herself into enjoying the shower. She scrubbed her scalp and skin until it was pink. After, she raked her stylers through her hair and then stood in front of the mirror to finger coil the curls around her face. Once she finished, she left it to air dry for a while and went to dress.

No one had said what they were doing today, but she knew it was just a rest day, so she kept her clothing casual. She pulled on some fitted dark denim jeans. They were torn and slashed through the thighs and knees. She grabbed a fitted short sleeve t-shirt with a number 86 across the chest like a football jersey. She liked it because the tighter fit made her look curvier, and she figured she could use all the help she could get in that department. A pair of sneakers finished the look.

After scrunching her hair a bit more, she went to finish her face and brush her teeth. She wore little makeup, but she put on some moisturizer and a little blush and mascara. She dried her hair, gave it a fluff, grabbed a lip gloss, and called herself ready.

This time before she went through the door, she knocked. When she opened the door, he smiled knowingly at her. She walked over and sat at the little table by the bed. "I didn't know exactly how to dress for the day."

Nicholas looked her over for a moment. "You look beautiful. You may be cold, though. Do you have a jacket?"

"Yeah. What are we doing today?" she asked as she peeked under the silver dome to see a grilled chicken salad.

"We can go to the local town center. You could get some birthday gifts or souvenirs for Penny, maybe. I'm sure there are some sites close by we could explore. It's really up to how you feel. We have a big day tomorrow, so we should keep it local and light this afternoon."

Sophia thought about it while dressing the salad. "Where is Martin?"

Nicholas sat and dug into his salad too. "He's gone to get some supplies and track down one more person we wanted to talk to before tomorrow. He'll meet us in the morning."

"I feel kind of bad that I don't know more about what you two have been doing, Nicca. Like I haven't been doing my part," she admitted.

He smiled at her. "You have done exactly what we asked of you, little one. Martin and I have been trying to gather information that might help you do your part later. Your part is coming, and it will far surpass anything Martin or I have ever done."

"I try not to think about that. The idea of me fighting or destroying or killing, maybe? It seems so crazy, and if I think about it too much, I panic."

Nicholas gave her a sympathetic look. "I understand. After tomorrow, I hope you'll have more answers."

"Ok," she declared. "I will not spend my last night before

adulthood sulking. I say we go to some local shops so I can buy Penny some gifts." She gave a half-smile to Nicholas.

He grinned. "Sounds like a plan to me."

Nicholas spent the afternoon escorting Sophia patiently into shop after shop. He offered his opinions, carried every bag, and never once rushed her. She took pictures of the quaint and colorful storefronts and made Nicca sit in a cafe with her and people watch. By the time they walked back to the hotel, she was feeling tired again.

"Miss Snow, I feel your tiredness. Why don't you rest for a bit in your room? I'll see if we can get into the restaurant here in a couple of hours." He handed her a card to unlock the door. "I'll be in my room in a moment if you need anything."

She gave a nod and took the room key. Their rooms were just off the elevator on the third floor. She walked up to the elevators and noticed two men waiting as well. The moment they noticed her, they turned to face her, and alarms went off in her head before they even spoke.

"Hey there, beautiful. Are ye going up with us?" the larger man asked with a leer.

She could tell they had been drinking and decided evasion was probably the smartest tactic. "No. Sorry. I'm waiting for someone."

She turned down the hall, spotted the stairwell, and darted through the door. She'd made it to the first landing when she heard the men bursting through the door.

"Hey miss, why the hurry? Come, say hi." The larger one was the talker for the two.

Sophia sighed. This was a stupid thing to deal with after a lovely afternoon. "I told you. I am waiting for someone." She continued jogging up the stairs.

When she got to her room, her key card didn't work. She must have taken the wrong card from Nicholas. She heard the guys burst through the stair doors and closed her eyes for a moment before slipping the card into her pocket and turning to face them. "Guys. Honestly, can we not do this today? I've had a really nice day."

The talker leaned over way too close to her face. "I can make your day nice too. I'm nice. Arnie here is nice. We can all be nice." He smiled.

Sophia smiled. "I didn't say I was nice." She grabbed him with both hands behind his neck and pulled down hard. She brought her knee up to meet his face and then let him fall. His head landed by her right foot, so she placed her foot on it and looked up at Arnie. "What do you think, Arnie?"

Just then she felt Nicca against her back. Arnie looked up from his friend on the ground, whimpered, and ran. She felt the anger vibrating off Nicca, but he leaned over her shoulder to look down at her foot. "Who is this, little one?"

"I don't know. Someone that wanted to ruin my nice day." Sophia could feel herself getting angry.

The floor rumbled.

Nicca reached his hand around and placed it flat against her ribcage. "Breathe, little one. I think you have taught him his lesson. I will take him from here. He'll not bother you again."

Sophia took a moment to calm herself before she nodded.

Nicholas chuckled. "You're going to have to stop standing on his neck, little one. Go inside."

Sophia looked down to see the talker trying to get her foot off his neck. "I can't. My card won't work. I think I took yours by mistake."

Nicholas took a card out and leaned over to open the door. "Go inside. You were amazing. Let me clean up here."

The moment Sophia took her foot off, Nicholas gently maneuvered her into the room and shut the door. She couldn't hear a thing outside, so she walked to the bed and sat down.

She wasn't sure how she felt about what she'd just done. Mr. Larry would be proud, certainly, but that guy was probably just drunk and thought he was being friendly.

Had she overreacted?

She laid back on the pillows, turned over to face the windows, and tried to pinpoint what felt different.

When Nicholas came to her, he sat on the bed and put his hand on her back. "Miss Snow, I felt a jolt of fear from you and when I checked, you were just going to the stairs, then I felt it again and you were just jogging upstairs, then I felt you a third time and you were having trouble getting inside. I thought you were worrying about something, it didn't feel like a physical threat. I didn't see the guys until the last moment. By then you'd handled yourself perfectly, but I'm sorry you even had to do it."

"It was different," Sophia whispered. "It was like I wanted to fight. Like I wanted to hurt him for trying to ruin my day. That's not like me at all, Nicca. Is this what's coming tomorrow? Will I change into someone like that?"

Nicholas wrapped the blankets around her and climbed into the bed on top of the covers. "You'll not change who you are. You will be stronger, but you'll still be you. I think today is a combination of stress, nerves, and fear. You will not turn into a monster. That's what I'm here for. What you did to that man was justified, but it's always difficult for a good person to feel good about being violent. It's the conflicting emotions inside you. Knowing you're right, but feeling guilt. Just rest. In a bit, we'll go to eat. You will feel better. Trust me."

Sophia closed her eyes. "I always trust you, Nicca."

CHAPTER 32

*S*ophia woke after a little nap and felt better. She checked with the brochure on the table to see if there was a dress code for the restaurant. It seemed like a nice place, so she decided to not wear her ripped jeans. She opened her suitcase and thanked the heavens Penny had suggested packing a nice outfit for "just in case."

She went to the bathroom to freshen up. Then she wiggled into the tightly fitted black dress. The bodice had a square neckline that cut just above her breasts. It covered her completely from chest to knees, but the dress still seemed to make her feel exposed. She grabbed strappy silver heels and put them on.

She gave herself one last check with a critical eye. She still looked like a teenager, but the dress made her butt look good and bonus, it gave her a hint of cleavage.

She put on some mascara, blush, and lip gloss and then knocked on the adjoining room door. It only took a few seconds before Nicholas opened the door.

He was standing, open-mouthed, in black suit pants and shoes. His white dress shirt was tucked in but not buttoned to the top. "Fuck me," he muttered.

Sophia looked down at her outfit. "Um... I packed a dress for just in case scenarios." Sophia pointed over toward her bed. "The brochure made the restaurant out to be pretty fancy, so I thought I should dress up."

Nicholas just kept staring at her.

Sophia tried again. "I take it from your reaction that I should change." She backed away.

Nicholas reached through the door and pulled her into his room. "Forgive me, Miss Snow. It always shocks me a bit to see you dressed up like this." He smiled. "Honestly, you're exquisite. An outfit like this is likely to draw attention, which will make me... grumpy. Just consider yourself warned, Miss Snow. I'm too overprotective for you to dress like this." He winked to lighten the comment and then turned to finish dressing.

"I would change, but it's the only nice outfit I packed," Sophia offered.

"Thank God. I couldn't survive a second outfit, I'm afraid." He turned around while finishing his tie. "You ready? I don't know how you will feel tomorrow, so I thought we could celebrate your birthday tonight." He looked a little unsure.

"Best. Birthday. Ever." She gave him her biggest smile.

She took the hand he held out to her as they walked into the hallway. When the elevator doors opened, he guided her in with a hand at her back. She felt beautiful and special, like a birthday princess. If people were looking at her outfit, she didn't notice. She just wanted to enjoy the few moments with Nicholas she had. He would probably always see her as something to protect, but for tonight, she was going to pretend something more could be possible someday.

Once seated, Nicholas spent the dinner asking her questions about her life. Just like every single birthday since she had turned seven. The meal was the fanciest thing she'd ever eaten, and the dessert had been an elaborate piece of art that they struggled to eat.

Afterward, Nicholas walked her to the courtyard behind the hotel. It was cold, but it felt good after the warm restaurant. There was a beautiful fountain, so they both sat on the side and watched the water. Sophia's real mom popped into her head as she stared into the swirling water. It always happened during times like this.

"Say it, little one." Nicholas leaned over and tapped her shoulder with his.

She looked up. "I was thinking of my mom," she said. "My real mom." She reached her hand into the water, but it was freezing, so she pulled her fingers away quickly and laughed.

Nicholas took her fingers and warmed them. "What made you think of her?"

"I often think of her when I'm in the middle of a fantastic adventure. I always wonder if she got the adventure she wanted." She closed her eyes for a moment before asking the question she had put off asking for a decade. "I never ask you anything about her, Nicca. But... is she still living?"

He didn't answer until she looked at him. "As far as I know, she is. I can tell you more facts if you like, but I don't want to upset you on your birthday. It might not be the story you want to hear."

Sophia stood up and walked a few steps. She didn't want to ruin her birthday, but she would probably think the worst now. She turned to face him and crossed her arms. "Tell me."

He answered. "Over the years, Martin and I have checked on her. I'm not sure what adventure she dreamed of, but I don't think she's destined to overcome her circumstances. She runs out of money from time to time, so I give her more. I've helped her get a place to live, even a job or two, but she always leaves. Currently, I don't know where she is, but she always becomes easy to find when she needs more... help."

Sophia frowned. "You mean money."

Just then a group of college kids walked through. A couple of guys started whistling at her and yelling, "Hey beautiful, come and party with us! We'll have great craic! Have mercy on a poor sod, why don't ye!"

Sophia laughed and then gasped when Nicholas was suddenly in front of her, wrapping his jacket around her. He pulled the front of his jacket tight around her and frowned at the boys walking away.

Sophia thought about what he'd said about her mom. Then she looked around at her surroundings. All the things this man had done for her. "I've turned into quite an expensive responsibility for you, Nicca."

He pulled her close by the front of his jacket and bent down almost nose to nose with her. "Not expensive, Miss Snow." He turned her into his side, and they began walking back inside. She looked up just as he looked down and declared, "Priceless."

CHAPTER 33

*A*s the elevator doors opened, and Nicholas ushered Sophia out into the hallway, she had a sense of coming back to reality. It was time to stop pretending and focus on what was happening tomorrow. She needed to put away her daydreams and focus on why they were there.

"Nicca," she began as they reached her door, "can you tell me more about tomorrow?"

He pulled the key card from the pocket in his jacket, still draped over her. "Yes, Miss Snow. I suppose it's time to talk about it if you're ready." He opened her door.

Sophia handed him his jacket and walked over to the couch against the window. She slipped her heels off and sat in the corner, tucking her feet under her. When she looked up, Nicholas was standing in the middle of the room, still holding his jacket, watching her.

"I'm ready, Nicca," Sophia said with determination.

He sat in the opposite corner of the couch. "Tomorrow we'll head to a place about a half hour south of here in the Wicklow Mountains. We'll park at a tourist location called Glendalough and hike to Ballinastoe Woods. It will take a while to reach the mountain the druids lived on. The area around the mountain is a tourist area now, but the actual mountain is covered in spells to repel hikers, so it's still largely untouched. Once there, I will set a druid circle for us, we'll get you as comfortable as possible, and then we'll wait." He gave a half-grin.

"That seems simple enough, I guess," Sophia answered.

He reached into his pocket and pulled out a blue box. She had ten other boxes just like it.

Nicholas explained, "I wanted you to have something to remember our time together this week."

Sophia opened the box. It was a white gold angel. The triangles that made its wings and body were green emeralds. The center had a gold Celtic knot overlay.

It was him, Sophia realized. Her Irish Angel.

She looked up at him, her eyes brimming with tears. "I love it."

He reached over and wiped a tear with his thumb. "Happy Birthday, little one." He stood and leaned over to kiss her curls. "Rest. I'll wake you in the morning."

She watched him walk to his room while she clutched the charm to her heart. It just wasn't fair, she thought with a sigh. Why did he have to be so perfect? Any man she tried to have a relationship with would always stand in a massive shadow. A guardian-shaped shadow.

After getting ready for bed, she dug in the carry-on for her charm bracelet. She couldn't wipe the smile off her face while she added it to the next link, but as she climbed into bed, she tried to focus on tomorrow. Her part in this crazy destiny was about to begin, and she really hoped she lived through it.

She still hadn't gotten that first kiss.

$\mathcal{N}$icholas leaned against the window, watching the world down below. He had a drink hanging forgotten in one hand. Being with Sophia was messing with his head.

How was he supposed to let her go into her trance or sleep or whatever tomorrow night? What if she needed help, and he couldn't get to her? With a low growl, he began pacing. All of his feelings were intensifying and swirling around inside of him. Her feelings were coursing through him as well, and it was making it hard to think straight.

He touched his heart and closed his eyes. She was trying to sleep, so he went to the bathroom, stripped, and got into a hot shower. He put his hands against the wall and just let the water hit him while he tried to clear his head. How was he supposed to walk away from her after this week? Would she understand or feel abandoned? Tonight had meant something. It was the very first time he'd been responsible for her birthday celebration. He had wanted to make it special for her. It'd ended up being special to him.

He pushed his head under the water, trying to calm nerves about tomorrow. He was taking the most precious person in his life into an unknown situation. He hoped Martin learned something from the woman he met with tonight. She descended from druids and hopefully, some oral stories had made it down her family line.

Nicholas finished quickly so he could call Martin. Thinking of earlier with a laugh, he pulled on clothes in case Sophia needed him. He was walking over to his phone when it rang.

He picked it up and joked, "Hey Martin, great minds think alike."

"What? You were just thinking about how amazing I am?" Martin asked.

"Something like that. What happened tonight? Anything that will help us tomorrow?" Nicholas was crossing his fingers.

"Maybe. She had an old hand-written letter in the old language. Her family passed it down with instructions that if anyone came asking for information, give the letter to them. So that could be something. It's more than we've gotten in quite some time." Martin sounded hopeful.

"We don't have long to study it, but hopefully, it will provide us with something. Good work, Martin." Nicholas needed to read that letter.

"I also asked her if she had ever heard about the druid power-awakening ceremony. She had only heard rumors about the 'old trances' she called them. She said the only thing she remembered is that it was important not to stay under too long," Martin said softly.

"How long is too long?" Nicholas wondered.

"She didn't know, but she'd always heard that the call of the drums was seductive, and if you stayed too long, you would be lost to them," Martin explained.

"Fuck!" Nicholas grumbled. "What the hell am I supposed to do with that? Fucking drums?" His feelings swirled again.

"We'll figure it out. She'll be fine. It's her destiny," Martin said calmly.

"Bring me the letter, Martin. I need to read it before we go." Nicholas felt like he was grasping at straws.

"I'll be there shortly," Martin said and hung up the phone.

Nicholas swore and threw the phone on the bed before picking up his drink. He had a sinking feeling that tomorrow was going to be a type of test for Sophia. He just hoped he could hold it together long enough to make sure she passed it.

CHAPTER 35

Sophia felt the side of her bed dip as Nicholas sat down. She was awake, but not quite ready to face the day. She felt his hand on her back, between her shoulder blades.

"I know you're awake, little one. Happy Actual Birthday. Time to see what the day holds for us," Nicholas whispered.

Sophia pulled the covers over her head. "No."

Nicholas chuckled. He pulled the covers back down, and Sophia turned over to look up at him. "My favorite time to see you is right after you wake up, Miss Snow," he admitted.

She frowned at him. "What? Why is that?"

He pulled on a crazy curl. "I don't know exactly. Your hair, your grumpy face, and your sleepy voice, I think. It only lasts for a moment, so I know that few have seen this side of you. It's a special gift."

Sophia stared up at him in shock. What the heck was she supposed to say to that? "Well... I can't feel grumpy after hearing that," she muttered.

Nicholas laughed and stood up. "Come to my room when you're ready. I have some things to share with you that Martin learned about last night."

Sophia perked up at that. "Oh, cool. Ok, I won't take long."

Nicholas responded as he walked away, "I almost forgot. Martin bought better outerwear for you. It's in the bag there."

He pointed to a bag by the door. "I'm sure you have good clothes, but it can't hurt to layer up. It gets cold at night."

She dumped the contents onto the bed and took in all the new gear. Hiking boots, big fluffy warm socks, some type of leggings, thermal top, and water-resistant jacket. They were beautiful and better than what she had. She began changing her outfit up in her mind as she went to the bathroom.

She stopped when she caught her image in the mirror. Her hair was going in every direction except the right one. This was his favorite way to see her? She shook her head and set about taming the beast that was her hair.

Once secured in a messy bun on top of her head, she finished her other toiletries and went to dress. She pulled on the new pants. They fit close like leggings, except they were thick with a layer of fuzzy warmth against her skin. Next, she used the new thick wool socks and hiking boots. She dug into her suitcase and got her favorite sports bra before donning the under armor top. She put on one of her t-shirts and a light jacket. Looking at herself, she decided that should be enough layers. She would take the big jacket for later in the evening.

She went to the door and gave a knock. Martin opened the door with a smile. "Happy birthday, lass!" He hugged her as she walked into the room.

Sophia laughed. "Thanks, Martin. Thanks for the new gear. It's great!"

"You're most welcome, dearie," Martin said with a wink.

Sophia looked around to see Nicholas at the table eating breakfast and looking at a couple of pieces of paper. She walked over and sat. "Have you eaten, Martin?" she asked.

"I just finished. You get what you like. I have a few calls to make. I'll duck into your room so Nicholas can catch you up." He grabbed his phone and some files and went next door.

Sophia looked at the food and began making a plate of eggs and toast. Her nerves had robbed her of her appetite, but she figured she should at least attempt to eat before a hike.

Nicholas observed her. "You doing ok, Miss Snow?"

"Yeah, Nicca. I'm nervous, of course, but that can't be helped.

I'm ok though." Sophia looked over at the papers. "What is that?"

Nicholas looked down. "It's what we wanted to tell you about. I don't know if it'll help, but I want to cover all our bases." He held up an old piece of paper.

She recognized it was written using the old druid language. "Martin got this last night?"

Nicholas nodded. "Yes. The woman he interviewed was of druid descent. Martin has spent a decade trying to trace family lines of the original druids from the old village. It has been almost impossible. He hasn't been able to build entire family trees, but he got a few limbs here and there."

Sophia sat up. "Mine?" she asked.

Nicholas froze for a moment. "Yes," he finally responded. "We can share what we have if you like, Miss Snow, but I would ask that we save it for a different day."

Sophia knew him well enough to know he said that to spare her feelings. Her tree must not be a happy one then. She nodded to him with understanding. "Ok. Another time, Nicca."

He relaxed a little and continued. "Martin found this woman on a message board online. Her name is Maria. She told Martin that this letter had been passed down through her family with instructions to give it to whoever came looking for information."

Sophia's eyes widened. "It could be for us then?"

Nicholas shook his head. "Don't get your hopes up. I think it's meant for us, but the information is still general. I don't know if it is telling us anything more than we already know."

Sophia slumped back in her seat. "It's frustrating guessing all the time. Why couldn't there be like a guidebook or something?"

Nicholas agreed with her. "Yeah, I asked that before. Jophiel gave an answer about the path to knowledge being just as important as the knowledge itself."

Sophia thought about what he said. "Hm, I guess. That doesn't mean I have to like it though." She crossed her arms.

Nicholas chuckled. "Here. You look at it before I give you my impression. See if it means anything specific to you."

Sophia reached out and touched the paper. The moment she

did, there was a zing of electricity running up her arm. Her face felt warm, and she knew her eyes were showing her magic from the look on Nicholas's face.

Suddenly she blinked, and instead of a hotel room, she was standing under a large oak tree. There was a lovely dark-haired woman in brown robes standing by the trunk. She looked to be in her fifties, but her eyes were shining with kindness and youth. She immediately felt at ease.

"Hello," Sophia said to her with a half-wave.

The woman smiled. "I am so happy to see you. Come closer, I have a message and not much time."

Sophia walked closer. "I'm Sophia."

The woman smiled again. "Come closer, I have a message and not much time."

Sophia paused. She got the sense this was not a real woman. Something about the way she repeated the sentence made it sound more like a recording. She walked cautiously toward the woman.

"Druids are not supposed to write our stories, but we are dying, and I don't know if any will be left to help the chosen girl. If you are hearing this, then I'm blessed that you, Liúsaidh, have found me. I hope the messages I have can help you defeat the one of the night."

She paused for a beat and Sophia focused hard to remember every detail of what she was saying. The woman turned her head slightly before beginning again. "There are few stories left. Even fewer about Liúsaidh defeating Lilith. Here is all I know:

When your power awakens, hold on tight. The pain will end.

Bring the thing that makes you calm. It will find you when you are lost.

You must make all into one before the night comes. Or lose yourself to madness.

Sometimes sacrifice is the way to overcome."

The woman smiled gently. "Thank you, Liúsaidh, for this opportunity to help you on this journey. May your life be filled with light and life. Peace be with you."

Sophia blinked and was back in the hotel, still holding the

letter. "Whoa!" Sophia said. "How long was I gone?"

Nicholas looked at her oddly. "You weren't, Miss Snow. I just handed you the letter, and your eyes lit up. No time passed." He looked concerned. "Martin!" he yelled.

Martin came through the door quickly, looking around like he was looking for danger. "What's up?"

Nicholas never took his eyes off Sophia. "Something happened when she touched the letter. Her eyes glowed. Then a second later she was asking me how long had she been gone."

She pointed at the letter and asked, "What does it say to you?"

Nicholas explained. "It just says that she knows she shouldn't write a letter, but there aren't many druids left to pass the knowledge to. She says the magic will tell you everything that's important, and that she is blessed to be a part of the journey. That's it."

Sophia paced again. Suddenly she stopped. "Does Lucy... no, not Lucy… more like LOO-say mean anything to you?"

They both looked at each other and shrugged. "No, lass," Martin said sympathetically.

Nicholas jumped up and walked to her. "Miss Snow, please, will you start from the beginning?"

Sophia sank onto the bed. "Who is Lilith?"

Both men rushed her at once.

Nicholas demanded, "Did you see her? Did she try to hurt ye?"

Martin put a hand on Nicholas's arm. "You're scaring her. She's safe here with us. Let her talk. Please," he said calmly.

He forced his body to relax. "Forgive me. I'm not happy that something happened to you, and there wasn't a damn thing I could do about it. I didn't even fucking know it was happening."

The only way they were going to understand what happened was if she just spit it out. She took a deep breath. "I blinked and, instead of here, I was standing underneath a big oak tree. There was a woman. She called me a word. It sounded like Loo-say. She said she hoped her messages helped me to defeat the one of the night."

Martin pulled out his phone and began looking something up. Nicholas frowned at him, but then nodded at Sophia to continue.

Sophia kept going before she forgot anything. "She said there weren't many stories left. Even fewer were about Loo-say defeating Lilith." She noticed Martin and Nicholas look at each other and tucked that away for later.

"Then she told me four things." Sophia closed her eyes and recited them word for word.

"When your power awakens, hold on tight. The pain will end.

Bring the thing that makes you calm. It will find you when you are lost.

You must make all into one before the night comes. Or lose yourself to madness.

Sometimes sacrifice is the way to overcome."

She opened her eyes and stared at them both. "I don't know what any of this means. Except the first one. It makes me think that tonight is going to hurt. It's going to hurt bad, isn't it?"

Nicholas softened his gaze. "I don't know. Maybe. But it'll not last, and you'll not be alone."

Martin spoke up while looking at his phone. "Sophia. I think maybe she was calling you Liúsaidh. It's a Scottish Gaelic word that means 'graceful light.' It makes sense she would call you light because Lilith means 'of the night.'"

Nicholas cleared his throat, which made Martin look up. He shook his head at him and Martin seemed to realize what he said out loud. "Sorry. I was thinking out loud there."

"Who is Lilith?" Sophia said with a determined glare.

Nicholas sighed. "We think that is who you will face in the end, Miss Snow. Or, at least, some part of her." He took her hands. "Let's save that battle for another day. Focus on tonight. Could the second sentence be about tonight too? Bring the thing that makes you calm? Does anything come to mind?"

Sophia's mind went straight for her bracelet. It was the first thing she ran for when she was anxious. She looked at Nicholas and gave one shoulder a shrug. "My charm bracelet?"

Nicholas's gaze softened, and he smiled softly. "Ok, Miss

Snow." He squeezed her hand. "And what about the other state-ments? Could they all be about tonight, I wonder?" He began looking off into space.

"I hope not," Sophia said. "I don't like knowing I have until nightfall before going insane."

"Well, lass, night could refer to Lilith too. Maybe it means you need to have your magic managed before she comes?" Martin guessed.

Nicholas nodded. "That's a good point, Martin. It feels right." He turned back to Sophia. "It also makes sense that you will have a certain amount of adjusting to do once all of your magic awak-ens. It'll be something no one can really help with because no one has done it before."

Sophia closed her eyes. "Great. Pain and madness is the fore-cast, then."

Nicholas made a sound of frustration, and Martin's arm tightened around her shoulders. "Now lass, you can't start the fight assuming you've lost. You're not alone. We won't let you fail."

Something was bugging Sophia about the letter. "Nicca, how was she able to leave me that letter? I thought magic died with Ney and her druid sisters."

Nicholas glanced at the letter thoughtfully. "It was very clever of her, actually. She was still a druid. She didn't want the knowledge to fall into the wrong hands, so she left her oral story attached to the letter using a spell." He looked back at Sophia. "A spell that only magic could activate. It ensured that only you could get that message. Only you have the magic to get it."

Sophia nodded. "Wow. It's a little overwhelming the amount of people who have worked so hard to ensure I don't fail." She looked meaningfully at Nicholas and Martin before reaching over and grabbing each man's hand. "I gotta make sure I don't let those people down."

Nicholas smiled, but it was Martin that answered her. "Nay, lass, it's us that'll no' let you down."

CHAPTER 36

Sophia walked to her room to get the heavier jacket Martin had given her. When she reached her bed, instead of picking up the jacket, she turned and sat down slowly. Suddenly everything was rushing at her at once. It had always been a part of her life. This idea of being a druid, having magic, and the looming encounter with evil. But that was just it—it had always been something that was going to happen sometime later. Suddenly, it felt like her time was up. She was hours away from pain she couldn't avoid. The evil now had a name, Lilith, and she could soon be fighting for her sanity. Even though she had known about it from the beginning, she wasn't sure she was ready.

Sophia sighed as she stood up and walked to the bathroom counter. She unzipped the inside pocket of her carry-on and pulled out her beloved bracelet. So many hours of running her fingers over the charms, reminding herself of the promise Nicholas gave her to always be there when she needed him.

The sound of a throat clearing made her look up from the charms to see both Martin and Nicholas watching her. She smiled at them. "It's the sound they make when I run my fingers over the charms. It relaxes me." She tucked the bracelet in her pocket and looked back up. "I'm as ready as I'll ever be, guys. Lead the way."

They were quiet as they went down to the lobby. The weather was thankfully sunny with clear skies. Sophia took off her light jacket and tied it around her hips while she and Nicholas waited for Martin to pull the car around. She caught Nicholas watching her, so she offered him a smile.

He turned away to look out over the parking lot. "Miss Snow. It has only just now dawned on me I have never told you this, but... I am very proud of you. You have embraced every task we have ever put in front of you. You never complain. You just accept and then do your best. You have far exceeded any dream I ever had for the girl... or... the young woman I hoped you would become."

Sophia just stared open-mouthed up at his face. He'd refused to look at her while speaking those beautiful words. It ticked her off because that wasn't like him. He was usually very direct and not looking her in the eye felt too much like an apology or a goodbye.

"Hey!" she scolded to get his attention.

He twisted to look at her, and she almost laughed at the confusion on his face. Instead, she waved her hand in a circle in front of him. "Whatever that was... stop it."

Martin pulled up in a Land Rover. "You say beautiful things like that to my face, Nicca."

She looked over to see him grinning.

"Yes ma'am," he said as they started toward Martin.

Sophia jumped into the backseat and looked around the back in awe. "Well," Sophia began, "I was going to ask what the change of car was about, Martin, but I can see it. Are we camping?"

Martin looked at her in the rearview. "Well, lass, we wanted to prepare for everything. It will be late and possibly cold, and we donna know how long it will take. We just want to be as ready as we can be."

Sophia looked back at all the gear piled up. "Martin. Are there like... five of you running around? How do you get it all done?"

Nicholas laughed. "I ask myself that all the time, Miss Snow."

Martin winked at her before looking back at the road. "Aye, I canna be tellin' all my secrets, now can I?"

Sophia laughed and looked out the window. She was trying not to get caught up in her emotions. If she gave in, she felt like they would pull her under completely, so she was fighting to be brave. She also wanted to enjoy the surrounding beauty. She didn't want to miss it all because of her fear.

She prayed. She felt like a lot of her conversations with God came through the people around her. When she opened herself up to accept guidance, she noticed that the answers she needed usually appeared through people. Sophia felt like God placed people in her path to give her the information she needed to move forward. Sometimes, it was a random conversation with a lady in a grocery store. Or of course it could come from someone she knew like Nicca. God had even used Sophia to answer her own questions. Many times, she found herself in a conversation with someone, giving them the very guidance she needed herself. Those lightbulb moments were her favorite.

She didn't feel the need to pray every day, but when she did, it couldn't be denied. Sometimes she needed to confirm she was on the right track, or clear confusion and settle her mind.

She spent the trip to Glendalough praying for strength to be brave. She really didn't want to crumble in front of Martin and Nicholas. They had so much faith in her, but she was human, and really didn't want to feel pain.

So she sat quietly, rubbing the charms on her bracelet and talking to God.

CHAPTER 37

*H*alf an hour into the drive Nicholas turned to Sophia. "Miss Snow, take a moment and call Penny. It's your birthday. She will worry if she doesn't hear from you. We should be there soon." He gave her a sympathetic look.

"Thanks, Nicca. You're right, of course." She called her number. Penny answered on the first ring.

"Soph? Hey!! Happy Birthday, sweet girl!" Penny gushed over the line.

Sophia couldn't stop the tears. She loved this woman so much. Nicholas's hand came over the seat and grabbed her fingers in support. "Hey Mom, thanks."

"How's your trip been so far? Are you loving it?" Penny said.

"It's so beautiful. Nicca and Martin are both making sure I have the trip of a lifetime," Sophia said.

"Oh honey, I'm so happy you're getting this experience. I can't wait to see all the pictures," Penny began. "I really miss you though. It's super quiet around here, and Sam is useless," she joked.

Sophia laughed. "Well, it's going fast." She paused. "I can't stay on the line, Mom. It'll cost a fortune, but I wanted to make sure we talked on my birthday. Also, have fun at your spa day tomorrow. Enjoy every minute, ok? Don't worry because I'm having a blast, and I'll see you soon."

"Ok, sweetheart. I love you, and I can't wait to see you. Have a great time!" Penny said cheerfully.

Sophia closed her eyes tightly. "I love you too, Mom. See you soon."

She hung up and looked up at two faces staring at her with concern. Sophia looked around to see they parked in a lot full of tourist buses and family cars. People were obviously taking advantage of the rare appearance of sunshine.

"I'm ok guys." She looked at all the gear. "Which of this stuff do I carry?" She just wanted to focus on anything but her emotions.

Martin dragged out the backpacks, and Nicholas stood at her door. She interrupted him before he could even speak.

"Nicca, the single biggest way you could help me right now is to not focus on my feelings. If I give in, then I'll lose it. I need to focus on things, like what do I carry? Where are we walking?"

Nicholas pulled her out of the car by the hands. He looked her over for a minute before nodding and reaching behind her to grab her jacket and shut the door. He gave her the jacket and pulled her to the back.

"Martin, how can Miss Snow be of help to us?" Nicholas asked him.

Sophia felt a tear run down her cheek. She furiously wiped it away and nodded her agreement with him to Martin.

"Well, lass. I confined most to the two packs. I have a duffle here that has some overflow goods in it. If you could carry it, that would be a big help. The straps convert to a backpack. Here, you could probably get that jacket into it."

Sophia nodded her thanks to him and grabbed the duffel as she lowered to the ground to unzip and put her jacket away. She saw Nicholas's fist clenched right by her face and knew he was struggling. The guys were having a wordless conversation while she pretended not to notice, but she couldn't do anything for them right at that moment. She was fighting enough just for herself.

She turned and followed the flow of people heading for a

building. She figured the guys would catch up, and she needed a moment to collect herself.

All the way to the building she concentrated on breathing in, taking three steps, breathing out, taking three steps. At the building, she leaned against the corner to let the guys catch up.

She felt blessed to have them in her life, because there was no way she could do this alone. When she could handle it, she would definitely tell them.

She smiled as they approached. "Sorry guys. I needed a moment. I just assumed we were going the way everyone else was going?"

Nicholas explained, "We will for a little while. I'd like it if you stayed behind me, but in front of Martin, please."

"Ok. Sounds like a plan," Sophia agreed.

They walked around the corner to see a type of walkway.

She stopped. In awe.

"Oh. My. God," she said. Her jaw was dragging the ground. She couldn't believe she'd been so lost in her head she hadn't seen the beauty before her.

Glendalough was easily the most beautiful sight she had seen in Ireland yet. Before her rose beautiful mountains covered in green. They were at the bottom of a valley that spread before them. Way up ahead on the path she could see what looked like church ruins.

Nicholas placed a hand on her arm. She breathed deeply. "It's so beautiful."

He smiled and looked at Glendalough. "It is, indeed."

She slowly began down the path. Nicholas jumped ahead of her, and she felt Martin behind her. Single file made it easier with the crowds of people.

The presence of tourists upset her, because it felt like they were intruding. It was impossible to talk, but after about fifteen minutes they made it to a point where the path forked. To the right were the ruins. Straight ahead kept to the side of the mountain.

Nicholas walked straight, but she paused, causing him to turn with a question in his eyes.

Sophia pointed to the ruins. "Can you tell me about these, Nicca?"

"It's the remains of a monastery, little one. They thrived here for many years. Ney and her sisters often helped them through rough times. These remains are from much later than Ney's time, though." He turned and began walking again.

Sophia kept looking at it as they passed the turn. "Why did they leave?"

Nicholas looked back to answer. "The vikings got them several times, but in the end it was the Normans sometime in the 13th century."

Sophia fell back into step. They were walking a relatively straight path, but it was uphill. It took about five minutes to crest the little hill they were on, and when they did, she saw water. It was still far away, but she caught a small glimpse, and she could see sheer cliffs of surrounding mountains.

She couldn't explain how beautiful being in the bottom of that valley felt. There were sparks of electricity humming through her as if the valley was giving her energy.

The tourists really slowed their progress, but eventually, they came to a sharp turn in the path. To the right and straight ahead was the water, but to the left, the path led into the woods of the mountain they had been walking along.

Most of the crowd were walking to the water and then returning to the parking lot. Very few were turning to hike into the woods. Nicholas stopped at the water's edge so they could take in the beauty, and a thought came to Sophia.

"Nicca! Is this the valley you told me about when I was six? The one you dreamed of?" She turned to him with wide eyes.

He smiled softly. "It's close, but this is not the exact one." He finally looked at her. "The lake from my childhood feeds into this larger one. We're close to home."

Martin suggested, "Why don't we make use of the beautiful sight and those tables there to grab some lunch. We have at least a three-hour hike ahead of us."

Nicholas led them over to the table that a group had just left. Sophia wasn't hungry, but she knew she needed the energy. So she grabbed water and a granola bar and lost herself in view while she ate. It made her feel strong.

Eventually she looked at the guys to see them staring at her again. "What?" she asked. "Do I have food on my face?" She reached up and wiped her mouth.

Martin laughed, and Nicholas smiled. "Your magic is showing." He looked at the table in front of her.

Sophia looked down and saw the sandy grit on the table moving into a swirling shape that looked like her mark. She startled and sat up straight, making the dirt fall through the cracks of the table and disappear.

She looked up apologetically. "Sorry... this place..." she trailed off.

"Aye," Martin agreed. "Even I feel it, I think."

Nicholas looked up into the woods. "The next part of the journey will be less crowded. It'll be more difficult, but not too bad. Are you ready?"

Sophia turned to look up the path. It looked dark compared to the open sunshine reflecting off the water. "Yup?" she said.

They laughed and Martin asked, "Are you askin' or tellin' us, lass?"

She smiled and helped them gather the trash and their bags. With one last look at the lake, she turned and entered the dark woods behind Nicholas.

CHAPTER 38

The moment they entered the woods, the temperature dropped noticeably. The trees and ground were covered with a fine green moss that gave off a dank, musty, earthy smell that wrapped around her senses.

There was a worn-down pathway, but all around the ground looked wet and dark. Roots of large trees came out of the ground everywhere, making it hard to look anywhere but down. It was actually a good thing, because she had to focus on what she was doing instead of how she was feeling.

They passed a hiker every few minutes, but nothing like earlier. The path wasn't too physical. It had been steep in the beginning, but they had been walking easily for the last ten minutes. It had eased up enough that the silence got to Sophia, and allowed her to get back into her feelings.

"Ok." Sophia finally broke the silence. "Someone tell me something."

Martin laughed behind her. "Anything?"

Sophia shrugged. "Sure. I mean, I was just trying to break the silence, but now that I really think about it, I don't really know much about either of you."

Martin replied, "And yet, you allowed us to drag you deep into the woods. That is either very brave or very... not."

Sophia smiled at Martin. "I'm serious. I've known you both

for a decade. Yet, except for that first week, our interactions have only been small moments, and you always make me do all the talking."

Nicholas stopped walking and turned to look at Sophia as she finished, "You know everything about me. I don't have a single secret, so I think you two should start spilling beans."

Nicholas crossed his huge arms over his chest. "To be fair, Miss Snow, no one ever had to make you do the talking."

Sophia looked on in shock as Martin, who was laughing, walked over to Nicholas and gave him a high-five. "Good one."

"Nope. Not liking that." She crossed her arms and began her silent treatment. She would show them.

She began walking the path again, even though she had no idea where they were going.

When she got even with Nicholas, he put his arm across her to stop her progress.

"Where are you going?" Nicholas asked with a smile.

Sophia looked away and pinched her lips together, determined not to answer.

"It appears now you *are* going to have to make her talk," Martin joked.

"What exactly would you like to know, little one?" Nicholas asked gently.

Sophia gave him a quick look. He looked genuine, and she really wanted to know more about them, but it hurt her feelings that they thought she talked too much.

She slumped her shoulders. "Nothing. We can keep walking. I was just filling the silence," she said sadly and tried to step forward.

Nicholas moved quickly in front of her. "Miss Snow, I apologize. Did my joking around hurt your feelings?"

Sophia shrugged. "It's fine. I do talk a lot around you. I never know when I'll see you again, so I try to pack everything into one conversation."

Martin put a hand on her shoulder. "Ah, lass. I'm sorry, truly. It was insensitive of us." He looked over at Nicholas. "Since when have you had to ask Sophia how something made her feel?"

Nicholas frowned. "I don't usually, but she is feeling... a lot. And it's all very strong. So my bad joke was lost in a sea of hurt. I'm sorry, Miss Snow. It was bad humor."

Sophia sighed. Everyone was on edge and emotions were high. She was being sensitive. "It's fine, guys. Sorry. I'm overly sensitive today. Let's keep going. It will help." She smiled at them both.

They hesitated for a moment before Nicholas turned and walked again. She stretched her neck and followed while taking a drink of water. After about five minutes, Martin spoke from behind.

"I've never had a girlfriend," he said matter-of-factly.

Sophia stopped, straightened, and slowly turned to face Martin with a straight face. "Sorry?"

He just shrugged. "I have never had a serious relationship. Thinking I never will."

Sophia fought a smile and heard Nicholas cough to cover a laugh. "Martin, I was thinking more like, what's your favorite color or what did you get for Christmas last year." She smiled at him in thanks. "You just jumped right in there with both feet, didn't you?" She walked up and gave him a quick hug. "Thanks," she whispered before turning around to walk.

After ten steps Martin spoke up again. "It's pink. My favorite color is pink."

They all broke into easy laughter. Sophia responded, "I remember now. You told me when I was young."

"See?" Martin said. "You know more than you think you do about us."

Sophia thought of another question as they kept walking. "Hey, how did you two meet?"

Nicholas looked over his shoulder and smiled. "I happened upon Martin one day getting his ass handed to him by a group of lowlifes."

Sophia gasped, "Oh Martin! That's awful."

Martin explained, "It's fine, lass. I was in trouble, but, thankfully, Nicholas got to me before any permanent damage was done."

Nicholas kept going. "He's been with me ever since."

They walked along a few more minutes when Nicholas paused. The woods looked straight out of a fairy tale. Not the happy ending part, but the dark part, the evil witch lurks in the woods with a poison apple part. It was seriously creepy. "I am so glad I'm not alone right now."

Nicholas looked around the woods. "The magic gives off a certain vibe. It's meant to repel normal people, and it's why we haven't seen hikers for a while now. For some reason they can't explain, they just don't want to be here. It'll work in our favor. We leave the path here, little one. Watch for exposed roots."

Sophia nodded and fell back in line while keeping an eye on her feet. She slipped a few times, but thankfully no embarrassing wipe-outs. They were walking at a sideways angle that was awkward. It was just what she needed. Minutes passed without her thinking about anything but what she was doing.

With no tourists' eyes around, they moved much faster. After about forty-five minutes, Sophia heard a roaring noise. It took a couple of more beats to realize it was water, and she got excited. There was a waterfall up ahead.

The land crested a few feet away from the edge of a river, and they followed it toward the noise. With every step, the sound of the water got louder and louder. She strained to see around the bend of the river, but the trees and stones were blocking the view. When they finally reached the bend, a large waterfall stretching at least eight stories high burst into view, and Sophia gasped as she looked up.

Nicholas turned and held out his hand, and without a thought, she took it.

He pulled, and she left the stone she was standing on. Sophia squealed in shock, and when she opened her eyes, Nicholas was laughing.

He was carrying her through the shallow water along the edge.

"Give a girl some warning next time, why don't you?" Sophia

grumbled good-naturedly. "I can walk through water, you know."

"I know, little one," Nicholas said.

She held on tightly as he made his way to the waterfall. She looked at the top. Were they going to climb that? She was fit, but that would not be easy.

Nicholas leaned close and said, "Not going up, Miss Snow."

She frowned, but he just smiled, and set her on the smooth river stones about ten feet from the falls. Water mist was hitting her face, and she thanked God she'd had the good sense to put her hair in a bun.

Nicholas positioned her to face the falls. He leaned over her shoulder and pointed to a spot just to the side of the falls. "We're going to that stone right there, Miss Snow. Put on your heavier jacket. It will block a lot of the spray from the fall."

Sophia's eyes grew wide. They were going behind the falls? Wow, she thought as she dug out her jacket and put it on, this was straight out of a movie.

Nicholas led her to the base of the falls. He flattened himself against the cliff and turned to hold out his hand again. She gave him a dubious stare, and he quirked an eyebrow at her.

She grabbed his hand and began walking along the ledge. After about twenty feet, they reached a bigger round rock they could barely fit on. She watched Nicholas as he ducked down and walked behind the water.

Sophia took a deep breath and followed.

"Oh, my goodness." Sophia said as she looked around the barely lit cave opening. "This doesn't seem real. It's straight out of Last of the Mohicans."

She looked out through the water. It was magical. Martin was just walking into the cave opening, and she couldn't help herself. She walked over to him while he was shaking water out of his hair. She grabbed his shoulders and began shaking him while yelling the famous words from the movie.

Martin slowly blinked. "Oh wow. You are such a dork, aren't you?"

Sophia laughed. She turned to look at Nicholas, who just looked confused. "Ah, come on people! Last of the Mohicans?"

He just looked at her with a blank face. "Geez... tough crowd." She wouldn't apologize. That was an awesome movie, and she silently thanked Penny for making her watch it.

Nicholas walked over to the corner. Well, it looked like the corner, but Sophia realized once she got there that it was an illusion. There was a long narrow corridor that stretched into the darkness.

Sophia gulped. "Someone please tell me we have flashlights."

Martin pulled at the zipper on her back. He handed a flashlight to Nicholas, who turned it on and began down the long hall. It was straight at first, but every once in a while there would be a fork. Nicholas never hesitated over which direction to take. Eventually they made a sharp turn, only to go a few feet and turn again. She bumped into Nicholas as he stopped abruptly. Sophia leaned around him to see steps carved into stone.

They were hard steps, especially for a short girl. Nicholas would step up, turn, and pull her up. She looked around when Nicholas lifted her up the twenty-first step into the sunlight.

They were standing in the middle of a trio of large boulders set at the side of the mountain which kept going up on her right. It was another illusion; she realized. They squeezed between a boulder and the mountain to emerge into absolute beauty.

Sophia stopped and looked around. "This is home, isn't it, Nicca?"

He nodded his head and turned to look at the forest. "This is home."

Sophia walked out into the clearing to get her bearings. They were behind and on top of the waterfall. Before her stretched another forest, but this one was lighter, more inviting. To the right, a mountain side kept going up. There was a path leading into the woods. The right side of the path was lined with moss-covered trees. The limbs curled overhead to touch the slope of the land on the left side. It created a tunnel effect. As they stepped along the path, it felt like they were walking through a tunnel back in time. It was possibly the coolest thing Sophia had ever seen.

She looked down at the wood planks they were walking on. "Who put these here?"

"I did," Nicholas said.

"By yourself?" She said with surprise.

"Not all at once. I did a little here, a little there," Nicholas explained.

Sophia asked the question she had been thinking all day. "Nicca, this is your home, and it was also Ney's home. So, are you a descendent of one of the families from Ney's time? And where is everyone? Why would they leave this place?"

Nicholas paused in front of Sophia, and she noticed his shoulders fall. She was about to reach out and touch him when he finally turned to her. She saw the genuine sadness in his eyes and braced herself for what he was about to say.

"It's complicated, little one. I'd ask that you wait until we get to the ruins before I explain. We're about a half hour away."

Sophia couldn't imagine what could be complicated, but she nodded anyway. She tried to relax and enjoy the beauty around her, but it was hard for her to avoid thinking about what was coming. When they walked out of this forest, how different would she be? And what story was so complicated it made Nicholas dread telling her?

CHAPTER 39

*N*icholas was suffering. His fears and Sophia's fears about tonight were messing with his head, and coming home was adding to his emotional state too. It was always sad to see this place, or what was left of it, anyway.

Then on top of that, after all these years, Sophia finally had to question his connection to Niamh. He'd made sure to never lie to her over the years, but she would see his omission as a lie. It had seemed less complicated, or maybe, if he was being honest with himself, it had been the easy way out. He hadn't wanted her to know she was here because of his weakness.

Why did she have to ask him now, he wondered? Tonight, it was so important to be on the same page. He would have to come up with a way to answer her questions without causing her to shut him out.

Keeping Sophia safe over the years had been so easy compared to this. He remembered once when she was nine, his magic had brought him to her. She'd been playing in the school-yard with friends, and he'd been confused because she looked happy.

Two minutes later a guy had shown up at the edge of the yard. Nicholas had watched in horror as the guy had singled her out and waved her over. Of course, his sweet Sophia had skipped to the stranger without a second thought.

210

Nicholas had crouched down behind Sophia and grabbed her hand.

She had turned around with a surprised, "Hi, Nicca!" launching herself into his arms.

He'd whispered to Sophia to walk back to her friends and not look back. She had touched his cheek like she does when she understands something is serious.

"Ok, Nicca," she had said and had promptly run away.

Nicholas had nearly killed that day. The disgusting coward had talked to Nicholas as if it was a normal thing, "Hey dude. I didn't know. She's not even my type. I'm more into the boys myself, you know. I just have a guy I know would have loved her, and I needed the cash."

Nicholas had dragged him behind the football shed and beat him almost to death. Then he'd stood there while he made the guy call the police and turn himself in. He hadn't left until they put the guy into a police car. Then he had visited 'the guy who would have loved her' and given him a similar heart to heart. The only reason he hadn't killed was the knowledge their time in prison would be worse than death. A much more fitting punishment.

Just thinking about that day sparked anger in him, but the point of that day was her complete trust in him. Dozens of times throughout her life, he had needed her trust in him to save her life. Whatever he needed her to do to be safe, she did without question. Tonight, that was more important than any other time, and right before the battle, he was putting a chink in their armor.

He looked up at the sky as they entered the clearing where the village used to be. The clearing was a huge circle with the mountain face still to the right. Trees, stones, and the remains of buildings made up the rest of the round shaped border. In the middle, there was still evidence of the fires that had always burned. The nostalgia that hit him was always a little sad and painful. He turned to see Sophia's face as she looked at it. For some reason, he really wanted her to like it.

She walked out ahead of him into the center and looked each

building over carefully, as if she was trying to figure out what it used to be. As she spun around, she came upon a building with two walls still partially standing. She walked straight for it with determination.

Surprised, Nicholas followed her.

When she got to the building, she reached out and carefully touched the edge of a wall. "Nicca?" She looked at him over her shoulder. "Did you live here in this home?"

Nicholas was shocked. "I did. How did you know that?"

She looked back at the building for a moment before shrugging and admitting, "I don't know. I feel you here." She walked on, looking at everything.

Nicholas turned to Martin. "Hey, could you set up the fire and tent? It's about to be dark, and I need to have a conversation."

Martin looked at him with sympathy. "Sure, no problem. Take your time. We can eat something when you both are ready. Midnight will be here soon enough."

Nicholas relaxed. "Thanks. Not sure if I said it, but I'm glad you invited yourself on this trip."

Martin laughed. "I know."

Nicholas walked back to Sophia and sent up a silent prayer that he would have the right words. When she turned, he noticed her eyes shimmered in the low light of the afternoon.

She smiled nervously. "You look really serious, Nicca."

"There is a really beautiful spot to watch the sunset, little one," Nicholas said. "I'd love to share it with you, and maybe we could have that conversation I promised you."

Sophia nodded. "I'd like that."

After a beat, he started for the old path leading to the cliff's edge. He held out his hand. She immediately grabbed it, and they walked along together. Maybe he just wanted to feel her trust, because he feared he was about to lose it. Maybe it was all the emotions of the day, and he just wanted some support and comfort. Either way, it felt nice, so he enjoyed the moment.

CHAPTER 40

*S*ophia was so over it. She had spent the entire day in knots, and a person could only feel this way for so long. Bring on the pain or whatever was coming and get it over with.

All of her swirling butterflies aside, she was excited to see the lake. She knew that's exactly where Nicholas was taking her.

She could tell a cliff was up ahead because the ground stopped and all she saw was the sky. The closer they got, the more the picture revealed itself. When they came out of the tree line, there was an open grassy area with big stones randomly placed around.

The closer she got to the edge, the more nervous she felt. It was quite a way down the mountain to the valley below. The lake was a turquoise color, just like he'd said. The green-colored mountains stretched on as far as she could see. No houses or businesses or electrical lines marred the vision before her. Just untouched nature. It was peaceful.

Sophia felt him tug her hand toward a group of stones. She took his cue and sat down, "It's as beautiful as you said, Nicca."

Nicholas looked out over the valley. "It's just as I remembered it."

She took in the changing colors as the sun set, and knowing

he struggled, she sat quietly. She didn't know how else to help him.

"I have to be honest, Miss Snow," he finally began. "I dread telling you the story I promised ye."

"I can tell," Sophia said. "But since I don't know what it is, I don't know how to help you."

Nicholas chuckled. "Of course you would be trying to help me." He turned to look at her. "I let you believe something not entirely true, little one. At the time, I believed it to be the simplest explanation. You were only six, but as time went on, I understood you would see it as a lie. I need your trust to keep you safe. That I am taking a huge chance with your trust right when I need it the most scares me to death." He pushed his palms into his eyes.

Sophia feared what he was about to say, but she longed to put his suffering to rest. "Just rip the band-aid off, Nicca. I will always trust you."

He scoffed and looked back out at the valley. "I'm not a *descendant* from Ney's time, little one." He turned to look at her. "I'm *from* Ney's time."

Sophia processed what he said. "You knew her... personally?" she asked in shock.

He nodded. "She found me wrapped in a blanket in the woods here and raised me as her son."

Sophia was shaking her head as she understood what he was saying. "But that would mean you're like... over a thousand years old or something, right?"

He answered apologetically, "Around thirteen hundred, give or take a few."

Sophia felt tears filling her eyes. "You told me you were eighteen, that's not an omission, Nicca. You said that to me. I thought you were like twenty-eight now. You've aged. You look older than when I met you."

He nodded his head. "I stopped aging at eighteen when Ney and her sisters did the first guardian ritual to locate you. I was frozen at eighteen until I found you and did the final ritual with you at the hotel."

Sophia felt warm tears sliding down her cheeks. Until this moment, she really had held onto the dream of having more with Nicholas when she was older, but he was thirteen hundred years old. He would always think of her as a child. She looked down at her feet. Suddenly the beauty before her just made her sad.

She really was over all of this day. "That's a really long time to wait for me. I can't imagine how much you have seen and done."

She felt him sit beside her. "Honestly, little one, I don't remember much of it before finding you."

Sophia broke at that. She was thin, fragile glass shattering in slow motion. She had secretly hoped one day he would see her as someone to love. Not a child or a responsibility, but a partner in life, and she had justified that things would change for them when she was older. Twelve years wasn't that big of an age gap, and she knew he cared for her. They had a connection like no other, but now, she felt the last strings of hope snapping and flowing on the breeze over the cliff. It had been a beautiful dream for her, but now she felt it dissolving. There was nothing she had to offer someone thirteen hundred years old. She really would always be a child to him.

Nicholas moved quickly, pulling her into a hug. "Please, Miss Snow. I'm sorry. I can't bear to see you this way."

Sophia just held on and let out what had been building all day. She'd have to deal with this new knowledge about Nicholas, but everything was hitting her at once. The truth was, they had a bond that nothing could break, and she knew he would give his life for her. That hadn't changed. She needed to remember that and focus on what was coming.

She leaned back, and Nicholas immediately began wiping her tears.

"I'm sorry. I'm just tired, Nicca. Can we go back to the tent now?" Sophia asked sadly.

"Please don't shut me out, Miss Snow," Nicholas pleaded.

"I'm not, I promise. I just need a moment," Sophia explained.

He brushed a loose curl from her forehead and tucked it into her scrunchie. "When you're ready, I'll tell you anything you want to know about my life here. Maybe for now, we should just focus on tonight?"

Sophia nodded. "Yes. I'll feel a million times better once tonight is over with. Then I'm sure I'll have all kinds of things I want to know. Like when is your birthday?"

Nicholas smiled. "It's the same as yours, little one." He touched her cheek.

"What?" Sophia gasped. "Every year when you visit me and give me a present for my birthday, it's also your birthday?"

He laughed. "Yes. Every year, my birthday is the same as yours."

Sophia frowned. "I feel horrible, Nicca. I've never given you anything. All these years, I hogged our day for myself. I feel really selfish right now."

Nicholas slowly stood while pulling her to her feet. He wrapped his arm around her as they began walking. "Every single year, for my birthday, I have only wanted one thing, and you are the only human being that can give it to me." He looked down at her questioning eyes and squeezed her shoulders. "Time with you."

CHAPTER 41

*S*ophia had been back at the campsite for five minutes when a very awkward situation presented itself. She wanted to avoid it, but there was no way around it.

"Um, guys?" she said hesitantly.

Both guys stopped working on the tent to look at her.

"I need a little direction on how to handle the... bathroom situation?" She felt like her face was on fire.

Martin began laughing. "I'll let you take that one," he said as he went back to the tent.

Nicholas laughed. "Believe it or not, we have a bathroom, sort of. Come on, I'll show you." He grabbed a bag and walked with her back toward the cliff. Halfway there, he turned and went deeper into the woods. It only took a moment, and they were standing by a fast-moving stream. Downstream a little way was a wide rectangle building.

Sophia turned to Nicholas. "An ancient port-a-potty?"

He laughed. "Yes, actually." He held out the bag.

She took it from him and walked a few steps toward the building. "What about snakes and spiders?"

He laughed as he started back toward the village. "It's Ireland, Miss Snow. Nothing to worry about here."

Sophia hesitantly walked to the building. Through the broken walls, she saw a stone slab seat with a hole in it. When she peeked through the hole, she saw the river edge had been dug out to go under the stone seat. The water swirled into the area lined with stones and back out into the rushing river. It was basically a constantly flushing toilet.

After a moment of hesitation, Sophia decided it was better than squatting in the woods, and her bladder was done thinking it over. When she opened the bag, she saw a roll of toilet paper and hand sanitizer. She set the bag up against the corner of the building as a makeshift trash can and stuck the toilet paper on a stick wedged in the ground. She quickly went, sanitized her hands, and then walked back to the village feeling much better.

When she got back, the tent was up by the mountainside and the guys were working by the fire. Martin was cooking something, and Nicholas was pulling logs around the fire to sit on.

She took a seat on a log and watched the fire. It was hypnotic.

"Nicca, is there something I can do to help?" she asked while staring at the flames.

"Not really. I was just doing things to keep my hands busy and pass the time," he explained as he sat down next to her. "I'm going to turn this area into a druid circle in a bit, but there's no hurry."

She turned to Martin. "What are you creating over there?"

Martin grinned at her. "I'm making award-winning baked potatoes. It'll blow you away just wait and see."

Sophia laughed. "I'm already amazed. It smells delicious."

Martin had indeed outdone himself. He roasted potatoes on the fire, warmed canned chili, and cracked open tubs of chopped onion and butter. It made for a pretty filling dinner under the stars. It struck Sophia again how grateful she was to have these two men on her side.

She cleared her throat. "I realized earlier today I've never stressed to the two of you just how thankful I am... that I have you both. I couldn't get through this without you. So... thank you."

Nicholas smiled at her. "I think you have it backward, little one."

Martin agreed. "Aye, we couldn't do this without you."

She smiled before confessing. "I'm nervous about tonight. The anticipation of pain has me in knots."

Nicholas moved over to her side. "Maybe it won't be as bad as you think, Miss Snow. We tend to blow things out of proportion in our minds."

She took a shaky breath before looking up at Martin and Nicholas. "Oh... I think it's going to be bad, guys."

Nicholas frowned at her before leaning closer to look into her eyes. "Miss Snow?"

She gave a one-shoulder shrug, "I started feeling differently a few minutes ago. It started as a kind of burning sensation low in my belly." She smiled at Martin. "At first I thought it was dinner, but now I realize it's something else. I can feel it growing."

Nicholas sat next to her and began rubbing her back. "I can't feel it. I'll set the circle now, little one. Hold on." He looked at Martin. "Can you grab that lighter and candle, those pieces of oak and stones I set by the tent, and run to the river and get a glass of water?"

Martin jumped up as soon as he began talking. "What is going on?" He was scrambling to grab the stones and sticks of oak. "It's still three hours until midnight. Why is she already feeling it, and why can you not?"

Nicholas took the items. "I don't know, Martin. We're in unfamiliar territory here. Let's just get the circle set, ok?"

Martin grabbed a cup from their meal and looked at Sophia for a moment before jogging off toward the river.

Nicholas kissed the top of her head. "Hang on, Miss Snow. I will set a circle for peace and protection, and then I'll be right back."

He went directly to the north edge of the circle close to the tent to set a piece of oak and lit the candle to set at the west point. He walked to the east and turned to Martin just as he ran up with the water. He put the water down and moved to the southern edge.

"Martin, remember to stay in the circle after I set it. If you have to move out for something, only move through this door

I'm setting here on the southern end." Nicholas made a doorway with a line of smooth stones. He took the longer piece of oak and set the circle by drawing in the dirt to connect each point going clockwise.

Sophia watched all of it with interest. She understood Nicholas better this time as he wished peace at each corner. When he finished, he turned and looked at Sophia. "Remember, this circle will help keep you centered and calm. Hopefully, it will help your feelings even out."

Sophia wanted to lie, to offer him comfort, but she knew it was pointless. "It still feels the same. Not worse though, so that's something."

Nicholas pulled her to her feet gently. "Come to the center with me, please." He walked her to the other side of the fire. Martin tossed him a sleeping bag.

Sophia stood there with her arms wrapped around her stomach while they stretched a sleeping bag on the ground. Nicholas helped her lay down. She looked up at the starry, clear sky. It was beautiful, and she felt her body calm down. Nicholas picked up her head to place a rolled-up jacket as a pillow.

He looked down at her. "Is this better?"

She smiled. "Yes, it is a little better. Thanks."

He smoothed the flyaway hairs off her forehead. "Just rest, concentrate on breathing, and keep yourself centered. If you're lucky, you could even fall asleep for a while."

She watched him get settled next to her, then she looked back up at the stars. She didn't think she would sleep, but she took in the expansive sky and centered herself, anyway.

She reached into her pocket and pulled out her bracelet. As the charms freed from her jacket pocket, she heard the familiar sound they made as they hit against each other. She rubbed them while looking at the stars, trying to guess which charm she was touching.

The last thing she remembered before slipping away was the feel of her Irish Angel charm between her fingers.

CHAPTER 42

*N*icholas had thankfully watched Sophia fall asleep about an hour ago. He picked up the charm bracelet and gently pulled her hand over to rest against his thigh. He wrapped the bracelet around her delicate wrist and was concentrating on hooking the clasp when Martin spoke up.

"Are you sure she's just resting?" he whispered.

Nicholas finally got the bracelet on properly, so he tenderly placed her hand back. "Not a hundred percent, no," he admitted. "But it's not her exact birthday yet, and she appears to just be sleeping. I don't want her laying here worrying, so I think we should just let her sleep."

Martin moved closer to the other side of Sophia and sat cross-legged on the ground. "Is there anything we can do other than wait?"

Nicholas looked over at Martin. "I don't know. All I can focus on is keeping her alive through whatever happens. Other than that, I think this is part of the battle she has to fight through on her own. Maybe that's why I can't feel it. It's not something I am supposed to guard her against." He put his head down and ran his hands through his hair. "It'd be fucking fantastic if Jophiel would show himself and give us a clue," Nicholas said in frustration.

"Yeah. That's a big reason I wanted to be here. In case he showed to help you," Martin agreed.

"Well, all we can do is what we are doing." Nicholas stared off into the woods.

Both men ended up laying down with their heads close to Sophia and gazed at the stars in silence. Nicholas tried to rest. He focused on her breathing, letting it lull him to sleep.

Nicholas's eyes opened suddenly at the sound of a whimper. He turned his head to see Sophia shaking.

He crawled over to touch her. "Hey, little one. How do you feel?"

He touched her forehead and felt the heat rolling off her. "Christ, she's burning up."

He noticed Martin moving, but he couldn't turn away from her. "Hey there, open your eyes for me." He put his hand under her head and gently pulled her up into a sitting position. He peeled off her outer jacket and tossed it aside. After looking her over, he peeled off her lighter jacket too and placed her head back on the ground.

Martin came back into his view. He had a bottle of water and a t-shirt. He poured water on the shirt and handed it to Nicholas, who promptly started wiping her face and neck. "What time is it Martin?"

"It's only a couple of minutes until midnight." Martin said nervously. "You can't feel what she is feeling?"

Nicholas shook his head. "No, dammit. I noticed nothing until I heard her." He squeezed his eyes shut to harness his anger. "Miss Snow," Nicholas said firmly. "Come on. Give me those eyes." He took her face in his hands and turned her toward him.

She opened her eyes slowly, looking confused at first, but it quickly turned to pain. She looked at Nicholas and his heart broke. "Hey, little one. How do you feel? What hurts?"

She struggled to talk. Her hand grabbed his shirt. "Ni...Nicca...it hurts so b..bad."

"I know, little one. I'm here. I won't leave ye." Nicholas was at a complete loss of what to do for her.

Her eyes took on an eerie glow, and she was shaking so hard. He grabbed her face and turned it back to him. "Keep watching me. I'm right here." He didn't look away but asked Martin, "How much time, Martin?"

"Seconds," Martin said.

Nicholas watched as Sophia shook harder.

Martin guessed, "Could it be a seizure because of the high temperature?"

"More water," he said as he held his hand out and grabbed the bottle. He poured the water across her neck and then held her to keep her from hurting herself.

After a minute the shaking stopped, and she stilled. Both men just stared at her, hoping that was it.

Her eyes opened, and the light in them began swirling. A low, tortured moan began deep in her chest and grew into a blood-curdling scream.

Nicholas froze over her with his hands in the air. Martin began pacing and running his hands through his hair. He didn't know what to do for her. He grabbed her hand and held tight while she screamed.

It seemed to last for minutes. Her scream ripped at his soul. Everything in him said to do something. He felt anger building, and he couldn't stop it. It welled up and burst free.

He roared. His body shook with rage. He wanted to kill something. He punched the ground. The pain helped, so he punched the ground again. He ripped his hands through his hair and pulled hard before slumping to the ground in defeat.

Martin spoke up. "Hold tight. She's calming."

Nicholas watched her. She wasn't screaming; she was just giving a few whimpers. He crawled back over to her and tried talking to her. "Hey there. Can ye open your eyes?"

She opened her eyes and looked at him with exhaustion. He stroked her hair and smiled at her. "How are ye feeling?"

She seemed to look beyond him, so he turned to look but saw nothing. He looked back at her. "Miss Snow?"

She looked at him finally and gave a weak smile. "Can you hear them?" she asked.

Nicholas looked up at Martin, who shrugged. "Hear what, little one?"

She whispered as she closed her eyes, "The drums."

A shock of electricity bolted through him. They'd forgotten about the drums. "NO!" He shook her. "No, don't listen to the drums!"

But it was too late.

CHAPTER 43

Sophia was burned alive, and then the charred outer shell had been peeled away. She held herself still for fear the pain would return. It was the drums that brought relief. She heard them in the distance, and the steady rhythm was intoxicating. Before long the sound of the drums became her focus, and the pain had stopped completely.

Now she was floating in a cloud. Her limbs felt light and weak, and everything around her was dark but comforting.

The floating sensation faded in stages. It began at her feet with a force pushing back, letting her know she was standing. Slowly moving up her body, she gained control and feeling and finally awareness.

A sensation of something behind her caused her to turn slowly. She saw a faint light in the distance. Taking it as a sign, she took a step toward the light. It got brighter instantly, so she kept walking.

She was happy to not be in pain, but she worried about where she was. And where were Nicholas and Martin? Had she died? With every step, everything around her got lighter and lighter. Before long, she could make out a person walking toward her. She didn't feel threatened or afraid, so she kept moving.

Eventually, she got close enough that the answer clicked into place. Between one step and the next, she realized it was Ney. Happy to see an old friend, she took off running and threw her arms around her as soon as she got close.

"Ney. I'm so happy to see you!" Sophia said happily.

"My sweet Sophia. You've grown up. I've waited for this day for a very long time." Niamh hugged her tightly.

"Did I die, Ney?" Sophia asked her first worry.

"No, my dear, I'm sure it felt like you did. It rarely hurts that bad. I'm sorry, dear heart. Having one magic awaken hurts. I cannot imagine having four," she said gently.

"What is this place?" Sophia asked as she looked around.

"It's hard to explain. It's nowhere, really. A place between places and times. Or maybe we're all just in your head." She smiled kindly.

Sophia frowned. "How could I be making you up? Nicca, says you were a real person."

Niamh smiled fondly. "Ah, my sweet Nicholas. You must tell him how proud of him I am. I miss him." She turned and began walking, so Sophia caught up to walk alongside her. Niamh continued, "I didn't mean you had made us up. I think maybe we all live on in the blood." She turned a grin to Sophia. "Magic."

Sophia smiled. "So I'm here for you to teach me how to use your magic?"

"I can teach you about my visions, but the others will have to teach you about theirs. I only know my own skill," Niamh explained. "It'll be dangerous because you shouldn't stay here long. You can easily get lost, and things lurk here that aren't good. This place is open to both light and dark, unfortunately. You have four different things to learn about so we shouldn't dally."

Sophia turned to Ney, determined to learn as much as possible.

Niamh began, "All magical skills come with free will, Sophia. Just as all life. There is a balance. You take the knowledge or power you have and choose to do good or bad with it. Because of that, always be conscious that you can do great good or terrible destruction. Decide what type of druid... what type of person you are."

Sophia shrugged. "That's easy for me, Ney. I'm a good person."

Niamh smiled. "Nothing is as easy as it seems. Remember, it's about balance. Nothing is ever completely good, or for that matter, completely bad. But yes, sweet Sophia, you are the light to balance the coming darkness. It would be hard to find the darkness in you."

Sophia admitted, "It seems like all of you were, Ney. You all gave up so much to save a world you wouldn't even be a part of."

Niamh smiled. "There is always more to a story. We were righting a wrong, my dear. It wasn't completely altruistic." She kept going, changing the subject quickly. "We must keep going, though. From me, you inherit the Power of the Mind. It always shows in the eyes."

Sophia nodded. "Yes. I could really use your help hiding that. The people in my day don't understand magic."

"I would imagine not. Humans aren't known for embracing differences," Niamh said off-handedly. "It's actually easy to do, dear. Envision covering yourself with a veil. It will mute your powers, which will help if you want a mental break from visions or your other powers. It's a good idea to put a veil in place to set up boundaries. For example, if you don't want spirits coming to visit you in your home, then place a veil before walking in your front door. It'll keep them at bay. But be careful. It will affect Nicholas's ability to sense you. It will put a barrier up between you two, so be aware."

Sophia nodded thoughtfully. "Ok. Show me how."

Niamh spent a few minutes explaining how to focus on a veil sliding over her mind and body. After three attempts, Sophia could do it for a few seconds.

"Continue to practice. After a few tries, it'll become second nature and something you no longer even think about," Niamh said.

"Ok. What exactly does the Power of the Mind entail?" Sophia asked, wishing she could take notes.

"Well, you are already familiar with this skill, but I will try to explain more. You can practice retrieving visions by attaching them to strong emotions. You don't have to just wait for a vision to hit. If someone comes to you looking for help, I suggest you gain as much information as possible and then focus on the emotion of that event. I don't know why, but emotion is the trigger. Your mind will take you there on that pathway." Niamh let that sink in before continuing. "Normally, we would practice. But we simply can't, my dear. You must focus and remember, then practice growing your skill later," she explained. "Every person will explain their skill to you, how it basically works, and the extreme of their power."

"The extreme?" Sophia asked.

"Yes, emotions are a huge part of your magic. Learn control because, Sophia, in a moment of anger you could accidentally kill or hurt innocent people. It's important to be aware of the possibilities so that you can avoid the extremes." Niamh looked serious.

"What is your extreme?" Sophia asked nervously.

Niamh walked a little while before answering. "When used with control, you can help people find closure, or answers, or make connections, but in the extreme you could literally scramble a person's brain permanently."

Sophia gasped, "Oh! I would never want that."

Niamh paused. "Unfortunately, the extremes exist for a reason. There could always be a reason one might need such a thing, but hopefully, that reason never comes."

Sophia was staring off into a dark nothingness, thinking about her words, but the sound of Niamh's voice brought her back. "My dear, this is Maria."

Sophia turned back to see a woman that looked very similar to the woman under the tree from the magic letter. "I think I might have met a descendent of your family," she said with a smile.

Maria nodded. "Yes, we're so honored. From us you have inherited the Power of the Body."

Sopha frowned. "How will I use that?"

"It came in handy for hunting, but mostly for you, it'll be a defensive skill," Maria explained. "The best way I can explain how to use it is to attach it to a visual. You can slow or freeze a body temporarily. I used to hunt rabbits by picturing the rabbit moving through molasses or frozen in a block of ice." She grinned as if remembering fun times.

Sophia tried to recap. "Ok. So Power of the Mind attaches to emotions and Power of the Body attaches to visuals."

Maria nodded sympathetically. "I can't imagine how you feel right now. I'm sorry. It will become like a second skin quickly. You can do it."

Sophia braced herself. "And the extreme?"

Maria dropped her smile. "If you lose control, you could reduce a body to extreme, crippling pain. You must not let negative emotions take over your vision of a person. Imagine envisioning your enemy burning alive or something worse. You could lock them in agony."

Sophia felt overwhelmed. "I'm human, y'all. Are you saying that if I slip up during a bad day and get mad, I could really hurt someone?"

Niamh stepped forward. "It won't always be that way. Everyone loses it sometimes, but when you lose your temper, you must always hold control over your magic. Separate the two, which at first is hard because emotions will rule you if you let them."

Niamh nodded to Maria who waved with a sad smile and then was gone. Next, a blonde woman stepped into the space next to Niamh. She had long wavy hair and blue eyes. Niamh introduced her as Agnees.

Sophia asked her, "What skill have you sent me?"

Agnees answered, "I gave you the Power of the Earth."

Sophia smiled. "I've already experienced a bit of that one."

Agnees laughed. "Yes, it's easily triggered. You have the power to mold, shake, or move the earth. It will respond to verbal command, even if you think the words, so be careful what you think in your head."

Sophia laughed. "Yes, I asked the ground to swallow me, and it nearly did I think."

Agnees sobered up. "In the extreme you can scorch the earth. Causing complete devastation of the ground close to you."

Sophia's mouth dropped open. "So basically I'm a ticking time bomb. How can I do all of this, Ney?" She looked to a very apologetic Niamh.

"It will not be easy, but I fully believe you can do it, dear heart. You were chosen for a reason. I assure you it was more than just the date of your birth," she promised Sophia.

Sophia looked to see the woman next to her had already changed to a beautiful older redhead. "Hey," Sophia said.

Niamh answered, "This is Bridget."

Bridget smiled kindly. "I gave you the Power of Souls. It is a blessing and a curse to have this skill. You can help the dead find answers for the living. You can speak for souls that can no longer speak for themselves."

Sophia felt a foreboding. There was a reason they left this one for last. "How do I access it? Do I call spirits to me?"

Bridget's eyes widened. "No! You mustn't call a spirit to you unless you are forcing it out. Spirits still have free will. If they wish to speak, they will appear. Calling a spirit is pointless, if they were going to tell you something, they would have already appeared."

Sophia frowned again. "Ok. I just listen to spirits that choose to show themselves. I don't actively do anything?"

Bridget nodded. "In a way. It's not like molding dirt. This is a skill that is used to bring balance and justice to the dead. They have free will, so you can't force them to do anything. Unless you go to the extreme."

Sophia sighed. "What is the extreme?"

Bridget looked at her sadly. "You have the power to force a soul from a body, Sophia. It's attached to moments of extreme love or hate. In those moments, you are in danger of killing the person you target."

Sophia covered her open mouth with a hand. She could really accidentally kill someone. "How could I accidentally kill someone while experiencing extreme love?" Did this mean she could never love anyone?

Bridget shook her head. "You misunderstand." She seemed to reflect on a personal story. "Imagine someone you love in agonizing pain and begging you to help them. If you aren't careful, you could accidentally kill them to free them from pain. Or maybe you witness someone you love killed tragically. You could accidentally kill an innocent bystander in your moment of pain from lost love."

Sophia begged her, "Please tell me how to make sure that never happens, Bridget. Please."

Bridget tried to explain. "When you are in that moment, concentrate on the emotion and not the person causing it. Feel love or even hate, but do not focus on a person. Center yourself on just the feeling."

Sophia nodded. "So accept the emotion and reject the vengeance."

Bridget nodded thoughtfully. "Yes. Exactly."

She nodded to her as she stepped away into darkness. Sophia turned to Niamh. "That's so much to remember, Ney."

Niamh put her arm around her, "Yes, dear heart. I'm very sorry. You can do it, though. Try to focus on one skill at a time at first. But remember, you are going to have to figure out how to assimilate them all into one fluid power inside you. I don't know how to help you do that because it's not something we've ever done. But I know that if you keep them separate and undeveloped, it could drive you mad. Face each one and master it, then figure out how to fit them all together in a way that feels whole."

Sophia felt tired. "Maybe I could just stay here."

Niamh cautioned her. "That is a dangerous way to think, my dear. This is nowhere. The troubles will come whether or not you hide here. You might as well give it your best. Besides, Nicholas will go crazy without you."

Sophia smiled sadly. "I love him deeply, Ney. I've never said that out loud before. But he will always think of me as a child. Sometimes, I wish I could free him from his responsibility, so we could both move on with our lives."

Niamh smiled with a sadness and understanding, "My dear sweet Sophia. No one could love him better than you. Nicholas has a great capacity to love everything and everyone... except himself. He will struggle to believe anyone could love him. It would never even dawn on him. He will have to be hit over the head with it, and even then, he may not believe it. He has had a long life to nurture his guilt and build up his brick walls." She reached up and touched Sophia's cheek. "Don't give up hope on him."

Sophia felt a spark of hope again. "Thanks, Ney." She felt a change in the air and looked around. "Will I see you again?" She frowned as she couldn't catch what was different.

Niamh turned to walk back toward the light. "I'm sure you will, sweet Sophia."

Sophia heard a noise. "Do you hear that?" she said to anyone that could hear.

Niamh had disappeared, but she heard her voice. "It's not for me to hear, my dear."

Sophia spun around. She couldn't place that noise, but she wanted to hear it again. She began walking. "What is that? Hello?" She began running.

Niamh yelled sharply, "Sophia, NO! Come back!"

The fear in her voice caused Sophia to freeze and turn back. She saw Ney fade back in, stretching her arms out. Her mouth was opened in a silent scream. Just as Sophia took a step toward her, she felt icy cold arms wrap around her neck, and Ney disappeared again.

"Why, hello there," a low female voice sounded in her ear. It caused a chill to run down her body. "So, are you the one meant to defeat me? Let's get a look at you then."

The arms around her squeezed briefly before a hand grabbed her shoulder and spun her around. Sophia had only a second to brace before she faced the most beautiful creature she had ever seen.

A tall woman with long dark straight hair stood before her with a smirk on her face. Pale translucent skin, large green eyes, and a perfect mouth with full sensual lips. Her body was built for seduction. She wore a soft green material wrapped around her like a toga. It showed off her large breasts, small waist, and lush hips. Sophia was so lost in the picture before her, it took a moment to understand what she'd said.

"Who are you?" she asked, afraid she already knew the answer.

The woman laughed. The sound rolled around her and through her. It seemed to echo. "You don't even know your nemesis? That doesn't bode well for you, dear." She spun around on a toe and took a couple of steps away. When she turned back, she smiled and curtsied. "Allow me to introduce myself. I'm Lily. I'm on my way between portals. Imagine my surprise when I heard the druid drums. I knew someone was getting their powers and came to see who the lucky girl was."

Sophia didn't know what to do, but she knew she wasn't ready to face her. She knew nothing about her abilities. She could hear the faint sound of Ney yelling in the distance.

Sophia turned and ran for Ney, but it was over before it began. She made it three steps before an unseen power grabbed her and held her suspended in the air. Lily sauntered around her like she was inspecting a bug.

"I don't know if I should be insulted. I knew they would try something. But you? You couldn't kill a fly. You think you can defeat me?" Lily reached a finger up and placed it at the base of Sophia's throat. The moment she made contact, pain sliced through her. It felt like a blade instead of a finger. Slowly she dragged it down her chest, slicing through her shirt.

Sophia let out a scream. The pain seemed to intensify. She felt like the skin was cutting open with her clothes. "It's almost too easy. I think I feel a little bad for you."

"Why are you doing this? I don't know who you are!" Sophia choked out.

"I think you do. I knew I was getting close to the portal I needed. It only makes sense I would find a druid awakening. It won't matter, though. You'll not stop me this time. No one will. Not druids. Not angels. And not God." Lily spit out. "I pity you." She backed up to look at her handy work before she continued.

"You're so eager to do His bidding. What do you think happens to you if I'm gone?"

Lily must have seen her confusion because she kept going. "I'm dark. You're light. They convinced you I'm bringing the world out of balance, right? But what about you? If I'm gone, then what?" She leaned close to Sophia and smiled seductively. "That's right. You'll no longer have a use. They'll crush you. You can't exist in a world without me. You need me."

"No," Sophia whispered. Surely she was spouting lies.

"Oh yes. Don't think for one second your loyalty will be rewarded." She pressed her lips against Sophia's ear and whispered. "He. Doesn't. Care."

Just then Sophia heard Nicca. "Sophia, open your eyes, baby." It made her whole body tingle. He was calling her Sophia?

Lily spun away from her, looking for the voice. "I know that voice." Her body stiffened. She turned toward Sophia and reached up to squeeze her neck. "They sent Nicholas to be with you?" She squeezed so hard Sophia couldn't answer.

Lily lunged at Sophia and screamed in her face. When Sophia blinked, she saw Lily change. Her face sunk in and yellowed. It looked like a skeleton covered with thin yellow paper. Her eyes became deep black orbs. Sophia blinked again, and she was back to being beautiful.

She leaned into Sophia and smiled.

Sophia was so confused. How did she know about Nicca? She wasn't able to think long because her hands were wrenched behind her painfully. Lily pushed her shirt open, exposing her stomach. "Let's say hello, shall we?"

Lily reached her finger out and began tracing lines on her. Sophia didn't want to be a wimp, but she couldn't stop screaming. She was slicing into her body. She was afraid to look down. How was she going to get out of this mess?

Lily stood up with a satisfied smile and pulled Sophia down until her feet touched the ground again. "I'm done playing. Now I'm going to kill you. Don't feel bad. This is actually me being kind. I'll be quick. I have to get to my portal." She grabbed

Sophia by the hair and pulled back harshly. Her finger raised and a long blade slowly emerged from the tip.

Sophia wasn't listening to her at all. Instead, she heard a familiar tinkling noise. She wanted to hear more. If she was going to die, she wanted to hear Nicca say Sophia again. She strained to hear him and felt a tug.

Her arms came loose and Sophia fell to the ground. Lily grabbed for her while screaming, "NOOOOO!"

The ground fell out from under her and everything slipped away into darkness.

CHAPTER 44

$\mathcal{N}$icholas and Martin paced circles around Sophia. She had been out for almost an hour, and Nicholas didn't know how long was too long. He was trying to stay calm, but each silent second ticking by was pushing him closer to the edge. He dropped to his knees and picked up her hand to feel her pulse and check her breathing. It was like she was sleeping peacefully.

He looked at Martin. "I don't know at what point we panic."

Martin stopped pacing and looked down at her. "I don't know. She seems peaceful for now."

Nicholas sat back on his heels and watched her, his anger and fear bubbling to the surface. Closing his eyes tightly, he threw his head back and yelled, "*Jophiel!*"

His voice echoed off the mountainside, but Martin simply shrugged and shook his head sadly. Out of the corner of his eye, he saw light.

Sophia was holding her body rigid, and her eyes were open and brighter than he'd ever seen before. He leaned over her and touched her forehead. "Hey, little one."

She didn't seem to hear him. The light in her eyes flickered.

Martin asked, "What's happening to her eyes? It's like she keeps turning it off and on or something."

"I don't know. Miss Snow, can you hear me?" Nicholas tried

to get her attention. After a minute the dimming stopped and she stared vacantly. "Miss Snow?" Nicholas tried one more time, but no reaction came from her.

Minutes passed, and she simply closed her eyes again. He sat back and just stared. He'd never felt so lost.

"Martin, why don't you exit the circle and take a walk and stretch your legs," Nicholas offered.

Martin shook his head. "No, I will if I need it, but I'm fine for now." He sat back down on the other side of Sophia.

Three hours later, Nicholas was lying on his back when he felt a heaviness growing in his chest. He tried to sit up and couldn't. "Martin?"

"I can't move," Martin said in a panic.

Nicholas looked as far as his eyes would let him. Sophia was unchanged, but Martin was frozen in a half up position with one arm out toward Sophia.

Martin pushed the words out. "What's happening?"

Nicholas wasn't feeling pain, really. It was more frustration. He was fighting his body and nothing was happening. "I don't know. I think it's her."

Minutes passed before he regained control in stages. First his head, then limbs, last was his core. Once he had control again, he jumped up and paced.

"Martin, there are four magical skills inside of her. One is visions, which are connected to her eyes, but another has to do with controlling the motion of living things," Nicholas explained.

Martin nodded. "So you think she is moving through all her new magical skills?"

Nicholas agreed. "I think so. The other two have to do with moving earth and talking with the dead."

Martin looked blankly at Nicholas for a moment before slowly turning to look at the mountainside looming over them. "Uh... Should we worry about moving earth?"

Nicholas looked up at the mountain. Understanding sank in at the precarious position they were in. She could bring the mountain down on them. "Taking her out of the circle could intensify the shaking and ensure we're all buried, Martin. You need to go at least to the river, if not the cliff. You should get as far as possible. I can't protect you both."

Martin thought over the options. "What if we quickly set up a new circle? You could run ahead and set it, and I could grab her and run for the new circle. We might get her to the new one before anything happens."

Nicholas thought it could work, but it would mean leaving her. "What if it happened while I was off making a new circle, Martin? Both of you would be unprotected. No, just go before the shaking starts. If we're right, it could last several minutes."

Martin looked at the ground. "Maybe it's stupid, but I just can't do it. I'll do my best to protect myself, but I can't just run off and stand like a coward in the woods." He looked up with an apologetic but determined smile.

Nicholas held Martin's gaze for a beat before giving a quick nod and moving on. "At least this means she should be ok until she's worked through the next two magical skills."

They waited hours for any sign of something. Nicholas was getting sick and tired of jumping at every noise, and he was starting to doubt his theory. They'd both taken short breaks, but Nicholas hadn't gone far. He was standing close to the circle, looking up to see where the sun was in the sky. It was midday, which meant she'd been out for close to twelve hours.

He finished his water as he walked back to her. Martin looked up when he heard him and started to say something when a low rumble started beneath his feet. He froze for only a moment before breaking into a run, jumping the doorway into the circle, and sliding on his knees to Sophia's side. Leaning over her body, he tucked her head under him, and looked at Martin. "Get away from the mountainside!"

Martin covered Sophia's feet and legs. "No! Just keep her covered."

Nicholas didn't know if it would do any good, but he began whispering to Sophia. "Calm down, little one. Come on, center yourself. You can do it."

The shaking increased, and he heard stones and debris falling around them, but thankfully, everything held. After a couple of minutes, it calmed down, and he slowly pushed up to look around.

Dust filled the air, but nothing big had fallen. He turned to look at Martin, who was also looking around smiling.

Just as he smiled back, he felt his hand sinking in the dirt. He jerked his hand out only to have his other hand sink. He pulled up onto his knees and looked at the ground. It looked like it was trying to swallow them up.

Sophia was sinking.

"Martin! Help! The ground is taking her."

Nicholas grabbed Sophia's arms and pulled her up, but the ground was acting as a suction. He pulled hard and wrestled her torso free, but as soon as he freed her, he couldn't do anything because his knees and feet were sinking.

Nicholas watched Martin put his hands on the ground by the doorway to find it solid. He pushed up and freed himself. "Stop moving. Think of it as quicksand. Here, grab this." He crawled free and threw one end of a sleeping bag at him.

Nicholas stopped moving, held Sophia's head and shoulders close to him, and grabbed the bag.

Martin wasn't pulling them free, but he was keeping them from sinking lower. "Don't stop, Martin. You're keeping us above ground," Nicholas said. "Just hold on until she stops."

Minutes passed and Nicholas and Martin were both nearing exhaustion. He focused on keeping Sophia's head above ground, but his entire body shook with fatigue.

He felt himself sinking lower, and Sophia's head slipping beneath the dirt. "Grab her! Please, Martin!"

Nicholas took a deep breath and let go of the bag and grabbed Sophia around the waist. With every shred of energy he had left, he pushed her above him toward Martin, knowing it would push him under. As the ground closed around his face, he tried to keep her up as long as he could.

Eventually, the burn in his lungs forced him to breathe. With one last push to keep Sophia above him, he finally gave into the darkness.

CHAPTER 45

*N*icholas heard a voice from a distance, like it was coming through a wall. He woke in stages. First the sound of Martin's frantic voice, then the need to breathe hit him. He tried to suck in air, but nothing happened. He cracked his eyes, saw the ground in front of his face, and could feel a hand beating his back. Something wet was on his face, and he desperately needed to breathe. He could feel Martin reaching around him, trying to force air out.

Finally, something dislodged from his throat and dust and dirt flew out of his mouth and nose. He began coughing and sputtering. A water bottle suddenly appeared, and Martin tried to wipe his nose and mouth. Nicholas took the water and drank, only to spit it out. After several attempts, the coughing subsided.

He looked for Sophia.

She was lying on her back behind Martin. Once he saw she was ok, he put a hand on Martin's shoulder and grinned. "What took you so long?"

Martin laughed. "Sorry, you're a heavy bastard."

Nicholas looked down and saw he was only free from the hips up. It had become solid again, so it took some digging from Martin to free him.

As soon as he was free, he crawled to Sophia and checked to

see if she was indeed ok. She was breathing fine, so he turned back to Martin and asked, "What happened?"

Martin pushed dirt back into the hole as he explained, "It stopped just after you pushed her up. I pulled her to the center and then pulled your arse out."

Nicholas closed his eyes tightly. "Thank fuck you were here."

Martin smirked. "Yeah. I know."

Nicholas laughed. He couldn't help but feel overwhelmed with how close he'd been to losing her. All the times he'd saved her throughout her lifetime, he'd never doubted he could. This was the first time he realized he could fail her, and that was not an option.

They spent the next couple of hours putting everything to rights. The circle amazingly seemed intact, but Nicholas closed and reset it, anyway. They fixed the ground, straightened the bag, and repositioned Sophia. After fixing the tent, they started a fire because the evening was coming again. After trying their best to wipe down their arms and faces, they took a moment to eat and drink.

Nicholas watched Sophia while Martin rested in the tent. He spent the time just being near Sophia and thanking God she was ok. He held her hand and watched the stars as they popped into view.

He was fighting sleep when Martin finally tapped his shoulder and told him to rest. It surprised him to feel possessive. He didn't want to leave her with him, but he was hitting a wall and wouldn't be any good without rest. The first skill showed after only an hour, the second after three, and the third after eight hours. If the pattern continued, it should be eight hours before the fourth skill. That was still a couple of hours away, so he should be safe.

He pushed his feelings aside and forced himself to walk into the tent and lay down. This horrible night was almost done. He didn't know how the last magical skill would present itself, but it couldn't be as bad as being buried alive.

He finally relaxed enough to doze, but currently, he was lying on his side facing the opening of the tent and the village ruins.

He hardly remembered the young, innocent, naïve man he had been here. His eyes drifted toward the woods, and he tried to stop himself, but it was too late.

"You did it! You found the site," Lily said as she ran for the pile of rocks that looked like ruins to Nicholas. He smiled. He loved pleasing her.

"I did." He couldn't help sounding smug.

She turned to him and opened her arms, and Nicholas went willingly. He wrapped his arms around her and claimed her sweet mouth. It didn't last nearly as long as he wanted before she was pushing him away, though. "If only we knew a way to make it work."

Nicholas sighed. She was so certain this ancient site still held power. He hated to disappoint her. "My Lily, I don't know how you think this place will help you find your brother. It's just a pile of rocks."

She gasped. "No, it isn't, Nicholas. It only looks that way. It's part of the spell. There's supposed to be a special person who can control it. The right person can bend it to his will." She looked over her shoulder and smiled.

Nicholas perked up. "If that's true, then I will be that person."

Lily laughed. "Oh Nicholas, it can't just be anyone. It takes a man above all men."

Nicholas felt his pride take a hit at her words. He wanted her to think he was that man. Why did she tease him so?

"I'm only trying to give you all you want," she continued. "I know you don't believe me, but I'm trying to find my brother so we can finally marry and be together."

Nicholas felt hope bloom in his chest. He walked up to Lily and kissed her gently. "I will do this for you." Then he walked up to the stones.

The moment he got to the first step, something in the air shifted. The broken-down altar changed. Nicholas was now looking at a large circle of symbols engraved in the mountainside.

He felt drawn to one symbol in particular. A large triskelion. His hand itched to touch it. He was so fixed on it, he didn't hear Lily approach him. Her voice made him jump.

"I wish I knew what to do," she said sadly.

Nicholas smiled. He knew what to do. He would help her find her brother, and then he would have her in his bed tonight.

With a smug grin, he walked to the stone calling him. He placed his hand into the picture gouged into the rock.

The moment he touched it, light shot from everywhere. His body vibrated with the light shimmering along his limbs. The center of the circle seemed to wake up to his touch. The light flowed from him into the rock. After a few seconds, the entire center was a bright swirling white, blue, and green light.

He pulled his hand free roughly and fell to the ground, but the gate remained blazing. He was trying to catch his breath when he heard Lily laughing.

"Oh sweet Nicholas," Lily said as she knelt beside him. "You never disappoint."

Nicholas wanted to feel pleased, but something about her tone gave him pause. He looked over to see Lily, but she was changed. Her eyes were empty and cold.

"What is this, Lily?" Nicholas tried to sit up straighter.

Lily pushed him down easily with one hand on his shoulder. "Nothing of your concern. Men are so gullible. I feel sorry for you, Nicholas. You have so much power, and yet, you are clueless." She slapped his cheek softly before standing and heading for the light.

Nicholas grabbed her hand. "Wait! What are you doing?"

Lily looked back at him. "I'm taking back what's mine." She jerked her hand free and walked into the light, laughing.

Nicholas sighed and sat up. He rubbed the grit from his eyes and shoved his hair back into the leather strap he used to hold it back. It did no good to dwell on those days. They just brought up his intense feelings of guilt and shame.

He felt a very unnatural shiver move over his skin. It made him freeze and listen carefully. He couldn't put his finger on it, but something was very different. He dashed out of the tent to see Sophia laying unchanged in the center. Martin stood still with his back to him.

"Martin?" he asked softly.

Martin didn't seem to hear him. He kept staring at a point

beyond the circle. Nicholas moved in front of him to block his vision and tried again. "Martin?"

Martin looked at him with tears in his eyes. "Do you see them?" he whispered.

Nicholas turned around and looked out into the abandoned village. He didn't see anyone or anything moving. "See who?"

The tears rolled down Martin's face. "My family." He dropped to his knees.

Nicholas looked out into the woods. Nothing moved. He put his hand on Martin's shoulder. "You mustn't look, Martin. It's a trick of the eye."

Martin shook his head. "You said the last power was talking to the dead. My family is dead. They're right there. They're dead because of me." He squeezed his eyes shut. "I'm sorry. I have to go."

Nicholas panicked. He checked Sophia, who was still resting, then focused back on Martin. "Martin, listen carefully. I don't know how spirits will behave once you leave the circle. I just don't know enough about how it works. They might be kind toward Sophia, but you're seeing something you aren't meant to see. If you leave the protection of the circle, anything could happen. I don't believe you killed your family, Martin. I don't know what happened, but I know it's not that. Just stay here and close your eyes. Let it pass."

Martin jerked his shoulder away from Nicholas. "No! You donna understand! I wasna there when they needed me, but I can be now. They must need to tell me something."

Nicholas braced himself to stop Martin. "No, Martin. Listen, if they wanted to talk to you they could stand here at the circle and talk to you. They must want to draw you out of the circle for some reason. It is a trap. I feel it."

Martin stood on shaky legs. "You donna understand."

Nicholas grabbed Martin's arms. "I know. Maybe after this is over you can try to make me understand, but Martin, you have to trust me."

Martin sighed and nodded to Nicholas. "Ok, fine."

Nicholas straightened and clapped him on the shoulder. "Good man, Martin." He turned to Sophia.

Martin muttered, "I'm sorry."

Nicholas turned back to see him breaking for the woods.

He dove at Martin and hit him at leg height, causing both men to crash to the ground. He scrambled to get a hold of Martin's legs, but he fought him off. Nicholas finally got a foothold and used it to move higher up his back. Martin clawed at the ground and tried kicking him off. Nicholas almost lost his position, but just as they reached the edge of the circle he got his arm around Martin's neck, locked his arm, and choked Martin out. He rolled back and held. "I'm sorry, Martin," he spat. "I'm trying to save you."

Nicholas, in his exhaustion, forgot that Martin had been training with Larry for years. He made the mistake of leaning back when Martin relaxed. He rocked his head back straight into Nicholas's nose at the same time he kicked back with his foot. Nicholas was stunned momentarily, which caused his grip to slip. Martin turned his head and pushed out with a punch to the ribs. He scrambled up and took off.

Nicholas rolled over to see Martin hit the doorway like it was a brick wall. Instead of running straight through, it knocked him flat on his back. Nicholas rolled up and spat blood on the ground beside him.

Martin rolled onto his side. He looked over at Nicholas as he pushed up to his feet, and Nicholas caught the gold flash in Martin's eyes.

Nicholas wiped at his bleeding nose. "Jophiel, you're lucky I'm tired, you fuckin' bastard."

Jophiel laughed. "Is that how you thank someone helping you?"

Nicholas saw red. He leapt at Jophiel and grabbed him by the throat, lifting him onto his toes.

Jophiel flashed gold again. "Careful, brother. I'm here to help you." He looked pointedly at Sophia.

Nicholas squeezed before tossing him away. "We've been

flying blind for almost a full day, Jophiel. We needed help ages ago."

Jophiel coughed and straightened his clothes. "You've done outstanding. Honestly, there was nothing more I could share with you. There are certain revelations you must make on your own. I can't interfere with that." He looked sadly at Nicholas. "Believe it or not. I'm on your side."

Nicholas waved him off and turned to Sophia. "Tell me then. What are you doing here?"

"I was going to show once this part finished, but I stepped in a little early to help stop ol' Martin here from getting himself killed." Jophiel tapped himself on the chest. "I kind of like this guy. I'm not sure why, but I've developed quite an attachment to him. Although right now he's throwing the tantrum of the century."

Nicholas paused. "So I was right? Leaving the circle was a trap?"

Jophiel grimaced. "That makes spirits sound so bad. They aren't, really. They stand back to show respect to Sophia. She's sleeping, so they are simply waiting at a respectable distance. You're protected by the circle. It's hiding you from them. If you step out of the circle, and they see you can see them... well..." Jophiel trailed off.

Nicholas was curious. "Well, what?" he asked.

Jophiel shrugged. "It's hard to explain, but basically, it's not meant for you to see them. So they will go kind of... crazy? I guess that's the best way to put it. They lose it and try to right the wrong. In this case, that could mean driving him off the cliff to join them."

Nicholas looked out into the trees. "Why can't I see them?"

Jophiel paused. "Hmm... perhaps Sophia's mark on you protects you. I'm not entirely sure. How curious!" He looked excited to come across a riddle he couldn't answer.

"Thank you for stepping in and saving Martin," Nicholas admitted.

"That's more like it, brother!" Jophiel smiled and walked over to Sophia.

Nicholas sat beside her. "Tell me this is almost over, Jophiel."

Jophiel looked over at Sophia for a moment. "It has to be. You have no choice. That's my original reason for coming to see you."

Nicholas sighed and dropped his head. "Explain. Please."

Jophiel sat on the other side of Sophia. "She'll be lost in the in-between if she doesn't wake soon. You have until midnight. After that, she'll not wake, my friend."

Nicholas panicked. "That's like... what... a couple of hours?"

Jophiel nodded. "Give or take. Yes. She has completed all of her magical skills. Now she must leave that place and return here... or be lost."

Nicholas brought his elbows to his knees and cradled his head in his hands. "What can I do? How can I help her?"

Jophiel shrugged. "That I don't know, my friend. All I know is that you have the knowledge you need to make it happen."

Nicholas grabbed his hair and pulled. "I'm really fucking tired."

"I know. You're almost through it. Hold tight. She's depending on you."

Nicholas sighed. "I feel like I'm failing her." He took his shirt and wiped the blood he could feel running from his nose.

He heard Martin respond, "I think that's my line."

Nicholas looked up to see that Jophiel had made his grand exit without a goodbye. He rolled his eyes. "Enough of the blame game, Martin. I'm just glad you're alive and not at the bottom of the cliff."

Martin looked back to where the spirits had been. "I'm sorry. I have... baggage... where my family is concerned, but I never imagined it would hinder my ability to do my job."

Nicholas laughed. "Martin. Nothing about what we're doing out here is your job. You aren't responding to emails and phone calls. You volunteered to come help. That's not your job. If you think it is, then I'll fire you right now."

Martin turned quietly back to look at Sophia. "You know what I meant."

Nicholas decided a change of focus was needed. "I did. Let's focus on Sophia for the moment. The sooner I have her awake and ok, the sooner we can get the hell out of here."

No sooner were the words out of his mouth than Sophia's body arched off the ground. He watched in horror as her shirt ripped down the center, leaving a trail of blood behind. He dove for her body and gathered her up in his arms, trying to hold the shirt to her wound. It didn't seem deep, but it was bleeding.

Her scream shredded the last of his control. "What the fuck is happening?" he yelled into the night sky.

Martin's mouth was hanging open in shock. "My God," he muttered. "Jophiel said we had the knowledge," he thought out loud. "Could it be referring to the things we learned before coming out here?" He looked up. "Bring the thing that makes you calm, it will find you when you are lost."

Nicholas panicked. "God. Her bracelet. Was it lost in the dirt earlier?" He dove for her arm. It was still there. He collapsed back down in relief. "Thank fuck."

Martin wondered. "If that's the right object she needs, why is she not waking up?"

Nicholas thought about it. "I don't know. I really think it's the bracelet."

Martin said, "I've never seen her wear it. Could that be part of the problem?"

"You're right. I've only ever seen her holding them. What did she tell us at the hotel, Martin?"

Martin perked up. "The sound."

Nicholas jumped. "Yes, she said something about the sound relaxing her." He sat Sophia up. "Hold her up, Martin."

As Martin held her up, Nicholas got behind her so she could sit against him. He placed her head on his shoulder while Martin took off the bracelet and handed it to him. He said a prayer and took Sophia's hand and ran her fingers down the charms.

At first, it wasn't doing much. "Please, wake up. Come back to me." He pressed his face into her neck and begged. "Sophia, wake up, baby. Please. Listen to the sound."

He handed the bracelet to Martin. "Please, keep making the sound closer to her ear."

Martin took the bracelet, and Nicholas gently turned her face to him.

Sophia's face twisted in pain, and her shirt ripped open again. Nicholas looked down. A loud cry wrenched from him as he watched words form on her stomach. Thin lines breaking her skin. In seconds, the lines formed symbols of his old language. It was Lily saying hello. Fucking Lily had his sweet Sophia.

"Oh, my God. It's her," Nicholas's voice cracked. His eyes filled with tears as Sophia's screams filled the air. He grabbed her shirt and tightly pressed it to the wounds on her abs.

Martin was cursing. "Who? Lily? What does that say?"

Nicholas couldn't answer him. All he could think about was Sophia. "Martin, the bracelet."

Martin jumped to her side and began making the charms hit each other next to her ear. Nicholas leaned toward her other ear and begged with every ounce of power he had. "Sophia, give me those eyes, baby. Come on, sweetie." He kissed her temple. "Come on, wake up. I need you to open those gorgeous eyes, Soph." He rested his forehead against her. "Please," he whispered.

"You never call me Sophia." Nicholas heard her say.

He pulled his head back with a jolt of surprise to see beautiful turquoise glowing up at him. He couldn't stop the strangled noise that escaped the back of his throat.

"Sophia," he breathed out. "You came back." He kissed her forehead, holding her to him for a beat longer than he probably should have. He couldn't describe the joy he was feeling. His sweet Sophia was back.

CHAPTER 46

*S*ophia couldn't quite explain how she felt waking up in Nicholas's arms and hearing him call her by her first name. She held onto his shirt while he hugged her to him.

When he let her go, she looked up and smiled at him. "Hey," she breathed.

He grinned at her. "Hey, back."

Sophia noticed he had blood on his nose and chin. Her smile disappeared. He had dirt and mud all over his clothes. "Nicca..." She looked over at Martin, who looked worse. He was covered in mud, too. And he had the beginnings of a shiner, but he was smiling ear to ear. The ground around them looked different.

"What happened?" Sophia asked.

Martin laughed. "What? You expected us to just sit and twiddle our thumbs?"

She pulled away from Nicholas. "How could you two get into so much trouble in a few minutes?"

Both Nicholas and Martin looked at each other.

Nicholas answered first. "Miss Snow, forget about us." He leaned toward her and put both hands gently against her face. "Are ye ok?"

Sophia took a minute to gaze into his beautiful soft eyes while she took stock of how she felt. She could feel burning down her front, but other than that she seemed fine. "I think I'm ok. I'm afraid to look down though. It burns."

Nicholas ran a thumb gently along her cheek before backing away. "Martin, do you have some first aid in those bags of yours?"

Martin ran to the tent. "One moment lass, we'll have you fixed up good as new."

Sophia squeezed her eyes closed tightly and grimaced while Nicholas helped her sit up. She breathed deeply and then looked down to see the damage. When she saw her stomach, she let the air rush out quickly and laughed. "Oh! That's not as bad as I thought it would be. It felt like she was slicing me open. These are just scratches. I don't know why it burns so bad though."

Nicholas gently touched one symbol scratched into her abs. "She was there? She did this to you, little one?"

Sophia could see tears welling up in his eyes. He looked shattered. She reached up and touched his cheek softly. "I'm ok now, Nicca."

"But you weren't," Nicholas said roughly and leaned away from her to dislodge her hand.

Sophia was about to respond when Martin came back with a first aid kit. "Here we go. Let's get those cleaned up and covered. You'll feel better." He was opening a bag of wipes as he talked and stretched a hand toward Sophia.

In the blink of an eye, Nicholas had the wipes. "I'll do it."

"It's all good," Martin said smoothly. "Here. Take care of Sophia." He handed over the antibiotic ointment.

Nicholas realized he was being an ass. "I'm sorry, Martin." He grumbled as he sat next to her.

Martin laughed. "It's ok. You'd think I'd know better by now."

Nicholas gave undivided attention to the wounds on her abs. Sophia grabbed her own wipe and began cleaning too.

"How did this happen?" Nicholas asked, refusing to look up from his task.

Sophia answered, "I'm not sure. One second I was with Ney and the next, Lily had snatched me away." Sophia paused in wiping at her stomach. She looked at Nicholas until he paused and finally looked up. "I was powerless against her, Nicca. She had control the entire time. There was nothing I could do." She hated the shaking in her voice.

He muttered a curse and wrapped her up in a hug. "Ye won't be, little one. You just got your abilities. You'll be ready next time."

Martin spoke from behind him. "I don't understand how she found you."

Sophia pulled back and wrapped her shirt gently closed. "I think I was in a place between places," she began.

"And times," Nicholas finished.

Sophia nodded. "She heard the drums and came to see who the lucky girl was." She watched Nicholas's eyes closely. She wanted to ask how Lily knew him, but she was afraid.

He could see the question in her eyes, she was sure, but he stared back blankly.

Martin interrupted the direction of their conversation. "How long does it feel you were gone, lass?"

"I don't know. It was less than an hour. Ney said we had to rush. It was too dangerous for me to be there long. Turned out she was right. Why? What time is it?"

Nicholas reached up and touched her cheek. "It's about midnight. The next night, little one. We've been here 24 hours."

Sophia's eyes grew round as she looked between Nicholas and Martin. "Oh. My. God. What happened to you two?"

Martin smiled. "We seem to have lived through the manifestation of your magical skills, lass."

Sophia frowned and looked over at Nicholas for an explanation. "I'm not sure what you were going through on your side. But here, we faced some... issues... connected to each of your new powers. We can explain more later. I think we should all get cleaned up and rest so we can hike out of here tomorrow. You should be safe now."

Martin spoke up. "Just please try not to do anything to wake up mother earth, dearie. That one was a little precarious next to a mountainside."

Sophia looked up at the mountain and then at their dirty

muddy clothes. She closed her eyes. She had an idea what these poor guys had been through while she slept. "I'm so, so sorry."

"Stop," Nicholas demanded. "It's why we're here, Miss Snow. Don't be sorry. We made it."

Martin reached over and touched her shoe. "Aye, lass. Don't worry yer mind."

Sophia smiled at them. "Thanks. Do you have something I could write on before I forget?"

Martin spoke up, "Let me get something for you." He jumped up.

Nicholas took one more moment to push her hair back from her forehead and smile at her. "I'm very glad to have you back, little one." He rose and pulled her up by the hands. "Let's get cleaned up and eat something. It will help us recover."

Sophia watched him close the circle. Then they all walked to the river and wiped as much filth off as possible. Sophia peeled off the layers down to her sports bra. She was thankful it had remained intact. That would have been embarrassing.

She didn't have clean clothes, so she shook out her lighter jacket and put it on. After doing the best with what toiletries and first aid they had, they went back to the fire. They sat in silence and ate granola bars while Sophia tried to write everything about her powers she could remember. She tucked the paper away and practiced pulling down a veil.

"What are you doing?" Nicholas asked sternly. He got up quickly and walked to crouch in front of her. "What did you do?"

Sophia smiled. "It's called a veil. Ney taught me how to hide my eyes... well... my magic really, when I'm in public."

Nicholas closed his eyes. "I understand the need for that, but..." he trailed off and looked away. "I just need to feel our connection, Miss Snow. Please, can you lift it?"

Sophia warmed all over. He missed her. She smiled and lifted the veil. "Ok, Nicca."

He smiled warmly and stood to walk away. "I think we should get a few hours' rest and then get out of here first thing." He paused and looked back at Sophia. "I know there are unanswered questions. I just think we'll talk better after rest."

Maybe they needed more time to process all they'd seen and felt, but one thing was certain, this experience had bound them. She trusted them completely with her life. She wanted to put words to how she felt, but nothing would come out.

It seemed the guys felt similar because they were just as silent. After a beat, all three walked quietly toward the tent. They needed rest, but no one was willing to leave each other to get it. Without a word, they all picked a sleeping bag.

Sophia thought about her magic. She was excited about learning how to use it, but terrified of hurting someone. She felt different now. Better, she thought. Like something she hadn't known was missing had been put back. She hadn't felt bad before, but now that it was awake inside her, she felt complete. She just hoped she could master it before it consumed her. Instead of falling asleep, she kept going between the facts she'd learned from the druids and the fear she'd felt facing Lily.

The pain in her head grew. She felt movement and turned her head toward the opening of the tent. Nicholas was moving closer. Without a word, he reached out and grabbed her fingers. It was the distraction she needed. She focused on the feel of his hand to force herself to relax. She fell asleep remembering the sound of Nicholas calling her Sophia.

CHAPTER 47

*S*ophia cracked open one eye. Light was coming in the front of the tent. She felt like a ton of bricks were stacked on her back, and she didn't want to move a muscle, but her bladder was screaming at her.

She pushed up with her hands and looked around the empty tent. She twisted around to sit crossed legged and pulled the falling scrunchie out of her hair. Her stomach thankfully felt ok. The scratches didn't burn anymore, but they felt tight and itchy. She put her head down and shook out her curls. She could not wait to get in a hot shower.

As she raked her fingers through her roots, she could feel grit. "Ugh." She pushed it all back up and secured it before walking out into the campsite. The guys were sitting by the fire. With a look around, she could tell they had already packed and cleaned up almost everything.

"Morning, guys. I hope you haven't been waiting on me," Sophia said as she sat on a log by the fire.

"Nay, lass. We only just sat." Martin smiled and handed her some water and a protein bar.

Nicholas smiled at her. "We were thinking we would pack up the tent while you get ready. Then we can get back to the hotel."

"Yes, please. I, for one, am looking forward to a hot shower."

Sophia was not happy about the long hike between her and that shower, though.

She stood with her food. "I'm going to head to the river, then." With a half wave she walked off eating her breakfast.

She reached the river and paused to watch the water while finishing her food. She focused on the rushing water because, like fire, it was calming. When she finally put the last bite in her mouth, she leaned down and washed her hands in the freezing water.

When she finished, she pushed up on her knees and turned to the little girl standing beside her.

"Hello." She decided talking to a spirit couldn't be much different from a live person. The girl looked young. Maybe seven years old. She had pale skin, big green eyes, and long curly strawberry blonde hair. Sophia could see little freckles across her nose and cheeks.

As soon as she'd spoken directly to her, the young girl smiled. "Hi. I'm Isla."

Sophia wasn't sure how the druid women used to interact with spirits, but she decided to just go with the flow. "I'm Sophia."

Isla nodded. "I know."

After a moment, Sophia figured the spirit was waiting on her, so she was honest. "Um. Listen. You're my first ever spirit conversation. I don't really know the rules here. Is there something you need to tell me? Can I help you in some way?"

"Not yet." She giggled, skipped away, and disappeared.

Sophia stared after her. "Hmm," she said thoughtfully. "Ok, then."

Maybe sometimes spirits visited out of curiosity? Weird. She was glad for the privacy though, because she needed a bathroom, so she ran to the ancient set-up and took care of business as fast as she could. She threw her breakfast trash in the bag and collected everything before heading back to the campsite.

The guys were packing the tent when she walked up. "Hey, I brought back the trash. Do you have a place for it?"

Martin pointed to a larger bag. "I've been using that bag to collect food trash, dearie. Just throw it there."

Sophia walked over and threw it away, then put the other items in the duffel. After a half hour, they were all packed.

Nicholas spoke up. "I think that's it."

Sophia smiled. "Great. Let's get this party started then." She tried to look excited.

They took a moment to look around. Sophia asked, "Nicca, do you think we'll ever come back to this place?"

He looked up at the sky before walking over toward the path leading to the waterfall. "I think anything is possible, little one. The magic in the ground here is fading year by year. Eventually, it won't be so hidden from the world."

Martin grumbled, "You mean someday it could be a shopping center."

Nicholas turned back. "Maybe, I guess. It'll probably become a popular tourist look out spot, or camping site, or something like that."

They walked on in silence for a moment. The sun was breaking through the trees and warming the air.

Martin broke the silence first. "Sophia, dear. How do you feel now that your powers have awoken?"

Sophia thought about her answer before speaking. "I feel more complete, but I'm terrified of hurting someone by accident."

Nicholas chimed in, "I can feel your magic."

Sophia looked at him, mortified. "Does it hurt you?"

He looked away from her. "No."

She grabbed his arm. "It always makes me nervous when you duck to answer. Promise me?"

He looked straight at her, and Sophia thought he... blushed? "Nicca?"

"I promise it doesn't hurt, little one. It's... pleasant." He seemed uncomfortable.

Sophia let him turn away and start walking. Did she just witness Nicholas get embarrassed? She looked over at Martin, who gave her a wink. She grinned and kept walking.

It didn't seem to take as long as she remembered to get through the waterfall and down the steep ledge. When they hit the main trail again, she got excited. She was so close to that shower she could feel it.

The trail was quiet today. No one seemed to be around, so they passed the rest of the hike recapping their versions of the day before. The guys listened carefully while Sophia told them what she had learned from the druid women. Then she had to explain the horrifying encounter with Lily.

Nicholas told what happened to them while she was under. It upset her. She felt responsible for what they'd gone through. Instead of feeling excited when they finally reached the car, she just stood there quietly while the guys loaded the car. Nicholas gently pulled the duffle from her back. "Miss Snow?"

"I almost killed you, Nicca," she said slowly. "Being around me means you could die."

He turned her to face him. "It's very hard to get rid of me, Miss Snow. Remember the vow made on that hotel rooftop?" He placed his hand on his heart. "I am." He moved his hand to her heart. "Ye are."

She scrunched her face up, making him laugh. "As long as ye are... I will be. You can't kill me unless you're already gone. And if that's true, I wouldn't want to be living, anyway. So no worries, yeah?"

She warmed at his words and gave a small nod. He reached behind her to open the door. She jumped in while he threw her bag in the back. The moment the car took off, she fell asleep dreaming of soap and hot water.

CHAPTER 48

The trip back to Tennessee from Ireland was easier. They left to come home a couple of days after returning to the hotel. She had loved Ireland, more importantly, she had loved being with the guys, but she was excited to see Penny and sleep in her own bed.

Martin was driving them to her house. It was about five in the evening. She didn't know what was coming next, and it bothered her. Would she see Nicholas anytime soon? Would she have to wait until her birthday to see him again? She really hoped not. This week had brought them closer than ever, and she didn't want to lose that.

"You know," Martin said from the driver's seat, "I learned a lot on this trip." He looked over at Nicholas. "I learned you give a decent fight."

Nicholas laughed. "I learned that you're very brave and very loyal. We would've been lost without you on this trip."

Sophia reached up to tap Martin on the shoulder. "Yes. I learned Nicca likes The F-Word."

Martin burst out laughing. "She's right. You love The F-Word."

Nicholas looked at Sophia. "I apologize, Miss Snow."

Sophia laughed. "I like it. Your accent gets strong and somehow when you say it, it just sounds funny."

Martin was laughing hard. "I have to agree with Sophia. When you're in the middle of losing your temper, I find myself quite entertained."

Nicholas stared at Martin, but when he heard Sophia giggle, she saw the corner of his mouth turn up. "Shut it, Martin."

"Yes, sir," Martin said with a smile.

She got a case of the nerves when they got to the house and was about to ask Nicholas to stay when she heard him tell Martin to wait in the car. She hugged Martin over the seat. "Don't be a stranger, Martin."

Nicholas already had her suitcase and carry-on, so they began walking up the sidewalk. "Nicca."

"Miss Snow," he interrupted her, "go talk to Penny. She'll be over the moon to see you again. Catch her up on the trip and ask about the spa day."

Sophia stopped. "Nicca, I..."

Nicholas grabbed her chin. "I'll come by later, before you go to bed. We'll have our closure then, ok?"

Sophia sighed. "Ok. You won't disappear?"

Nicholas smiled. "I'll return in a couple of hours." He kissed her forehead and turned to leave.

Sophia watched him walk away briefly before hearing the door open behind her. A screaming Penny grabbed her up in a bear hug.

Sophia and Penny brought her bags in and then she spent the next hour over dinner telling Penny everything she could about the trip. She decided not to give the details of getting her powers or about getting into an altercation with Lily. Penny knew she was different, but they had an unspoken rule to keep the sharing to 'need to know.' She knew Penny would help in a heartbeat with anything she needed, but Sophia's instincts told her it was easier this way.

As she sat talking with her, she realized Penny looked differ- ent. Her hair was cut from her spa day, but it was more than that.

"Mom, did you enjoy your break?" Sophia asked her. Sam

began rubbing against her legs and purring so she leaned down and picked him up.

"I did. It was quiet and a little lonely at first. I had trouble figuring out what to do with myself. But then, one evening I saw a book on my desk I had been hoping to read for a year now. So I sat down and read the whole thing. It was amazing!" She smiled at her.

"And? Did Mr. Larry stop by?" Sophia asked hopefully.

Penny reached over and swatted playfully at Sophia. "Don't you even try that. I called him as soon as you left and let him know you were gone so he wouldn't waste a trip."

Sophia slumped in her chair. "I know you both like each other. Why not see if it can go anywhere?"

Penny paused in thought. "I appreciate what you are doing, but I think you misunderstand Larry's intentions, Sophia. He's just being nice to me. That's all."

Sophia realized Penny didn't know her potential. She was going to have to resort to smarter tactics, so for now she dropped the subject. "I think I'll get unpacked. Maybe start some laundry. I know I have a couple of days left before school starts, but I'd rather get a jump on it."

"Ok sweetie, I'm really glad you're back. I'll go start the wash." Penny headed for the laundry room.

"Thanks, Mom." Sophia ran upstairs, pulled out enough clothes to fill a load. Then she spent some quiet time getting everything unpacked and sorted.

She had to work at keeping thoughts of Lily and her new powers from overwhelming her. Feelings of doubt, insecurities, and just plain fear were creeping in.

She flopped down onto the bed, and immediately, Sam jumped up. "Hey, buddy." He crawled up the bed and bumped his head against hers. She laughed and began rubbing his head. "I missed you too."

The doorbell rang, causing Sophia to jump. She raced down the stairs yelling to Penny, "I got it, Mom. It's just Nicca."

She opened the door but didn't see anyone right away. She

turned her head as she stepped out and saw Nicholas leaning against the railing by the porch swing, looking as beautiful as ever.

"Come talk to me, little one." He smiled at her.

She shut the door and walked to the swing. It swayed gently as she sat, and she stared down at his feet stretched out in front of her. One large boot was crossed over the other. She didn't know how to ask him not to leave her again because she didn't want him to reject her.

"Look at me," Nicholas said gently.

Sophia looked up slowly, and she felt her magic swirling. She saw him tense and grip the railing with both hands, so she quickly put her veil in place.

"No." Nicholas shook his head. "Don't. Please. Just tell me what's on your mind."

Sophia dropped her veil. "Are you disappearing again? Are we going back to how it was before?"

Nicholas looked at her hard before answering. "I'm not sure we can ever go back to how it was before, little one. Things are different, don't you agree?"

Sophia nodded. "I feel different."

Nicholas stood straight and turned to face the street. "It's important for me to focus on your safety, Miss Snow. That's why I keep my distance. The longer we spend together, the harder it is for me to do what I am supposed to do."

Sophia looked down. "It's too late for that, Nicca. Maybe when I was younger, but after this week? You just go back to never talking to me? It's... well, it's not fair. What about what I want? Does that matter?"

Nicholas turned to her. "Of course it matters. You don't know it, but having me around would be a huge distraction for you as well. You have school to finish and powers to master."

Sophia shook her head. "You underestimate me, Nicca. I'm not asking you to move in. I just wish you would drop by more often. Or heck, maybe let me have your phone number and text you sometimes. I just want your friendship. It's all I've ever wanted. An honest to God friend. I just don't understand why you have to ghost me all year. Not now... not after this week. It's too late for distance, Nicca."

Nicholas stared down at her. "Honestly, it was too late for distance the first time you sat on that wooden crate and started swinging your pink flip-flops." He smiled. "I've only ever tried to do what's best for you."

Sophia smiled. "I know. I never doubt that."

Nicholas pulled her out of the swing by the hands. "I have to go." He reached into his pocket and pulled out her bracelet.

"Oh my God! Nicca, I thought I lost it in the woods during all the craziness." Sophia's hands covered her mouth.

"I had it cleaned. I'm sorry. I should have told you I had it. I wasn't thinking," he said. He pulled a hand away from her mouth and set the charms gently in her palm.

"You were thinking. About me. Thank you so much, Nicca," Sophia said with her whole heart in her eyes.

He sucked air in and leaned away from her like she had hit him in the chest. She was going to have to figure this magic out. It made him uncomfortable, judging from his reaction.

"Lily isn't here yet. Try not to think too much about her. Focus on learning. I'm always around––always." He kissed the top of her head and pulled her in for a hug.

She hugged him tightly, knowing it would be the last time she saw him for a while. She wanted to ask him about Lily, but something stopped her. The words wouldn't come.

When he pulled away from her, she felt her magic follow him like it was trying to hold on too.

"Miss Snow, I can't move," Nicholas said with humor.

Sophia's eyes widened. "Oh, my God. I'm sorry." She tried to focus on a visual that would unfreeze him. She settled on just thinking of him running. It took a few beats, but finally he moved again. She giggled. "I guess that's one way to make you stay."

Nicholas grinned at her over his shoulder as he ran down the steps. Sophia went to the front post to watch him drive away.

As Nicholas opened his car door, he paused. "Miss Snow, you'll find my number already in your phone. Drop me a text whenever you like." He hopped in the car and drove away, leaving a smile on Sophia's face. She laughed as she turned to head into the house. Maybe life would be a little less lonely now.

CHAPTER 49

*N*icholas didn't know how long he'd been running. He was soaking wet and his muscles were burning. It was so much harder this time to stay away. That one brief day spent disconnected in the woods had done a number on him. Seeing her almost die had switched something on inside of him.

He couldn't stop thinking about her magic and how it felt when it reached out to him. When she'd asked him about it, there had been no way to explain it to her without sounding like a pervert or embarrassing them both. It swirled around him like a very inappropriate caress. He shook his head to clear it. Yeah, no way he could have that awkward conversation with her.

Basically, to sum it up, he was miserable. She needed to focus on getting back into some type of routine, and her new magic would be enough of a distraction without him around muddying things up.

"You think you've run far enough away from her?" Martin said from the side of the treadmill.

Nicholas slowed the speed and lowered the incline. "What do you mean?"

Martin smiled sadly. "I'm not blind. I've watched her grow up for ten years too. You two have a connection no one in the universe could ever understand. No amount of running or beating yourself up will change that."

Nicholas frowned at him. "What are you trying to say, exactly?"

Martin explained, "Nothing really. Just, if you want to see her, simply go see her."

Nicholas jumped off the treadmill and grabbed a towel off a side table. "You sound like you're trying to be a matchmaker, Martin. She is fucking sixteen if you haven't remembered that."

Martin spun around angrily. "I know she's 'fucking sixteen.' I will be the first to admit I don't understand the relationship you have, but I do know you'd never harm her. You'd never do anything inappropriate toward her. Geez, give me a little credit. I was there, and I saw you when we thought she wouldn't wake up. I felt it too. I just hate watching you moping around punishing yourself. If you refuse to visit her, then let's figure out what the hell to do about Lily. There's no point sitting over here staring at her window like a little sad puppy dog."

Nicholas stared at him for a minute before nodding curtly. "You're right, Martin. I'm sorry. I'm finding it harder to go away this time. It was... difficult... for me in the woods. We should try to figure out how Lilith hopes to become whole by coming here to this time. What is here that she needs?"

Martin smiled. "That's the Nicholas we need right now." He turned to walk out of the room, but just as he left he ducked his head back. "You know she won't always be sixteen."

Nicholas threw his towel at Martin's head. "For fuck's sake! Martin, you fucking bastard." He yelled to the sound of Martin laughing down the hallway.

～

Sophia worried about starting back to school with her magic. It had only been a couple of days and she was nervous about it. She smiled down at her phone. Nicholas had sent a text wishing her luck at school. He was trying to give her what she asked for, and she loved him for it. Life was finally going to be perfect. Well, as perfect as it can be with power she couldn't control and a psychopathic monster after her.

Penny knocked on her door. "Hey sweetie, Martin is downstairs. Says he needs a quick word."

Sophia frowned. "Really? Ok." She hoped nothing was wrong with Nicholas.

She ran downstairs and didn't see anyone, so she checked the front door and saw a shadow through the glass. When she opened the door, she knew right away it wasn't Martin. It was the way he held himself. When she looked into his face, she saw the flash of gold in his eyes. "Jophiel?" she whispered.

Jophiel smiled. "Ah good! Of course, you remember me. You're a smart girl. Would you be kind enough to take a short walk with me?" He gave a small but formal bow.

Sophia nodded as she stepped out. "Is everyone alright?"

"Oh yes, dear. I apologize. Everyone is fine. I would appreciate it if you'd try to keep your emotions calm. I'm bringing you knowledge meant only for you. Martin will have no recollection of this talk, and I hope to keep your guardian's eyes off it too," he explained with a wink as he led her down the steps.

"Um... ok. I'm not that good at keeping things from Nicca, to be honest," Sophia said.

"I understand. This is nothing insidious, my dear. I simply want to point out a few things you may need to help you develop your magic," Jophiel explained as they turned down the sidewalk.

Sophia perked up. "I could use any advice you can give me."

He laughed. "Yes. Well, I know you begin school tomorrow, and you probably worry that veiling yourself also blocks Nicholas."

She nodded. "I need to keep a veil up almost constantly in public, but then it mutes the connection with Nicholas, and he doesn't like that."

Jophiel smiled. "No, I imagine not. The druid sisters gave you a lot of excellent knowledge. They gave you what they know. But they... are not you, my dear. With all of your powers, you can move beyond their limits."

Sophia frowned. "You mean I can do more than they said?"

"Sure." Jophiel shrugged. "You could probably do just about

whatever you wanted, but to be more specific, you need to think of the things they taught you as 'the basics.' If they said you can move dirt, take it another step, move rocks, trees, plants, or maybe even something sitting on the ground. Also, the sisters focused on the extremes. I know you fear them. It's scary to think you could create great pain or even cause death. But remember, my dear, just as I always harp on about free will, I also stress balance."

Sophia agreed. "Right. So I have to stay away from the extremes and master my magic, I already know that."

Jophiel shook his head. "No child. The sisters only focused on the destructive extreme, but there is an equal power on the other end of the spectrum."

Sophia cringed. "Jophiel, are you saying I have a whole other set of extremes I have to prevent myself from doing?"

Jophiel leaned over and placed his hands on her shoulders. "What I'm saying is that while you may possess the ability to force a soul out, it also means you could push one back in." Jophiel looked at her meaningfully.

"So it's possible for me to save someone, as much as kill someone?" She liked those odds better.

Jophiel kept going. "Like I said. Your magic is beyond theirs. What you could do is yet to be determined. I simply want to impart that you should not limit yourself. Just because they didn't tell you it could be done, doesn't mean you couldn't do it. Be creative."

Sophia nodded. "Ok. Think outside the box. I think I get it, Jophiel."

He nodded and turned them back toward the house. "You know, most people never know who their guardian is."

Sophia looked up at him. "I didn't know that. Is that why he tries to stay distant?"

Jophiel laughed. "Oh, sweet Sophia. He's a lot of things, but distant is not one of them. Most guardians are never born and raised on Earth. They just pop into a body like I have and quietly protect the mission. No. Nicholas being raised by the druids, roaming the earth for so long, and then living alongside you while you grow up is all unique, wouldn't you say? He took one look at you, Sophia, and demanded the guardianship. No one else had a chance. I have to wonder why that is? It's all very interesting," he explained as they strolled along. "You, I find very interesting too. Did you know you picked this role as well?"

Sophia stopped walking. "What do you mean?"

Jophiel nodded. "You weren't born accidentally into this role. You knew exactly what you were signing up for with this life. And you embraced it, happily, so I have learned." He leaned over and whispered, "Angels can be such gossips, I'm afraid."

Sophia couldn't believe it. "So I chose this role? On purpose?"

He laughed. "I know! So interesting, right?" They walked a few steps before he continued, "I'm concerned that when it comes time for you to face your purpose, his feelings may make it impossible for him to let you." Jophiel stopped and turned to her. "You should know that you may have to make him let you. It will not be easy, and it should be a last resort, but if for some reason your mark no longer fit into his mark, your connection would be severed."

Sophia gasped. Her hand flew to her mark. "I could never do that, Jophiel."

Jophiel nodded sadly. "I know, dear, but you should have the knowledge. You should have options. As I mentioned... last resort and all..." He turned them back up the drive to her house.

"One last thing to be helpful." Jophiel stopped at the bottom step, and she stepped up and turned to him. "Druids never had to worry about details because they only had one skill to master. You have four, so details become more important. You don't have to do a blanket veil. You can choose what to veil. If you want a mental break from spirits, then veil your mind. If you simply want to hide your eyes, then just do it." He smiled kindly. "If you want to mute your connection to Nicholas, you could veil just him too."

Sophia wondered, "What do I veil to do that?" She could think of a time or two in the past that some privacy would have been nice.

Jophiel grinned and leaned toward her. "I think we both know what you need to veil to hide from him, sweet Sophia."

Sophia reddened. "My head?"

Jophiel winked. "Is it? Perhaps I was mistaken, then." He turned to walk away. "Don't worry, dear. Your secret's safe with me."

CHAPTER 50

*L*ife settled into a routine for Sophia. For a while, it was almost back to normal. The exception was getting to text with Nicholas a little and the growing, swirling storm that was brewing in her head.

At first, things were going along ok. School was a little more stressful, but once she nailed keeping the veil in place, she felt more comfortable and could concentrate.

She worked with the veil first, and once it became second nature, she started freezing things. After a few weeks, she could freeze and unfreeze specific parts of a creature. She could freeze a squirrel and then free the tail. She even froze Sam and then laughed while he angrily swished his tail at her and growled. He forgave her after tons of belly scratches, and it made for some fun afternoons.

Next, during the spring, she tried to manipulate earth. It was more difficult, ironically, because it was the easiest to trigger. So far she could bend trees, mold dirt, and even pick up and throw gravel. She couldn't seem to figure out how to curb her mouth, though. She was constantly thinking of the time she almost buried Nicholas alive. It made her paranoid, and in the end, for this magical skill, she decided to keep a veil in place. If she needed it, she would simply have to lift the veil first.

Once she settled on that, she tried to work on spirits, but

strangely, the only spirit she ever saw was Isla, and she wasn't ready to talk. That left her with her natural-born ability.

She wanted to access a vision on purpose. The last connection she had knowingly made was about Penny and Mr. Larry, but they had turned out to be stubborn and nothing had worked to nudge them together.

It was the end of summer. She'd had nearly a year to work on her magic, but she had hit a wall. The last month she hadn't progressed at all, and a turbulence was growing inside of her. Sophia didn't know if it was because she had stalled or if something else was happening.

Something like a growing madness.

She had started researching Lilith and read everything she could online about her, hoping something would trigger a vision. So far, nothing. Each story was more outrageous than the one before it, and she didn't know what to believe.

A depression had settled over and around her like a fog. Her senior year would start soon, and she couldn't bring herself to care. Each day that passed, a thicker shell grew between her and the outside world. She could tell it worried Penny, and the last time Mr. Larry had come over, she'd seen the concern in his eyes, too.

She thought having Nicca a little closer would help, but it hadn't. Lily's words about there being no place in the world for her kept rolling around her brain. She had to admit it made sense, and she was terrified that Lily had been telling the truth. Lily was the extreme darkness, but Sophia was an extreme too, just the opposite end of the spectrum. What if there was no place in this world for her either?

Then came the morning she had to admit something was wrong. She could hear voices. She couldn't understand any words, but the sounds of whispering were filling her head, and it was driving her mad. She couldn't even focus enough to get out of bed. All she could do was face the wall with her eyes tightly closed and try to drown out the whispers by humming.

Lost in the chaos, she didn't even feel Nicholas when he

appeared. She didn't see him watching her with fear and sadness as she rocked in bed with her hands over her ears.

"Little one," he began as he sat on the edge of the bed and touched her back.

She didn't hear him at all.

He turned her to him and pulled her hands from her ears. "Miss Snow, talk to me," he pleaded.

She opened her eyes and focused on him, but the sound didn't stop. She pulled her hands free and covered her ears, "Nicca, I can't stop the noise."

He pulled her hands down again. "Tell me what the noise sounds like."

"It's whispering. Constant whispering. It won't stop," she said as a tear fell down her cheek.

"You must make all into one before the night comes, or lose yourself to madness," Nicholas repeated the prophecy given to her by the druid.

"I know! I know! Don't you think I don't know? I've been working on it, but I don't know what else I can do," Sophia said desperately.

Nicholas wiped a tear. "I know. I'm sorry. Have you tried to veil yourself?"

Sophia nodded. "It worked for a while, but not now. I just need a break. I need it to stop."

"I never felt the connection drop." Nicholas frowned.

Sophia admitted, "I didn't veil you. Only my mind."

Nicholas looked impressed. "You can pick what to veil? Can you veil just your ears?"

Sophia thought for a moment. Anything was worth a try so she tried. Then shook her head. "Still there."

Nicholas nodded. "I'm here. Go ahead and veil everything."

Sophia veiled everything and saw Nicholas reach up and touch his mark. She gave him a sad smile. "Sorry."

"It's ok. I want to make sure we try everything," he assured her. "Let's think about the sentence. You must make all into one. I know you've been working on your powers. When I ask, you just say it's going fine. Have you hit any roadblocks there?"

Sophia nodded. "Power of the Mind and Spirit." She squeezed her eyes shut again.

He waited for her to gather herself before prompting her. "Why have they stalled you?"

"I've only had one vision about a connection, but the people are being stubborn. The only spirit I've seen came to me that next morning in the woods. She's been with me since, but won't tell me what she wants. She just hangs around sometimes. No other spirits have shown themselves so I can't work on that, Nicca." Sophia was getting more desperate by the minute.

Nicholas brushed her curls away from her tear-stained face. "How can I help you?"

Sophia laughed painfully. "Unless you can get Penny and Mr. Larry to see they are perfect for each other, or make Isla talk to me, then I can't think of anything. It seems I'm destined for straitjackets and padded walls."

He looked away for a moment. "Why didn't you tell me about the spirit? Isla, you said?"

Sophia looked confused. "I'm not sure. Something told me I should keep it to myself. I got the feeling she knew who you were." Sophia stopped. "Well actually, now that I say that out loud. Not you. Martin. I think it's his sister, Nicca," Sophia said as if she was just realizing it.

Nicholas wondered out loud. "I listened carefully to you tell me how each power worked. You said a spirit spoke to you only of their own free will. So Isla told you these things?"

Sophia paused. "No. I just... kind of knew it?"

Nicholas asked her, "Is it possible the Power of the Mind told you things about the Spirit? That the two overlapped?"

Sophia's eyes widened. "Could it be as simple as that?"

Nicholas shrugged. "So far, everything we have learned about your abilities has come from revelations. Why not? Knowledge is power, right? When you see a problem, don't think about which power you use. Just like Larry teaches you when you fight, put it all together to solve any problem in your path. Instead of four different languages, put them all together to create your own unique language."

Sophia thought it through. "So my visions gave me the knowledge to handle the spirit better. Or maybe in a fight, I freeze my attacker and throw a rock or a tree at him?" Sophia smiled.

Nicholas smiled, then widened his eyes. "You can throw a tree?"

Sophia giggled. "Don't mess with me."

She noticed Nicholas was smirking, which made her pause. Her eyes grew round. "The voices aren't as loud!" She launched herself out of the bed at Nicholas.

He caught her with a laugh. "I think it's even bigger than that, little one. I suspect you have to put the complete picture together. Not just your magic, but all of your skills. Everything you've learned from me and Martin, the druids, and even Larry."

Sophia pulled away and nodded thoughtfully. "Think outside of the box… be creative." She remembered Jophiel's words.

Nicholas smiled. "Exactly. I suspect the more you do that, the better you will feel."

"I'm ready." Sophia heard a voice coming from right behind her.

She gasped and spun so quickly, Nicholas pulled her to him out of instinct.

"What is it?" he asked while looking around the empty room.

"It's Isla. She startled me." Sophia relaxed, but she felt Nicholas pull her closer. Isla was standing on her bed, bouncing up and down.

"Have you been waiting for me to realize all of this before you talked to me?" she asked Isla.

Isla smiled. "I was only trying to help. Only one of us can talk at a time so I was holding the spot while you figured things out."

"Thank you, Isla. That was very thoughtful. Tell me. How can I help you?" Sophia asked her.

Isla twirled a curl around her finger, looking shy. "I really want to talk to Martin."

Sophia knew immediately this would be uncomfortable and painful for Martin, but she also suspected it was time. She touched Nicholas's hand on her stomach. "It's ok, Nicca. I'm going to need to see Martin." She gave him a sad smile.

Nicholas watched the place Isla was standing, trying his best to see something, but he looked down as Sophia's words and understanding dawned. He gave her a serious nod. "Ok, little one."

He put his phone to his ear without looking away, watching her carefully while he told Martin to come. It wasn't until he put his phone away that he reluctantly let go and walked to her desk chair. He sat, crossed his arms, and glared at the spot he seemed to think Isla was.

Isla leaned close to Sophia. "He's pretty. Grumpy. But pretty."

"Yeah, he is." Sophia giggled, and Nicholas looked sharply at her.

She tried not to laugh, honestly, but Isla had produced a daisy and was holding it under his nose. Turns out, a grumpy, sullen man sniffing a flower is hilarious.

Isla dissolved into fits of laughter. Sophia hoped all spirits were this delightful.

The door to her room opened, and Martin appeared looking curious. She said a quick prayer that she would say the right thing. "Martin, wow, you got here fast. You must have been close by."

Martin grinned. "I try to stay where I might be needed."

She could see the resemblance between Isla and Martin in their smiles. "Martin, unfortunately, I do need your help today. I have a feeling it won't be fun for you. I'm sorry."

Martin stopped smiling and stepped into the room, closing the door. He tried once more at levity. "Well, it canna be swallowed-up-by-the-earth bad, right? You know I'll help anyway I can, lass." He kept looking over at Nicholas, sitting quietly.

Sophia explained, "I've been struggling with my sanity, Martin. Today I really thought I was lost for good, but thankfully, Nicca helped me realize something that seems to hold the madness at bay."

"That's great, lass. Why do you look like you are about to tell me my dog died?" Martin looked nervous.

"You have a dog?" Sophia asked before shaking her head and getting back on track. "Sorry, you can answer that later. I'd hit a roadblock with one of my powers, Martin. The Power of Spirit. I couldn't move forward and learn this skill, because the spirit, the *only* spirit, that appeared to me in the woods, wasn't ready to talk."

While she spoke, the blood drained from Martin's face. "No, lass." He turned to leave the room.

Sophia froze Martin without thinking. She realized she couldn't force Isla to talk, but she could damn well force Martin to listen.

She walked around to face him. "I'm sorry, Martin. She's ready to talk now. Give her peace, please."

Martin was straining against her power, but he couldn't move anything except his head. Finally, his head fell. "Damn you, Sophia."

His words hurt. The moment the pain hit her, Nicholas jumped up, growling. "For fuck's sake, Martin. She is trying to help you."

Martin looked at Nicholas. "Fuck you, too. You donna understand. Neither of you do."

Isla stepped up beside her. "He doesna usually curse so much. He'll feel bad about it later, Sophia. Donna worry."

Sophia looked down at her and smiled. "I know, Isla."

Martin blanched at her words. Tears filled his eyes. "Isla?"

Sophia nodded. "She's been hanging with me off and on since the woods, but she only decided to talk today. It's a shame, really, because she's hilarious. It obviously runs in the family."

"She was the best of us all." Tears filled his eyes.

Isla nodded up at Sophia. "I really was."

Sophia laughed. "She agrees with you, Martin."

He laughed through his tears. "Please, Sophie. Free me."

Sophia looked at him for a moment, then at Nicholas to get his opinion. He nodded to her. She freed Martin, and he fell to his knees and continued to cry. His position brought him almost face to face with Isla.

Isla looked at him sadly. "He punishes himself every single day that he wasn't with us when it happened. It's time to stop."

Sophia repeated her words.

Martin shook his head. "I should have been there. Instead, I was off flirting with some girl, and I canna even remember her name. I was angry with Da." Martin was struggling to talk through his tears. "I told him I was a man and could do what I want. Apparently, that was to abandon them when they needed me the most."

Isla looked to Sophia, who nodded and repeated her words. "Stop it, Mac."

When he heard the nickname, Martin broke down.

"If you had been there, it only would have meant your death too. We were all thankful you weren't there. Do you hear me? We were glad you weren't there. Da loves you. We're all proud of you," Isla continued.

Martin shook his head. "At least I could have fought. I could've died defending my family."

Isla touched his face. "Our destinies here were complete. Yours wasna, Mac. You were always meant to end up right here with Nicholas and Sophia. Your family is so proud you are going to help save the world."

Martin furiously wiped his eyes before looking at the ceiling. "I miss you, Issy, so goddamn much."

Isla smiled. "How can you miss me? I'm right here. Quit your moping and get it together."

Martin laughed. "Yeah, ok." Martin wiped his eyes again. "I'll make you proud, I swear it."

Isla shook her head sadly. "You already did that. There's never been a better brother, Mac. What I want is a promise to go out and live your life. It's ok to be happy. This 'poor me' business is boring."

Martin laughed. "Ok, Issy. I hear you."

Isla nodded up to Sophia. "Thanks, Sophia. Help him remember my words. Kick him in the butt if he needs it?"

Sophia laughed. "I will, Isla."

She looked fondly at her brother. "I love you, Mac. Be happy."

Sophia said it to Martin, who nodded through his tears. "I love you too, Issy."

Just like that, Isla turned and skipped off. She disappeared about the time she hit the bed. Sophia watched in fascination as she wiped the tears from her face.

A noise made her turn and catch Martin just as he grabbed her up in a bear hug. "I'm so fucking sorry, Sophie, lass. Thank you. Thank you. Thank you." His voice trailed off as he squeezed the air out of her.

"I'm happy I could do it. It saved me too, Martin." Sophia smiled as she noticed the whispers were completely gone.

Martin pulled away. "I'm sorry, but I need a little time to myself," he said to Nicholas.

"Take what you need," Nicholas assured him.

Martin turned to leave, but when he got to the door and turned back to Sophia. "I'll never be able to repay you for this." He paused. "Although, I could have done without the freezing part." He smiled.

Sophia laughed. "Sorry. Not sorry."

As he left, she watched Nicholas prowl toward her. He wiped a tear from her cheek.

"So fucking proud of you, little one," Nicholas said gruffly.

Sophia smiled. "Couldn't do it without you, Nicca. I would be in that bed over there going insane. Thank you, once again, for holding me together."

"Gotta go. See you on your birthday," he said with a smile.

She nodded. "You better."

He winked and disappeared.

Sophia spun around in her now empty room, taking in the emotions of the morning. It had been quite the roller coaster. Thank God, it was ending on a note of hope. A sound had her turning back to her door to a confused Penny.

"Did I hear voices?" she asked.

Sophia couldn't help it. She burst out laughing.

CHAPTER 51

*S*ophia was in a pickle. She was stranded on her birthday, her phone was dead, and she was still at the mall. Sighing, she put her phone back in her bag. What good was all her magic if she couldn't charge a phone? She had been shopping with her friend Brandy, who unfortunately had become ill and gone home.

She looked at the big clock hanging above the food court. There was enough time to walk home, she supposed. If she took a few shortcuts, she could probably get home in an hour.

As she strolled across the parking lot, she thought about life. The whispering had stayed at bay and her school schedule was easy. So far, most of Senior year was about pictures, prom, deciding colleges, and making memories.

She was enjoying it, even though she preferred to watch from the sidelines. That had never changed throughout high school. Always separate. Always different.

She had tried this year to be more involved and make deeper connections with kids at school. It was the reason she had met Brandy at the mall today, but Sophia was starting to accept that she would always feel alone.

She kicked at the gravel as she turned down a side street. Her thoughts turned too, and as always, they settled on Nicholas. She wanted to talk to him about getting more involved now that school was finishing this year because college just wasn't the path for her. She wanted more action.

She turned down the side of an abandoned strip mall and startled when she realized there was a guy leaning against the wall looking at a cell phone. He was a teenager, but Sophia didn't recognize him from school. Something about him sent up red flags, and she was learning to listen to her instincts.

He laughed when she moved away. "Don't be scared of me, honey. Why don't you hold up a minute and talk to me?"

Sophia smiled politely but kept walking with a firm. "No, thanks."

"Hey! You think you're too good to talk to me for a minute?" he asked, challenging her.

She passed by him, tossing over her shoulder, "Not too good, but I'm just in a hurry, and I don't have a minute." Something told her this would not end peacefully.

"Hey!" he yelled. "You don't got a minute for me, eh?"

She could tell by the sound of his voice he was walking toward her. She sighed as she turned and dropped her bag lightly by her feet. What was his obsession with 'a minute'?

He got right up in her space. "Yeah. That's what I thought. Hey girl, what's your name?"

Sophia grimaced. She could smell the stale smoke on his breath. Did this really work for him? Like ever? "My name is I'm in a hurry and you are making me late on my birthday."

His face slid quickly from what she suspected was his 'seductive face' straight to his 'enraged face.'

"You bitch!" he yelled and grabbed her by the neck with both hands. He pushed her against the wall and squeezed.

Sophia had to admit, she hadn't anticipated he would jump straight to attack like that. She had to give him credit for the element of surprise. Luckily, she tucked her chin just as she'd been taught, brought her right elbow up high, and twisted hard to the left, pulling down.

His hands ripped off her neck, and he was pulled down and off balance. It left him wide open to her right hand, so she made a fist and swung back hard to his groin and immediately doubled up with an elbow to the stomach. He yelled and pulled up, which made him a prime target for anything she wanted. She settled on a kick to the gut, and he fell to the ground.

She had to admit; she had enjoyed that. She walked to her bag, and as she pulled it over her shoulder, she spoke to Nicholas. "Thanks for letting me handle that one, Nicca." She looked over her shoulder at Nicholas leaning against the wall with his boot on the thug's face.

"What in the actual fuck, Miss Snow? Why are you in this place, with this trash?" Nicholas pulled the teen up by the hair. He leaned over and said something in the guy's ear before slamming him against the wall and letting him slide down. Stepping over him, he walked to Sophia. "Answer me, Miss Snow."

Sophia started walking again toward home. "Phone died."

Nicholas caught up quickly and fell in step with her. "You couldn't have borrowed a phone from someone?"

Sophia slowed. "Hmm, I suppose that could have been another solution."

They walked a couple of steps before he stopped and turned her to face him. He gently pushed her chin up and looked at her neck closely. Once satisfied, he looked her in the eyes. "Happy birthday, little one."

She smiled. "Thanks. Happy birthday, Nicca."

He grinned and winked. They began walking again. "Why did I not get a warning? I barely felt anything wrong. If distracted, I would have missed it altogether."

Sophia shrugged. "Maybe because he wasn't a genuine threat to me? I wasn't that concerned. More annoyed. It's probably time for you to let me fight my own battles anyway, Nicca."

Nicholas wrapped her hand around his bicep. "I did not enjoy seeing his hands around your neck. I wanted to kill him."

Sophia agreed. "I didn't enjoy having them there, but I did enjoy removing them myself. It made me feel strong. You gave me that. I may have done the action, but you gave me that gift with Mr. Larry." She squeezed his arm.

"Well. It makes your birthday gift perfect this year, that's for sure," he said off-handedly.

Sophia gave an excited little hop. "They're always perfect. What is it?"

He laughed. "You'll see later." He dug out his phone and called Penny. "She'll be along in a moment," he said as he put his phone away.

"Boo," Sophia pouted.

Nicholas laughed again. "I won't go until she comes. We might as well keep going."

They walked for only a few minutes before she saw Penny's car coming up the street. Nicholas placed his hand over hers. "Enjoy your birthday, little one, and your gift."

She stopped and looked up at him. "I'll still see you later?"

He smiled as he leaned over to open the passenger door. "Of course, I still need my birthday gift, remember?"

Sophia grinned from ear to ear as she jumped in the car with a quick 'Hey' to Penny. Nicholas leaned over and waved while telling Sophia, "Buckle up, little one."

"Does he need a ride too, Soph?" Penny asked once he'd shut her door.

"No. He's fine, Mom," she said. "Sorry about this. My phone died on me."

"It's ok, sweetie. I'm just happy you're ok," she said pulling into traffic.

Sophia watched the scenery fly by. She wanted to feel bad about getting violent with another stranger, but she just didn't. He'd brought his violence to her, and she had answered. All she could think about was Nicholas. And her present. She was excited to see what her present was now.

CHAPTER 52

a car. He'd bought her a car. Sophia was still in shock. She'd taken a class this year and gotten her permit, but she'd never guessed it would be a car. It was a gunmetal grey Nissan Maxima, and it was so beautiful, she was afraid to drive it. She just sat in it with her hands on the steering wheel and pretended.

It made her even more nervous about her gift for Nicholas. What do you get someone who has everything? She looked over at the wrapped gift on her desk.

"Why do I detect nerves, Miss Snow?" He stood with his arms crossed at her door.

"You got me a car. That's too much, Nicca." Sophia stood and hugged him. "I never expected you to get me a car."

She felt his hand against her hair. "It was time. You need to go more often than Penny can accommodate. It only made sense. Do you like the model? Penny assured me the Nissan would be more appropriate than the models I suggested."

She laughed into his chest. "It's perfect. Too perfect." She pulled away and turned to her desk but suddenly got too nervous.

Nicholas placed his hands on her shoulders. "Hey. What's this? You're never this way around me. What's wrong?"

She laughed. "I don't know. Just nervous."

He spun her around. "Out with it."

"I want to get more involved, Nicca," Sophia admitted. "I'm finishing school this year, and I want to contribute more. Maybe I can use my magic. Get through the fake and figure out what's true. I just want more control."

He walked over to her desk chair and sat, so she followed and sat on the bed. "Don't you want to go to college?"

She shook her head and held up her hands. "Why? This is my life, isn't it? We have to be getting close to her arrival. I just don't think I could put much effort into college classes when this is what I need to focus on."

"I'll admit. The thought of you being able to help through magic is appealing. We have collected a lot over the years, and we've had no way to discern what's true," Nicholas conceded.

Sophia put her hands together and bounced. "Is that a yes, Nicca?"

Nicholas gave her a half-smile. "It's a maybe, Miss Snow. But nothing until after graduation, and you have to promise me that if you change your mind and decide you want to pursue a degree, you'll tell me immediately."

Sophia decided to take what she could get and not push it. "Thank you." She smiled.

Nicholas looked at the gift. "You haven't opened all your gifts."

"It's... well... it's for you, Nicca." Sophia's face burned.

His grin returned. "I told you what my birthday gift is, Miss Snow. You shouldn't have purchased anything."

Sophia felt stupid. "It's not a car or anything. It's not a big deal."

"Hey," Nicholas said firmly.

She looked up at his tone, and he watched her thoughtfully. Then he placed his hand on the gift. "This is why you're so nervous."

Sophia shrugged a shoulder. "I just feel silly. There's nothing I can give you, you don't already have."

Nicholas drummed his fingers against the present for a

moment. Then he sat up as he decided something. "Come with me." He picked up the gift and held his other hand out to her.

Confused, Sophia grabbed his hand and let him pull her down the stairs. He walked to the kitchen and grabbed her new keys off the counter, waved at Penny, and then pulled them out to the front porch.

Setting his gift down gently on the swing, he tossed her the keys. "Take me somewhere, Miss Snow."

"Where?" She stared blankly at her keys.

"Wherever you want, little one." He winked and walked by her toward the car.

Sophia laughed. "Um... ok."

They got in, and after an awkward few minutes of taking stock of where everything was, she took off down the street. "I can't believe I'm driving in my own car."

She took him to Sonic. "I don't understand, Nicca. How have you never been to Sonic? It's like the king of drink combinations."

"I don't know, but I'm happy you're setting it right for me," he joked.

Sophia ordered and the two of them laughed and talked about her year over blue raspberry slushies. By the time they pulled back into her driveway, she was feeling much more herself.

As she hit the button to lock her doors, she looked over the car with pride. "Thanks again, Nicca. It's more than I ever imagined."

He wrapped his arm around her shoulders as they walked to the front porch. "I'm glad, Miss Snow, and you're most welcome."

She walked over to the swing. He picked up the gift and sat next to her, crossing one foot over his knee. "I want to explain something to you, Miss Snow," he began. He leaned toward her and placed a large hand on the present in his lap. "I meant every word I said to you in Ireland. All I've ever wanted for my birthday was time with you. That's not a line or something to say just to make you feel good. It's the truth. I can't go to a store and buy that. It's something that only you can give me. Spending the evening in your new car and trying Sonic for the first time is a birthday memory I will cherish." He tapped the gift in his lap. "This is just a bonus."

Sophia's eyes welled up with tears. He always said things that shot straight to her heart. "Ok," she whispered quietly.

He pulled a little blue box out of his pocket. She smiled and grabbed it. When she popped open the box, she threw her head back and laughed. It was a cute little Volkswagen bug with yellow and pink accents. "You got me a car," she whispered as she closed her fingers around it and clutched it to her chest.

He pushed hair blowing across her face back over her shoulder. "Never feel nervous around me. It doesn't sit well with me. Ok?"

She nodded. "Ok."

He smiled and finally opened her gift. He looked over at her with a smile as he opened the top of the box. When he looked down, his smile disappeared.

Sophia nervously began over-explaining. "I rarely see you wear jewelry, but I thought this matched the leather you often tie your hair back with."

He reached in and pulled out the leather hair tie. Woven on the end of a strip of leather was a tiny silver charm. It was her mark, a triskelion. In the center of each spiral was a turquoise stone.

"It's you," he whispered.

"I... well... yes. I thought this could be your version of my charm bracelet." She laughed at how silly she sounded.

He looked up with so much emotion that she stopped breathing. "It's perfect, little one." He immediately put it in his hair, which warmed her heart.

She explained, "The rest is just... I don't know... a tradition I guess."

He glanced at her before pulling back the tissue to see a framed picture. It was her favorite senior picture of herself. She had gone to a local waterfall in a neighboring county. It had been her idea because she wanted to honor her time in Ireland behind the waterfall. She was standing in water up to her knees in a summer sundress with her hair down. It captured her goofing off. She'd been splashing the water when the photographer had taken the picture. Water drops surrounded her, and she was laughing.

She tried to read his face, but it was as hard as stone. She saw a muscle tick in his jaw. Was he mad at her? Sophia explained, "I know it's weird to give a picture of yourself to someone. It's one of my Senior pictures, and it's tradition to give them to family. I didn't know anyone other than Penny that might want one. I thought maybe, wherever you live, you could add this somewhere... or something." She felt pretty lame.

He touched her hair in the picture. "This is the life I hoped for you."

He set the picture on the swing before pulling her into a hug. "Best birthday ever, little one," he whispered in her ear.

Sophia's magic swelled, and he pulled her tighter in response. She couldn't breathe, but she didn't care one bit. Sadly, though, the words she knew were coming came next.

"I have to go," he mumbled and finally released her.

She walked him to the front steps. He stepped down and turned around, walking backward while holding her picture to his chest. "Until next time, Miss Snow."

She grinned. "Not my birthday, Nicca. I graduate in May."

He left in the next blink. She sighed and looked out into the night. Maybe once she was eighteen. Maybe once she worked more closely with him. Maybe then he would see her the way she saw him.

CHAPTER 53

*A*ll of her "maybes" were slowly turning into big fat "nopes." Sophia was losing hope that Nicholas would ever come around. Mainly because he was avoiding her.

"Coward," Sophia muttered under her breath. She was folding laundry at the kitchen table and contemplating how her year hadn't gone quite the way she had pictured.

In her mind, she was going to graduate, turn eighteen, and then a huge light bulb moment would happen for Nicholas. He would take her all over the world, and the three of them would discover the Lilith mystery. They would defeat Lilith before she even got here, and then she would live happily ever after with Nicholas by her side.

"Hmph," she said. None of that had happened. Well, she'd graduated and turned eighteen, so technically two of those things had happened, but that was beside the point.

He was giving her bogus tasks to keep her busy. Even worse, he was doing it through Martin. He wasn't even speaking to her directly.

She grabbed a stack of clothes and ran upstairs to put them away. It was time to get a job and maybe find a place of her own. She'd been naïve enough to think she would be so busy helping the guys that she wouldn't be able to work, but they were underestimating her once again.

She caught herself in the full-length mirror. She now stood 5'5" and was a little curvier, thankfully. When she looked at herself she saw a young woman, not a child. Her hair was darker, but still long. She had been considering cutting it, but hadn't gotten the nerve yet.

She grabbed her bracelet and looked at the new charms. He had given her a graduation cap at her ceremony, and then on her birthday he'd given her the world––a golden globe. He told her that the world was hers, and he would make sure she had every part of it she wanted. His words, as always, had gone straight to the heart, but he only visited a few minutes with her and left abruptly.

Shortly after, Martin began contacting her with random tasks. Read this and see how you feel. Look at this and tell me if you have a vision. Blah. Blah. Blah. Sophia rolled her eyes and put the bracelet back on the table.

Who was he kidding? She was naïve, but she knew busy work when she saw it. She went back downstairs to make dinner. Now that she was out of school, she tried to do things around the house to help Penny more. It was a Tuesday. Why not make it a Taco Tuesday?

She laughed to herself while pulling ground beef from the fridge. A movement at the counter caught her attention. It was a spirit named Oliver that had been hanging around for a couple of weeks. He looked to be about eighty, and he always popped in this way––always sitting at the kitchen counter. He was a big guy with a full head of silver hair. He looked like a guy who had been fit, like ex-military or police, but years had added pounds and wrinkles. No amount of years had taken the twinkle from his eyes, though.

"Hey, Oliver," she said.

"How about a beer for old time's sake, Soph," he said wistfully.

"What, they don't have beer on your side?" she said curiously.

"Aw, it ain't the same gorgeous," he said sadly.

She blinked. "So they do have beer over there?" It surprised her.

"It's not the beer I miss. It's the pretty girl pouring it for me." He winked at her.

Sophie laughed as she pulled out a chopping board. "Oliver, there's a lot of women today who would take offense to that."

She heard him grumble under his breath. "Not the pretty ones."

Sophia began chopping lettuce and onion. "You gonna talk to me today, Oliver?"

"I'm talking to you now, ain't I?" Oliver said with a smile.

"You know what I mean, ornery man," she said kindly. "Gonna let me help you with whatever brought you here?"

He sat quietly for a beat. "Your smile brought me here, Soph."

Ok, she thought, so not today then. "Ok Oliver, I guess I walked into that one."

CHAPTER 54

When Penny got home, they ate and talked about maybe shopping over the weekend. Now she sat on the porch swing trying not to focus on Nicholas avoiding her. Instead, she wanted to be proactive and come up with a logical solution, but she couldn't do anything if she couldn't physically talk to him.

She had tried texting, but he wasn't responding. She had tried to connect through Martin, but he made excuses. She didn't know what else to do.

She considered, for a split second, that if she got into trouble he would come, but she immediately dismissed it. It seemed wrong, like she'd be using his need to protect her against him. Besides, the idea of finding trouble on purpose didn't seem very intelligent.

She used one dangling foot to push the swing back and forth slowly and pulled on the frayed hem of her cutoff denim shorts. She couldn't believe she had no way to find him.

As if on cue, her mark tingled, and she knew he was checking on her. "Come see me, Nicca, please."

She waited for a beat, but nothing happened. She sighed heavily and leaned her head back. It'd been worth a try. She didn't know exactly how it worked. She asked him a couple of years ago, and he said it worked a lot like her Power of Body. It was visual. He pictured her mark fitting into his and BAM; it brought him to her.

BAM, that's it, she thought. She sat up straight and grabbed her mark. Could it work in reverse, she wondered? A tingle of excitement raced through her, telling her it could. Jophiel's words came back to her. Be creative. Don't set limits on what she can do. Think outside the box. Sophia buzzed with excitement. She wanted him to see her as an adult. Well maybe, she needed to act like one first. Sitting here waiting for breadcrumbs didn't feel very adult. She needed to take charge.

She stood up and looked around. Should she tell Penny? What if she ended up in a foreign country? Could she get back? She felt her back pocket to check for her phone. Surely she'd be fine as long as she could call.

Ok, she needed to quit stalling and do this before she chickened out, so she closed her eyes and pictured Nicholas's glorious chest. She felt deep down that she needed to be as specific as possible, so she drew the mark on his chest in her mind. Once she felt it was complete, she pictured the mark behind her ear. She felt magic swirling inside her, so she knew she was on to something. Taking one last breath and crossing her fingers, she pictured her mark pulling from her and resting over his heart. And then she waited.

She thought she would feel something. When she didn't, she figured it didn't work, so it surprised her when she opened her eyes and was in the middle of a street.

"Oh!" She jumped and turned. Where in the world was she? She turned and looked again. It looked like her neighborhood, just a different street maybe.

Completely defeated, she slumped her shoulders. "Balls!" she said and kicked at a rock. She needed to figure out which way was home from here.

She walked toward the end of the street to see if it was familiar. As she turned to go to the sidewalk, she looked up at the house in front of her. Nothing about it seemed special, so she kept going. It wasn't until she'd walked about ten feet that she stopped and straightened. Slowly, she turned around and walked back to the house and stared.

In the driveway were not one, but two familiar cars. It couldn't be, could it? Could they have been in the same neighborhood the whole time? Tears filled her eyes.

She walked closer to the house, and when she reached the garage door, she walked to the side and looked in the backyard. At first, she saw nothing, but as she turned to go back, her eyes caught the top of a very familiar play set.

Immediately she veiled her heart because she didn't want him to feel what she was feeling. He lived here. Right next to her. And he never told her.

Tears rolled down her cheeks as she calmly walked to the front of the house. When she reached the front door, she considered just going home and pretending she didn't know, but she rejected the thought because she knew she could never do it. She knocked, took a step back, softly crossed her arms, and waited.

It was Martin who answered. He opened the door with a smile but, almost comically, she watched all the blood drain from his shocked face. "Sophie, lass," he whispered.

She couldn't say anything. She told him with her eyes how betrayed she felt, and he at least had the decency to look ashamed. After a moment of awkward silence, Martin backed up and opened the door wide.

She found herself drawn to the back door. When she looked out the window, she had a view of the top level of her home. She could see her bedroom window even. All these years, she thought.

Martin tried to speak behind her. "Sophia, listen, I know how this may seem…"

Sophia interrupted him. "Stop, Martin. I don't want to hear all of your well-meaning reasons. I'm struggling with my emotions, and I don't want to hurt you. So… just stop."

There was a long silence before he mumbled, "Aye, lass. I'm sorry."

Sophia closed her eyes and put her forehead against the glass.

She was trying hard to reel in her emotions. She'd told Martin the truth. As angry as she was, she didn't want to hurt him.

"Martin!" She heard Nicholas yelling. "She veiled herself and isn't answering her phone, I have to…"

"Christ…" Martin muttered under his breath as Sophia slowly turned to face Nicholas.

Nicholas stood across the room holding a phone in his hand. He looked like he'd been running. He was staring at her as if he couldn't believe she was real. "Miss Snow, your eyes… I… How…"

If Sophia hadn't been so devastated, she would have laughed. The great Nicholas Stone was tongue-tied. Her magic pulsed. She was trying to keep it separate from her emotions, and it was making it hard to talk. She turned to look into the backyard.

"Is this where you both would watch me? Maybe laugh and make jokes about how naïve and stupid I am?" she managed with difficulty.

"Have I ever given you one moment that would make you think I would talk about you that way, little one?" Nicholas said earnestly.

Sophia squeezed her eyes shut tightly at his nickname for her. She shrugged one shoulder. "I suppose it's easy enough to pretend anything for only a few minutes a year." She heard him suck in air as if she had punched him, and dammit, she felt bad about it.

"Please, we'll talk this through, but I need you to lift the veil. I need the connection back, please," Nicholas said.

"Trust me, Nicholas. You do not want to feel the connection right now," Sophia said calmly.

"You never call me that," Nicholas whispered.

"Maybe it's time naïve Sophia grew up." She turned to face them both. "Am I so awful to be around?" she asked, hating the quiver in her voice.

"Being around you is the only time I'm truly happy," Nicholas confessed.

Sophia stared at him unbelievably. "I find that difficult to believe at the moment."

"It's why we live so close when we're here," Nicholas admitted while looking at the ground.

"That makes little sense to me right now. You could have been working with me now, but you're avoiding me. Why get my hopes up and tell me I could? Why send me bogus busy work?" She could tell from their looks she was right about the work. "Maybe you're stuck in your research because I haven't been a part. Maybe I could take one look at it and have a dozen leads. I could be the missing key. Who knows?"

She looked up at the ceiling. "I understand shielding me when I was younger, but I'm old enough to be involved in things that affect my life. That's what I would have told you if you had only let me talk to you." She looked over at Nicholas. "You know. I don't know why I am sparing you my feelings, now that I think about it. You want our connection back, Nicholas?" She lifted the veil and watched him fall to his knees and clutch his chest in pain. "There. Now you can feel what I feel."

Martin took a gentle step forward. "Lass, please. We're sorry. We never meant harm. I know deep down you know that. You're hurting right now, and I understand why, but don't do something here that you can't undo."

Sophia looked away from Nicholas on the ground to Martin. "What exactly did you think I was going to do? Hurt you? Kill you? Is that why you stay away? Are you scared of me?"

She looked down at Nicholas and realized Martin was right. Emotions were too high to talk right now. All she was doing was causing pain like a wounded animal striking out. She went to the back door and veiled herself again.

Over her shoulder, she explained, "I will unveil myself if I get into trouble and need help. Otherwise, leave me alone." She left without looking back.

She made it three steps before they burst through the door. She warned them. "Stop. Don't follow me." But they just kept walking. She felt her magic swirling like a tornado in her core, kicking up dust and rocks and grass. She turned, hair blowing wild and eyes of turquoise fire.

"*STOP!*" she yelled. She froze them as the ground around

their feet became soft and they sank to their knees before it became solid again. She stomped up to them and cringed inside when they shielded themselves with their hands. It brought her up short and everything halted.

"What exactly do you think of me? I'm not a monster. I just want you to listen to me. Leave me alone," she said to them.

Nicholas looked up at her with pain-filled eyes. "I just want to fix it. You're not a monster. I just want to talk to you and explain myself. I don't want you to hurt like that. Ever."

Sophia leaned her head back and laughed. "Oh, that's rich. Perfect, in fact." She looked down at two confused faces. She walked up to Nicholas and leaned down. "You don't get it, Nicholas. My entire life I've sat right over there, feet away from this spot, and craved just one more minute with you. One more conversation. I sat over there in anticipation, gladly accepting any small breadcrumb of attention you showed to me. Not once have you ever had to wait for attention from me because every time you wanted it, I was standing there waiting to give it to you. All I've ever been is your stupid, gullible, naïve pet. But guess what, Nicholas? Your pet has grown up. And now, *you* will wait for *me* to be ready to talk to you. I will let you know if that happens or if I am in trouble and need your services. Until then, leave me *alone*." With that, she turned and walked toward her backyard fence. When she was close, she lifted the veil on her mouth. "Move!" The fence post in the ground flew back and took the section of the fence with it. Sophia was too hurt to be impressed as she stepped through and walked to her house.

CHAPTER 55

*N*icholas and Martin dug themselves out of their dirt prisons. He was panicking because she was completely veiled, and he could barely feel the connection.

He'd thought that finding out they lived one street over might be hard to bear, but he'd never in a million years anticipated it being this bad. He didn't know how she'd found out. Who could have told her?

"Martin," he said desperately.

"I know. It'll be ok." He was brushing the dirt off his pants. "This is Sophia we're talking about. She'll understand."

"Martin, you didn't feel what we did to her. It shattered her." He started for the hole in the fence.

"Nicholas!" Martin grabbed his arm. "You'll not get anywhere right now. Respect her wishes and give her space. She'll work through it and come talk when she is ready."

Nicholas grabbed his hair and pulled in frustration. "I can't protect her like this. Fucking hell, why did I push her away? Why didn't I just let her help more?"

Martin sighed. "Honestly, I think the idea of being around her more is a little scary for you."

"What? That's crazy," Nicholas said dismissively.

"Is it? I think you work very hard to give her the life you

think she deserves, but you haven't let her decide if it's the life she wants," Martin reasoned.

Nicholas looked over at the hole in the fence. "I can't protect her like this."

Martin scoffed, "If I didn't feel like complete shite at how we made her feel, I'd be standing here completely impressed. She handled two fully grown men like we were rag dolls."

Nicholas turned around to face him. "Two grown men who didn't want to hurt her, Martin. What if they did? Or what if a third man was hiding she didn't see?"

Martin blanched. "God. Well, she said she would drop the veil if she was in trouble."

Nicholas yelled in frustration and put his clenched fists up to his temples. "What if it blindsides her while in her car? How is she supposed to have time to drop her veil then?"

"Jesus. You sit around and think up all these scenarios?" Martin looked over at Sophia's home. "You can't talk to her right now. You'll do more damage. I promise you that. She should be fine for a few days."

"You don't understand. Sophia is mostly light. Beautiful light that draws more darkness than a normal balanced person. Haven't you always wondered why she is so good, so agreeable all the time? She goes along with the flow and stumbles into trouble more than others. It's why she needs a guardian in the first place."

Martin sighed. "Seriously, at the very minimum. Give her a few hours. Let her work through the hurt and calm enough to talk with you."

Nicholas turned and walked into the house. He didn't know what to do with himself. Every second of his existence revolved around her. He reached in his pocket and pulled out the leather she'd given him. He rubbed his fingers across the turquoise stones. She looked so fierce while putting them in their place. Wounded, but savage and commanding.

She thought he saw her as a child, but he hadn't thought of her that way for a while now. Young, yes, but not a child. He wanted desperately to be a bigger part of her life, but he didn't deserve her. Her smiles, hugs, laughs, and even kisses should go to someone better than him. He only allowed it on his birthday for selfish reasons.

When she asked to work closely with him, he'd wanted it, but he knew he wouldn't be able to resist getting even more possessive. That wouldn't be fair to her, so he'd convinced himself he could send her things through Martin and keep her happy while still keeping his distance.

Maybe Martin was right. Maybe he'd decided what her life should be without really stopping to ask what she wanted. She was right, too. He treated her as naïve, and once again, he had underestimated her.

He put the leather in his hair to feel closer to her, like a lovesick fool. He sent up a prayer that she would have mercy and talk to him soon before he acted like an idiot and begged her.

Is this how she felt, he wondered? All these years. Lying in bed waiting for him to decide to show her any attention. The thought of that made him sick. He owed her a huge apology. He just hoped he had the chance to give it.

CHAPTER 56

*S*ophia went through her closet to find something to wear. She didn't know where or what for, but she was going out. She was well on her way to being nineteen years old and had never just... gone out.

She settled on a pair of black leather pants.. She found a racy leather top left from a Halloween costume last year. It wrapped over the shoulders like a tight tank top but, just under the breasts, it turned into leather strips that criss-crossed her abs. She looked in her mirror and shrugged. Not bad, she thought. She grabbed her leather moto jacket to cover a little more of her skin. No need to be too showy, she thought. She was slipping on combat boots when Penny opened the door.

She looked her over carefully before asking, "Um... I was wondering if you might know about a piece of fence missing?"

Sophia almost laughed at her confusion. "Yeah. I'm sorry. I..." She stopped as a thought occurred to her. "Did you know the guys lived right there?" She got up and pointed out the window.

Penny's eyes widened and walked over to look where she pointed. "I didn't. I knew it must be close, but I never asked."

Sophia paused. Honestly, she'd never asked either. Would they have answered honestly, she wondered? "I just found out, and... I kinda got upset. I'm sorry about the fence."

Penny stared back at her outfit. "Are you going somewhere?"

Sophia collapsed onto the bed. "I just want to go out. I've never done it before, and I need to go somewhere he can't find me. I'm angry, and I don't want to talk to him."

Penny sighed. "You know, I've never pushed you to explain certain things. My purpose was just to love you. I knew you would share anything important, but maybe I should have pushed harder. Maybe I used that as an excuse because the thought of what you're facing would probably terrify me."

Sophia smiled sadly. "You've been everything I ever hoped for in a mom. You know that."

Penny nodded. "I always tried to do the best I could for you. I don't know what happened earlier, but it must have been bad for you to be running away from Nicholas. That man would die for you. If you're Earth, he's the moon. I understand wanting to get away, but driving off in anger isn't safe. What if I go with you somewhere?"

Sophia teared up. "I just need to be alone, and I can't explain it. I promise to be careful, but I need to do this."

Penny pressed her lips tightly together and nodded. "Alright. Keep your phone on you, ok? Don't get mad if I keep checking on you. I'll leave you be, as long as you answer. Deal?"

Sophia jumped up and hugged her. "I love you, Mom."

She grabbed her phone, ID, and check card and tucked them in her pockets. As she was heading out the door, she heard Penny yell, "And fix my fence!"

She hit the road, cranked up the radio, and drove around for about ten minutes. When she reached downtown and saw the interstate signs, she went for it, following the signs for downtown Nashville.

She felt compelled to go into the city. Maybe she wanted to go back to her roots, where everything began for her and Nicholas. She knew deep down he hadn't meant to hurt her. She believed that he and Martin cared deeply for her and only wanted the best for her, but today had just been the last straw for her. They seemed so dead set on what needed to happen.

It was *her* fight. *Her* life.

Neither one had asked her opinion about how her life should

go. She had tried to insert herself into the action, and they had treated her like a child who couldn't contribute at all. It hurt.

It embarrassed her how she'd behaved with them. She'd gone over there to show him she was an adult. Instead, she'd thrown a tantrum. Now that the adrenaline of the moment had ebbed, she felt genuinely bad for the things she'd said to be hurtful. She should have just let them apologize and explain all their good reasons.

As she got closer to the city, she got nervous. She didn't know the city well, and she didn't have a clue where Nicholas had found her. A dirty alley close to the bars is all she remembered.

She parked and started walking. It felt powerful being out in the city on her own. Kind of thrilling. This was the feeling she'd been craving.

It was early evening, and darkness had set in. Thankfully, the streets were well lit, and she was close enough to the main streets and shops that people were about. She wandered around the tourist shops still open just passing time and thinking about life.

By the time she reached the main strip of bars, tourists packed the street. Walking along in front of a bar, loud country music would blast out, only to fade again until she came across the next hotspot. People of all ages moved in groups, laughing, drinking, and singing.

She noticed quite a few homeless begging or hopefuls singing on the sidewalks. She didn't remember it being like this. What stuck out in her memory were the smells. Old, stale beer and cigarettes, fried foods, and sweaty crowds. It was a little overwhelming.

She had to admit, a part of her was looking for her mother in every face she passed. She often wondered what it would be like to see her again. What would their conversation sound like? Would they even recognize each other? She just didn't know.

She came upon a kid playing the guitar on the sidewalk. He was good enough that a small crowd had gathered. Sophia looked around and noticed a piece of concrete that stuck out of the building behind her. It made a type of ledge that looked perfect for people watching. She reached up and grabbed a piece of decor to pull herself up. Once settled on the concrete ledge, she tried to make herself as small as possible to not attract attention from the crowd just below her.

Watching the crowds and listening to music, she thought about her mother. She thought about Nicholas. She thought about Lilith. Time ticked away, and she tried to imagine herself slowly becoming a part of the building.

She was tired. Having a looming battle hanging over your head had a way of wearing a person down. Whatever the outcome, she just wanted to face it. If Nicholas wasn't her future, then she needed to get this Lilith business behind her so she could figure out how to move forward.

She didn't know how much time passed. Her body had been in the same position for so long it was feeling frozen. When she stretched her legs, it was hard to move. Maybe she *had* become a part of the building, she thought with a scoff.

There were still people, but the crowds had thinned out. She timed her descent so that she came down softly behind a group as they passed. She had sulked enough for one day and was ready to head home.

She had to turn down a side street to get to the parking garage. Something made the hairs stand up on her arms. She looked all around her but couldn't see anyone. When she entered the parking garage, she felt zings of electricity buzzing down her limbs like little warnings. Her power was telling her trouble had to be lurking close by, but she couldn't see it. She didn't know if she should run for her car or run away. She paused for a moment to listen and see if she could get a sense of things.

She couldn't see or hear anything moving, but she was learning to trust her instincts. Her decision made, she slowly stepped back to exit the garage. Just as she passed the brown stucco wall of the building, she realized her mistake. She assumed the trouble had to be in front of her when, in fact, it had been behind her.

She didn't expect the arm that came around her from behind. An intense smell of sulfur hit her nose just as a creepy child-like voice whispered in her ear.

"I found youuuuuu." The words slithered over her skin.

Her training kicked in, and she tucked her chin to block being choked and kicked back hard to connect with his knee. She heard him cry out in pain, and he loosened his grip enough to break away. She dropped her veil and took off.

She ran away from the main streets, because she didn't want to expose her magic. If she had to use it, she wanted to limit the chance of being seen. She turned down a quaint strip of shops that were all closed and quiet at this hour. One shop down, she passed an alley that stepped down.

She ducked into it and hunkered down against the wall, trying to disappear. Her breathing was heavy and her heart was racing. She was pretty sure she had connected well enough to slow him down, but the adrenaline was telling her to keep running.

"He'll not bother you anymore, little one," she heard Nicholas mumble behind her.

She whirled around, ready to attack. "Geez, you frightened me." She sank down to the step behind her.

"I apologize. I didn't mean to," he muttered. He looked carved from granite. His fists were clenched. She looked up to see a muscle twitch in his jaw. His eyes looked like ice.

"You're angry," Sophia said.

"I'm upset. I don't understand why you're in this place. I don't like being cut off from you, and I don't like seeing you run away in fear," he said, getting angrier with each sentence.

"I don't know who that person even was. I didn't even see his face, much less provoke that trouble. It was different, though. He was different. Something was off about him. I dropped my veil as soon as trouble found me. In fact, I went out of my way to avoid it, I swear," Sophia said earnestly.

She saw him breathe deeply. "I don't want to fight with you. I'm sorry. If I hadn't messed up so badly before, if I'd been more open with you and not pushed you away, none of this would have happened. I blame myself," he said sadly as he walked over and sat beside her.

Sophia slumped her shoulders. "I didn't behave well earlier. I should have let you explain, but I was hurt, and I threw a tantrum." She looked over at him. "I knew, whatever your reasons, you probably meant well, but at that moment, I didn't care. It hurt. I want so badly to be a bigger part of your life, and I just don't understand why you don't."

"I do..." He started passionately but stopped and calmed himself. "I do. It's complicated for me, but it still doesn't excuse how I behaved. You're right. I always underestimate you. I don't mean to, trust me. I just want to do it all for you. I never wanted any of this for you. I hoped I could fix everything so you wouldn't have to worry about any of it."

She placed a hand on his arm. "I signed up for this. It's my fight. It *has* to be me."

Nicholas stood, walked to the opposite wall, and leaned his hands against the building like he wanted to push it over. "No, little one."

Sophia was done. He'd just dismissed her comment as if she couldn't possibly know what she was talking about. He would never see her as an adult unless she made him. Ney's words about having to hit him over the head jumped into her mind. They were spinning circles here, and she needed to take charge. She stood up.

"Kiss me," she said with a confidence she did not feel.

He stood up straight and spun around. "What did ye say?"

She knew he'd heard her. "I want you to kiss me." He just stood watching her. She launched her attack while he was stunned. "There is no human being better suited for me than you. You are hard-wired to my feelings. Do you know how many women would kill for a man to know how they felt instantly? Throughout my life, I've tried to look at other men, but they all fall short because none of them are you. They can't care for me the way you can. It seems completely natural to me that the progression of our relationship would always lead to this. Kiss me. You once told me to wait for someone who at least tried to deserve my affection. No one works harder than you. I will walk out of this alley and find someone else to be my first kiss if you say no, but no one will take care and make it beautiful for me the way you would. Kiss me, Nicca."

A long silence followed. Sophia stood listening to her heart beating in her ears. She watched him fighting an internal battle she could not help him win. She couldn't do more than straight out ask him. He either accepted it, or he didn't. She stood silently and begged him to accept.

The moment his eyes dropped and looked down her body, Sophia caught fire. She felt his eyes as surely as if they were his fingertips. He was not looking at her like a child. He wanted to kiss her. Whether he did was still up for debate, but he wanted it. She could feel it.

He prowled toward her slowly, giving her a chance to back out. Every step he took toward her pulsed through her body, and she was finding it hard to breathe.

When he reached her, she had to tilt her head back to look up at eyes of green fire. Could he feel the fire inside of her? She felt his fingertips graze her abs as he lifted his hands slowly up to slide along her shoulders, pushing the jacket off. She felt the leather sliding down her arms, revealing her bare shoulders. The cool air and his touch caused goosebumps to raise along her skin. Her eyes closed at the sensation.

"Jesus," he muttered.

She opened her eyes to see him looking at the skin exposed between the strips of leather stretched across her stomach. He wrapped his hands around her waist and stroked his thumbs gently over her bare skin, sliding just below her breasts. The sensations running through her body were overwhelming. She was at his mercy. She couldn't breathe or move. And she didn't want it to stop.

His hands slid down to her hips, pausing only a moment before squeezing and lifting her. She gasped and grabbed his shoulders as he stepped forward to place her against the brick wall. He pressed his hip and thigh against her to hold her in place and moved his hands up to her face.

"Give me your eyes, Sophie," he whispered.

She looked up from his lips to his eyes. He shook his head.

"Sophie, please," he said roughly.

Understanding dawned, and Sophia lifted her veil. He pushed his fingers into her hair and just looked. "So fucking beautiful," he whispered.

He leaned in slowly, killing her with the anticipation. The moment his warm, smooth lips touched her, she felt her magic swell. It was a teasing, gentle kiss, barely touching the corner of her mouth. He pulled back, only to lean back in and kiss her fully on the lips. Again pulling away.

She whimpered, thinking he was stopping, but he wasn't. He was teasing her with gentle kisses along her mouth that were driving her crazy. He kept softly kissing her lips until she thought she would explode.

The moment she needed more, he felt it, of course. And he gave it to her. He kissed her firmly while tugging gently on her hair to pull her head back. When his tongue touched her lips, she gasped in surprise and he slowly pushed his tongue inside her mouth, deepening the kiss.

Her magic pulsed as his tongue massaged hers in the most sensual way. It caused a low growl to come from Nicholas, and the tone of the kiss changed from gentle to passionate. He lifted her thigh higher on his hip, pressing into her core and making Sophia moan.

And then, just like that, the best moment of her life ended.

He ripped himself away from her with a loud cry. She fell down the wall, catching herself, while she watched him walk to the opposite side of the ally and punch the wall.

She stood there and watched him pace back and forth before punching the wall again. She felt the beginning of her heart cracking. He was going to reject her after all it seemed.

"Don't you love me?" Sophia asked, her voice cracking.

His back was to her, but she heard his reply, anyway. She saw his head fall forward as he whispered, "Fiercely."

"Please, make me understand," Sophia begged.

He spun in a burst of anger. "It's my fault. You're here

because of me. I fucked up, and now you're being punished for it. And here I am again, unable to put my feelings away and do right by you." He pushed his fingers roughly into his hair.

Sophia looked at him, confused. "I don't understand. How can this be your fault? I chose this life. Jophiel told me. I chose to be in this life with this purpose. You didn't force it on me."

"Jophiel?" he said angrily. "I'm the person who opened the guardian gate and let Lily through the portal. Yes, I knew her. I saw the questions in your eyes in Ireland, but I was too ashamed to confess. Would you like to hear the gory details? Want to be an adult? I was eighteen, and she was beautiful. I fucked her. She gave me a sob story about being separated from her brother." The heat suddenly left his words, and he slumped his shoulders and leaned back against the wall. "I didn't know I was a guardian, but she did. She knew the gate would open to me. I wanted to impress her, so when she told me she knew of a way to get him back, I jumped to help her. I opened the gate, and she laughed and walked right through. Right to here. Right to you. I don't deserve you. I did this to you."

Sophia just stared at him. His words were like little knives to her heart. She had known. Deep down, she'd figured out it was something like this, but hearing him say the words were crushing her soul. "So I'm your punishment then?"

He blanched and looked up at her. "What? No, I…"

She interrupted him. "You fucked up. You feel guilty about that. So you've chosen to view your long life and your responsibility to protect me as your punishment? This is your penance to make right what you feel is your wrong." The tears that had filled her eyes while talking spilled over her cheeks. "You will never love me. You could no more love me then a prisoner loves his cell."

She turned and walked a few feet down the alley. "So exactly how does a life with us not together work? Have you thought about it before? Because I have." She turned back to face him. "Am I destined to be alone or do I date and marry someone else? If I do, every time I have an orgasm are you off somewhere in the world feeling it like some twisted remote threesome?"

"Stop," he begged, closing his eyes.

"No, I would genuinely like to know how you see this playing out. How far does this self-induced punishment go?" Sophie said.

"Once we defeat Lilith. You'll be able to veil me more often. You'll be freer to have a life separate from me," he explained sadly.

Sophia blinked. "Wow." She wiped a tear angrily. "You have thought it through." She turned away from him. When she looked at her feet, she noticed a piece of glass reflecting light.

Jophiel's words came back to her in an instant. She leaned down and picked up the glass. It felt cold in her hands. She knew what she was about to do would hurt, but it was the only way.

She sighed and asked the sky. "What is it about me and fucking dirty alleys?" She turned slowly to face Nicholas.

She watched as their current location dawned. "I would never abandon you." At least he looked genuinely sorry, she thought.

She took a few steps closer to him. "Yes, you will, but before you do, I want to say something. Jophiel told me you were adamant about being my guardian. Demanded it. Why couldn't you think, instead of a failure, that my guardian must be a super strong extra special person willing to make a tremendous sacrifice? Maybe you looked through time and saw me failing. No support. No magic." She stepped even closer, feeling certain with every word. "Most guardians aren't born and raised. Did you know that? They just pop in like Jophiel. Maybe being raised by the druids so they would then send me their magic, was part of *saving* me? What would be so wrong with thinking that what you've done for me is give me a fighting chance instead of fucking up?" She shook her head and took another step forward. "I've thought my entire life that if I could just make friends, if I only had family, I wouldn't be lonely. Life would be perfect, and I could accomplish anything." She squeezed the glass into her palm. "I'm realizing just now that I was wrong. All I need is myself. I will not be your prison. I free you from the punishment you're so determined to put on yourself. You've been the best

possible guardian, Nicca, but I'll finish the fight on my own."
Sophia raised the glass to her mark behind her ear.

Nicholas frowned. "What are you doing?"

Sophia took a beat to look at him one last time, and then she
dug the glass in and cut. She felt the blood run down her neck.

Nicholas's eyes grew wide, and he cried out, "NOOO!!" He
began running and then disappeared.

Sophia stood frozen until the pain hit her. Her mark felt like
it was on fire, and her heart was shattering into tiny pieces. She
fell to her hands and knees and cried.

"What have I done?" she whispered as the pain consumed
her. She concentrated on the cement between her hands and the
emotions surging through her. Here in an alley was probably the
best place for her to have a breakdown. She really didn't want to
kill someone.

CHAPTER 57

*N*icholas blinked and was in his home. He spun frantically in a circle, not exactly sure what to do first. He tried to go back to her, but nothing happened, because he couldn't feel her––at all. Martin ran into the room as Nicholas ripped his shirt off.

"What…" They both looked at his very naked unmarked chest.

The tattoo was gone.

Nicholas felt his skin where his mark should be. "I think she…" he couldn't even say the words. He spun to face Martin. "I need you to kill me."

Martin blanched. "What are you talking about?"

Nicholas grabbed Martin by the shirt. "The last thing I saw was Sophia slicing her neck with glass and now my mark is gone."

Martin's face went white. "My God. What does killing you do?"

Nicholas gave up trying to convince him and ran to the kitchen. "If I live, then I know she's ok. If I die, then I want to be dead, anyway. She did it because of me." He felt his voice break and the tears on his face. He went to the butcher block and grabbed a knife from the block.

"Actually, dear brother, she probably did it because of something I said." Nicholas turned at the sound of Jophiel's voice.

He started for him with the knife before remembering it was technically Martin's body. He tossed the knife and swung at his face with his fist. "You bastard." Nicholas leaned against the counter. The void left where Sophia used to be was sucking pain from everywhere. "You fucking bastard," he whispered as he bent over and held his head in his hands.

"She is ok. I'm really sorry. It was important for this to happen," Jophiel said while wiping his nose.

"And talking to her without our knowledge? Did Martin know you kidnapped his body to whisper your secrets to her?" he said bitterly.

Jophiel laughed. "I gave her knowledge that I didn't give to you, but it wasn't to be nefarious. It was important knowledge for her to have that the druids couldn't give her."

"I just want you to tell me how I get my mark back," he demanded.

"I'm sorry, again. I cannot do that. She's right. You don't accept her as an equal in this fight. You hold her back, thinking you're keeping her safe, but you underestimate her. Now, to her credit, she is fighting to be accepted, but she doesn't really believe in herself either. This needs to happen, brother. You and she both need to see that she can stand on her own feet."

Nicholas stared at him with a blank face. "How the fuck do I keep her safe if I don't even know where she is?"

Jophiel gave him a sad look. "You don't my friend. She has to fight her own battles for a while."

"No," Nicholas said, shaking his head. "I don't accept that."

"You must. It is done," Jophiel said, and then he left.

"That bastard," Martin muttered. "I didn't know. I swear it."

Nicholas brushed him off and walked into the living room. Kissing her beautiful mouth had been the single best moment of his existence, only to be followed by the very worst. He didn't know what to do with himself. His body trembled with pain and desperation.

He looked down in front of him and saw a chair. As the rage built, he felt himself lifting the chair and throwing it. After that, things became blurry. When he finally calmed enough to note his actions, he was on the other side of the room with a piece of unidentified wood in his hands. He was breathing heavily and standing in a destroyed living room. Martin came into view. Fluff from a pillow landing on his shoulder as he leaned calmly against the wall.

"You feel better?" he said sarcastically.

Nicholas dropped the wood. "I kissed her," he said, bringing the pain back again.

Martin's eyes widened. "That took longer than I thought it would, honestly."

Nicholas frowned at him. "Don't be like that. It wasn't like that, and you know it. She asked me to kiss her, and I couldn't say no to her. I wanted it too badly to say no."

"And then you freaked out about it," Martin offered matter-of-factly.

"No," he said. "Well. Yes. Maybe." He fell into a broken chair.

"There is no one more perfectly designed for her than you. The sooner you accept that, the better for you both," Martin said as he walked to the fridge to grab some water.

"She said the same thing to me." He turned up one corner of his mouth, thinking about her very well laid-out argument of all the reasons he should kiss her.

"I think she's right about a lot of things. We keep selling her short, and she needs to be a bigger part of this," Martin said carefully.

Nicholas nodded. "I'm realizing that, but I can't do a damn thing about it right now."

Martin thought. "Well, she has to come home eventually, right?"

Nicholas sure hoped so. He needed to see her like he needed to breathe air. He swore he could still feel her smooth skin on his fingertips. She had tasted like cinnamon and smelled like vanilla.

A switch inside of him had flipped the moment she'd asked him to kiss her. It had released all the feelings he'd been putting in a box, and he didn't think he'd be able to put them back.

CHAPTER 58

*S*ophia didn't know how long she had been crying and staring at the concrete between her hands. It scared her to leave the alley because she didn't want to do anything extreme. Her mark still burned, but it was the void inside that hurt the most. She felt empty. What in the world was she supposed to do now? She had felt so certain that she had to do it, but now what? Nicholas had always decided on the big stuff. Now instead of just being alone, she was lost *and* alone.

"Hey honey, you ok?" She heard a woman's voice. It startled her, but she was afraid to look up.

"I'm fine. Thanks." She hoped the woman would keep walking.

She heard heels on the cement approaching, and a pair of gorgeous shiny red open-toed heels moved into her field of vision.

"You sure about that? Not a normal thing to see at two in the morning. Anytime really, if I'm being honest. Not judging, but are you like, giving an imaginary friend horsey rides or something? I saw a show on late night tv. Some people like that kind of thing."

She sounded so serious that Sophia laughed and looked up. She heard the woman gasp and remembered her veil was not up, so she quickly slid it into place before looking back at an absolute vision of beauty.

She looked like a 1950s pin-up model that had stepped right out of a magazine. Her dress was navy blue with white polka dots. The bodice was tight and fitted. It pushed her ample breasts high. There was a thick strap of material wrapped around her neck, holding the bodice in place. From her waist down, her dress puffed out to below the knee from several layers of petticoats. She'd done her midnight black hair in a 50s style with big pinned curls on each side of her head and the rest of her long straight hair falling down her back. Her fair skin contrasted starkly with her black hair, blue eyes, and red lips. Sophia's eyes immediately went to her dimples as she smiled at her.

She remembered herself and made an apology. "I'm sorry about that, uh, crazy contacts," she said as she sat back on her feet.

The woman gave her a look of doubt. "Look. I just wanted to make sure you didn't need some help. I could walk you somewhere if you want?" she offered.

"That's super nice of you, but I don't know where to go." She surprised herself by being honest.

The woman looked her up and down for a moment before she seemed to decide something. "I'm Sugar," she said and turned to sit delicately on the step behind her. "Please don't tell me a gorgeous girl such as yourself is out here in this alley because of a man?"

Sophia smiled sadly. "I've loved him my entire life, but he's determined to punish us both by denying how he feels. I ended it just now, and I was sitting here trying to figure out what happens next."

Sugar nodded sadly. "Ok. Well, I suggest you wipe the slate and start over. New job and or a new place to live. That's what I am hearing. Sounds like you did the right thing. If you love someone, let him go. You know the saying. If it's meant to be, you'll find your way back to each other, but until then, pull yourself up by your bootstraps. Be strong. Nothing will scare a man more than showing him you can make it on your own without him just fine." She snapped her fingers. "Whips him right into shape, just like that."

Sophia laughed. "I'm Sophia," she said softly.

"Well, Sophia, strange eyes and invisible horsey rides aside, I think we might be able to help each other out," she said.

Sophia considered the interesting woman in front of her. She needed to stand on her own two feet. Maybe it wasn't how she had planned it, but it was sink or swim time. She needed to shed her childhood and step out into the real world. Her own sort of metamorphosis, and she wanted to start with how she looked on the outside. "I don't suppose you have a pair of scissors?" she joked.

Sugar tilted her head and turned to the bag on her shoulder. She pulled out an enormous pair of sewing shears with a black plastic guard on them. Pulling the plastic off, she grinned. "I'm in. Sounds fun. What are we cutting?"

Sophia's eyes grew round. "You carry those in your purse?"

Sugar shrugged. "It'd surprised you how often I need them."

Sophia stood with a gentle smile. She glanced up at the sky. It would be just like God to bring her a friend the very moment she decided she didn't need one.

Just when she was about to answer, a motion caught her attention. Sophia looked up and saw Oliver standing at the top of the steps.

"I'm ready, gorgeous," he said softly.

She glanced at Sugar, and Oliver nodded his head. She sighed. "I want to cut my hair. Game?" she said with a small smile.

"Sophia, are you sure? Your hair is beautiful, and I highly advise avoiding long-term decisions when emotions are high."

Sophia shook her head. "I don't want anything drastic. Just cut it shorter."

Sugar nodded. "Got it. You like cupcakes?"

"Um, who doesn't?" Sophia asked.

"Right? Well, this right here," she hit the wall next to her left shoulder, "is my store. I was up late trying to do the books. Love cupcakes. Hate paperwork. Anyway, how about we stuff our faces and contemplate hairstyles on Instagram?" she suggested.

Sophia felt her anxiety subsiding. She looked at the fond way Oliver was staring at Sugar. Hopefully, what he needed to say wouldn't be too painful. She had reached her limit.

She nodded to Sugar. "I'm in. Sounds amazing." She started for the steps and remembered something. "One sec." She pulled her phone out and texted Penny a quick message explaining as simply as possible what she was doing and promising to contact her soon by email. Then, with a deep breath, she threw her phone as hard as she could into the dumpster.

Sugar smiled and nodded. "Bad ass."

Sophia grinned, and they walked off to consume their weight in cupcakes.

ACKNOWLEDGMENTS

I know. I know. Cliffhangers are awful! Don't worry. The next chapter of Nicholas and Sophia's journey will continue in *Sophia's Moon*. (Coming very soon!) Follow me on social media for release information.

I would like to thank my mom, Mary, and my husband, Philip, for being my biggest fans. Your support means the world.

ABOUT THE AUTHOR

I was born in Texas but moved early in my life to Louisiana. I was raised as a farmer's daughter. I grew up doing all those stereotypical things a girl on the farm does. I had strays for pets. I was a card-carrying member of 4-H. I showed livestock, entered cooking contests, and sewing classes. I rode the back roads and listened to country music. I was at the dinner table every night and in church every Sunday.

I went to Louisiana Tech for my bachelors of science and graduated with my teaching degree at twenty. I taught Family and Consumer Sciences to high school kids, and I LOVED it.

I met the love of my life online before online dating was even a "thing." In 2010, he moved to the United States. We moved to Tennessee to be closer to my family, which is where we still live today.

One last thing: Follow me, and if you haven't already, visit my website and sign up for my newsletter so you will hear all the good stuff!!

MeredithHowlin.com

CPSIA information can be obtained
at www.ICGtesting.com
Printed in the USA
BVHW071730070521
606757BV00002B/149